The
Golden
Codex

William Sandberg

EXPLORA BOOKS
700 – 838 West Hastings St. Vancouver, BC V6C 0A6
www.explorabooks.com   Phone: (604) 330 6795

No part of this book may be reproduced, stored in a retrieval system, or transmitted by any means without the written permission of the author.

Because of the dynamic nature of the Internet, any web addresses or links contained in this book may have changed since publication and may no longer be valid. The views expressed in this work are solely those of the author and do not necessarily reflect the views of the publisher, and the publisher hereby disclaims any responsibility for them.

ISBN: 978-1-83430-129-7 (Paperback)
978-1-83430-130-3 (Hardback)
978-1-83430-147-1 (eBook)

© 2026 William Sandberg. All rights reserved.

The Golden Codex

Table of Contents

Chapter 1: The Foretoken 1
Chapter 2: The Apprentice and the Seed 13
Chapter 3: The Transmutation Game 35
Chapter 4: Marron's Gambit Declined 56
Chapter 5: The Ilyaan, the Codex and the Tree 71
Chapter 6: The Ghenjil's Way 96
Chapter 7: At the Dahi's Lodge 117
Chapter 8: The Serpent's Feather 145
Chapter 9: Initiation in Cuzco 161
Chapter 10: Intervention Intervened 183
Chapter 11: Behind the Artwork 205
Chapter 12: The Cord in the Labyrinth 223
Chapter 13: The Curtains Open 239
Chapter 14: The Seruwani Council 259
Chapter 15: Drag Race 277
Chapter 16: Strange Attractor 291
About the Author 307

Chapter 1
The Foretoken

It was a place where open wounds still slept unhealed. He hadn't crossed the threshold of the mottled brick storefront since the days of his youth, his aversion due neither to negligence nor forgetfulness. Jim Ralston had sworn a binding oath to himself that he would leave it behind him in the unspoken past. A return to this place, where the promises of youthful trust had been broken, and everything had gone so very wrong, was never in the cards. Yet, like a thing ordained, he was here again, and without full comprehension, he knew nothing could have kept him away.

He strode to the vacant counter at the far wall with a swagger that belied his qualms and called out, "Tom, I'm here. Got your message."

As he glanced here and there, he took in his surroundings. The room spun around him and an eeriness took hold of him, as though he had never actually left the dark staid interior that still troubled his dreams. He found himself scanning the silent wall clocks, paintings and bric-a-brac, then the empty street outside the front window, and finally the eternally curtained windows of the facing buildings across the street. The odd passing car or covey of schoolkids glued to their cellphones faded away like ghosts. All seemed motionless, even time itself.

His reverie snapped like a dry twig. A somber, older man emerged from the shadows of the back room. He wore his customary blue smock. Ralston recognized him instantly and marveled at the years his old mentor wore on his face. But the twinkle in Tom Aimesworth's eyes had not faded over the decades, and Ralston felt a heart-warmth that he had not had in many years. If anything, the man looked more like a kindly old mahir now than he ever had in those early days. He was the man who taught him all the things beyond the five senses, even those he could never fully come to believe in.

Outside, the evening cast its long purple shadows through the front windows of the store and reached like fingers that encircled the two men. Almost in mimicry, they interlocked their fingers, touched thumbs and shook hands in the old secret way as they once had done decades ago when the Kopendres Ordinath held sway in their lives. It was an unconscious artifact of the syndicate's powerful grip on the lives who touched it, even two who had escaped it long ago.

"Nahiti taji. It's so good that you came, Jim-tatsa-satjim," the storekeeper almost whispered in a hoarse voice. "We're alone here, so we can speak freely."

Jim had neither heard nor spoken Dirshani in decades. He realized he was expected to dust it off and respond with a formal greeting to his former mahir. To his surprise, the despised lessons of his youth were not in vain; the formula rolled off his tongue effortlessly.

"Nahiti taji, tewantsa mahir-satjim. It's great to see you again after all these years, but tell me, Tom," Ralston said as he caught the older man's gaze, "Why the urgent message? What's up with that? You remember—

life, limb or liberty? We swore an oath: no meetings unless there was certain danger. It's risky—anyone could see us together here."

"Yes, I kn-know, Jim, but they c-can't, really," the man replied with a slight stutter, "It's safe here now. I received word in secret from the Dahi, and I've been asked to relay it to you only, and only in person. This is the sole shielded enclave where I can do that without risk of … what can I say? … monitoring, or God forbid, attack. Not that I'm expecting anything of the kind."

"Attack? For real, Tom? You're blowing smoke at me." Ralston smiled like a skeptic who scoffed just to hide the hint of a long-forgotten fear.

"It's happened more times than I can count—always dirty, underhanded and hard to prove. Don't worry, though. Relations with our former associates have been placid of late."

Now in his mid-forties, Ralston struggled to remember his early life in this place. So prosaic, humdrum in a way, yet the venerable store remained a place of awe and terror to him. He shuddered at the thought of standing directly over the lower chamber, separated from it only by the worn oak floorboards he stood on. There he had been lured and, with craft and cunning, inducted into a cult locked in secrecy. It still radiated a singular potency that he found unsettling. He could feel the pull of it in this place. He took solace that the man who stood before him was the one who once took his hand and led him away from that thralldom.

"You swore you'd never go back to Sunara, Tom, not in this life." Ralston almost accused the man, then instantly regretted his high tone. The orb of Sunara was a place unthought of for years, but Tom's mention of the Dahi brought it back to him, and in a cultish way that left him cold. And for Ralston, any being as powerful and benign as Tom's Dahi bordered on pious delusion.

"Jim, I was trying to free Cynthia from the Kopendres. That's the only reason I'd journey to the Dahi for help—at least before I cast off the shell of this old world. I only wanted the same freedom for her that I, myself, treasure. I hoped that she could somehow inherit it from me when I meet my omega."

"And did you? Free her?" It came out of Ralston's mouth like an unbeliever's taunt. Then he softened his expression and backtracked.

"Sorry, Tom—didn't mean it that way."

"Sadly, no." The other man paused. "Vic Marron may have been blindsided by you and me, and it's plain he's given up on us. But he still holds his claim to her—his grip's all the tighter. It's like he sees some use in keeping her—like she's a bargaining chip or something. I shudder to even guess. The Dahi has neither power nor influence in the matter. But listen, that's got nothing to do with why you're here. He gave me a foretoken concerning your son."

"Is that all? It can't be too important, then." Ralston laughed as he let off a sigh of relief as if nothing coming from a hypothetical higher orb could have much impact on his current life.

"It's urgent."

"So, Tom?" Ralston said tersely without looking at the other man. "Tell me." He found himself in both fear and yearning for Tom's reply, and his body tensed involuntarily.

"You needn't ask. You and I know the story, Jim. We know why they're hellbent to punish us—the only ones who got away with the unpardonable sin. We took all the arcane knowledge they piled into our hearts and heads, then used it against them."

"Story? I get the sense that's only the half of it. What's the rest?" Jim asked, as though his repressed memories were an indemnity. His words sounded more like feigned ignorance and he knew it. He wiped his brow and tried to look indignant, as if he had been summoned on a trumped-up rumor.

"Well, I'm sorry to have to remind you. You know the rest as well as I do, Jim. My firstborn—taken as the property of the Kopendres—in payment for my willfully-gained freedom from them. Now," Tom faltered, then regained his voice, "the same ruling has been applied against you, satjim. It's retribution for following me from the rank and file of the Ordinath into the free life. Plain enough for you?"

Ralston gasped as he took it all in and reeled with shock. "You mean ... Piers? They want my boy, Piers? And after all these years? God, he's only fourteen."

The shopkeeper silently nodded, then said, "More than just want him. Legally, they already have him."

"No. No, they do not. There's been some mistake, Tom," Ralston said quietly, his jaw relaxed. He shook his head. The look of fake indignance returned.

"He's been entered into the kravl inventory of the Kopendres Syndicate—the slave registers, as you and I once knew them. His calling-name is Taighen, under your old clan, Uchundar. It's probably purely bureaucratic for the time being."

"Bureaucratic? My ass," Jim countered, roused from disbelief.

"It's sinking in, is it?" Tom whispered.

"He's been targeted. That's the only reason the Kopendres would put out any coin on the legal side," Jim shot back, fully-awakened to the new reality.

"Strange things have been going on lately. You'd never guess what manner of power beings have been sighted here. I just know it's somehow tied in with this. I'd tell you more, but you wouldn't believe me."

"Ilyaan? Elaari? Ruakon? Don't get me started on that rubbish. And please don't tell me you're seeing things, Tom, and talking to them." Ralston scoffed. He remembered enough to list off some of the higher beings held to be endowed with powers beyond the sentients of the lower orb. But there was no reverence left for the lore he once committed to heart, only derision.

"I just said I wouldn't. But something's brewing. There could be a big end buyer who's sighted him. Or a small independent hunter who's speculating the resale profit on him. It's just paperwork for them, and it might explain the sudden flurry of activity by the syndicate. They're quick to react to market demand or they wouldn't have survived as long as they have."

"What about legal action? Is there a countermotion we could put through the courts in Irupaan?"

"Now, don't you get caught up in fantasy, Jim," the old man chided. "At this late date, the claim can't be rescinded in the Kopendres courts—neither in the halls of Irupaan, nor here. It's sown up tighter than a stuffed turkey's gullet. There's only one strategy that will work. He'll need to be primed, trained and initiated to survive this. Pure and simple. I shouldn't have to tell you that we need to start soon—before they move in on him."

"We're right under the nose of the Ordinath, Tom. What can any of us do? Can't we contest this with that greedy bastard Marron? It's all his doing— probably another of his gambling debts," Ralston cried out. No sooner had he said it, he realized that if there was a way, Tom would be the first to tell him.

"No, Jim, it's imperative that you bring your son here," the storekeeper urged as he shook his head. "And say nothing to Vic Marron, or anyone else for that matter. They must never find out the Dahi has warned us, or that we have so much as the slightest inkling what's going on. Trust me. They've put their best watchers on him, or soon will. Your boy could be taken immediately if they get wind of you and I talking loudly or acting stupid. No, no. I'll train him in the skills he needs, without their knowledge or sayso."

"But they'll just claim him when they're good and ready anyway. He'll wear the star just like us," said Ralston, despondent. "You know how they operate. What the devil can I do? Move somewhere the hell and gone where they can't find us? What can I tell him?"

"Jim! Get your head working. They can find him anywhere. Stay here where it's safe. And whatever you do, don't tell Piers the least thing at all about this—for his own good. It has to be occultus, right?"

"So, what's the plan?" Ralston sighed, resigned to hear any option that remained.

"I'll give him a job here, just as I did when you were a teen. I'll teach him everything he'll need to know, but on the side. Knowing you, he's a bright one. But I'm just as subtle in my ways as I was with you—he won't even know he's being initiated. He'll just feel the power growing in him over time. I'll let it seep in nice and slow, or in big gulps if he can take it."

"Sounds vaguely familiar. By the way, I knew what you were up to back then, Tom. About as subtle as a herd of elephants, and twice as ornery," Ralston said softly, reveling in the moment to take a gentle jibe at his ex-boss.

Tom gave him a look of mock disapproval, then smiled as if the memories took shape before him, of the two of them at work together in this store. It was obvious to both that each remembered the old days differently. The realization helped lighten the mood, if only for a moment.

"Jim, just let me be as clear as those hand-polished crystals that dangle from the chandelier over your head. I'm not guaranteeing there'll be no abduction if you send him to me. Are we clear on that?"

"Yeah. The rest is charted where the Ilyaan shine from their sky-palaces, the Ruakon fly the night skies and the greedy virs build their empires below—if you can believe all that crap, I was fed. If any of it's true, it almost doesn't matter what I do."

"It matters in heaps, fells, and mountains, man. What I'm telling you is that when it happens, he'll be strong enough and have the training under his belt to make his way in the upper domains—and he'll be able to thrive, and even find his way back here if that's what he wants. He'll have the immanent seed of freedom planted in his deepest ground."

"Yeah, guess he'd need that in short order," Ralston acquiesced. He bristled slightly at the zeal the old man still retained. He could almost hear the broom-sweep of so many years of fruitless labor in a cult they had both rejected.

"He absolutely needs that and the vital knowledge and the skillset that goes with it. And you know something else? It may even dissuade them from taking him as a child if he's getting a superior level of training here. You don't want him to end up among the Ilushi outcasts, do you? Or enslaved on a root farm or worse?"

"No. Of course not." Ralston paused, then asked, "So that's the whole plan? All you can give me, Tom?"

"That's all I can give you. It's a tall enough order just to do that."

"Just you, old man? All on your own lonesome here? From what I've heard, you've lost all your apprentices and so-called followers. Are you sure you're up to it? Teenagers can be a handful. I taught him manners, but he's bull-headed sometimes. He's curious as hell and has a mind of his own." Ralston looked skeptical but flashed a smile as if he wanted to believe.

"Well, I would expect nothing less of a young Uchundar, and a Ralston to boot," the older man responded, laughing. "And after all, I'm never really alone, Jim. You know that. I always have you to fall back on," Aimesworth joked, then turned serious again. "Cynthia's only too happy to help, too. She's my right arm here. She won't leak any of this to the Kopendres, either. We can trust her."

"Yeah, of course I trust her. But you think that's going to be enough? This is going to be a hell of a climb for an innocent kid."

"Give him credit, Jim. He may prove less innocent than you think. Once he has shown himself capable in the high arts there will be no intervention, no induction to the Ordinath and no star on his wrist. I'll promise you that much, as long as we can deliver on the basics of survival."

"One condition, Tom. He's no lab rat. I won't have him subjected to what went on down there in that hell-hole," Ralston demanded, his eyes directed towards the unseen chamber beneath them, then at Tom.

"That's all been closed down, Jim. After Aston passed, I told the Ordinath they had no place here anymore. It took time, as you might have guessed, but with the Dahi's help I banished them from here, and there's an end to it. Vic's still sore about that. But there's no, absolutely no entry for them here. And they know it. It's a stronghold."

"And the training—he'll get none of that mind-bending nonsense they used to brainwash us with?"

The shopkeeper shook his head, eyes closed.

"Remember Aston Dixon? What a total screw-up!" Ralston went on, unable to stop himself, "The force-bindings, the purging, the godawful transmutations that either never quite worked or missed by a mile. The fake explanations? Telling us we were like young astronauts training to ride the wahan to Sunara—or God knows where? The man was certifiable. All the while, ol' Vic and his crew just smiled and looked on. I mean, wadda load o' crap!"

"Jim. Listen. Closely. Those days are all over. Long ago. And as for the wahan to Sunara, you were never forced to enter any transorbal tunnel or manifold that would take you to another world—not on my watch. I would have intervened unless you were willing and absolutely ready for it."

"We were just kids—green as grass—scarred for life. That's my point, Tom. The Ordinath was everything to us; we were stupid, faithful kids. And we failed at everything that mattered to us." Ralston gave his friend a scowl that was anything but kindly, though couldn't help it. There were almost tears in the corners of his eyes, for he knew that Tom had not only seen it all happen to him, but to his own daughter as well.

"Now, now, there'll be none of that—I swear to you, Jim. Piers will need to be immersed in the forces that operate in the chamber, even so. He'll damn near have to become a master of them. But it will be done under my guidance and control. That and his own sense of natural discovery will be the key to his survival. Even Marron and his Ordinath have nothing like what remains intact here, and he well knows it. He designed most of it, after all." The old man seemed so sure of himself, his eyes flashing blue and bright.

Ralston fell silent for what seemed like an eternity. He saw nothing else but his son, his wife, the times they had shared, playing as though by an endless river. He had nothing else that mattered to him.

"So, you're saying it's a safe place for him here? No lingering traps?" Ralston asked, resurfacing from his thoughts.

"None. It's as clean as a pastry chef's apron, and it's a fortress unlike any you'll find in the two lower orbs. There's anti-surveillance filters and adaptive high-frequency noise emitters in every wall. Even the window glass has time-warps riddled through it. They may try to lip-read or hear us, but all they'll get is distortion. Even from their own bugs."

"That's comforting Tom, but it's not what I mean." Ralston's voice broke and warbled slightly.

"Fine. I take your meaning. Absolutely no traps, Jim. And he'll be left alone if they see he's under my wing. They've learned by their own misadventure that I have strong allies who will stand with me on this. The Ordinath won't risk an intervention once he's settled into training. They wouldn't want to jinx it."

"And he'll initiate in the full doctrines of the elect? In the Dahi's lineage? Under you as his mahir?"

"He'll initiate here when he's good and ready, I swear, and grow into manhood with a fighting chance. You know that's bone-deep true. I pledge that not only to you, but to the Dahi as well. And you can trust he'll hold me to it or see me die trying."

The storekeeper fixed his gaze on Ralston's helpless eyes and chopped his words into sound bites. "Listen, Jim! I hear you. It's hard, it is—to keep the faith. But you know about the disappearances. Every day the secretly indentured—abducted to the next orb—a goodly number of them children. I don't need to tell you: they're never found. They never return, Jim, or those that do are little more than zombies. Don't be another sleepwalker—you have no excuse. Just know that you're not alone. We're with you on this, but this's our last chance to save him from the Kopendres and whoever else is pulling their strings."

"How do we know for sure who's behind this, Tom?" Ralston's morose tone revealed he had wandered to the edge of his hope, where cliffs plummet into the dark unknown.

He hadn't expected an answer, but Tom struck back like a blacksmith before the anvil, his voice a hammer. "Doesn't matter! The Ordinath will do the dirty work, or someone they're planning to sell him to. They've shown their hand, I tell you. We have it on the best intelligence. The soul hunters have been let loose. We know by the Dahi's grace they've almost got him in their sights, Jim. They're so close, all they have to do is reach out and pull him from the branch."

"When?"

"It can happen at any time, I tell you. The Marpole wahan is in a lunar mode—peaking in two or three moons after the eclipse. At most. Then say goodbye. He'll be gone forever," Tom said, voice rising.

Jim Ralston turned his eyes towards his old mentor in silent assent.

"Arrangements are in place. Clear it with your lady wife any way you can but come back with him on the cusp of the lunar eclipse next week. Don't fail me. Don't fail your son. We can plant the seed of freedom in him, so tend ready the land. You know exactly what I mean. Nothing can defeat it. Surely you still believe in that."

Chapter 2
The Apprentice and the Seed

The brick-red moon had settled well into the eclipse, but still lit their path as the two figures approached an aging store with wide awning-shaded windows. The quiet street was nestled in a bland South Vancouver neighborhood known more for grocery stores and gas stations than curiosities from the past. For those to whom history mattered, it was the site of an ancient nation and a village as old as London or Rome. But outside of a plaque on a cairn in a nearby park, nothing of that past remained above the asphalt and concrete. The two who approached the store plied the seas of a new future, and their port awaited them. Smiling, his father opened the door for the tall dark-haired boy. It was a gesture not lost on either. He would be the first of them to enter the softly-lit interior of Aimesworth and Dixon Antiques.

This was to be Piers' first real job. Though he was quietly anxious, he put on a brave face, embracing the moment with an outward air of confidence. The discordant clank of the bell above the front door loudly announced them. Startled, the boy's green eyes widened. Banished forever were the boyish fantasies about the far-off world of work. This was the real world his father often spoke of as though it were humanity's final destination. He knew he was entering a new phase in his life and that it seemed nothing less than an espousal, a day to remember, for better or for worse.

As he walked towards the empty counter, every manner of oddity swept past his gaze. There were the vaguely familiar Ming blue and white Kraak ware, crystal decanters and gnarled walking sticks. There were also things that Piers now saw up close for the first time: gilt-lacquered oriental cabinets, etched renaissance armor, followed by an inlayed Micronesian mask, ornate silver candelabras and several tottering grandfather clocks. Above them all, a cloud of cut crystal hung from chandeliers. It formed a soft rainbow dazzle that rivalled the milky way. The stale spicy aroma of oiled oaken floorboards permeated the subdued atmosphere and filled his lungs like a walk in the forest. A strange new forest at that.

He was drawn in by it but watched his way as he stepped quietly over to the greenish glass counter full of military medals, coins and estate jewelry. Beside him loomed a baroque brass cash register. The two of them finally leaned gingerly against the thick glass countertop, each reluctant to break the silence as if they might scare away the fish from a bend in the river.

As he slipped easily into boredom, Piers gazed lazily at a framed print on the wall show: Athena emerging from the head of Zeus with the silent Eileithyia looking on. He looked away, unable to decode it. The engraving had disquieted him, and he fidgeted ever so slightly. Responding, his father mumbled, "He knows we're coming, Pike," then muttered something about just waiting there and being patient. An odd clock that displayed the night sky with an ashen full moon sounded four chimes. *Must be the moon in the eclipse's umbral stage*, the fourth of seven, the boy thought, impressed by the clock's precision. In moments, the grey-haired and dusty Tom Aimesworth appeared from the back room.

"Jim Ralston, a pleasure to see you again. And I take this to be your son Piers?" Aimesworth exclaimed with a smile as he wiped his hand on his stained blue smock and offered it to Jim, then to Piers. Piers instantly noticed a small faded tattoo on his wrist just like his father's: an orange eight-armed star circumscribed by a thin circle. As soon as he saw it, he knew it was something he was not to ask about, no matter how much curiosity overtook him.

"Yes, Tom," Ralston replied. "We call him Pike. He's the one I told you about. I thought he might be the right man for that job you mentioned."

Aimesworth was already scrutinizing the younger Ralston with gleeful attention. "I like that name! So, Pike, you've come here looking for some hard work, I see. And by cloud of earth's shadow, the full moon shall give no light as the ship of industry puts to sea."

"Yes sir," was all Piers could manage to say with a nervous smile. The strange little quote Aimesworth had delivered threw him off-guard, until he realized he was the ship of industry. A blush swept over his cheeks.

"And did your father tell you much about the job?" Aimesworth's tone was probing, as if he wanted to know just how much the boy knew.

"Not much, sir, just that you need someone to clean up some rooms for storage and help moving things."

"That's about it, and that's what it's all about. And if you're willing to learn this trade and work hard, I'd say you've come to no better place." Aimesworth grinned. "There's no sales work involved—m'daughter and I'll take care of that. But sometimes the customers need help loading a purchase, and I need help moving new stock into place. My back isn't what it was once upon a time. There's also the cellar that needs cleaning out, and that will take much of your time here. I've got to find more space for storage in this old place. It's the only warehouse I've got, you see."

Aimesworth went on to assure him that for a fourteen-year-old, he looked tall enough and strong enough to handle most of the stock, and that movers could do the rest. There was only one thing that Aimesworth had a penchant for repeating, as much to the father as to the son. "This store has some valuable merchandise. I can't stress enough that broken items must be paid for, by staff or customers." At this, Jim assured him that Piers was a very coordinated and careful young man, and he would not be likely to put any of the inventory at risk. A curt nod and a wink between father and son served to further emphasize this.

At Aimesworth's suggestion, they toured the main floor back rooms and then the cellar. The rooms at street level were confined to a shipping area just back of the storefront, a tiny washroom for staff only, and a workshop cum office and storage area where some furniture was under repair on the bench. Piers took careful note of each room and its contents. As they began the descent down the narrow basement staircase, he noticed a strange bronze plaque above the door. It bore a Latin motto that he could not make out, but which seemed to call out to him. In a mere glance he retained only the word "occultum."

Their affable guide fumbled with the light switch at the bottom of the stairs, and soon the room was illuminated by a dim yellowish array of ceiling lights. Piers noticed an old unused coal furnace nearby and a blocked chute that opened onto a still plentiful pile of coal. Piers remembered the more modern gas furnace on the main floor and surmised that part of his job would be removal of the unneeded coal.

Aimesworth noticed his gaze and offered bodeful confirmation, "I've got someone to take that away, but it needs to be brought up to the back-alley entrance." Patting him on the back, Aimesworth chuckled, "It'll take no time at all, Pike!"

Piers looked at a large collection of white church-style candles on a long shelf, then looked over a pile of crates filled with antique pop bottles bearing forgotten names like Kik and Wishing Well, as well as the more familiar brands. Then there were medicine bottles and quart sealers of a bygone age and a large 1920s coffee grinder that was taller than he was. On one shelf, he noticed a jam jar that bore a gummed brown paper tape, hand marked "Rare Left-handed Jar." He couldn't resist trying to open it as the two adults smiled and looked on.

"Well, it's not any pastry-chef's apron, but I guess it's safe enough," Jim Ralston said under his breath as he scanned the dusty room.

"Just like you remember it? Right?" Aimesworth answered back with a knowing smile.

Ralston gave no reply but continued to survey the walls of the place as if he sought something long forgotten.

As they surveyed the general state of chaos that filled the windowless room from corner to corner, something caught Piers' attention on a far wall. He blinked at first, then focused on it—another bronze plaque with a large symmetrical tree-like bas relief and inscriptions in a foreign script on various parts of it. It glinted in the flashlight that Aimesworth kept gesticulating with as he spoke. To Piers' agile imagination, it was mysterious and a portal to the unknown. His father suddenly noticed it too but squeezed his hand and gave him a shake of the head that seemed to advocate caution and feigned disinterest. It was only then that Piers understood that his father held a deeper aversion to the place than could be easily accounted for. Aimesworth noticed the gesture and looked askance, but nothing was said.

Aimesworth prepared to lead them up the stairs again with an impatient wave. Piers and his father were to mount the stairs while he commandeered the light switch. By now, Piers was resigned to show no more curiosity than necessary and silently marched up the stairs. They waited as the older man switched off the basement lights and trudged up the stairs, speaking of potential dates the job could start and announcing the wages.

Aimesworth poured a neat whiskey for Jim and himself and fixed a less heady shandy gaff for Piers. Then, after a toast to the three orbs, he regaled them for a while with his upbringing in a place called Merthyr Tydfil in Wales. He spoke fondly of his English father and Welsh mother and how they moved from place to place around Britain, blasting in coal mines and clerking in shops, their brood of children in tow. Piers could tell it was part of a collection of stories that could last an evening and then some, but a wink and a nod from his father seemed to put a shorter end to it. The strange astronomical clock chimed seven, as if to remind them all that the eclipse was formally over. There was little more chatting after that, for it quickly led to formal handshakes. Piers was puzzled by the odd handshake the men sealed it with, but otherwise the meeting had gone well in his eyes. He was relieved to have it over when Aimesworth kindly and firmly shook his hand in the normal way.

Then, as if on cue, the Ralstons smiled, said their goodbyes to Aimesworth and departed under the moon's fullness, freshly emerged from the eclipse. Piers felt a twinge of disappointment, sorry to have missed it. *By cloud of earth's shadow, the full moon sheds no light as the ship of industry puts to sea*, an absurd little voice in his head repeated. All he could say in reply to himself was, "Shut up." His father heard it but took no notice. Jim's eyes had that faraway look of someone who had long been in denial but was now forced to confront a greater reality.

As Piers looked back, he saw the lights extinguish in the storefront and made out the featureless stance of Aimesworth, who watched them vanish around the corner. There was a strange restlessness about the man. He almost seemed anxious for them to leave, even excited—as if he suddenly had something important to attend to.

Just two days after the eclipse, and on his own, Piers entered the door under the sun-bleached green awning of Aimesworth and Dixon Antiques. He fought off nerves as he waited for his new boss to appear. The slanting rays of the late afternoon sun crept under the awning and flooded the front windows, turning yellow in the aging sun shield that had been pulled down, covering the window. The yellowish cast of the antiques gave him a moment's unease. It was like a fish tank in time. *But where are the fish*, he thought. In no time, he noticed a stuffed sockeye salmon trophy mounted on a wooden plaque on the wall. He smiled as he imagined it swimming in the yellow light around him. His daydream was broken as a bevy of old clocks chimed the hour in a grand fanfare.

Then Aimesworth came up from the cellar and stepped up to the counter with a broad smile for his young employee. "Pike! So fair a sight to see you this fine day. You're right on the chime o' the time. Eager to get started?"

"Absolutely, Mr. Aimesworth, I'm pumped." Piers flashed an ingenuous grin in the yellow light. "Well, my dad says I'm ready. Sure hope so, anyway."

"Ah, he's almost right about that. But there's one thing you're missing—a smock like mine to protect your clothes. That's very important in a trade like this one—it's like having a uniform in the army. So, I had one delivered yesterday, just your size."

Aimesworth went on with the rules and regulations of his store and the careful attention Piers would need to pay to the dusting and cleaning of inventory. There would be floor sweeping and vacuuming in the retail area, as well as small projects in the workshop as needed. He would need to lift the heavy things with his legs, not his back. Anything substantial would need two people, and he must avoid at all cost a hernia or sprain. Aimesworth said all this to him in a very exacting but kindly tone. As Piers put on the starched blue smock he felt ready and eager to begin. There would be much to learn, but the place had started to grow on him. In a way, it was like a school but exciting, important and mysterious in a sense that no other school could ever be.

After a brisk and tutored sweep of the front floor and the backrooms, Piers followed Aimesworth down the narrow staircase to the basement. "This lower area hasn't been cleaned in years!" Aimesworth warned. As he looked over the area, he saw the empty wall where the bronzy plaque had been. It had recently been removed, but Piers felt it best not to seem too inquisitive.

"Mr. Aimesworth, could I ask how all these things ended up here?" he enquired.

Aimesworth replied with a laugh. "Well, I'm mostly to blame for that. Whenever we had something that was a slow mover in the store, or took up too much space, I moved it down here. In years past it was my partner Aston Dixon who stored part of his private collection down here. Most of that's gone now, but I know there's a few of his choice items still rattling around. That old coffee grinder would be one of them."

Then Piers felt bold. "What about that strange metal thingy that was on the far wall the first time I was here?"

"Oh, foggertybobbit! Aren't you the observant one, Pike? Odd you should mention it. I kn-know the piece you mean," Aimesworth responded with just a hint of hesitation. "It was an original brass from Dixon's catalogue of what they call yantras. He had over a hundred, he did, by the time he passed on. They came from his travels in North India and other collections he acquired over his life."

"Were they just to look at?"

"I can't rightly say to you what he saw in them, but as they say in the trade, who can account for taste?" After a pause, Aimesworth continued, "Over the years, most got sold off to collectors who knew 'im, and them as didn't. But that one piece remained until yesterday. Never would have thought it'd be the last of a hoard to scatter to the four winds. But they're all gone now—the end of an era. The last ship has left the harbor. And it's done it in style, I might say."

Aimesworth seemed ready to turn to other things, but Piers couldn't leave it at that and pressed for more, asking, "Where did it go?"

"Well ... a new customer asked me if I had anything matching its description," Aimesworth obliged him, but only after a guilty pause. The question almost seemed to have caught him off guard.

Aimesworth was ready to leave it at that, but the boy kept staring at him. He carried the answer along as if telling a tale, "... So I came down here, took it off the wall and brought it up for a showing. He actually bought it for the inflated price I quoted, no questions asked. The whole thing took minutes. That just proves to you that sometimes fortune favors the bold. Anyway, I have my carrying charges to think of."

Aimesworth's voice faded slightly as his gaze fell on a chaos of crates and boxes in the far corner of the room. His eyes resembled those of a dead fish, as though he knew that he and the boy were being watched and had to be extremely careful.

"I saw it on the weekend when we were down here. I got a feeling I knew what it was, like I had seen it before—but of course I hadn't," Piers said, pensively, still focused on the plaque.

"Oh, I really don't see how you could have, Pike," Aimesworth mused as though woken from a trance, "That was a one-of-a-kind item. I don't expect to see anything like it again. Y'may find it hard to believe, but there are things in this world you only see once."

"There were words on it too, I think."

Aimesworth agreed with a wink but was as quiet as a poker player with three wild deuces and a pair of aces.

"D'you know what the words said? I couldn't read 'em. It was a language I've never seen. It looked so beautiful, that writing."

The old man nodded and pursed his lips as if in affirmation.

"The most beautiful I've ever seen. I wish I knew someone was going to buy it. I might have asked you the price."

Aimesworth smiled at the innocence of the boy for his thought of buying the yantra. Perhaps something in the boy reminded him of another at that age, starting out and still ingenuous. Then he looked troubled, as if he wanted to spin another white lie but was honor-bound not to.

"You've good eyes. It's a language that you'll s-someday know as well as the th-thoughts that flow from your heart, Pike, old man," he stuttered, close to maudlin, presaging the future as if it were the past. The shopkeeper seemed suddenly regretful at his show of emotion, as though he'd given too much away. Piers just looked at him, puzzled and expectant. Aimesworth kept his silence, waiting for the moment to pass. But he hurriedly relented under the boy's unabated gaze.

"It's a poem of sorts, once sung, 'tis said, by a high being named Osiris, but it's older still—beyond ancient old, written by the nameless ones at the universal dawn," Aimesworth went on. "It's called by many 'The Seed of Life'. There. Now you know. Happy?"

"I never heard of it," Piers spoke up, not knowing whether he should have.

"Oh well, it goeth by other appellations," the shopkeeper muttered to himself as if quoting scripture. His unsettled eyes darted around the room as if he could see something the boy didn't.

"What do you mean, sir?"

"Ah, yes ... 'The Gates of Paradise' I've heard it called, and among those of my former order, 'The Prime Manifest'. That's such a giveaway. And it's exactly what the customer called it. He'd come a great distance— from Australia, I think. He somehow knew it was here, too. I never cease to be amazed at these people. There's no addiction like it. The collecting bug, I mean. It's a cult in itself. They hope to own whatever void infests the heart." Aimesworth bit his tongue and looked away from Piers' enquiring eyes.

"What's so important about it? Why would someone come across an ocean for it?" Piers could see he was on a roll and that there was much more to extract from this charming old gentleman. He only had to lead him on, then pull the line in, like he had hooked a trout.

"Oh well, the world's a village market, and every seller has a buyer somewhere else. If they can wait long enough, that is. That's what this business is: waiting for the fish—like an eel skulking between the rocks." Aimesworth grimaced in mock disapproval of his profession.

"Okay, I get that. But that plaque was different, wasn't it? The man from Australia knew it. I knew it, too."

"I'd go so far as to say you're forcing me to indict myself, young man, you're having me on over a piece o' brass. Yes, indeed, there's more to be said. I just thought you might find it all a drudgery, judging by your age and all. Anyway, putting that aside, let me tell you about that poem and get it over with. I suppose the powers that be would approve—better early than never." Then he muttered as if talking to some third person in the room, "Though I shudder to think of the consequences if this doesn't take."

"So, there is something ... special about it." Piers brightened, then toned himself down. He had already learned that firebrand eagerness often attracts a bucket of cold reality.

"You happen to be right. Just hearing it can change a life or save it, you know. It'll take you deep where none can touch you. And the knowing ones say impossible things can be done by those who remember its words at just the right time. I've heard said it can get you through the antechamber of the Orbis Tertius. It's not a spell, though, or just any tidbit of petty magic. And it's not without its dangers, make no mistake. Lord knows, it's how I got started in all this." The old man cast his eyes ruefully around the cellar again. He seemed almost regretful he had spoken so long about Dixon's brass yantra and was plainly getting anxious to drop the subject again.

"Guess I've told you too much as it is," Aimesworth muttered as he looked here and there. "It's like I've walked to the end of the plank and have to take the dive."

Piers noticed the man's peculiar behavior again, as though he knew someone was watching them—someone his words seemed to be directed to from time to time. Did he beg permission from an unknown presence? Piers wondered if he had asked for too much from the man.

"Can you tell me how it goes? The words of the poem?" Piers was driven to know that much, then he would leave it alone.

Aimesworth wiped his brow, his hands following furrows dug by time. "Yes, I suppose so, Master Ralston, since you're so taken by that old departed plaque. Now, I'm trusting it won't be wasted on one so young as yourself—I can't help but wonder if we're getting way ahead of ourselves here. Yet, as they say, once the sap flows in spring it doesn't stop, does it? I'd give you what they called in days gone by a 'declamation', but you'd like to hear it rendered as a song. Would I be right?"

"Yeah, a song's good," Piers nodded vigorously as he settled onto a nearby stool.

"And me without my ukulele. Guess it'll have to be *a cappella*," the shopkeeper whispered. Then he came back with a more serious precondition. "Only if you keep it an absolute secret between us. It's supposed to be for initiates only, occultus, you know. Even so, I hope you'll always remember it. I'm not saying you'll ever recite it yourself someday, but you might well need to. So, keep it tucked away in that clever head of yours, and some day—when you call it in earnest—it will seep and trickle into your heart, and you'll do things none of us have ever dreamed of."

Then he steadied his voice to a hush and began what seemed to the boy an old-style folk tune. The cavernous room soon echoed with his practiced voice.

> *A true seed once found,*
> *Then planted in style,*
> *Shall come to your aid*
> *'Gainst all days of trial.*
> *It gives light and life*
> *At Will's own command.*
> *So till the soil well,*
> *Tend ready the land.*
> *The tree shall grow tall*
> *And bounty bestow*
> *From wind-swept branches,*
> *To bright flowers' glow,*
> *For in the fullness,*
> *'Twill a nameless voice wake*
> *And call you to reap,*
> *Then true life partake.*

The refrain, sung between each stanza, spoke of something called a "jaadentril". Afterwards, Piers asked what such a thing was. But the singer just rolled his eyes and shook his head, as if he didn't know, wouldn't dare to tell, or couldn't remember. Piers sealed that word away in his memory. It seemed important.

"Let me tell you something, Pike. A carny knows his trade and I know mine. Don't yearn for the objects that hang from these walls. That's for the marks who come through the door. We sell them packages of time—a long lost time, a better time or one they think was richer in the things that matter to them—but that's all most of these things are, crystallized time."

"If they're just time, why do people want 'em?"

"Ah! It's bred in us, Pike. Time's a thing we all desire, an addiction, and all the more the older we get. Yet it trickles quickly through our fingers just as we crave it the most. Some equate it with gold in that way, and perhaps there's a part truth there. Some even find the way to attract time to them, just as others attract gold. Time is a great charlatan, though. Few see that he's both a lover and a trickster, but he's all of that. You'll be taken in by him, like the rest of us. But you'll come to see his true nature long before you reach my age. I can only hope you learn how to beat him at his own game. That's a cryin' need we call survival."

"What about the yantra and the poem on it, is that all it is? A trick?"

"No. Not at all. It belongs to another category entirely—the timeless domain of the precious thing. Things are precious by the material they are made of, or the workmanship of their form, or in the case of the yantra, the rarity of its meaning. But here's the rub that few understand: you needn't own a precious thing to possess it hook, line and sinker, Pike."

"I don't understand ..." He blinked.

"Just take it with you in your heart and you'll be all the richer: you'll never need a brass trinket to hang on your wall if you frame it in the powers of your mind and enshrine it in the aura of your soul—for it becomes a new and better thing. The wise call it philosophical gold. And you can take that to the spiritual bank," the storekeeper said and looked the boy straight in the eye.

"And after that? It can't be a trinket on the wall in your mind forever. Can it?" Piers countered instinctively, his eyes wide with an almost wanton wonder at the wisdom that poured out of this man.

"That's a precocious question for one so young, Pike," Aimesworth replied thoughtfully then softly continued, "for after that comes the raging fire that only you can light. It consumes all objects in the entire cosmos, leaving only the Void. Few of us ever stretch ourselves that far, satjim, for it leads one to the mind-heart of the *Memra*, the union of light and dark. Trinkets are no longer needed there."

Piers was about to open a fresh cascade of questions but was abruptly stopped by the wave of Aimesworth's hand.

"I can answer no more, Pike, so be satisfied with that. So, if you've understood all I've told you, it's time for me to start asking you the questions."

Piers could tell the time for profundity had come and gone. The little séance of kindred soul bonding had passed, and it was time to stumble back to reality. He fumbled his boss's name then smiled self-consciously.

"I'll remember that, Mr. Aimes ..., uh, Aimesworth."

"Something of a mouthful, isn't it? You call me Tom. Everyone else does. From now on, we're satjim, you and me. That means friends—and good ones too."

"Yes sir, I mean Tom, that is."

Aimesworth fell silent for a moment, then his voice picked up tempo. "Now that the music lesson's over, young Pike, I'd like to show you how we can get all this coal up the stairs in potato sacks. You'll be pleased you learned this next trick, and so will I that you have."

Aimesworth quickly proceeded to show Piers how to fill the sacks with a scuttle and place them near the stairs for transport to the back-alley above. The sacks were to be filled to no more than a boy could carry, of course, and Piers was warned the boss would be watching. After a few minutes of instructive help, the old man left Piers to finish his first task on the new job. It would prove to occupy the rest of the afternoon, and then some.

While rhythmically shoveling coal, Piers tried to remember Aimesworth's song. But by midafternoon it had largely evaporated from his memory like a dry puddle. The only lines he could remember were the strange ones from the refrain, "So Jaadentril grow / And Jaadentril climb, / Your treasures are safe / In the deep folds of Time." It echoed in his mind like a mantra—one that he couldn't rid himself of.

It seemed to mean so little, given that the rest of the song had fallen into fragments. Even so, something of the sense of the whole poem remained with him. In part, it was the simple and ancient image of a seed sprouting and becoming over time's ribbon a life-giving force: seed to tree, tree to seed. *That's the whole sum of it,* he thought—that and the mysterious secrecy to which he had been bound. Nothing like it had ever happened to him before. It had made the whole afternoon enchanting and singular—as if he were the sorcerer's apprentice or some such. Could it be that he was an initiate now? Probably not. It was just a word he had heard and would continue to hear bandied about when Tom and his father met. He laughed inwardly, not knowing what that word even meant.

That was only the surface of a deeper pond. Mostly what drew him in had been the rapture in Aimesworth's face and voice when the old man imparted the words to him. It was as if an orator or spellcaster had emerged from an antique land. Though jocular and even borderline avuncular, the man also seemed like a tightly closed book, even devoid of emotion much of the time. Yet a bottomless well had surfaced in those words the old man sang. Piers clearly saw that he, a mere schoolboy, had opened a channel to its waters simply by the asking of a question. In doing so, his world had become a larger place, as if some archaic resonance had been transferred to him.

He recalled a physics experiment in school. He had been called up by his science teacher to help enact the experiment in front of the class. He was asked to observe a tuning fork the teacher had him hold by its ball-end against a resonator box. He remembered watching the teacher strike middle C on a piano. He witnessed the tines of the fork vibrate for the longest time, unaided by anything but the air that surrounded them. He could hear and feel the vibrating tines too, though only slightly. The feeling he had then was one of delight and wonderment. It wasn't much different from what he felt now. Piers noticed that the whole room vibrated in a similar way, but he couldn't account for it.

An hour before closing, Aimesworth called Piers to come up top and meet someone. Piers was mortified. He looked like a coal miner, covered in black dust from his face to his tattered running shoes and laces. He tottered briefly and found his balance on the stairs with a heavy sack, then decided to take it back down to the cellar. Hands free, he brushed himself off as best he could, smeared the dust from his face and emerged in the office area to the laughter of Aimesworth and a woman in her thirties. She immediately extended her hand to him.

"Hi, Pike, I'm Cynthia, the junior Aimesworth around here. You didn't know we had a coal mine in the basement, but it looks like you're in the thick of it already." She smiled.

"Yes ma'am, very much. Pleasure to meet you," he said with a toothy smile that vastly outshone the rest of his face.

"He's a polite one and hard-working too. I'd say Tom has landed a real catch for this old place. Unlike some of the attitude we've had in the past, not mentioning names, of course," she said as she turned to her father.

Her bright blue eyes drew his gaze, and her silken voice charmed his ears. She had none of the brusque manner that Piers sometimes detected in Aimesworth senior. Cynthia had him in her spell without trying to in the slightest. Piers knew what a crush was, and he knew he had to fight it. But the feeling was infinitely agreeable and hitherto unknown to him. She was definitely different from any of the girls he knew at school. *If only she were younger*, he thought.

Aimesworth chimed in curtly, "Cynthia will be at the sales desk from Tuesdays to Thursdays, Pike. So, she's in charge here when I'm away."

"Understood. I'll do my best to be a help," Piers replied in subdued tones, but he had already warmed to the idea of working with this vivacious and charming woman. As he returned to the cellar to continue filling the coal sacks, it was with a renewed sense of optimism, and the time seemed to pass quickly. *It's so much better than school*, he thought. *No exams; I get paid. And I can talk to Cynthia.*

At closing time, Aimesworth came down to speak with Piers, pointing out the stack of old crates in the far corner. "Pike, we need to go through all those crates tomorrow. You'll need a hammer to pry up the lids on some of them, so get one from the upstairs workbench. Go very slowly and carefully with them. They may have valuable contents that I've forgotten about or never knew about in the first place. There could be china, glass or other breakables like that. I'm trusting you to be mindful.

As soon as you find anything that you think is valuable, let me know immediately—I trust your judgment, so don't hesitate. You can start on that tomorrow as time permits."

Piers agreed to start on the crates after the bulk of the coal was stowed above in the alley. As he finished up his work for the day, there was an excitement he felt incapable of containing. It seemed to emanate from these crates. Although it would be drudgery, he looked forward to satisfying his curiosity and finding out what was inside them. Perhaps there would be nothing at all, of course, but just at this moment he sensed the presence of something. Oddly, he couldn't tell if the presence was actually there, or if it would be there sometime in the future.

In a moment of whimsy, he chose a large black piece of coal from the pile, blew on it for luck and placed it on the topmost crate. Not a speck of dust remained on the coal lump, and in the dim light of the cellar it seemed like a trans-dimensional window into darkest space. He had never seen such an open piece of velvet darkness, as though its vacancy extended far beyond its boundaries. For a brief second, he felt in his heart that this one object could touch, permeate and engulf all things. The feeling of communion with the coal lump soon subsided, but it left him with the sensuous echo of a transit, a transference of energy between distant places. It gave him a shiver as he clawed himself back to reality. Panting, he felt as if he had returned from a deep mine shaft, so narrow only his body could fit between its walls.

As he turned to leave, he noticed the familiar cult-mark: a circled asterisk painted in red on the side of the top crate. It was worn and scratched, and the crazed vermillion paint had crackled and darkened with age, but it was a circumscribed star nonetheless. Scanning the other crates confirmed that it was unique in that respect, as though consecrated in some way. It suddenly struck him that of the people closest to him, he was one of the few not so marked.

Then he cut the lights and went upstairs. Piers left after goodbyes to Cynthia and her father. On closing the front door of the store, an awareness arose in him that a great trust had been bestowed. One that he meant to live up to.

Chapter 3
The Transmutation Game

The next day, Piers entered the front door of the store at his usual afternoon time and greeted Cynthia, who stood behind the counter. She smiled at him and enquired about school.

"Pretty dull. There's a math test tomorrow," he replied glumly, but was secretly glad she had asked.

"Well, it's been a slow day here, too, but no tests that I know of." She laughed, and this brought out a wry smile from him. "Do you want to work upstairs today? Tom's away for a couple of days with sellers in Victoria," she continued.

"I promised Tom that I would finish the coal sacks today, then get the crates opened." With a mock frown he proceeded to the back room closet where the smocks were hung. After donning his smock, he descended into the lower level with a nod to Cynthia. Minutes later, he was engaged in the stygian task of lugging coal sacks up the stairs and out the back door to an area protected by an overhang and a plastic tarp. Everything seemed almost normal, but there was something that gnawed at him, a change that Piers could not identify.

When he returned to the cellar, he looked at the shadowy pile of crates again and it came to him. The lump of coal he had placed there was gone. It must have fallen off. But there was no trace of it on the floor, and all the other coal had been bagged the day before. It was odd, but he shrugged and got back to business. He took the first crate off the top of the pile. It was more like a thin-planked hardwood case or drawer with a nailed-on top. After prying up the top slats, he found it was empty except for some old straw and a piece of coal. Piers was sure it was the one he had placed on top of the crate the day before, or one that looked identical.

Logically, it has to be another one, he thought. For why would anyone open the crate, put in the coal lump, then neatly tack it all shut again, all without any trace on the dust of ages on the slats and not a single sliver of wood out of place around the nail holes? Yet no matter how hard he tried to convince himself that it had to be another piece of coal, his body told him otherwise. "Occultum!" he said to no one in particular, then wondered if he had used the wrong Latin ending. Suddenly agile, his thoughts darted back to the crate game, for he twigged to what now transpired. And the game was already in play. An opening challenge, nothing less, had been issued. It was his turn to make a move.

On impulse, he blew a cool stream of air over the piece of coal as he had the day before, then set it back in its bed of straw. He no longer thought of it as for luck, though. It was an ancient priming, this ritual of air on black stone. It was the gift of life to an inanimate corpus. It was an act of creation, the feeding of an invisible flame. By now, he guessed that the stone was not coal. It was a thing consecrated for him from long-lost time. He pushed the slats and their embedded nails back on the dark, heavy crate, resealing it. Finished with it, he slid it over into a dark corner of the room. Piers then lit some of the candles on the shelf and dribbled wax on the mouth of an old Kik Cola bottle. He followed that with a hobble skirt Coca-Cola and a Mission Dry and stuck the lit candles on top of the molten wax. He then put the bottles on top of the crate. He told himself this provided better light and allowed him to proceed with the rest of the crates. There was another purpose though, but not one he wished to recognize. Even the act of thinking it would tip his hand to his unseen opponent, a being as real as himself but far more practiced, subtle and game-wise. For Piers, the candles were a taunt to terror and a magus' flourish. *Why hide? Show yourself. I dare you.* Win or lose, it would all come out when the game was over; he felt sure of that. In the meantime, he would learn it as he played it, and he would play to win.

Then, in the flip of a moth's wing against his ear, cold rationality dowsed his ramblings and he scuttled all thoughts of invisible players and imaginary games. Work called.

With a sigh, Piers turned his attention back to the pile of crates. Some were empty and had no top. One did contain old bone china teacups and saucers nestled in the now familiar straw packing. Piers carefully brought the teacup-filled crate to Cynthia and she asked him to put them on the workbench. She would go through them with her father later and enter them into inventory. Oddly, she insisted he carefully take out the cups and take the crate back to the depths. He could tell she wanted nothing to do with it.

Another crate had an ivory and ebony chess set, each piece wrapped in the same straw as before. He thought the board under it might be a fine chess board to go with it, but he was disappointed to find a dusty old snakes and ladders board with strange writing on it. *Worthless*, he thought, *it's such a stupid kid's game*. Another had what seemed to be old masons' tools and surveyors' instruments. It became clear that it would take another day to empty and unload the rest of the crates, so Piers dowsed the candles, turned off the lights and went up the stairs with the last of the items he had found. He said goodnight to Cynthia and left with his study books as she closed the store.

The next day he arrived in the afternoon as usual, his head filled with the questions on the test. He hadn't put as much into studying as he had intended, but thought he had at least passed the test, and possibly better.

"So, how was the test?" Cynthia queried him. "Was it as tough as you thought it would be?"

"Not too bad," Piers replied. "I think I aced it, actually. I'm out of this world at solving polynomials, you know. Simple ones, anyway."

"Yeah, pride cometh before a fall," she shot back sternly, but in jest.

"That sounds more like your father talking!" Piers laughed, to which Cynthia said nothing. He instantly regretted the quip and launched a flash change of subject. "You know, that basement has a weird vibration, and it's starting to get to me. It would be a great place for a really spooky Halloween party, eh? I'll be glad when I finish cleaning it out. Working up here is way better."

"Funny you should say that," Cynthia responded slowly." I've never actually been down there since I was seventeen—a little older than you."

"That a fact? Not that I blame you," Piers shot back in mild disbelief.

"I just have odd feelings about the place. And memories I'd rather forget," she answered. "I know it's silly, but it's like I'm still a little girl—I get Daddy to go and get things that are down in the scary darkness. If he's not around, and customers ask for something that may be downstairs, I tell them it's in storage. Then when they come back I show them whatever he was able to find down there."

After a pause, she said in utter sincerity, "I don't think I'll ever go down there again. Not willingly, at least. He won't board it up, though. So, door's always open."

She seemed to recover her previous train of thought and smiled reassuringly. Piers was confused and tongue-tied for a moment, then, in an attempt to break the silence, he asked, "You mean there's something dangerous there? Or a ghost or something?"

"I'm sure it's safe enough, especially if you're not connected to this place and the things that went on here years ago," she said in a low voice, adding, "but be careful down there, especially when you're digging around in the old crates and boxes. You might just stir something up."

"I think I already have," he answered nonchalantly as he went down the stairs, smock and hammer in hand. She turned to look at him, to tell him something, but he was quickly outside earshot.

Once he was surrounded by the cool musty cellar, Piers forgot the conversation with Cynthia and he surveyed with utmost attention the entire domain before him. While he looked for any changes that may have occurred overnight, the thought of what he was doing made him laugh at himself. It was ludicrous to expect anything to have happened in this confined space. On the other hand, there was a definite vibration, subliminal and inaudible, and he felt a creepiness, as if someone were watching him from the shadows. *If so, who is it? The gamester maybe?* Piers realized that none of this made sense and that his mind could well be playing tricks with him. Whatever he'd awakened, all he could do was swallow it and move on with the job, mind over matter. There was nothing he could detect that might indicate a physical change from what he remembered, so unpacking proceeded.

As Piers opened the first box, he found old sheet music and a creamy parchment-bound book dated in the 1700s. The book contained bizarre pictures of flasks, retorts and furnaces that brought out a giggle from him. Even to a fourteen-year-old, the phallic symbolism was unmistakable. He carefully wiped the dust off and took the items upstairs. Cynthia was with a customer, so he left them on the office desk. On his return to the basement, he looked up again at the remaining bronze plaque above the stairs. He noticed the word 'VITRIOL' at the top. Perhaps an advertisement? It seemed like something a pharmacy might sell. The rest of it meant nothing to him but burned itself into his memory as he quickly scanned it. He'd seen it in the old velum book too. *Visita Interiora Terrae Rectificando Invenies Occultum Lapidem. Whatever that means. Have to run it past Tom sometime.*

He was about to open another crate when he suddenly noticed something. The crate he had resealed and kicked towards the wall the previous day looked as if it had been moved. But not by him. Nor by Cynthia, judging from her aversion to the underground realm. Aimesworth had said he would be out of town for two days, so he couldn't have moved it either. It was now oriented in a north-south alignment, parallel to the stairs, and perpendicular to the way it had been the previous day. He recalled another favorite physics experiment: magnetized needle floating on cork. *That's stupid. To do that, it would have to be in a different kind of field. Not electromagnetic. Not gravitational. And the gritty old floor's got way too much friction.*

Piers examined his memory. *Damn! Why hadn't he noticed earlier this morning.* It had seemed unchanged then. He must have kicked it again without noticing. *Yes, that's it,* he thought. But why had the three bottles and their candles stayed in perfect alignment just the way he had placed them yesterday? *They should be all over the floor.* Piers was dumbfounded. Someone unknown to him had been messing around, right down here in the cellar, he reluctantly concluded. *Maybe a customer? But Cynthia wouldn't let a customer come down here on their own, or would she?*

He had read of poltergeists in one of his mother's magazines, but his sense of rationality prevented him from accepting them as an explanation. The place was windowless. The once-functional coal chute was bricked in long ago. He scanned for a hidden door in the wall or a trapdoor in the floor, but no other entrance existed save the stairs from the street level store. Then he looked for a hiding place where someone could have stayed in daylight hours then emerged at night to move the crate and escape by the stairs. It took seconds to realize how futile all this was. There was no rational explanation but that some unaccountable agency or power pervaded. Just as Cynthia had hinted.

He carefully took the bottle-mounted candles off, lit them and set them aside on the floor. Then he knelt near the crate and opened it. He loosened each nail with care and placed the slats beside him in precise order. He sensed, he knew, the vibrations so whispered, he was back in the crate game—a place where chaos reigned and ordered ritual was the only weapon. Nothing less than sublime concentration would net a victory this move. He calmed himself heardbeat by heartbeat and removed the straw tangle by tangle. What emerged from the straw packing was no longer the expected coal lump, but a sheet of brilliant yellow metal that reflected the flames of the pop-bottle candles on his face and on the wall behind. For just a moment he felt a sudden joy, as though he had turned a shady street corner and walked into the blaze of the full sun. Then he carefully held the object in his hands—hands that trembled like butterfly wings, then steadied themselves without his intervention. The sheet had a heaviness and pull, like the lead sheeting used to cover power lines or for making fishing weights. But in no way was this dull, cold lead. This metal had a seductive warmth, reflectiveness and ductility to it that suggested only one thing. *Gold.*

Piers could see that the sheet was embossed with a bas relief of unintelligible glyphs and forms, each of them repouséed from the hammered back and delicately engraved on the polished front. As he tilted the sheet gently, the designs darted across a molten sea of reflected candlelight like liquid fire. With great care, he gingerly touched the cool, electric surface. Whatever he had uncovered was not an illusion, but heavy, solid, real and like nothing else Piers had ever seen. He lost a clear sense of time as he admired the treasure, then broke himself from the enthrallment it had cast on him.

With deliberation, he checked the crate side panel and confirmed that it bore the unique ruddy asterisk, the only one so marked. He looked again at the rectangular sheet that he had laid on the straw and now realized for the first time that the piece was unfinished. Only certain parts of the surface were completely engraved and burnished—others were vague and without distinct contours. In these areas some faintly executed designs appeared only as pinpoints, ready to be engraved, hammered and embossed into complex patterns yet to be imagined.

Nothing of this saddened him in the least. It was like a work that the artist had chosen to prove his technique, or perhaps one that was set aside temporarily. The black-brown patina on the engraved crevices and pin marks showed age, perhaps antiquity, but Piers knew he could not be the judge of that. Cynthia was with a customer, and he could hear their random footsteps above him. There was no need to divert her for this. It could wait for Aimesworth senior. He would know what to do.

Piers quickly repacked the precious object with plenty of straw. He groped through the packing to find the coal so he could remove it, but it was gone without trace. A growing vacancy invaded the pit of his stomach, but it was quickly overtaken with an irrepressible sense of discovery. It was as if, at the age of fourteen, he had discovered a lost continent or new species of sea worm. After a careful and reverent repacking, he stowed it in an obscure walk-in closet under the stairs. Then, he closed his eyes. Every scratch of the object's surface and every glyphic form of its front face stood out in his photographic mind's eye, reminiscent of an old-time sepia photograph.

He turned the basement lights off, his eyes still closed, and mounted the stairs. He left the three candles burning in their bottles on the vacant floor where he had placed them. There was no way he would walk up those stairs without illumination, even if his eyes were shut. As he moved up the stairway, he sensed for the first time that a sea of energy surged beneath him on the cellar floor. He shuddered and quickened his step, taking two steps at a time to reach the top before giddiness engulfed him. *Squirelly fear*, he thought, his spine locked into the thrill of it. He made sure the door at the top of the stairs was firmly closed before he turned his face towards the smock closet and opened his eyes.

He left the building with a wave to Cynthia, who was too busy with her customers to wave back. He got only a nod from her as he closed the front door of Aimesworth and Dixon. Her eyes were still visible to him as he looked back from the street. Their serious expression seemed to say to him "You've stirred something up," but then she resumed smiling at the customer as she wrapped the Regency bone china teacup the woman had just purchased.

Piers walked homeward, repelled at the thought of his golden trove being sold like that cup. But he could never bring himself to steal it and hoard it away. It was the property of Aimesworth and Dixon, and it had to be honorably turned over regardless of what anguish it might bring him. He also began to seriously worry about the "Things that went on down there" that Cynthia had hinted at. The apparition of this object bore too many hallmarks of a magic trick. Except that it wasn't stage magic in the normal world that Piers knew, and there were no hidden compartments in the crate. The eerily excited feeling in his stomach lingered on through dinner and into the evening. His slight fever and loss of appetite prompted his mother to suspect that a virus was the cause. He smiled at that but retired early to a night of restless sleep.

Piers awoke to leaden skies and a general feeling of heaviness, then he suddenly remembered the gold sheet and retraced its flowing lines and reliefs in his mind. His memory was clear, but the disquieting realization of yesterday returned. It seemed no matter how many ways he thought it over, there was no way to account for how it appeared in the starred crate without the presence of an unknown agent who had access to the store after hours.

Then the memory of a dream from last night came to him. He was in the store basement in the dream, looking for a place to shovel the mounds of coal that lay around. There was nowhere to put it but the old furnace, so he shoveled as much as he could into the maw of the blazing old metal monstrosity. Then a fiery tree sprang forth from the furnace and grew up and up and up, like the beanstalk spoken of in the books of fairy tales. The tree turned green at first, then turned more golden as it branched upward. The higher he looked, the more brilliant the shower of stars that appeared above him. And there it ended, as the tree continued to grow without limit.

He insisted on going to school, in spite of his mother's better judgment. His father laughed and said he had never seen a boy pass up a day in sickbed unless he had a secret rendezvous at school. Piers laughed with him and winked but said nothing. It was not a work day for him at the store, but he was determined to show Aimesworth what he had found the previous day. The miracle was beginning to weary him, and it was time to share it, if only to bring it to closure.

After school, Piers arrived at the store at his usual time, finding Aimesworth by himself at the front counter. "Pike!" he exclaimed. "You're off today, boy. No need to show up here. You can go play soccer with your buddies in the park."

"Tom," Piers blurted out, "I need to show you something I found yesterday in the cellar. It's not like anything I've ever seen. There was no time to tell Cynthia yesterday—she was with a customer."

"It's all right, Pike, take your time. I'm sure it can wait 'til next week, but there's not much going on this afternoon. Foggertybobbit! Let's have a look," Aimesworth relented and met Piers' gaze with a calm but slightly apprehensive look.

Piers led him down the creaking stairs and immediately opened the stair closet, then took out the crate. Aimesworth noticed the candles mounted in their bottles, raising his eyebrows but saying nothing. Piers carried the crate in both arms, placing it on a sawed-off backless chair by the stairs. He carefully removed each nail from the crate top. A moment of doubt hit as he pulled off the first slat. *What if the treasure changed back into a lump of coal?* His mind flitted through the little gamebook in his head.

It was an attack a ruthless opponent might play. He shuddered at the mortification of it. He could almost hear Tom say, "Pike, boy, you're havin' me on!" Then he saw a bright glint peek up at him through the straw. His confidence returned, he tore off the slats one by one. When he fully exposed the metallic sheet, he looked up at the older man's face, seeking approval, anger, amazement or any other reaction that might bear witness to the reality of the singularity before them.

Aimesworth removed the object with great attention. He hefted it and inspected the front and back of it. Wordlessly, he darted up the stairs with Piers following. They came to rest in the workshop, where Aimesworth deftly ran an edge of it against his black touchstone and opened a bottle of aqua regia. Piers said nothing but watched intently. After testing against various gold needles and examining the minutia with his loupe, Aimesworth finally spoke to him.

"Lo, the heavenly choirs! Ain't it a symphony! Its high-karat gold, that's for sure. I'll have to check its volume and weigh it to make sure it's not p-plated or f-filled, but from the heft of it, it's surely close to twenty-four karats, through and through. How'd you ever find a rarity like this, Pike?" Aimesworth inquired. His voice carried a hint of tension.

Piers recounted a concocted story of just finding it in the crate, as is. This seemed to satisfy Aimesworth, but he paused and asked, "You're sure it was in that same crate you just opened?"

"Yes, Tom. That was the one. It has a red star on it," Piers said. "With a circle around it, just like the tattoo on your wrist," he was about to add, but didn't.

At this, Aimesworth looked slightly perplexed, saying to no one in particular, "I know that crate, and it's been empty for years. Cleaned it out myself. How did this get in there? Crikey! I've never seen anything like it in my life." He then turned to Piers and reassured him, "I'm sure you had nothing to do with putting it in there. My memory must be failing me. I've no idea how it arrived here. It's obviously very valuable and even more so if we can establish provenance. I'll need to get an expert in here to assess it."

"Can't you tell where it came from, Tom?" Piers asked, still guilty his sanitized story was taken at face value, but more than ready to move on.

"No, not really" Aimesworth replied. "It's not old Celtic or Norse, certainly not Mycenaean or Minoan." He went on in a whisper as he eliminated sources: Scythian, Middle East, Aztec, Mayan, or the prehispanic Andes.

"And I haven't the expertise in Shang dynasty or south Asian gold, but, based on the script-like elements and design, it's not outside the realm of temple or imperial treasury art. Any attribution like that would make it museum quality and worth a bundle, I'm sure." Aimesworth paused. It almost seemed his heart raced as he stared out the barred window that looked onto the alley. "This has something to do with Dixon, I suspect. But it's not listed in his collection catalogue. I'm quite certain he never spoke of it to me. What was the old coot trying to hide—squirreling it away like that? Probably paid a fortune for it. Then forgot it was ever there," he muttered.

"I'll leave it with you, Tom," Piers said quietly as he moved towards the doorway. "I just wanted to make sure … you knew … about it." His voice mimicked his retreating steps.

Before abandoning it to Aimesworth's cradled fingers, he scrutinized it one more time. What met his eyes shocked him. The size of the sheet was the same as before, about the size of an oversize book binding. But the decorations on its surface had changed. Piers compared what he saw with his memory of it from the day before. A significant area of new decoration had invaded areas that had previously had only pinpoints and scratchings. It seemed to Piers that at least a quarter of the surface had been worked and completed overnight.

Who's done this? Elves? He faintly smiled. *Not likely.* Whoever placed it in the crate also reworked it with the same skill as its creator, matching detail for detail and patina for patina with the original. To Piers, the chimerical object was at once a source of wonderment and anxiety—more than a boy versed in high school physics experiments could fathom. He realized now that his silence about the object's formation had become a tangled web, a deception he had woven from his own disbelief and a growing suspicion that Cynthia's fear of the cellar was well-founded. The dumber he played, the more it would entangle him.

Overwhelmed, he excused himself as Aimesworth wrapped the object in a cloth bag and slipped it inside the office safe. Piers could only stammer, "Y-You maybe should photograph it," as he left the room.

Aimesworth nodded his head in agreement to him, imploring, "Pike, mum's the word on this. I want you to know it's very important, this finding of yours. But keep it under your hat for now. We haven't the security for anything like this, and I don't feel inclined to walk it to the bank."

Piers silently acquiesced and left quickly, glad only that the abomination was firmly in Aimesworth's custody.

After that incident, a strained hush pervaded Piers' after-school job at Aimesworth and Dixon. Piers was able to quietly finish the cleanup in the basement and sweep it out with minimal direction from Aimesworth. The crates were emptied, a few put up for sale and the rest broken up for disposal. Of the latter, one was the star-marked crate. He noted that none of them had false bottoms or any other unusual construction.

For his part, Aimesworth was more taciturn and evasive by the day. He appeared to want to suppress the memory of the gold sheet almost to the point of disavowal. Piers clued-in that any talk with Cynthia was off-limits too. She doubtless had heard the story of what had been uncovered but had been coerced into silence on the matter. The three of them were like three soldiers in an outpost, knowing a military secret yet duty-bound to never discuss it.

Can an object have such power, Piers wondered, that it blankets and controls all it touches? He no longer looked forward to work at the store and hinted to his parents of quitting. They counseled against that. The underlying hope was that things would improve. But they knew nothing of the root of the problem. Piers had pledged to withhold from them the existence of the gold sheet and that he would do.

The "Nexus," as Piers privately called it, was in a coil of mutation and took on new forms within the safe to which it had been permanently confined. For Piers, the Nexus experience extended well beyond the few times he was given the opportunity to see it. He fretted about it as though it were a growing child. He could feel it in constant change, as though it roiled and foamed in a cauldron, transformed by an organic will into something he could not imagine. Yet he remained intimately connected to it. His dreams were of its many glyphs that took shape from dots and scratchings to full engravings and delicately embossed contours in and around them, like dancers at a masked ball. But more than some self-generating automaton, it was a force. And though separated from it, he felt conjoined to it.

He could see the evidence in Aimesworth's tired eyes. It spoke beyond mere words. Piers was aware that the old man also sensed and monitored the object's daily transmogrification. It could not be the work of a prankster. Not unless it was Aimesworth himself who masterminded the whole thing. But that was flawed too. There was no evidence of evil intent or malicious greed in the man. He gave the impression of one resigned to an erstwhile prophesy, unable to stop the hidden machine that was at work, and barely aware of what had taken hold of it.

It was Cynthia who broke silence with Piers. She came over to him while he was sweeping the front showroom one afternoon. As she dusted and arranged the china dogs and cats on a nearby shelf, she said quietly to him, "Father has asked a consultant to come—one who can assess the, ah, 'artwork' you found. He's coming over tomorrow morning to take a look at it."

Piers said nothing at first and kept sweeping. The whole thing sounded so ordinary. Even a browsing customer would have thought so. Then he stopped. He shook his head and looked at her. "What use is that? It isn't something that anyone actually made somewhere else, long ago. It's still being *made*."

"No, Pike, I've seen it myself," she countered, as though she had just heard a heresy. "It really is stabilizing. And it has an antique patina as genuine as I've ever seen. It comes across as a real old treasure of some kind. There's been some time warping going on around it, but less than before. Dad's tried the most bizarre things you could imagine. It's all beyond me, but I think it's in stasis now."

Piers said nothing immediately but kept sweeping. *She doesn't get the point.* Then the words he had stoppered up for days burst out of him, "What is it about that place?" He pointed downwards. They both knew he meant the chamber beneath them. Eyes trained straight at Cynthia, he continued, "I had the feeling you were going to tell me about it once. Why did that thing just appear and start changing? These things don't happen by themselves. Someone is doing this." He continued thinking out loud, "Y'know, Dixon didn't stash it in that crate like Tom thinks. It really was empty when I first opened it. And there was no false bottom—Believe me, I took that crate apart, Cynth. So's there such a thing as real magic? You two aren't magicians, are you?"

"Stop, Pike, you're going down a false trail. I can't tell you why, and I know more about it than I can say right now," she confided, "but I think you should be here when Mr. Marron comes. My father is against it. I don't know why exactly, but it seems he's afraid for you."

"No worries, eh. I can hold my own when it comes to sneers, jeers and put-downs. Anyway, I don't have any say in what happens to it. It's for the grown-ups to decide—as usual. I'm just a kid who works here after school, that's all. What right do I have to poke into any of this?" Piers replied in a dejected tone.

"I believe, in fact I know, you have a say, Pike, and I think if you speak with your father, he will agree and back you up," Cynthia implored.

"My dad is in the dark about this. I promised Tom I wouldn't tell," Piers flatly countered, but he took her point. "I'll talk it over with Tom, if you think it's so important."

Piers leaned his broom against the wall and searched out Aimesworth in the workshop. He confronted him directly and kept his voice straight and true. "Tom, tell me I'm out of place saying this, but I'm feeling like I have a stake in what's going on with that gold sheet in the safe. Cynthia says I should be in on the meeting you have tomorrow with Mr. Marron. Do you agree?"

Aimesworth seemed shocked, like a man newly fallen from a trance. "Pike, I'm sorry, it's just not a good idea that you be there. You must feel you've been sidelined, of course, but sometimes in business these things happen. And I'm not sure your direct involvement would be in your own best interest anyway."

"Why not, Tom?" Piers asked. "I know this thing I found is not normal. It's solid, but changes over time. It looks old but just appeared on the scene days ago. This is bothering me, and I want to know what happened. Did I do something to make this happen somehow?"

"I understand your feelings—they are true to the bone and need answering. But you're young, and the world is dangerous and complex, more than you could possibly know. I swore to your father to protect you and teach you, but I don't have an explanation that would make sense to you. At least not from the physics we all think we know."

"I get the situation. I just don't think anyone gets my situation."

"I'll say it again, there's a danger, Pike. And yes—there's things you don't get, and they might hurt you."

"Okay, Okay. So, teach me how. Then maybe I'll protect myself."

"All I can say is that these things can happen of their own accord and we can either accept them, and even gain from them, or pretend we don't see them and that nothing is happening," answered Aimesworth. "That's the only way I can say it."

"Yeah, I suppose," Piers said without conviction, then asked, "So what's happening tomorrow?"

"I've brought in another experienced dealer to consult for provenance and selling price. He will write up an appraisal that I can use to sell the item. It doesn't matter to him how it came into our hands, as long as it's legal," Aimesworth responded. "But he may clue into what's been happening here, so I want to steer him away from any speculation along those lines."

"How could he know, Tom? It's only just turned up. And it's not stolen. Don't ask why—I just know that."

"He knew Dixon and me years ago and belonged to a group of so-called initiates who met here in the old days, down in the cellar. That's occultus, secret knowledge, so don't spread it around. He's the one who painted the Kopendres Star on that box you opened. There's even an outside chance he and others might lay claim to the artwork itself. Just leave that part to me. I won't let that happen."

"Could he even say that?" Piers was alarmed and strangely possessive. "That's just plain wrong. It's not his to take."

"You don't know the whole story, and nor should you. Don't worry. I have it covered, Pike. Possession is nine-tenths. And that's all I'll say about that, other than that's that." Aimesworth was firm on that point.

At those words, Piers felt a cold chill run through his body. The whole affair sounded like nothing he wanted anything to do with. He began to regret having asked about the gold sheet in the first place. Maybe it was just like the chess set and the china cups—just something that had been lying around in a wooden box from decades past. Maybe he just got the boxes confused. *No, no.* He didn't. Or just another illusion in a place that spawned myriads of them. *Too solid to be an illusion. I'm a rat chasing my tail. Have to stop this now.*

"I'm just like you, Pike. Amazed and afraid. I'm afraid to read it—afraid lest it make sense to me. I just want to get it out the door as soon as possible. But it's a business we run here, and there's a proper code to follow. I don't know if I'm totally in the right here, but I can only do what I'm used to doing as a dealer. If that fails then you'll see, we'll chart another course right quick, but the student of the higher arts must first use normal means to restore normality. Trust me on this."

"That means finding a buyer and selling it," Piers said condescendingly, as though he spoke to a robot.

"Someday you will understand this. And when I do sell it, I'm going to give you one-third of the selling price as a finder's fee to you. I think that's more than fair." Aimesworth talked like he had just stepped up to a first sale to an undecided customer. It was a thing he did often and well.

Piers felt torn. In his heart, the Nexus seemed a part of him and intrinsically belonged to him. In his mind, it was different. He didn't know what it was or why he was the one it seemed to come into existence for. Or whether Aimesworth was right to frame the whole thing as a business transaction like any other. Yet the promise of a reward was very appealing to his fourteen-year-old sensibilities, and that became a strong factor in his shifting attitude. He shuddered like a nail pulled between two opposing magnets.

Aimesworth gazed at him as if he had only just seen the boy through his once-young eyes, then muttered, "... gan fod aur yn hysbys mewn tân."

Uncertain of how he should react to the utterance, Piers just stared at the man in bewilderment.

"Just a snatch of a saying ... such as my mother would have said in my old homeland, Pike. They say a true friend is known in adversity as gold is known in fire."

"Sounds true and wise, but it's beyond me what you mean by it," Pike said. They both laughed a little at the oddness they had stumbled into.

After a well-timed and thoughtful silence, Aimesworth relented. "All right Pike, it means I've decided I'll let you stay for the blessed meeting.

But you're going to have to be a silent partner in this. And invisible. I don't want Marron to know about you because if he thinks you started all this somehow, and succeeded where the Ordo Stella Kopendres failed, you may become a target. In fact, you could become more important than that gold sheet in there"—Aimesworth indicated the safe as he spoke—"Or a hundred like it."

"The Ordo … what?" Piers questioned. The fear he had felt before poked its head out of the bag again.

"Let's just call it the 'Ordinath.' It's that secret society I mentioned. You needn't be concerned about it if all goes well." Aimesworth brushed off the question.

"I can be quiet as the grave, but how can I be invisible?" Piers probed, still interested despite Aimesworth's sober tone.

"Ah! The easy part," laughed Aimesworth. "No real magic needed, only a little conjuring. See that smock closet over there? It's a tight fit, but there's room enough in there as long as you don't move or make sounds. Marron will have no reason to suspect you are here, and you will hear every word that goes on. I'll lock it so you won't be discovered if he gets sly enough to poke around. Cynthia will know about it too, so in the unlikely circumstance that something happens to me, you'll be safe. What do you say?"

Piers raised his eyebrows at this, then acquiesced with a wry smile. He tried to fit himself in the closet and found it could easily accommodate him after some cardboard boxes were removed. They both laughed at his antics but were satisfied it would work. By the time he left the store, he was uplifted that Aimesworth had restored his trust and brought him into the fold with Cynthia and himself. They were a team again. It still nagged him that the details of Marron's past were unrevealed, but he understood now why Aimesworth had kept everything confidential. It was merely a business deal, after all. There was no need to complicate things. That night, Piers slept easily and dreamt of flying. As he woke in the morning the sun shone from a cloudless sky. Excitement buzzed around him like a golden swarm of bees.

Chapter 4
Marron's Gambit Declined

t was Saturday, and school was as far from his mind as a raincloud on a sunny day. Piers got up early nevertheless. Then he readied himself for the meeting at Aimesworth and Dixon. There would be no soccer in the park today, said a stern inner voice. He had phoned his guitar teacher the previous night to cancel the usual lesson. He was free of all obligations. Cynthia had given him some recent photographs of the Nexus. He had hardly looked at them the previous night, but now, sitting on his bed in the morning light, he visually devoured them, taking in each new strand of details. He attacked each photograph as might a surgeon pouring over x-rays, assessing the patient's prognosis.

The design was almost complete, and he measured the area of worked field against the total area. Ninety percent, he reckoned. Whether it was pre-Columbian or Shang Chinese, he had no idea. But he knew in his heart the flowing designs were made up of repeated elements—elements that suggested a language or script and that expressed something intelligible. Was it a directed message, or a universal statement addressed to no one in particular? Without more knowledge, he could only compare the patterns in the Nexus to a turtle's shell, cracks in paint or veins in a leaf. But the knowledge that came from his heart said otherwise.

Piers used his mind like a sponge to soak up the symbolic flows that erupted here and there, running like streams across a page of hieroglyphs. He gradually picked out a general trend. There were often two parallel staves or guidelines that framed the glyphs. "One above and one below," he whispered. The subglyphs between the upper and lower staves were made up of strokes. There was something referential about them, but he couldn't place what it was that brought him to that conclusion.

It's like the cryptograms in the newspaper, he thought, *but it doesn't appear to be an encryption of something in a natural language.* It was idiomatic, highly redundant and quirky, but the idea grew on him that the visual idiom of the Nexus was more than an abstract design and had its own semantics. Perhaps the glyphs needed to be unfolded or decompressed. If so, that ciphertext analogy was apt.

He looked at the clock radio on his night stand. It was time. He stowed the photographs in a desk drawer and set out in advance of the meeting. On arrival, Aimesworth greeted him brusquely, his mind clearly on the tactics that would soon follow.

"Hurry, Pike, he'll be arriving. I've got to get you hidden away posthaste—before old Vic comes sauntering in. I don't want him to lay eyes on you. Just humor me." Aimesworth visually panned across the room in a nervous but unflustered way, monitoring the details as if planning to direct a movie scene.

It was easily as exciting and fearful as a stage production at school—the kind where an actor had to emerge by a trapdoor from under the floor. He'd never done it himself, but he'd seen the bullies stuffing younger boys into the sub-stage chamber during lunch hour, when no teachers were near. Shaking this from his mind, Piers responded to Aimesworth's promptings. He was quickly seated on a small stool inside the smock closet, and the door was closed on him. As Aimesworth turned the key he heard the lock click shut. Piers suddenly felt vulnerable. *What if Tom forgets to let me out?* Cynthia was not there, and there would be no one else to remind him. He could only trust that she would come to his rescue if he needed her.

"Are you comfortable in there, Pike?" came the dulled voice of Aimesworth from the other side of the door.

"Yes, Tom," he shouted bravely from the dusty enclosure. He felt like a magician's hidden assistant getting ready for the big performance.

"Good. Don't say a word, cough, or move so much as a mouse twitch. You read me? We can't let him know about you at all," Aimesworth continued.

"Roger that," shouted Piers, "No sound." He cleared his throat and coughed to make sure he would sustain a long period of silence in the dusty darkness.

"And remember, Pike, the living gold will sell itself. It will go where it is meant to go, or wait wherever its destiny demands. In the end, we are only the midwives and instruments of its journey. Okay, son?"

"Yes sir. Understood."

The rehearsal now over, the next few minutes seemed interminable. Only a small shaft of light came through the keyhole and a narrow slit along the bottom of the door. He heard the safe being opened and something taken out. Piers knew that it was the Nexus. His connection with it was now so strong that the impulse to leave the closet just to see it anew and handle it again almost took over. But he remembered the locked closet door and his promise to be silent and invisible.

He could faintly hear the doorbell and a muffled conversation at the front of the store—even the locking of the front door of the store, the clacking of the "closed" sign and the dimming of the lights. Then the conversation came nearer, and he heard individual voices and words. Piers strained his ears and could hear Aimesworth talking to Marron. Then an odor of strong cologne reached him in his dark cocoon. It was an unfamiliar scent, and not one he enjoyed being subjected to. *The eagle has landed*, he thought.

"Well, here's the piece. Take as much time as you need to look at it, Vic," Aimesworth said cheerfully.

At first, there was nothing in the way of a response, but presently a low, elderly and articulate voice said, "Tom, I think you've got something unique here. As you said on the phone, it's not oriental, not European … nor from the middle east. I think we can rule out those possibilities."

In an attempt to fill in the aural vacuum, Aimesworth then suggested meekly, "It could be New World pre-Columbian, but I just don't know the field as well as you."

More silence. Then Marron slowly responded. "Not any pre-Columbian culture I know of, old boy. The motifs are not right. Not Mayan. Not Aztec. Not coastal or inland Peruvian; possibly atypical Nazca, but that's a stretch. There appear to be glyphs from an unidentifiable language. Any luck decoding them? I'll need that magnifier you have over there. Could be connected to the Fuente Magna bowl inscriptions, but that's controversial and another long shot. We need something sure-fire."

As Aimesworth passed the lens to Marron, he commented on the quality of the gold, "It's easily a twenty-three or twenty-four karat gold by my tests and weighs a good thirty-seven ounces."

"Hmmm, you know, I'm looking at these glyphs, and I'm suddenly seeing something familiar. Amazing what the right magnification can do!" Marron almost whispered, "Did you make this? Is it a transmutation?"

"Make it?" Aimesworth snorted. "Foggertybobbit! This artifact was *discovered* here, not *made*. I'm surprised at you, Vic. We don't do forgeries, or anything of the sort. You should know that."

"Don't take offense, Tom," the voice of Marron continued softly. "I mean, did the object appear or seem to materialize downstairs near the old furnace, where we used to meet under the Ordinath's aegis and celebrate the grand equinox rituals? You remember. You can't have forgotten that."

"You mean the old days when Aston Dixon ruled the roost." Aimesworth came to the point with a note of unconcealed disappointment. His face must have given something away, for Marron immediately pushed on in this direction.

"Yes, it's certain that's where this took form. It's not from any material culture on this planet, Tom. It could be a latent effulgence from one of our rituals back then."

"Whoa there. No, no, no. It's just an abstract design. There's a bit of marginal insular design here and there—probably nonindicative—it could be from anywhere. For all I know, it's the cover plate of a medieval Albanian codex aureus. I don't want to crowdsource it to all the flaming internet yahoos yet. Not without some solid attribution. That would spoil it for any future sale. That's really why I called you in, Vic. I need a solid provenance with your name stamped on it. So far, you're way out in left field. Let's get back on track. Please."

Piers could tell that Aimesworth was irritated and reacted by pushing back a little too hard. It was clear that Tom's worst reservations about the consultation were surfacing early. Marron, to the contrary, showed no signs of getting on track.

"Tom. Look at these glyphs covering most of the surface, that's Brahan. Compressed into an indicial formalism, I'd say, but everything points to a Northern style. Dirshani, yes, unquestionably, pre-classic too. Yet highly reticulated—an impenetrable read, I agree. It could even be pre-Raanic. That'd be a real find. We'll have to unfold the glyphs to fully understand them. You know only too well what I'm talking about, Tom. I can barely believe what I'm seeing here." There was something desperately appealing to Piers in all this. It was as if Marron had directly intimated to him a deep affirmation of a miraculous encoding, a language, an art of highest sophistication. Piers desired nothing else than to be a brahanin, a master of this crypto-semantic subspace, for he was sure both Marron and Amesworth were such.

"I share your disbelief, Vic, but not much else," Aimesworth interjected.

"Can't you see, Tom? It's a deep correspondence from Sunara or even beyond. Speaking for the Ordinath, we were never able to accomplish an operation of this subtlety in all our years of labor!" Marron enthused.

"Ridiculous. It's as likely as not to be one of Aston's collectables that he brought home from Jove knows where on one of his picker trips. But whatever it is, it's crass gold, not metaphysical, and completely terrestrial in origin. Look at the engraving and the hammered repoussé on the back. It definitely shows a master's hand, but there's nothing here that points to an unearthly origin. Have you considered a connection with the shamanic Bronze Age European gold hats or the Scythians?"

"No. You and I know there's good reason not to."

"Good old Orbis Primoris without a doubt. That's the only working assumption I can accept," Aimesworth snapped back at him. It was a challenge and invited a fitting response.

Marron broke in strenuously, "I can't disagree more, Tom. Surely you can detect the vibrations it gives off when you handle it. There are incredibly ancient substrate waves—that can only come from a transmutation from something completely unobtainable. I almost hesitate to suggest it, but an ingredient like Konespaar?"

"Now it's getting ridiculous, Vic. Where would I get anything like that? The Kuiper belt? A rogue comet?" Aimesworth laughed in derision, but his voice broke in the oddest way, almost a choke, as though he'd miscalculated on a grand scale and only now saw the canyon of his deficit.

Piers was intrigued by this new word "Konespaar" but his position as a silent partner permitted neither direct inquiry nor audible show of amusement at the thought of the Nexus emerging from an extraterrestrial source. He knew too much about what really took place not to laugh at such a preposterous thought. Then he stopped smiling. Marron had ferreted out too many other insights to be dismissed as a crank. In fact, from the sound of it, he was leading poor old Tom around by the nose. Piers scoured his memory for anything he had seen or handled in the cellar that could have come from outer space. Nothing came to mind. There was not so much as a tektite in the cellar, let alone a nicely-mounted meteorite or moon rock. Aimesworth might later fill him in on Konespaar, but the latter's initial reaction to Marron's suggestion offered little promise of that.

"Sense the tril emanations. The metal is fresh," Marron continued, oblivious, "even if it's highly patinated by micro time dilations. Look at the seconds hand on my watch flit forwards and back when I bring it near the thing. The formations are fluid and barely set in their final matrix. The tempering takes time to settle in, you know, sometimes years. You should have mellowed it with the white ashes of alder and birch if you really wanted to fool me. It's a great stabilizer." The word "tril" was unknown to Piers, but he knew it could only refer to the metal that looked so much like gold.

"Yes, I tried that, Vic. Whilst I'm not denying there were stability problems with it, they've abated now. That damn cellar still imparts spatial and temporal disturbances that are easily picked up by some antiquities. I've seen that a number of times in the past, especially with the objects that have steeped down there in the Marpole fields for a long time."

Marron's patronizing silence stung like a bee to Aimesworth, so he returned to his rant to vent further.

"Regardless, it's not a conjuring from another sphere of existence like Sunara or whatever you're suggesting. You're talking about a feat that hasn't ever been done in living memory, at least not in the two lower orbs. I can't swallow the idea at all!" Aimesworth raised his voice almost to a bark.

"Dixon couldn't connect to the higher orbs without the Ordinath's active participation. He didn't possess the ohanic art to open this kind of Nexus on his own. And you certainly didn't do it unaided, either. But, obviously, someone did," Marron flatly countered him. Piers' ears picked up at the word 'Nexus'. That was his private word for the object, but Marron now referred to it by the same. *And what did he mean by a connection?*

"Vic, I'm paying you to find a credible provenance and price this thing. Credible. Try focusing on that. I don't need fairytales from the foolishness that went on here in years past. If it's what you say it is, then it's worthless to me beyond the high gold content. I may as well have it assayed and sell it for bullion," Aimesworth pushed back.

"By now I'm certain of what this is, Tom. I know you didn't casually find it, nor did you fake it," Marron flatly replied. "Someone else learned the opening ritual and used the rectified enclosure that we prepared here years ago. Your daughter is scared stiff of the sanctum, and fear bars all subtle action. Jim Ralston hasn't been near here in years as far as I know."

"Come now. Jim didn't do this. Doesn't know a thing about it. I challenge you to ask him yourself."

"I believe you. He was never much of a prospect for this kind of work anyway. And your other acolytes have drifted with the four winds. We picked up one or two in the Ordinath, and I can tell you they have little grounding whatsoever in this art. So, we're running out of candidates, unless there's someone you'd care to mention."

"There are no candidates! And whatever you think is going on here just isn't," Aimesworth shot back at him.

"Someone initiated an exchange transmutation right here on your watch. I feel it from the vibrations coming off it. They're palpable, and just barely stable." Marron went on, ignoring him, "It has the hallmark of a first attempt. Precocious but struggling, and certainly drawing on help from the other side—maybe a power being? Elaari, Scenai, even Ilyaan? But there's an unconsciousness about it—an unstudied certainty in every act. I *know* this profile. It's like the directed energy of a poltergeist but harnessed and onepointed. I'd almost say it was completely casual, like moving pieces on a child's board game."

Then, after a few seconds of dead quiet, the chain of clues linked together in the only way they could. Marron slammed his palm on the desk. "It's a kid, isn't it?"

His face must have frozen into a wooden stare, for Ainsworth said nothing. The man was not often at a loss for words.

Marron paused as though caught in a moment of self-congratulation, then continued in a gloating tone, "My watchers tell me you've hired a young man to help around the store. A teenager, they say. They don't know who he is, yet, but I have my own theory on that. Maybe he's just someone you need for the floor sweeping and heavy lifting, but based on the timing of this appearance, I'd say he's much more useful for other things. It sounded an awful lot like you'd gotten yourself another dud apprentice. But this one may be the real thing."

Marron seemed to wait for a response, but Aimesworth was still dumb with shock. Piers imagined Tom's lower lip twitching. Anytime soon, the stuttering would start, and Tom would fight with any kind of mind control he could summon just to squelch it. But it would roll out nonetheless, mangling his words like a broken zipper caught in the pull.

"You'll recall I'm a face reader, Tom, and I can read yours like a book. You sent a guileless adolescent down to the sanctum to open the Nexus vortex. He's unknowing, of course, but must have a natural potency in the ohanic ways. That's the only way you could have induced the opening of a transorbulence. Brilliant! You know? You're far more useful to me free than you ever were as a kravl!" Marron persisted, chattering excitedly, as if to himself. The word "transorbulence" caught Piers' attention. It somehow sounded to him like a scientific or mechanical contraption between orbs. *But what orbs? And my plays in that crate game weren't like working any machine I know. He was closer when he said it was like a board game. One with bizarre, unwritten rules and a real opponent.*

Then Piers muffled his thoughts. A new fright invaded his mind. *Intruder alert.* Marron was sensing his neuron chatter. He was peering through a window into Piers' mind, if only for a moment. In a watchspring's flicker, Piers froze his thought train to a block of ice and clicked into neural lockdown. The alarm bells faded to silence and Piers reengaged as the men's conversation shifted into gear again. Sweat ran down his forehead and stung his eyes.

Flustered, and approaching desperation, Aimesworth interjected, "L-l-look, with all due r-respect, that's none of your concern, Vic. Regretfully, I'm c-c-calling this so-called c-consultation to a close. Fact is, I expected mmuch more from you. I need something saleable, and you only give me crazy suppositions. It's not at all what I'd hoped for. I'll pay you for time spent, but it's over as far as I'm concerned."

"I'll waive my fees if all you care about is the commerce, Tom, but tell me the name of your protégé. Let me meet him. There are still members of the Ordinath who'd love to work with him, train him. Is he here? It's like I can sense him right in this room. Can I talk to him now?" Marron pleaded, then added in a hushed undertone, "Don't worry. We can buy off the boy's parents if that's what's holding you back. And if they don't see it our way, we have the means to coerce the level of involvement we need from him. Our methods are very sophisticated, so you won't have the least culpability in this. I don't need to add that you won't ever have money problems again, either. Think 'finder fee', Tom. This'll bring you a fine retirement. You deserve it."

"God, No!" Aimesworth quickly cried, "Not now, not ever. He doesn't work here anymore! There is no boy! It was me. I found it!"

Even Piers was struck how unconvincing this outburst sounded, but he stayed as erect and still as a totem pole and made not a sound lest it betray him in his hiding place. Once more, he broke into a sweat in the enclosed space of the dark closet. The only emotion he felt now was a profound fear of exposure to Marron and the shadowy clan he represented. The penetrating scent of Marron's cologne was enough to make Piers sneeze, but he covered his nose and clamped it hard to prevent certain disaster.

"Very well, then, keep the boy to yourself for now, and I'll pay you for the Nexus, Tom, and on top of that I'll give you better than market value. Would you bite at eighty thousand?" Marron calmly and evenly intoned, and after a pause, continued, "All right, an even hundred thousand. No? How about one hundred twenty thousand? Hell, I'll go up to four hundred thousand if we can wrap this up soon. That's way beyond the jeweler's scrap value. Is it a deal?"

"Damn it, Vic. This is no auction, and it's not for sale to you and your Ordinath cronies at any price," Aimesworth said hoarsely as he returned the Nexus to the safe, shut the door and twirled the dial.

"I'm stunned, Tom. Absolutely. It's senseless. You can't flog a rare Nexus accretion like this to the unwashed masses. I'm the best buyer you'll ever find for this class of object. But if you are bent on destroying the fruit of a true transmutation, then at least make me a plaster cast or a good hi-res photograph of it. I'll pay cash for those too," Marron continued coyly, obviously hoping to snatch a partial concession from Aimesworth.

Piers could hear Tom's fingers drumming against the table, as if to signal a response. But Tom fell mute again. Piers couldn't tell if he was actually considering the offer, or too shocked to respond.

"We need to translate the inscription out of the old Raanic-style Dirshani Brahan. We need to imbibe it deeply and understand its origin and significance. It could even lead us to the jaadentril of all jaadentrils. I can't stress enough how important this may become, surely you …" but Marron was cut off abruptly. Aimesworth had found his tongue.

"Jaadentril indeed! No more talk like that! I'm escorting you to the front entrance, Vic. We're calling it a day."

Muscles tensed, Piers strained to hear just one of them shine a glimmer on what a jaadentril might be. Amesworth had evaded him the last time he brought it up. He sensed he was finally on the verge of an answer, if they could only drift back into a civil exchange.

"Tom, listen—" Marron tried to launch a final salvo, but it was not to be.

Aimesworth quavered with emotion. "So sorry we couldn't do business today, but I know all about your interests, arcane and otherwise, and I did not invite you here to go tilting off in that direction. Now let me show you to the door." Aimesworth got up, his chair screeching against the floor planks.

Marron reluctantly rose and followed him, saying only, "You're either naïve or plain stupid if you think you can contain this, Tom. You just fumbled over a cosmic tripwire by what you've done here. There will be consequences. Especially if you try to destroy that thing, whatever it is. And I hope all that talk of the jeweler's kiln was a joke. This object has a will of its own, and it's downright dangerous to the uninitiated."

Aimesworth stuttered back, "I f-find this unprofessional in the extreme, Vic. And I'm inc-inc-inclined to report you to the an-antique dealers' association."

"That's right, tell on me! And to the dealer's association? See what good it does you! I have them in my pocket," Marron shot back, mockingly. "Tom, I was warned you had become very retro of late, and I didn't believe it. Now I see it's true. Fair warning? Don't fight this. It'll take you down with it." Marron kicked his chair in disgust and moved closer to the closet. "Just keep in mind I'm a fair and generous man, Tom. And if that boy is already mine, perchance, I'm willing to let him stay with you for protection and training. I can see you've done a very decent job with him. Extremely so. For now. But the day will come when he takes his place with me, or whomever I sell him to. Understand? And I decide when that day is, Tom, not you."

After another dead hiatus in the conversation, Marron added, "And another thing to keep in mind: what's inside him can be extracted, if you know what I mean. If he's as green as this tril, you'd have to lay down a titanic coil of energy within and around him to keep me from getting it all out. Don't oppose me in this, Tom. I don't believe for a second that you hold that kind of strength in you. And a mere boy on his own has no power against the will of the Ordinath and the Syndicate. We can gut him like a chicken on its way to dinner."

A chill stabbed Piers like an icicle. He had no idea what Marron could be referring to, but that was the last coherent sentence he heard of the progressively strange conversation. He could only hear vague perfunctory farewells in the showroom, the front door slamming and the lock clicking shut. After a minute or so, Aimesworth opened up the closet to a grateful Piers and told him that waiting would be a good idea. Marron was gone. But now there were other matters to attend to.

Chapter 5
The Ilyaan, the Codex, and the Tree

Piers blinked, dazed at the light, then finally sneezed at the full scent of Marron's cologne permeating the room. He had an alien sensation that he had just lived through a meeting that would echo through his life. The feeling it gave him was unexpectedly euphoric, though it made no logical sense to him why. Then euphoria morphed into guilt before he could enjoy the sweetness of it. He could see that Aimesworth was highly agitated. He quickly focused on Tom's voice.

"I'm ashamed and weak with anger at that fiasco. I can hardly speak, Pike," the old man paused, taking a breath and looking at the floor. He lapsed into a stutter, "But I d-deeply apologize to you for this. I never wanted for you to hear all that. N-n-ever."

Aimesworth gazed at Piers intently, as if seeking some sign. But seeing the boy's confusion, his tone darkened. "You must be very c-c-careful,

Pike. You mustn't work here or have contact with us anymore. These p-people Marron is mixed up with will be on the lookout for you. Now, m-more than ever—they'll hunt you like a pack of wolves. They cannot be allowed to find out who you are for sure. It's for your own good. I'll call your father privately and send your pay to the house with a letter of recommendation." He looked away, and his hands trembled as he fiddled with a stuck desk drawer.

"But you're my mahir, Tom. I know what that means now. Dad filled me in on how I'm supposed to be a student, a tatsa. I know I'm not the best at this stuff—I don't even know yet why I'm supposed to be doing it. But I'm trying hard." Piers was reeling with a new loss, and he had a hard time pushing back on a sense of betrayal.

For a moment, Aimesworth was lost in thought, then he ruefully continued, "I'm truly sorry, Pike, son. I never thought our time together would end like this. You're easily the best tatsa I've ever had. And I won't even ask what you did down there to trigger this. Maybe nothing. But that bastard senses that you brought this on, and right now it's the only thing that matters. If you did actualize this by your own instincts, there may be little more for me to teach you anyway."

"It's way too soon to cut me loose. There's too much I haven't learned. It's all just beginning to come together for me," pleaded Piers.

"Sometimes beginnings and endings are the same thing—you'll get used to that in life. Either way, you need protection. So, from now on, don't come near this place, and don't associate with Cynthia or me. It's not out of anger I repeat this. It's out of flat-out fear for you and yours. They've caught your scent. You have to run like a deer for the bush and stay under cover. Can you try to understand that? You're in survival mode." Piers nodded, crestfallen at what he heard.

Aimesworth looked out the cloudy window into the alley, as though expecting to see someone or something. Seeing nothing, he turned again to Piers. "I guess it was foolish to dream I could sell off an artifact like that and get Victor Marron to cooperate, but I was just trying to keep this place financially afloat. And don't think those figures he was throwing at me weren't tempting. No fool like an old fool. Right?"

Piers had no words but looked at Aimesworth's eyes for meaning. He saw only gloom and desolation.

Aimesworth sat at his desk and took a breath before continuing. "I do have one last picture of the object, and I'm giving it to you — you keep it hidden, and don't show it around. It's only safe to keep it if no one knows you have it. That includes your parents. Occultus, understand?"

Piers twigged on the Latin word. It seemed to sum up his entire experience in this place. Aimesworth took a large manila envelope from his desk and handed it to him. Piers accepted it without expression.

"One other thing, Pike," Aimesworth said in a low hoarse whisper, "and I know you will think this downright peculiar, but you need to take possession of a great secret from the upper orbs. A name. It's something that our Victor didn't think of, and it's far more powerful than the ham-fisted tricks he assumes I deal in."

"What is it, this, ah, secret name?" Piers hesitated, his green eyes locked on his mentor's face. There was something quirky, yet beguiling, about Tom's request.

"It is your true name since long before you were ever born down here. It's a powerful seal and transcends all other names and epithets. It will protect you from those who would enslave or entrap you or deprive you of life and its highest qualities. That is not to say you will never suffer defeat, but it will aid you in gaining recovery and victory. Do not write it or confess to anyone that this ritual ever occurred. Keep it only in your mind and memory. Once it takes effect, your enemies will suspect it. So keep them guessing. Do you understand me?"

"I think so," Piers replied, unsure how else he could respond.

"That man who just left us must never know it. He's no friend to you, so stay clear of him and make no alliance with the Ordinath or any other Kopendres scum. Even for your parents or friends, and definitely no one else who might claim you or call you his property. Tell it to no one. Promise me that and swear it in your heart to the Highest Essence."

"I promise not to tell it to Mr. Marron or my parents or anyone else. I, ah, swear to … the …"

"Now say: *Memra Itan Watetsuan.*"

Still disoriented, Piers repeated the words to the best of his ability.

"Good. That translates as 'sworn to Memra forever.' You've taken an oath to the *Memra* now—don't forget that. That's the cosmic heart-mind, the highest consciousness."

"And that means …?"

"It's imprinted on the blank page of all futures and potentialities, binding on all parties in perpetuity, including a witness like me. Believe me when I say that you need this protection now more than ever. We must complete the ritual without delay. They won't be expecting this at all. It'll smart like salt in their eyes." The old man chuckled on the last sentence.

Aimesworth's eyes radiated a new strength. He majestically rose, stood and had Piers stand before him, laying his palm on Piers' forehead. He solemnly incanted something in a language unknown to Piers, then switched to English.

"Under the powers invested in me by the Dahi Utanjil of the Durzh and with the full approving force of the lineage Iridas, I, the name-giver, bestow to you the knowledge of your primal name Taighen of the secret root of Kaatsuan, to be fully known as Taighenkaatsuan from ageless past and in perpetuity. By it you will receive the doctrines of the elect, the fullness of their power, and the protection of the Nexus. With the potency of the highest, I declare this shall be known only to the Imaros, who is the Great Intelligence, the Unara, who is the Great Heart, their beloved union the *Memra*, and to the Ilyaan, the Yondai and their bonded minions, to the Dahi of the lineage and to me, the name-giver. To all others this name is sealed under perpetual taji. Swarn to Memra in perpetuity. *Memra Itan Watetsuan!*"

At Aimesworth's prompting, Piers repeated the last phrase. The words still had no meaning to him, but this time they fell off his lips in the most natural way, and he could feel their vigor rattle up his spine. *Ah! The trinity of those god-words. Imaros – light-father. Unara – darkness-mother. Memra – allness-child, logos-sophia.* He had only ever heard his father utter the supernals in curses, but they vibrated with a mantric potency when Tom intoned them. *Ilyaan, Yondai, Dahi.* More incomprehensibles he would have to learn later. *Perpetual taji.* Now. The sound of this jolted his mind like the lightning bolt that flashed through Franklin's kite-born key.

He knew from conversations picked up around the store that *taji* meant an event that kept happening, an insistant, driven recurrence that occurs in a fixed topos, associated with an agency of actors, not the type who appeared in theatres, but sentient players, maybe just one, drawn into the same situation or scene again and again, as if rehearsing a script. Like reincarnation, Hamlet's soliloquy, school on Monday, the full moon or soccer matches. They were all tajis, and taji was the force, the one true binding that ties the cosmos to its spine of order and renders time but a dullard's illusion. It was no stretch; this "Taighenkaatsuan" would come crashing back to him each passing storm like an onslaught of breakers driven shoreward.

Aimesworth patted Piers on the shoulder and smiled. "You may use the primary name Taighen in the higher orbs or among the knowing ones down here. You may attach your father's clan name to it: Taighen-Uchundar. But the primary and secret root in full form is unspeakable unless in the company of an Ilyaan or one of the other realmless power beings. Do not even tell weaker vessels that you are the holder of a *nomen mysticum verum*, lest they try to discover it. Right now, it's the most precious thing you have, and it's linked to the Nexus. Obey this code! Self-betrayal of the true name means certain death-thralldom. And that is endpoint. Omega!"

Again, Piers nodded as if he understood the monologue, but his eyes said otherwise. *Ilyaans yet again? Realmless power beings?* The thin sliver that he could comprehend and put in words amounted to less than a fingerprint on the surface of his youthful mindset. But he knew the prevailing attitude towards the "higher orbs" in the world of his experience, parents, friends and opponents alike. It was clear that he now had a fresh set of enemies he had never reckoned existed. So there was no danger he would let pass the merest scintilla of the pact he had entered into with Aimesworth. And the secrecy of the name was the long and the short of it.

"Taighenkaatsuan," Tom Aimesworth said softly to him once more, patiently, with a teacher's emphasis, then added, "Make sure you know it, for when you need its energy and protection, you must silently repeat it within. Add the words 'I am that' after it and the energy will flow within you with a power proportional to that which is requisite."

"Taighenkaatsuan, Taighenkaatsuan, Taighenkaatsuan, I am that," Piers whispered to himself, as though it were a mantra. He had no idea what had just happened or what impact it would have.

Piers looked to his name-giver in silence. For his part, Aimesworth seemed overwrought and disillusioned again.

"I'm a stupid ass, you know. Not equal to mentoring the likes of you at all. And I'm afraid the cat's out of the bag, Pike. By bringing Marron into it, I've hoisted myself on my own petard!" Aimesworth half-muttered, then added, "And almost taken you with me."

Impulsively, Piers put his hand on Aimesworth's shoulder to console him as best he could. Aimesworth immediately felt buoyed by the energy that seemed to radiate so freely from the boy.

"Even so, Pike, with such little exposure to the old Marpole power fields that flow deep through here, you've learned all you need to survive on your own in the lower two orbs, and then some. I'd even wager you could teach me a few things some day!"

"Not any day soon, Tom." Piers permitted himself a chuckle.

"All this will die down by and by, and you can seek out Cynthia when the time is right. She's an acolyte of the higher arts in her own right and can finish the work I started with you. She and your father wear the Kopendres star like me, but you must trust them to keep you free of it when I'm gone. When the time comes, you will mind her, won't you?"

"I promise, Tom." He could only think of one thing: why his friend and mentor spoke of a time when he would be 'gone', but he choked on the words. "And ... what will happen to the Nexus?" Piers compulsively asked instead, almost regretting the words as he spoke them.

"Without contest, it is the first strike of an artisan of the highest order, a rarity in the lower orbs. That's what the man told us, and now, after being dragged kicking and screaming, I've come to believe him. But if that's so, I must destroy it whilst I can, Pike."

"But he said …"

"Yes, I know what he said, and he's right. No work for the uninitiated. But I was long ago instructed in the necessities of this grave and serious art, and now I must carry out what I was taught — none of us can keep your Nexus now."

"Why not?" Piers uttered, bewildered.

"Remember Dixon's yantra, the one you took to so much when you started work here?"

"The Seed of Life. I'll always remember that," Piers replied, reassured by the thought of the old brass plaque that had once graced the cellar walls. The sight of it and the sound of its poem were enshrined memories.

"Well, the fact of the matter is, there really never was a customer, Pike—not of the connoisseur variety. I bald-faced lied to you about that. When I saw how you looked at it that night, and the fear in your father's eyes when he saw you communing with it, I knew, I knew, I knew. I had to destroy it, precious though that old icon was."

"Why? I can't believe it, Tom." Piers felt himself pivot into a new shockwave.

"After you and your father left, I took it down, cleaved it with an axe and cast it into an ingot in the workshop kiln—the very next day it was off to the scrap metal dealer. He bought it for a trifle, as far as the selling of it goes, and that's the only iota of truth in what I told you." Aimesworth grinned at his facetious attempt to lighten the mood, only to realize it was salt to a raw wound, quickly adding, "I'm ashamed to say."

"And did you lie about the poem, the words, the history, what it means?" Piers was still trying to come to grips with Tom's confession. He needed to know who and what he could trust. And while his mind couldn't convict, his heart felt something just this side of a betrayal.

"No, lad. I could never do that. I was true to my calling—I gave you your first initiation in its full pleroma, as my lineage decrees. You're quick enough to have known that, aren't you? It was just as I had been initiated before you, and my mahir before me, and back through the generations. It was in a little antique store in Northeast Yorkshire, just like this one. I was a fourteen-year-old apprentice and an initiate to the higher mysteries and the doctrines of the elect, like you."

"And they zapped a frigging yantra for you?" Piers shot back with schoolyard sarcasm, dubious about this latest yarn.

"It's a necessary sacrifice, an old tradition called the *tatzirion*, and you should feel honored by it. Each time, a consecrated relic is cut asunder, arm from shoulder, leg from hip, and melted down in advance, and its core vibrance is transferred to the acolyte through a recitation. Like the song I sang for you."

"It's strange. I got the impression the yantra was made for someone else—a hand-me-down. Like King Tut's tomb."

"You're full of insight, Pike. Aston Dixon brought back that yantra from Srinigar in the Kashmir for your father's tatzirion, not yours. We had so many hopes for him."

"And it wasn't ever hacked up and melted. Why not?"

"Why go into that, Pike? Don't some things deserve to be forgotten?"

"No. I need to know. I think you owe me that much, Tom."

"Jim failed the test, arse over elbow, if you must know. He never made the joining, the communion with the yantra's inner seed."

"What's that about?"

"In the high arts, we call it first conjunction. It means a linking with the energic essence of the yantric field. It's either there or it isn't. That entering is the sign we look for. Cynthia, in turn, never achieved it, nor any of the other acolytes we trained here. N'ery a one."

"Yeah, I remember what you're talking about—the feeling, the vibration. I had it."

"You had it in spades, m'boy—like a salmon hatchling hellbent to swim downstream the raging canyon to the sea. You were the first to enter the precinct and make the join. And without a thimbleful of training. My boy, that yantra was for you from the day it was made and its seed is planted deep in you, now and forever, like a shield and a buckler, as the Good Book says."

"Speaking of vibrations—there was someone else there besides you and me. I felt we were being watched and I know you did too, Tom."

"Yes. Yes, Pike. A very powerful being, Pike. It would be hard to miss him, given your sensitivity to the greater real."

Piers continued to stare at him, and Aimesworth knew that holding back was not an option. "You've heard me speak of the Ilyaan race. Well, say no more of this Ilyaan for now. The first part of his work is done. You won't be seeing him for a long time. Not in this orb, anyway." Aimesworth's voice fell to a hush.

"What's an Ilyaan, Tom? You keep mentioning them. To me they're another name for zero. I need to know what I'm dealing with."

Tom shook his head. "Your father wouldn't want me telling you tales that he says he doesn't believe in himself, so don't you mention this to him if you don't want an angry jibe. Realmless power beings like the Ruakon, Elaari, Yondai and Soenai—they turn up anywhere they pretty much please. Let's just say they hold gigantic energies and wield that power at the behest of the Great Intelligence—here, or on a plane far higher than our material world.

The Ilyaan are the most potent of 'em all."

"I didn't see anything like that."

"If he'd shown himself, you might've just taken fright, I'm guessing, so that's why you can't see him. Fear is like radio static. It fouls the connections in this work."

"Will I ever? As you did?"

"Not as I did. I'm sure you will when you're ready, but he'll likely be younger."

"Why's that?" Piers gave a quizzical look, edging into disbelief.

"Born from the Father of Light's star point projection, they travel through childhood and age much as we do until they reach the apogee of their journey. Yet they are symmetrical in time, a thing we can't fathom. Unlike us, it's not over for them—they turn in their orbit like planets do, rejuvenating as they turn and approach union on the final course, younger and younger, 'til they merge with the Ultimate in final infancy."

Piers shook his head in disbelief. "Okay. Just tell me one thing. What was he doing down here?"

"I can't but guess his full mission, even though he stated his purpose as plain as I'm standing here. I don't think it was intended that I remember all that he said to me." Aimesworth planned to leave it at that, but piercing eyes told him he had to continue.

"It was a month before you came here," Aimesworth relented and went on. "A charming young man rang the bell on the counter. He appeared to be a workman in coveralls, asking to inspect the gas lines in the cellar. He had some kind of work order that he waved in front of me. I didn't even look at it—seemed a fake, I thought. I remember wondering if he was one of those young con men you hear of so often. They always want to see your furnace, then tell you need a new one. I told him the old furnace hadn't been used in years and it was for coal anyway, but he was insistent."

"So, you sent him on his way, then. To protect the sanctum."

"No—and as you say, I should have. There was something commanding in his manner. And I noticed the glow of his hair and eyes. I thought he was an albino, at first, but even his skin gave off a soft, clean light tinged blue. I knew at once what he was—a nameless one—and that I was honored to obey him as he obeyed the Father of Light. It's ingrained in me, you know. The training and all."

"The training?"

"You'll soon receive the mysteries of the three orbs, as the wise say. It may not be through me and it won't be through your father, but someone will step up to the urgings of the Imaros and Unara, and their union, the *Memra*. That's why I've already asked Cynthia to do the honors when and as the time is right for you. Time is on your side, so don't fret about it. The first error in the art is haste, as the knowing say."

"Tell me more about this Ilyaan you met. What did he want, Tom?" Piers was wide-eyed by now, and he knew he was swallowing Aimesworth's ramblings like a hooked fish.

"I led him down the stairs, and he looked in wonder around the place, even enraptured, I might say. I had to stifle a sheepish giggle. The place was in the usual mess—old pop bottles all over the place and the coal pile drifting here and there. He glanced at that derelict furnace. I could see it in his eyes; he knew right away it was a disguised athanor. He knew it held a coelem to the high places. I could see the satisfaction in his face—he'd been searching for it like the magi of the east. And for a long time."

"What did he actually say to you down there? Tell me, Tom. Don't ask me why, but I really need to know this."

"He asked if anyone else had entered the sanctum before him, and he warned me not to let other strangers enter. 'Allow no sulphur here,' I recall him saying. It was almost as if he had a rival he wanted to exclude."

"But then you brought dad and me down there, didn't you?"

"Yes, but you and Jim are not strangers. That he made clear enough to me —the line of Uchundar is welcome here. All but one of them. He didn't say who, but I believe I can guess."

"So that's all he said to you?" Piers was fully drawn into Aimesworth's tale. He no longer cared if it was true or false. It was real.

"He told me he was there as a witness to a great work, a *magnum opus*, so I gave him my blessing and promised him access to the precinct. He mentioned the formation of a codex and that a ghenjil of the line of Uchundar would hold it, but that it was occultus and I was to say no more of it. There was no mention of you, Pike, except in a very elliptical way. He said I would be a mahir again, but not for long."

"Ghenjil? What's that?"

"Patience. We'll cover that ground tonight. But Pike, realize that nothing he told me after that made much sense to me, and what I remember has now come to pass like a *déjà vu*. I remember him saying his work would be in two coils of a zirion. He looked hard into my eyes. I have to say it hurt like a hell-blast and gave me the most terrible headache. Bastard that he was!"

"That's so fucked! If I ever see him, I'd wanna make him pay for that," Piers exclaimed.

"No, Pike. And never you try to hurt him on my account—not that you can take on these powers in any meaningful way." Aimesworth laughed as if dealing with a spirited chihuahua.

"So, how do you get back at him?"

"Just show compassion for him. Forgive him for being what he is, grand though that is, and the nature that rules him. All creatures under the *Memra* are vulnerable. I have the feeling he might even need you someday, amazing though that sounds, and I know you'll help him. Won't you?"

Piers held back to process what he was hearing, then replied, "Ah, that's a bit warped, but okay, if you say so. But first tell me how it ended between you and him."

"I don't know enough Ilyaanic, I'm afraid, so I babbled something to him in Dirshani—I can't remember what. Then he did the strangest thing, Pike. He took a rock from his satchel, a rock as black as coal, and placed it in the coal pile, random-like. I was not to touch any of it. I could only think of the saying: taking coals to Newcastle. It seemed just as pointless. I think that's when I thought of hiring someone like you to clear out all the coal and be rid of it and all. It's clear to me now: he planted that thought in my mind. It's almost like he knew all about you, or maybe someone like you he was searching for. Then I can honestly say he gave me a last directive and vanished without awaiting the slightest answer from me."

"I still don't see what really happened. I didn't follow any rules. I didn't know beforehand what I was supposed to do. And I still don't understand what part the Ilyaan had in it," Piers confessed.

"In truth, he did little more beyond putting a black rock in a pile of coal."

"What's the sense in doing that?"

"On the face of it, none at all. A treasure hunt, maybe. Or so it would seem. But Vic let slip something about a Konespaar as the *prima materia* of the transmuted Nexus. That's a black rock that happens to be the original matter of the cosmos, used by the Yondai at creation to form all that we see, feel or are. Nowadays, primeval Konespaar is the rarest of minerals, bar none. Most of it was used up at the cosmic dawn."

"Never heard of it. Where would you find stuff like that, anyway?" "Astronomically, they say it can only be found far beyond Pluto, even past the Oort cloud in interstellar space. Who's to know, really? There's no source of it on Earth. But somehow, if we can believe Vic Marron, you found it lying in a cellar coal pile. Do you remember anything like that?"

"It's getting a little misty, but I remember grabbing a strange chunk of coal from the pile. It sure was black, as black as outer space, and the vibes it gave off were out of this world. I felt like I was falling into it when I picked it up. Like it had a pull on me. This'll sound freaky, but I blew air on it. Next day it showed up inside the crate I'd put it on. Like it was alive. I don't know why, but I blew on it again and repacked it in the crate. Then I left it alone, like it was a move in a board game. Like I was waiting for the other side to make their next move."

"Did it come in fits and pieces, this game you played?"

"Nah. It was all one thing, Tom. Like it never started or ended—the board was set up long ago, just waiting for a player to make the first move. And I never saw the other player. Maybe it was the Ilyaan."

"How did you feel as the game proceeded? Different?"

"Tired and feverish. I felt like something was dissolving in me—even while I slept. But alongside that, another thing was forming too, rising out of the water, if you like. The Nexus."

"I'm talking about your subtle energies interacting with a transorbulence channel, Pike. But fair enough, you've answered me figuratively. The crate was just a lower vessel in the train, the chest of Osiris to the old ones. The waters of transformation were inside you."

"And the black stone?"

"Ah! The Konespaar was your prima materia—the green seed of the wise. Not just the menstruum of this world, but of your Nexus as well. I'm sure it was given to the Ilyaan by the Imaros himself—the fair one we call the Great Intelligence and Father of Light. It was a touchstone to test your instincts and intuition, to test your fitness. May his will surround us like a castle wall."

"Fitness? For what, Tom?"

"The Work of Creation, Pike—for that's what you did. It's work once consigned to the Yondai, fearsome, invisible immensities at the dawn of all being—but you've done it, too, now. Fools like Vic and I can only dream of the forces you fused and harnessed in that old cellar."

"And the visitor I couldn't see?"

"For all the world, it appears the Ilyaan came here to witness you pull down this Nexus and form it with the transmuted matter of the Konespaar. It has to be a coil in the cycles he spoke of—a zirion—a great and important recurrence—an event that he long searched and waited for."

When Aimesworth saw Piers' vacant eyes and dropping jaw, he drove the nail in deeper. "You know, let's call it a magnificent surprise that keeps happening when you least expect it. Like an ice age melting, or the return of a comet, or a volcanic eruption. Just as nature has its zirions, a sentient can experience zirion too, but it's grander still—it's not tied to a single place—it follows and finds you anywhere in the cosmos, not the other way around, if you catch my drift. Some might call it destiny."

"So, history really repeats itself," Piers laughed. "Every Monday is like every other Monday. But seriously, I sort of see what you mean. I just can't believe all this stuff is connected."

"Well, neither could I. We must thank our flaming consultant, I suppose. None of this seemed connected until Vic Marron damned near drew me the picture tonight in this very room. And I couldn't accept it, dolt that I am. I'm sorry it took me so long to see it plain and simple for what it was and is."

"This Nexus or Codex, as the Ilyaan called it—what do you think it is?"

"Well, he didn't so much as tell me anything that stuck in my old brain, Pike boy. But years ago, in the old country, I was taken aside by my mahir and versed in the doctrines of the *Torvaaden*. It was all very hush-hush—you can be sure—but my old mahir must have had a flash and foreseen that I would need to apply that knowledge someday. Today's that, I can only suppose."

"This thing you just said, Tor- something. What's the connection to the Nexus?"

"The gold sheet that sits in that safe over there could very well be what the knowing call the *germinatus* of the *Torvaaden* Codex. I'm beginning to think Vic had a hunch what it was—he just wasn't letting on. I can tell you one thing: it's far more valuable than any of the fancy offers he made me. No figure can be named, Pike. True and sure, it's priceless." Aimesworth's voice trailed off to a mere whisper.

"Codex? That some kind of book, maybe? A story?"

"The *Torvaaden* is a self-organizing text—a zirion that spans all wisdom held by the orbs of the cosmos. It's vast beyond imagining and has a will of its own. It's so seldom among us that all wisdom-lovers rejoice at its appearance. Oh, I could show you old books from as far back as the 1600s that call it by other names, and even wood-cuts that—"

"Tom. Tom, you're going way too fast for me. So, it's all good, you're saying? Whatever I did was for the good of all, then?"

"For the true wisdom seekers, yes. But the dark-hearted seek only to own, harness and use it for selfish magic. When they have it, it's never for the good of all."

"They can do that?"

"It's a toxin to their dry and crumbling souls. Yet crave it they do, as an intoxicant or a last-hope medicine. They crave to see themselves at the center of the Allness. They covet it as a key that can open any lock, unbind any binding, tell all origins or fates, or lead them to the corridors of power and riches."

"Sounds like it's a book that tells the beginning and end of everything? And how to do all sorts of magic?"

"It's neither a book of creation, nor of doom. And it's definitely not a spell book. It's the *prisca sapientia*, the pristine wisdom of creation. A remote diamond among the analects of unknown authorship, it offers neither purpose nor theme. Its true art you must study within. And when you do, you'll find it's more like a spherical mirror—it reflects us all but teaches us the worth and divinity enfolded in others."

"Sorry, how? It still doesn't make any sense to me."

"Like a tree, *Torvaaden* is static yet mutable, always growing, always dividing and always unified. All its parts are rooted in a core indicial complex from which its corpus can be regenerated anywhere and anytime. It is so like a tree that long ago the wise ones remarked that it was to the soul what the jaadentril, a living tree of living gold, is to the mind, eye, and hand."

"Jaadentril. That was in your song, the one on the yantra. I asked what it was, and you wouldn't answer me ... then."

"You weren't ready, but you've proven yourself. Jaad-en-tril. Means 'treeof-gold' in Dirshani. The 'philosophical tree', the wise often call it, for it is living gold, *tril*."

"So, finally, you're telling me—it's a golden tree that grows from the ground? There really are such things? These jaadentrils?"

"They exist in every orb of the cosmos—sure as I'm standing here. But they're precious hard to find, Pike. You see, most of us walk in the shadow of the jaadentrils—we stumble by them but never see them in their timeless glory. We never access their power, life-flow or freedom, even though we trek through a forest of them and could reach out and touch them if only we knew how or cared to. We too often deny ourselves the medicine of joy as we trudge towards our omega."

"You're saying I'm like that, too ... that I'll never see one."

"Perhaps you'll prove me wrong. That's if you become a ghenjil as the Ilyaan said. If you master the art of the ghenjil, you'll find many a jaadentril, and even forge and fashion them through your own mastery of their energies. And that's a rockier road again than any you've yet travelled, but I'm not saying you don't have the wherewithal." Tom laughed.

The mahir and his tatsa talked, laughed and even cried at times, through the afternoon and into the evening. The time meant nothing to them—just water flowing down the rich, green and fast-flowing river of life. Each knew it was their last time together in this orb and the only opportunity they had left to lay a firm foundation. It was nothing less than the foundation that Piers would need to stand his ground against the Kopendres Syndicate in the years ahead, and he drank it inward like a thirsty weed. Tom kept it to basics, skirting away from the theoretical backbone he loved so well, for he knew it was the meat—the practical training—that would keep Piers out of trouble and stave off an abduction. Details could be left for Cynthia later, but today it was the essentials.

At the end of it, both were exhausted. Piers switched the topic back to the Nexus and his relationship to it. "And the Nexus—the sheet thing that came from the crate—it's not the whole codex, but a core indiciality-whatever?" "Aye, boy. The indicial complex—the germinatus that regenerates the rest of its vast tapestry of wisdom, like a weaver at his loom. When the codex manifests, it's the indicial complex that takes material form. It's written in a highly compressed and almost unreadable dialect of brahan. And always engraved in the finest philosophical tril, by that I mean gold, and not just any tril, but purest tril from the seed of a jaadentril." Aimesworth rolled the 'r' on tril as though sanctifying it.

"So, you're saying that gold sheet I found—"

"You did more than find it—you pulled it from a place high above us and a deep place inside you. It's a union of the two that you crafted. That was your second conjunction, boy."

"Conjunction? I've heard you use that word. Still murk to me."

"The *coniunctio* of the wise. A sacred wedding between your inner and outer selves. Your yantra's seed was the first. Your Nexus, the Golden Codex, was the second. And on this day, you've finished another, Pike. Your secret name is the third conjunction, as it always should be."

"So, I'm done, right? Tell me there's no more."

"I must prepare your fourth in seclusion, before I cut my stakes here. Don't worry, I'll leave you clues. It's always a treasure hunt in a faraway place. A transformation of the second and a seedbed to the fifth. But it's not for a few years. When your basic training is covered."

"How many are there?" He sounded hopeless.

"For the novice in the high arts, a set of seven, each a gateway to the next and each a shield to the ones before it. Every conjunction will have its proof—an artifact of passage that is the seed of what follows. A song. A nexus. A name. And so on."

"And the others?"

"They'll come of their own accord and needn't be rushed. They're sealed in hermetics, you know, for your own protection. They must all surprise you with maximum entropy. That's the power of them. I'd break my oath as a mahir if I spilled the flask now."

"Just a hint, then?" Piers flashed his mahir a look both penetrating and skeptical. Aimesworth sighed. It was hard to deny a face like that, but the old man knew the only safe answer was a riddle.

"The fourth you will hold within, yet in your hand, a relic of the second and a last gift from your mahir. And from what you don't cast to the winds like wasted seed, the fifth will be your own masterwork entirely—the serpent's feather, a powerful work of light and dark. It will bind you to your life's burden yet astonish the wise and warn you of danger. Fast on its heels, the sixth will be sealed by the worthless coin that someday buys your freedom. Then you'll be an *initiatus*, an artisan fit for the journey, willing or not."

"And the seventh?" Piers felt a shudder as he uttered the words.

"That's when you pull up stakes. For you, the seventh leads beyond this orb to the path of Measureless Essence and the topos of the *Torvaaden*. It's as clear to me now as the shine in your eyes. And it's clear to our unseen visitor, the Ilyaan. Remember, though: to all other watchers the conjunctions must be hidden until they happen. Occultus."

Piers shook his head at Tom's verbal knotwork, half in wonderment and half in disbelief. "So where do you think the Ilyaan is now, Tom? Far away?" His voice was wistful, even sad.

Aimesworth lowered his voice to a whisper. "He's with us right now, Pike —I've no doubt of that. I can't say where all this will end, but sure as stars you'll meet him again—long after I've crossed the river, my young satjim."

For Piers, the threads of Aimesworth's story had every hallmark of a madman's ramble. But the details rang true, and it connected all the facts he had witnessed. He thought about the rock that he had put on the crate. It had to be the stone the Ilyaan had left in the pile. It moved inside the crate as if someone was coaching him in a new game. He followed the game and learned it quickly—as if he already knew it. And now it had become this golden sheet bearing a web of inscriptions. More than ever, his impulse was to save it somehow. But he needed to know more.

"You still haven't explained the yantra and the Nexus. Why do we have to destroy the finest? Things that are rare, beautiful and should be kept? Because it's part of another ritual?"

"No, Pike, there's no hocus pocus here. If Victor is correct, I'm very afraid of what lies inside this Golden Codex—the meanings it holds. I told you: it's a key that unlocks an unimaginable power to those addicted to such. That's why he and the Ordinath want it; others too, I'm sure. And it's why we must contain it and seal its essence within you. You must be its enigma to the sentient cosmos. You're the only place it's safe. Remember how I once told you that you can save an object in your heart and mind with the right preparation and intention? I can't say more, but I'm confident you'll prove this in your own time. It'll never abandon you."

"So, what do we do, Tom? Wait for the Ilyaan to show himself and take charge?" Piers was suddenly feeling the weight of the cosmos on his shoulders.

"Sad to say, no Ilyaan can help us now. The task belongs to both of us, me to extract the elixir and you to contain it like the flask o' the wise," Aimesworth answered, then took Piers by the shoulders and looked at him squarely. When their eyes met, he spoke again.

"Even so, it may be the ruin of me to take down the seed of a jaadentril, drain it of its vibrancy, reduce its philosophical menstruum to a new and higher essence, and its flesh to the crass gold calx of this world. Yet, by the Great Intelligence, you will share in the earthly value of the calx as I promised, and much more: all its primal essence shall be invested in you."

"Why did all this happen to me?" Piers questioned, not really hoping for an answer.

"You have the curiosity, the will to learn, and there's a tendency you have to avoid the straight lines and think in curves. Sometimes it's the shortest way from A to B. All that, and your memory is a bottomless sack. You've shown you can follow the thread to the center of the ever-changing maze, then follow it back again. Yes, that's all it takes. But to know it firsthand can't be had by rote-learning. You just have to go down the shaft, enter the center of the earth and, by righting the balance, find the hidden stone. It's what's behind the artwork that counts."

"And you, Tom? What's your part in this? Are you supposed to show me the way or something?"

"Nothing but a catalyst. I'm just the fool who was there and couldn't see the greatest event in centuries as it happened right under my nose. But through our talking, the scales have fallen from my eyes."

"You know? I get the feeling there's a downside to this," Piers said in a facetious tone.

"It all comes at a price, Pike," Tom answered him in earnest. "The knowing ones you meet, good or evil, will see it in your eyes as easily as I— that's your vulnerability, and I have the feeling it may be your strength too."

"What is it they'll see?"

"They'll well-nigh see you are the *Torvi*—that rare and special carrier of the *Torvaaden* in all its subtle glory."

"*Torvi?*"

"At any given time, there's at most one Torvi, and it's been eons since there was one living among us. We've come through some very dark ages. But you must learn to be wary and shield your eyes from those of dark intent. And let no one know who and what you are until you are very sure of their intentions."

"And why is that?"

"I've warned you: the *Torvaaden* is dangerous. An ignoramus who stares into the sun will be blinded, but the Codex is far more treacherous. It's lethal to the unprepared, so you must be a guide and a guardian to them, and never give them more than they can handle."

"I don't know, Tom. I'm not ready for anything like this. Is there a way to just reverse it? Turn it off? You said I was to be a ghenjil and hunt for jaadentrils. Isn't that hard enough all by itself?"

Aimesworth gave him a rueful smile and shook his head. "Be strong, son. Know that your secret name protects you and the *Torvaaden*. Till the soil and tend ready the land, for like Dixon's yantra, the potency of the Codex is your dichotomous seed—half presents as the jaadentril's seed, source of your ghenjil-nature, and half is the void-flower that feeds the Torvi-wisdom within you. They're melding together as we speak. And in the gestation ahead? Inseparable. As the *Torvaaden* says, when the flower falls from the vine, the twin fruitions will take form and ripen. So will it be for you."

"This isn't one of your stories, Tom, is it?" Piers gave him a wary smile.

"On my honor and on that of the lineage that begot me, the last words the Ilyaan said to me were this: 'Take nothing of the essence, though it may call to you like life itself. It's for the ghenjil alone. Him. The elixir belongs to the *Torvi*, none other.' In both ways, he meant you, Pike-satjim."

The old man's tears streamed down his face, and his words hit like a crack of thunder, drifting off into silence. Though they made little sense to Piers, the keywords 'ghenjil' and 'Torvi' had unlocked the dual seals of his destiny—they were the answers to all his doubts and the guideposts to a new territory. The way forward was an overgrown trail, but tangles and brambles could be set aside now. Another realization loomed. He sensed that the journey with his first guide to the wilderness had led them to a sudden cleft. Only one of them would forge onward. Aimesworth solemnly shook hands with him, his right hand to Piers' left, to seal the pact. Without explanation, he insisted that Piers grasp his right hand, interlocking middle fingers to middle fingers, index finger and little finger tip to tip, and thumb to thumb. Piers had seen this done before. This was a rite of passage. As their hands released from the clasp, he stood alone before the mountain.

"Pike, one last thing! When you need an ally you can trust, or advice you can follow, seek out the Dahi I spoke of. He's your champion. He carries your true and secret name in his heart and will always safeguard your path."

"How'll I find him?"

"There's no need to puzzle it out. He's the wisest mortal I know. He travels through space and time like a vir, but with none of their inflated selfregard. Remember that in your greatest need, he will know of it beforehand and find you. Now be on the lookout for any Kopendres watchers on your way home. Hide before they see you, Taighenkaatsuan. And always seek your precious freedom. Always. From this day forth, it's hurtling towards you at the speed of starlight."

Aimesworth's parting words to Piers caught the boy by surprise, but the time for questions had passed. Aimesworth had closed his eyes and moved towards him with his index finger firmly pressed against his lips. After a parting hug, Piers left by the back door and quickly darted up the alley, questions racing through his mind.

Chapter 6
The Ghenjil's Way

Once home, Piers immediately sealed Aimesworth's manila envelope, scrawled it "private", and hid it behind a dresser in his room. It would collect dust there, he knew, but it would be safe. The next day, his father came to his room and spoke with him about the loss of the job. Beyond his expectations, the talk with his father helped him to focus on normal life and become grounded again.

Piers was determined to put this all behind him, get another job and get on with life. As it happened, Aimesworth had spoken on his behalf to the manager at the nearby groceteria and there was an opening there he could fill. As time passed, there would be no further talk in the Ralston home of the Aimesworth and Dixon antique store. Tom Aimesworth's name was seldom mentioned again, like the name of one who had faded from living memory. Marron and his ominous *Ordo Stella Kopendres* would become an even more distant, though still troubling, memory.

Regardless of his efforts to put the Aimesworth and Dixon experience behind him, the latent image of the Nexus would not leave him alone, no matter how he might try to ignore it. He retained a detailed mental map of its glyphic content and other-worldly embellishments, even down to the threadlike filigrees and fey reticulations. At times, he would take pencil or felt pen and draw the strokes and graphic elements of the compositions as he remembered them, as though they could speak to him if he mechanically recopied them over and over again. Then he would gaze at them on his desk, dancing across the laid-out scraps of paper and envelope-backs from his private file-box.

Dixon's yantra pattern appeared here and there in the overall design. He had no inkling why, but it drifted in and out the deeper he peered into it. Under sufficient probing, the golden layers of the Codex flaked apart in his mind, tearing like tissue and freeing ever lighter from its inner reaches to shine out through the cracks and tears and illuminate him. The inner landscape invited him. There were orbs and orbs within orbs; stars and stars within stars. There were golden trees that he knew to be jaadentrils, and they knew him, mirroring his face to him from polished bark. There was row on row of tangled glyphs that could be teased apart into garden plots of cursive forms. Some gazed out at him with trance-like devotion, the stares of faces in a forest of totem poles, or on stacks of cedar bent-boxes in an endless museum. Others writhed and flexed like garter snakes, eager to inform and enchant him, but stone-mute and condemned to slip away into the shadows of his mind. He felt like an explorer wandering inside a silent kaleidoscope that some drowsy giant had left unattended. But without a key or guide to its meaning it was a lonely land.

Eventually, he made small discoveries of how the glyphs were composed. When combined, the forms took on flavors and colors that, to Piers, transcended their mere values. As his analysis continued, the arbitrary numeric encodings he assigned to them combined with one another to appear as scenes or tableaus in his mind's eye—tantalizing in themselves but as removed from reality as the ships in bottles he remembered at Aimesworth and Dixon's. To him they were miniature ships with an unknown cargo, setting sail for exotic ports, leaving him behind on his drab shore.

Piers drew on deeper instincts hinting to him that the glyphs conveyed a hidden gnosis as well. He could not determine just what that knowledge was or how it applied to him. The original metallized Nexus no longer mattered to him, wherever it was. It was the mere crust of a more fundamental impulse that Piers had inwardly acquired in the aftermath of the Aimesworth and Dixon experience. He had absorbed the abstraction of the entity so profoundly that it now nourished itself and grew within him as an independent operative. He sensed full well the dangers of this fixation becoming obsessive, even a substitute for human relationships.

Outwardly, Piers strove to maintain a balance that belied any concerns that others might otherwise have had for him. He appeared to all who knew him to be a well-adjusted, happy teenager. Given his natural transparency of expression, the golden glow of the Codex shone through his ready smile. In the years that followed, he excelled in science and mathematics, soccer and guitar lessons. He got on well with the staff and customers at the groceteria after school and on weekends. And the iron will he developed to contain and rein in the internal Nexus stood him well in the achievement of the goals and ambitions of conventional life.

The prodigious memory skills of his childhood, if anything, intensified. He could recite the periodic table of elements as if it were the alphabet. Long nineteenth-century ballads were a specialty. He kept these talents to himself, but it became harder to do so. As time passed, the sheer energy of the *Torvaaden* Codex increased, as though an exterior power were feeding it and nurturing its growth.

It became evident that the light of the Nexus would not tolerate competition from darker domains. Though the murky world of supernatural spells, charms and mind-altering drugs was a magnet to some of his teenage friends, Piers quietly avoided all contact with these influences. If taunted by them, he would feign amused indifference and jokingly quote from some inner voice that he had only come to know since harboring the Nexus, "To see is to touch, to touch is to know, and nothing is invisible, untouchable or unknowable." Like a solo mountaineer bivuacked tight against the north flank of an icy summit, he waited in Unara's night for the morning light of Imaros, liminal to a dawn ascent to Memra's nonduality. For though he could not read them, these unsharable god-thoughts were the peak transcendence of the Codex, etched into him with a burin tempered in starfire. But they left him mute, these thoughts. He could no more explain them to others than a closed book can recite its own contents. And for reasons made all too clear to him, that book would remain shut. Tight shut.

His winsome grin and love of sophistry confounded his enquirers enough to end all serious questioning. But the forced laughter and puzzled stares he provoked came with a cost. Those who might have sympathized with him on the deepest level were ultimately driven away, along with the science and lit nerds and the musicians. Even the jocks, who appreciated his soccer skills, saw him as a strange hybrid and kept him at arm's length. It was a technique most of the girls his age unconsciously adopted as well, and for much the same reason. With extroversion a failed option, he became the quintessential boy who was always alone, his only companion an ageless text that resisted all his efforts to decode.

He became drawn to women older than himself, one in particular. He thought of Cynthia often, but dared not contact her and break his pact with Aimesworth. Of all that had happened in that brief Aimesworth and Dixon period, he cherished her kindness and encouragement the most. He also knew she would be the one person most likely to quench his curiosity for what really happened. His father seemed indifferent and would seldom answer his questions. Even the fact that he and the Aimesworths had the same wrist tattoo was treated like a state secret. But associating with either Tom Aimesworth or his daughter could implicate Piers with the Nexus, especially for those who could harm them all.

Even if not seen by the Ordinath directly, rumors could find their way to them and offer them clues of his identity. He imagined that even phone conversations were monitored by the Ordinath but was self-aware enough to laugh at his own reaction. Distance and caution, he reluctantly accepted, were the safest protections. At times, he felt resigned to the life of a fugitive, an inch away from paranoia. His unconscious demeanor had a way of attracting the worst energies.

Taunting and bullying occasionally found their way to him, as though his predators were in league with the Ordinath. Once he was crammed into the dreaded trapdoor chamber under the school stage by an impromptu gang. Practical jokesters? At least that is what they passed themselves off as. Piers was certain they were just the tools of Marron. They had long scattered by the time a kindly janitor heard his patient knocking and released him. The man urged him to name his tormentors, but, knowing the adolescent code of all boys, was unsurprised by Piers' silence.

Outside of an abiding fondness for Hesse's *Siddhartha*, Piers developed a voracious appetite for spy novels. He took on the unconscious habit of looking over his shoulder now and then just to see if anyone was observing or following him. It was an odd feeling that he wanted to shuck but found it inescapable. Paradoxically, closed spaces seemed safe and did not rekindle the memories of the infamous meeting with Marron. He felt exposed in broad spaces, when he smelled certain odors, or heard certain timbres of voice in crowded places. Any one of them could trigger an immediate sensation that he was in danger, the rumblings of a panic attack.

The fear he had felt in Aimesworth's closet resurfaced at these times. It also pounced on him when he relived that fateful meeting. He could almost smell the acrid odor of cheap cologne whenever he thought of it. Cynthia always came to mind when he felt this fear, her presence manifesting as a guide who would lead him home through the dark forest. Piers never gave up the hope there would be a time when they would meet again.

Then the fateful day came. It was nearly three years since Aimesworth and Dixon. Jim received a call from Cynthia. Tom Aimesworth had died after a lingering illness. His store had been closed for a year and sold off at a loss. Grief-stricken and not a little apprehensive, Piers showed up with his father at the funeral service. Naïvely, he was determined to console Cynthia as best he could. He had, of course, no idea how to do this. She had been very close to her father, and Piers was now forced to reexamine that bond if only to be a help to Cynthia. He listened to two short eulogies by Aimesworth relatives. They were touched by the difficulties of his final years, and Piers thought immediately of the last time he spoke with Tom.

The confusion, fear and doubt he felt then melted into the framed image of a slightly younger and smiling Thomas Aimesworth on a small easel by the pewter-grey coffin. Piers wiped a tear from his cheek in mild surprise. Then a tall thin man in his seventies took the lectern and began the final eulogy. Bearing thick bluish-white hair, he wore a black pinstripe suit and surveyed the congregation with steely eyes. Piers seemed to be in a stupor for the first few words of his address, and then a jolt went through him. *The voice!* And the faint scent of acrid cologne that had not quite penetrated the room. In a split second he realized that this man he was seeing for the first time could only be his archenemy, Victor Marron. His spy novel training kicked in immediately.

Piers slowly glanced at Cynthia from his seat in the fourth row, moving only his eyes. She sat motionlessly in the first row on the other side of the room, her blonde hair and black hat in perfect contrast. He could see no reaction from her, but it was clear to him that the ubiquitous *Ordo Stella Kopendres* was present, to forgive and see off their erstwhile brother Tom, yet make a show of force to boot. He would have to avoid all unnecessary attention. That would rule out any overt conversations with Cynthia. His gaze fell to his shoes for the rest of Marron's eulogy. His mind so gripped by terror, he later would have no recollection of what Marron said or when it was over.

It seemed to last for hours, and Piers was overtaken with the image of a hawk surveying a lush field of rabbits in various poses of eating, hopping and resting. One of the rabbits was frozen in position, just like the fourteenyear-old boy who had once sat bolt upright in a closet for what seemed an eternity. Nothing had really changed, except that now, for the first time, the rabbit had seen the hawk, its wings and its talons. And he understood tacitly that some of the rabbits surrounding him in the green grassy field were secretly hawks ready to morph and move in on him without notice. It seemed to him that they were all waiting for a single blade of grass to move.

Piers suddenly became aware that someone was tapping him on the hand. It was his father. "Pike, are you with us?" he enquired. "It's over. We should make an act of presence here and go talk to some of these people."

"Uh, I don't think so, Dad. I think I just want to go home. Can we go now? Or I'll just wait in the car if you want to talk to people," Piers answered, shaking off his daydream.

"Why?" asked his father. "Don't you feel well?"

"No, I don't. Headache," Piers said, looking for the quickest way to exit. "Can't we just leave without talking?"

His father just smiled and said, "Well, we can't go without talking to this man," indicating a smiling Victor Marron, who had moved up beside them.

Piers just froze and kept his eyes on the ground, saying nothing.

He heard his father speak as if at a distance. "Victor, I'd like you to meet my son, Pike."

"Pike, it's a pleasure," doted Marron. "I'm sure you're tired of hearing that you're the spitting image of your father when he was your age. Even the emerald eyes!"

"No, not really, of course," Piers replied through clenched jaws, looking up with a shudder, "but n-nice to meet you."

He felt forced by courtesy to look Marron in the eye, and he did so hesitantly. It was a time for his iron will to rein in the Nexus and cloud his face in opacity. He silently uttered his secret name to himself and affirmed his identity with it. Nothing must get through, he told himself as the obligatory handshake took place. In seconds the cordial Marron had already nodded a casual goodbye to him. With a pontifical air, Marron had moved on to other admirers who were eager to glad-hand him. Piers took a deep breath and felt the bone chill slowly depart on the exhale.

"So, how exactly do you two know each other?" Piers whispered as he looked at his father and the departing Marron.

"Victor gave me my first job when I was around your age. He has an antique store, like Tom's. Then I worked at Tom's place for a while, around the time Aston Dixon passed and Tom needed the help," his father answered tersely.

This surprised Piers, who had no idea his father had any connections to Marron. It was evidently one of those military secrets the family was so good at keeping. He immediately felt more at ease. His father had some history with his adversary, and that could be useful. In the next half hour, Piers found out that his father was known to just about all the 'Ordinath' people in the room. Piers found himself being introduced to one after another and observed first-hand the rapid-fire sequence of secret handshakes his father engaged in with great skill, spiced now and then with unintelligible salutations. Piers could only marvel at Jim's *savoir faire* with all this occult stuff.

As they made the rounds of the crowded room, it gradually became clear to him that his own father was nothing less than a member of some standing, though definitely not as active as he once had been. It was like finding out that his father was secretly a member of a notorious motorcycle gang. Not only that, many of the faithful looked on Piers with varying degrees of adulation, awe, or jealousy.

He was dumbfounded as they flashed their tattooed wrists bearing the Kopendres star insignia and shook his hand in ritualistic ways. A few even whispered among themselves the name Taighen-Uchundar as he passed, like it was some kind of mantra. He had fantasized once or twice about what it would be like to be a celebrity, but never seriously thought he would experience attention of that scale—especially at a funeral. He reciprocated with frozen smiles, studious attention to the obsequious compliments, and faraway looks to his father that begged for deliverance.

Cynthia left very shortly after the end of the service, as soon as the casket left the building. When Piers looked around for her, she was gone.

"Not to worry, Pike, we'll be seeing her soon, I'm sure," Jim said, reading him with ease.

When they were back in the car, Piers asked, "Dad, I've got a thousand questions. For instance: what was that language you were speaking to them in?"

"It's just a jargon they use in the Ordinath. A twilight lingo, as they say," his father replied as though they were discussing the weather. "You would have learned it if you had been able to stay at the store. Tom was going to teach it to you."

"You mean you were going to pay him to give me lessons, just like guitar?" Piers asked, incredulous.

"No." His father laughed. "Tom suggested it without any word from me. He wasn't really under the Ordinath's thumb, as you may have noticed, but he still held to some of their ways. That, and the fact that it would be outside the control of Victor may have made the idea of being a mentor to you attractive to him, I guess. Tom really wanted to show the Ordinath he was strong and independent of them. I think he saw you as a potential protégé—more than a tatsa. You know, farther down the road."

"And why do all these 'Ordinath' people kowtow to this Mr. Marron? Who is he?"

"He has a very high rank in the Kopendres organization, and locally he carries the stick for just about everything that goes on. He's what they call a vir. Do you know what that is?"

"Not really, but he knows about this secret Nexus business that got me fired," said Piers. "Does he know it's me? That I'm the one who made it happen?—At least Tom believed it was me."

"Yeah, Pike ... Vic knows. It didn't take him long to figure it out. And you're right, you actually did open a Nexus on which a golden transmutation membrane formed. That makes you a very special person. Other than Victor himself, maybe, no one else around here has ever done that, though it wasn't as if they didn't try hard enough."

"It's not just the gold sheet. That's gone with Tom. But there's more to it. It's like a piece of eternity inside me. Do you understand what that is?" For the first time, Piers opened up to his father about the *Torvaaden* and might be getting some serious support.

"Yes, sort of—Tom told me—it's way above my head. I confess I distrust the pompous words of the virs and dahis, but that's all we have. They say the meta-lesion seems to have taken on the imprint of a singular artifact. Something called a stasis zirion. It's like a piece of the foundation of the cosmos. It's a part of you now. Permanently."

"So, it's just Control-C Control-V? Do you believe that?" Piers noticed his father said nothing about the *Torvaaden*, or his being the *Torvi*.

"I'm inclined to, but I don't know if Tom could ever see the fullness of it. It all happened on his watch and he felt awful about it. I hate it too, but I don't blame him for it. He did his damnedest to protect you. I still don't know who did this to you, or if it really was anyone."

"Why do you hate it?" Piers was saddened and suddenly felt very alone. It was clear Tom had never told his father about the Ilyaan or the *Torvaaden*. They truly were occultus, and it struck him now, with Tom gone, only he and Cynthia carried that knowledge. His suspicions turned to Marron, though. Marron knew as much as Tom did, and more. Then there was the mysterious Dahi. Only Tom had ever spoken of him as a real person.

"Good question." His father broke into his thought-train. "Before your time, it was supposed to be me, then they tried using Cynthia. I guess it's something I couldn't ever do for them. Neither could Cynthia. That's why we got passed by after we became too old to be useful to them. Tom had a chip on his shoulder about that. Me, too, I guess. It's like we were nothing but livestock to them."

"Marron told you to get me that job at Aimesworth and Dixon two years ago? To turn me into some kind of freak?"

"Not at all! I don't take orders from him, Pike. It's not like that. I'm free and clear of those people. But I'll admit I wasn't always. That job you had at Aimesworth and Dixon? It was Tom and the Dahi who pushed me. Tom said you were at risk. You needed protection, pure and simple. What would you do if it was your kid?"

Piers had no ready answer and decided to change the subject. "I was really afraid of those people back there at the funeral. Some of them are just plain creepy."

"Don't be afraid, and never show them fear. Tom either hid or destroyed the original accretion, so you're the only one who retains the Nexus essence now. That's your protection, so never give it up to them. They need you alive and happy. You want to know something? The only reason they were even talking to me was because you were with me. That's how important you are to them. I'm just a pariah from the past."

"How do you know this, Dad? That I *have* the Nexus?" Piers said after a long pause.

"I can see it when I look into your eyes, Pike."

"Ha! You wish!" Piers laughed, but he couldn't help feeling that if his father could see the astral glow in him, others could too, and that might include Victor Marron. It all seemed to be falling out just as Tom had warned.

"Just don't tell your mother about any of this stuff. *Capiche?*"

Piers knew this signaled the end of this conversation, and any further revelations, for now. They fell silent, driving through the traffic and the rain that had crept up on them. As they neared home, it was a relief to Piers that his father would not be driving to the graveside ceremony. Had they gone on to the cemetery, there was no way Piers would have abandoned the safety of the car if Marron and his followers were there. Despite the largely friendly encounter with them, he'd had more than enough of the Ordinath for one day.

In several months, Piers had put the events of Aimesworth's funeral behind him. He still had not spoken directly to Cynthia, but by eavesdropping on his father's phone calls, he became aware that a plan was afoot to have her teach him in the ways of the Ordinath. It seemed that Marron was orchestrating his training with an eye towards inducting the younger Ralston into the organization at some future date. Jim Ralston had initially harbored and vocalized strong reservations about involving his son in a group he had rejected in his own youth. He was apparently yielding to the subtle but unrelenting influence of Marron, though.

To Piers, there seemed to be little regard in either camp for his own input. He told his father in no uncertain terms that regardless of what Marron wanted for him, it was not going to happen. Only when it was agreed that Marron would not be involved, and that Cynthia would do all the teaching, did he come around. As the planned start drew near, he was even becoming enthusiastic towards the idea, but tried not to let on.

For the first time, Piers arrived at the Aimesworth family home in Shaughnessy and was impressed with its faux Victorian grandeur. He was just as taken in by the grounds, landscaped with ornate trees, including a carefully locked lattice-enclosed bonsai garden. On the other hand, it became instantly clear that it could soon be someone else's. There was a

"For Sale" sign on the front lawn. Cynthia met him at the front door as she was seeing off a couple and their real estate agent. As Piers entered, a small van arrived with the banner of Marron Antiquities on its side. For a moment, Piers thought this an ill omen. Then two men from the van announced they were to collect some furniture, and Cynthia showed them the tagged items to take.

That taken care of, she and her student retired to the study. She couldn't resist commenting on how he had sprouted up since she last saw him, and how much he resembled his father even more than the last time she had seen him. Piers just rolled his eyes and agreed, smiling at her with the full luminosity of the Nexus. It was not lost on her in the least, and she gave him a look of both fascination and cautious probity. She knew the Nexus would empower Piers in the work ahead, but he would also need maturity and dedication to advance in what was before him.

They had coffee, then Cynthia seated herself across from Piers at a wellworn table and started the initial lesson. She opened with, "Your father said you wanted to learn the Dirshani language, a very old koiné language spoken in north and central Sunara, and also Brahan. That's one of the three high art forms of the Orbis Secundus, and it's the core semantic structuring component of the Nexus. The two subjects go together, so I'll teach you what I know of them in parallel. Did you bring an engineer's notebook with numbered pages?"

"Yes, but first of all, what's the Orbis Secundus?"

"It is more fundamental and elemental than this physical world, 'Monra Morasa,' which we take as the Orbis Primoris. That's the orb we are operating in now. In Dirshani, an orb is 'monra' and so the Orbis Secundus is 'Monra Sunara,' or just 'Sunara.' It's a realm of existential experience that is beyond the material world, Pike, and for most, an unperceived dimension. We call our conscious world phenomenal, but there are other phenomenal worlds. Someday, you may experience them. With a little training …"

"Can you describe this Sunara orb?"

"All orbs have what wise ones call a *spiritus mundi*, a world spirit or consciousness. It is said to draw on your perceptions and supply you with a realistic material environment, if you were to transfer your consciousness there. To understand it, be aware that you are entering into metaphysics, but the reality of the subject matter should be clear to one who has seen and heard what you have experienced. As for Sunara, there are dangers there and terrible power holders, but there are some nice spots too. Or so I'm told."

Cynthia went on to answer a barrage of other questions from Piers. He finally asked how the two orbs connected and whether one could travel between them. He knew this was a loaded question, yet he felt compelled to ask it. She showed him a blown-glass model of three ovoid orbs in decreasing size, each atop a larger one, centrally connected with vertical glass tubes.

Cynthia carefully pointed out the tubes, saying, "There's a point of contact where great power accumulates. That is where the knowing ones enter interorbal transit. It's called a wahan. That's a Dirshani term that means something like a soul-gate. Its form is that of a spinning tunnel of energic membranes, I'm told."

"Your father knew all this. He could transit the wahan, I'm sure. Can you, Cynthia?"

"Yes, he could, and no, I lack the needed talent for these things. It's extremely difficult because of the energy and insight needed to gain entry to a wahan. It's like a standing wave between the orbs, or even within a single orb: from one place or time frame to another. They form a network of channels that connect and span the cosmos. But only for the knowing ones, not a kravl like me," she laughed in self-deprecation.

"That's the only way to transit between orbs?"

"For the soul-complexes of sentients, yes. But then there is the minor connection: the transorbulence, or nexus conduit, like the spectacular one you opened three years ago. They are moveable threads, tendrilations or tubuloids that allow objects, energy and information to pass between the orbs. They form semi-permanent linkages between worlds. You're the only one we know of who has created one in recent times. And before you ask, it's nowhere near like opening a persistent wahan. That would need an active agent on the other side to set it up, or the powers of a vir."

"Virs. I've heard of them. They are powerful and knowing beyond other sentients of Morasa, but are Mehenti, like us. My father discussed them with me. He called them 'sorcerer princes'. Told me to steer clear of them."

"They certainly don't need a wahan, if that's what you mean."

"So how … how do they make transit?"

"It's supposed to be occultus. They have something called an 'ethris'—that's the limit of my knowledge. Don't let anyone know you've heard this. If you really want to learn more about these things, ask Victor. Doubt he'll tell much, though."

"He's one of them, isn't he?"

"Um … yes," Cynthia answered reluctantly, then quickly added, "although he doesn't publicize it. And I wouldn't mention it if I were you. Truth is, he's a well-known vir in Sunara, but he keeps that quiet here. Never cross him, Pike. He's still sore about what my father did with you."

"It's cool, I'm just curious. So, a transorbulence is what I set up to bring down energy to make a Nexus with the black stone. But I gave up the Nexus to Tom. How did it get back to me?"

"Tom separated the physical calx of the Nexus from its volatized energeum. The residual energy of the Nexus was transferred to you by a very difficult process. Painful, too."

"How?" Piers asked, then as a darker thought arose, added softly, "Did this have something to do with his illness?"

"I—I really hoped we wouldn't have to go there. But I have to say that I think it did, Pike."

"Tell me what happened—if you can." Piers was shaken, but he didn't shy away. "I need to know even if it hurts to hear it."

"It was a long sublimation process that involved successive purifications. When the stars were right, especially one he called the *stella signata*, he stayed up late at night annealing the gold sheet, pickling it in boiling acid and immersing it in the white ashes of alder and birch, over and over again until morning. Separation of the magisterium, he called it, separation into the white ethesia and calx. Gradually the Nexus essence underwent reductions and coagulations that transferred its energy to you like sap flowing up from the roots."

"Nothing you've said makes the least sense to me, Cynthia."

"Neither to me, I have to admit," she smiled. "He kept saying that you were becoming its ethris. It was the one thing that gladdened his heart, right up to the day he died. He said you had achieved pleroma, fullness, and he had an ecstasy about him when he said it. I had no knowledge of what he was trying to accomplish, but you must have felt it happening over the past two years."

"Now that you mention it, I felt something like a rush. But I thought it was something normal, like growing pains. Or maybe the flu, or night shivers," Piers responded. The odd nocturnal pain had always been inexplicable, but now he knew its source. Moreover, he knew why it had ceased shortly before Aimesworth died.

"Along with all of that, there was the founding of the purified goldcalx into a set of ingots. I helped him do all this as well as I could, but he lost his strength during the ordeal."

"He put too much into it?"

"He was frail near the end. He wanted you to have it all and took none of the essence for himself."

"Why did he waste himself away like that? You must have tried to stop him. No one asked me about any of it, Cynth. I'd've spoken up and said no. Absolutely would've said no." Piers fought back tears at hearing this revelation, guilt-laden he had not met with Aimesworth and convinced him to save himself.

Cynthia put her hand on his to comfort him and said with great conviction, "Look, I'm telling you this openly and with total honesty. He came to accept you as a unique person, Pike, one who may find a jaadentril. Even more, but I never knew the breadth of his mind on this."

"Is there anything more you can tell me about him—what he thought or said to you?"

"I do know he saw in his heart and mind what you may someday accomplish. He sometimes called you the Jaadentril's Seed. I can't get into that right now, but that's what he believed towards the end of his life, and he wouldn't let go of it. He was like a man converted. Nothing else mattered."

"I can't understand. Why do people get so caught up in this? It's selfdestructive," Piers anguished. His mother's warnings about the weird ways of his father's family swept over him like a North Pacific wave.

Cynthia was nearing her emotional limit, as was Piers. She responded, her voice cracking, "Just as Victor pigheadedly held to the notion that your father could be forced to do this at one time, and that I might have been ready for it when I was a teenager, my father chose to believe it was your destiny, too. He let his business and his health go to make sure the path would be clear for you."

"He said some of this to me the last time we talked, this 'destiny' idea. I had no idea it would take over him. I feel guilty—like I should have stepped in." His gaze fell. He couldn't look her in the face.

"Don't blame yourself, Pike. I tried to get help for him, but the doctors just called it dementia and said I'd have to just see him through it. It didn't help when he told them an Ilyaan had spoken to him about you. I know you don't want to hear this, but I can't sugarcoat it, and I miss him dearly. Frankly, I would rather he was here too."

Wiping their eyes, they both understood that the lesson was over. Piers went home and with tear-stained face told his parents what happened. He didn't want to go through it all again with them, but if he tried to conceal it, he was sure it would get back to them anyway.

More alarmed than sympathetic, his mother glared at him. "Drop these ridiculous lessons, Pike. It's not doing you any good just to end up obsessed over an ill-begotten old myth like Tom Aimesworth was. It's plain delusional to be sucked up into someone else's dream world and I fear it like the plague. He was a nice man and a good friend to you, his daughter, too. I'm not speaking ill of them. But you have a whole life ahead of you, and we're so proud of you. Follow your own path in this world, not hand-me-down notions from an age of ignorance." Her voice trailed off like a dry creek in summer.

All three understood her words echoed his father's past. It was a common enough family discussion, unresolved at the best of times.

Jim said nothing at first. Then he softly suggested a middle road. "Learn the lingo, Pike. It may help you later in life. And try to learn enough brahan to understand the Codex, because it's going to save you one day. Old Tom must have seen something in you that made him think that way. But don't be given over to the Ordinath like those people you saw at the funeral. Keep a healthy balance. You're young and you should enjoy life and plan for your future like it's your own. Even when others seem to be in control, keep your heart free of any shackles. That's the best advice I can give. I know you'll make the right decision."

Piers' mother shook her head in barely concealed dismay. She made it evident this was not the type of backup she had expected. With a final shake of her head, she left the table without another word to either of them.

Chapter 7
At the Dahi's Lodge

At a match the next day, Piers made a discovery about life. As he scored a decisive goal with a swerve shot, it came to him that fear could neither free him, nor save him. It could only cripple him. He needed tools to take him farther down this road he was on, strong and finely made tools that would unlock the jammed door that confronted him. The only tools he knew of for sure were the Dirshani language and its written form, Brahan. He had only one way to acquire them. To his mother's continuing disapproval, he continued with Cynthia's lessons.

In a year, he was fluent enough in Dirshani to have chatty exchanges with Cynthia and more furtive ones with his father when they were chopping firewood, out of earshot of his mother. Dirshani sign language was included in the curriculum, and Cynthia was a master of that. They laughed and joked with one another as Piers gradually gained competence in fluent hand and facial expressions. This was the start of his understanding of soul, for he learned it is by physical and aural means that soul locks with soul and achieves communication, mind to mind. It was a thing he would never forget.

While the brahan lessons were slow at the beginning, he found a way to apply his glyph-scribing abilities. With a growing knowledge of its swirling radicles, diacritics and ligatures, he began the task of unfolding and transcribing the Codex from memory onto paper and interpreting the glyphs. This took weeks of detailed work on his part and concentrated efforts by Cynthia as well. Piers tried to extract her promise that none of the glyph plexes, or their numeric encodings that he still used as a crutch, would be shown to Marron.

She reminded him that of all of them, only Marron and a few close associates had the skill in brahan to fully interpret his ambitious work. Piers fell silent when she suggested he involve others, especially Marron. He also had a hunch that a number of Cynthia's own interpretations had the nuanced tone of Marron stamped on them. His suspicion grew that the two were in a *sub rosa* collaboration, but he was willing to put it down to the difficulty of the brahan subtexts of the Codex.

All the same, it led him to look critically at what he was taught. With regret, he learned to hold back. He expressed his private thoughts less freely to Cynthia—a fact not lost on her. Random parts of the work were routinely withheld from her, or modified, just to ensure Marron and his cohorts could never acquire the full image. He had every expectation that they knew what he was up to, yet in the face of all their erudition and deductive skill, Piers was confident of one thing. Marron and the Ordinath had no way to force his inner brahanic tangles into the light of scrutiny, much less decrypt them without his permission.

Cynthia seemed to sense that Piers' restless energy would soon take him from her orbit, so she announced a change in the course of studies.

Piers knew the Mehenti were the highest order of sentients of Morasa, and they included homo sapiens. The Dirush were the ascended Mehenti who had transorbally migrated from Morasa to Sunara over the millennia. She would teach him Dirush doctrines, history and philosophy, in an effort to round out the more survivalist curriculum that her father had originally planned. These would be the gateway to the doctrines of the elect that Tom had spoken of.

He learned of the three principal orbs and the wahans that connected them. He was shown another blown-glass three-orbed flask that served as a model of that cosmos. It was silvered on the inside, and he had a triple view of himself whenever he looked at it, as though he were disjointed into three levels of being. He was also shown antique maps and porcelain models of the Monra Sunara, its rivers, lakes and mountains, its cities and towns and imperia.

Cynthia warned him again about the virs who controlled the geopolitics, fought wars and mandated laws, treaties and taxes. These evolved Mehenti fascinated him, for of all the physical sentients who had made transit to Sunara, they alone learned the arts of transcendence, power and mastery over other Mehenti in their domains. He further learned that their art was a closed book, but that it involved mastery of Avda, Brahan and Ohan, the three treasured artforms of Sunara. And another, a forbidden word she had only briefly mentioned before, the "ethris". This time she revealed it was more than a substitute for wahan transit inside and between the orbs. It was the source of their viric powers.

He also learned of the few northern free lands where the virs had limited power, or none at all. The southern such territory was the Hodenvaal, and he made a note of it. It had once been the center of a great empire, and its proud capital, Raa, was the envy of the orb. There was nothing left of its imperial past, but a forlorn settlement called Durgos near the old ruins. To its west was M'kesh, the homeland of Vir Draaxis and the Kopendres Syndicate, an imperium ruled from the city of Irupaan. To the south was Parún, a sprawling *viraaj* or empire, under the control of Vir Sephros. He ruled from the fabled city of Zirindar and his restless armies were feared throughout Sunara. For Piers, this all had the aura of make-believe, and in time it began to verge on the tedious. In that, he was not unlike his father, a thing Cynthia delighted to point out.

The course material he was drawn to lay in cosmic anatomy: the ten *chonas* or classtypes of the Kolvani, categories of sentient suprema and beings that make up the cosmic consciousness. He knew that he, and everyone else he knew, was of the Mehenti chona. Beneath the power beings, but the crown-holders of intellect, love, science, art and war, they had evolved quickly and assumed control of their footings in the Monra Morasa. But his favorite of the Kolvani was the noble Ilyaan. The little Cynthia could tell him about them fell far short of his curiosity, but it fed his desire to someday travel the wahan and meet the one who left him the Konespaar and played the strange game that led him to the recreation of the *Torvaaden* Codex.

In contrast to the Kolvani, the Dirush philosophies were a favorite area of discourse for Cynthia, and she exposited on them with relish. Piers found most of it dry and elusive, but his interest lit up slightly when she opened up the doctrine of *Veridos*, or non-exclusive truth, to him. He immediately saw that the entire universe could very well function without Aristotle's law of the excluded middle, but he voiced little satisfaction with the dearth of practical application. She mentioned Brower's mathematical theory of Intuitionism, and the non-exclusionism celebrated in Aymara grammar as human examples. Piers tried not to yawn his way through this, his patience in tatters.

When he no longer had new material to add to the large pencil on paper brahan, he phoned Cynthia and abruptly cancelled all future lessons. Then he opened the envelope Tom Aimesworth had given him three years earlier and compared what he had produced with the last photograph of the gold accretion he had transmuted. In every detail the pencil transcription was as good as the photo, or even superior in accuracy. So, he carefully inked in the drawing. The night the last ink was dry he burned all his Nexus photographs and file of sketches in the backyard barbeque. There would be no chance of breaking Aimesworth's last directive to him, to keep the image occultus.

He was seventeen years old now and wanted to close the book on the Ordinath. There was no turning back. He boldly called Marron the next day. He announced his intention to terminate all relations with the Ordinath and Cynthia's training. Like his father before him, he was summarily cut free without the expected entreaty to reconsider, or even so much as a comment. Neither Marron nor his followers ever made any effort to persuade him otherwise and join their circle. It almost seemed they were disinterested and had moved on to other things. For his part, Piers wasted no time pondering. The silence from Marron was odd, even ominous, but no—he saw no regress to the past.

Weeks later, Cynthia called him and asked him to agree to one last session. It would not involve the brahan glyph-writing or Dirshani grammar drills. She promised something different. She met him at the trendy coffee shop that now inhabited the shell of the former Aimesworth and Dixon store. When he arrived, he smiled at the location she had chosen, ambled over to her table with a flourish, and said, "Nahiti taji, Cynth. Hey! Look around at this place. Everything changes. Guess I've changed too!"

She agreed, "Change is the only constant, or so says Heraclitus. When we're finished coffee, I want you to look around and tell me two things here that haven't changed, and I don't mean the seedy old floorboards or the wall paneling."

Piers silently scanned the room, impressed mostly by the conversion from an austere antique store to an inviting spot to relax, drink coffee and socialize. The tide had come in and washed away the old detritus. The customers were completely different from those who frequented Aimesworth and Dixon. They actually seemed to enjoy the surroundings in an unashamed, hedonistic way. Not that the old museum-like atmosphere was completely eradicated. It was softened, brightened and buffed— consumerized and made comfortable with cheap imitations and décor.

The fake antique chinaware that he spotted on shelves here and there were obviously new. In a corner, however, he recognized Dixon's ancient coffee grinder that used to be in the cellar. It seemed smaller than the first time he saw it. But that was when he was 14, and not as tall. It was a fine decorative feature and one that Piers surmised must have been haggled over by the new owners when Tom was negotiating the sale.

Then he spotted the etching of Athena's birth, the adult goddess fully sprung from the head of Zeus. Aimesworth must have given it to the new owners. Piers still didn't relate to it personally but could appreciate it had some significance to him. It spoke to him of the mystery of creation, and more privately the Nexus within him. On this viewing, he couldn't help but think that the figure of Eileithiya, the goddess of childbirth, bore a strong resemblance to Cynthia. Then he looked at the other prints and photographs on the wall. He picked out another of the framed photographs from the old store. It was a 1912 tinted photograph of the Marpole Bridge in South Vancouver. They seemed an odd pair, but they definitely were the only framed items left over from Aimesworth's collection. Like a proud schoolboy, he announced triumphantly to Cynthia, "Made three finds!"

"That many? So, tell me what they are," Cynthia demanded. Her eyes showed a relish for his youthful enthusiasm.

Piers rattled off the three items, and Cynthia complemented him on his keen eye. The coffee grinder was obvious, but her interest was centered on the two framed images. "What do they mean to you, Pike?" she prodded him further.

"Birth and transformation," he volunteered after a moment. "The goddess is borne in the first picture and the bridge takes travelers to the other side of the river in the second, transforming them. But you can reverse it and say that Athena is transformed out of Zeus' head and the bridge bears travelers to a new world on the island. So, it works in two ways, like the nonexclusionism we studied."

"Write the brahan glyphs for these, here, on the napkin," she urged him in an effort to capture his thought process. Without hesitation or protest, he took out a pen from his pocket and deftly inscribed the swirling forms. She scrutinized it silently for a second or two. Then, in admiration Cynthia took the napkin, folded it into her purse, and said, "That's beautiful work, Pike. So quick and clean, yet subtle. You even included the coffee grinder as subradicles for grinding and washing. Right? That's clever. I've never seen the talent you have for this in anyone else. You're already way beyond my abilities. Can I keep it as a memento?"

It was a *fait accompli*, so Piers nodded and smiled, inwardly shameful that he had never before given a personal gift or remembrance to his first and only teacher in the art of Brahan. A scribble on a paper napkin was hardly a fitting gift, but it had been accepted before he could offer it. It mattered little that he had given up the only paper record of the glyphs or that it might end up in Marron's collection. They were already burned into his memory. Deeper still, they had traveled much further, into the *Torvaaden*. Just then, he fleetingly registered something like the hearing of an echo. They were already there or had always been there. Mind tattoos.

"Pike, you remember what my father promised you about the gold?" Cynthia casually changed the subject.

"I only remember him say that I would share in it. A third, I think. We shook on it. I haven't thought about that in ages." Piers strove to anticipate what she was getting at.

"Well, he gave me the large ingot when we finished the casting, but not the smaller one for you," she continued. "He wanted it to be a test for you when you were of age and trained in the arts. I guess that means now, because you've decided you have learned as much as you can from me."

"What kind of test?" Dead curious, Piers ignored the plaintive note in her voice and focused on what she had to say.

"When he was still in good health, he took his toolbox and went off on his own for a day. He told me that he hid the ingot somewhere. He never told me where, just that it was within a half-day's journey on foot." Cynthia spoke softly to make sure no prying ears could intercept her disclosure.

Then she added, "Those images you found just now, those are his final hints, and they were purposely left here for you. They form a thing called a taji, a fixed point of the transform between then and now, between the old store and the new café. I can't fathom what they really mean, but maybe your new glyph tells you more than the pictures do."

"Hmm ... maybe so," mused Piers, tentatively. "The glyph pulls the inner meanings of the taji together. It forms the essence of it. Don't you see? Isn't the glyph I wrote just a transform of the one for wahan?"

"I don't follow," Cynthia said, perplexed. Then her eyes lit up. "Wait, I see what you mean. There's a transformation that takes your glyph and turns it into the wahan glyph, and vice versa. It changes the soul radical into birth, and the gate into transformation, then adds new radicals that relate to the grinding and washing. But does that get us anywhere?"

"You're on the right track, but you've forgotten one thing," said Piers pointedly. "Something is created in that transform—gold. And gold is transformed by the river in the Orbis Primoris. It is ground up and washed by the river, like Dixon's coffee grinder, to form nuggets. The upshot: the transformation says the only way to find the gold is by finding the soul-gate, the wahan. And the only pointer in Tom's taji is the Marpole Bridge."

As Cynthia struggled to see his point, Piers continued as though it was obvious, "So there's a meta-taji that maps gold to gold as a fixed point but transforms the wahan to the Marpole Bridge." She stared blankly at him.

"Mystery solved," he concluded in the most off-hand way he could manage.

At this point, Cynthia had given up the fight to understand him. He had clearly gone beyond her personal comfort zone with his logic. She looked away from him. Brahan tajis were abstruse and notorious for dead-ends where the light often failed.

"I'm not sure this line of reasoning is what Tom intended, Pike. It's just that there's a fourth conjunction this is supposed to …" She was doubtful, and her face showed it.

Breaking into her thought chain, Piers summarized, "Cynthia, I know where it is now, but I'll need your help. Can you take me there and stay with me until I find it? I'm sure it's what Tom wanted."

"Only if you think I can help. Where to?" she shot back without further thought. But she regretted her words instantly.

"The Marpole Bridge."

"The old trestle bridge in the photo was on the north arm of the Fraser, but it's been gone for years. I think there's a rail bridge there now. If I'm not mistaken, it's a swing bridge that lets ships go upriver to New West. You're not going to go walking on it to cross the river, are you? Your parents would never forgive me if a train came along, or the span opened up with you on it."

"No, of course not, but I need to follow the call. It has to be now," he urged, then added, "After all, you started this."

Cynthia relented with a sigh. They got up from the table and piled into Cynthia's pale blue Honda. A short drive brought them to the foot of Oak Street. Piers darted out of the car and looked around. There were only nondescript industrial buildings—a concrete factory and large blue warehouses spanned the west side of the street. In the near distance to the east, the Oak Street Bridge loomed above the river. It hummed with rushhour traffic. The low-lying Marpole rail bridge was in front of it, almost invisible. A chain link fence separated them from a vacant lot leading up to the railroad line.

"Cynthia, I need to get into that lot across the street. Any ideas?"

"It's not like there's a welcome sign, Pike. I don't even think they would let you in there if you asked them over at those buildings. We'll have to go down to the river and see if we can sneak in along the shore. Maybe Dad marked a trail for us. Let's go, but be careful."

When they reached the river, Piers was mesmerized by the brown muscular flow of the Fraser as it surged relentlessly towards the Pacific Ocean, replete with powerful whirlpools and eddies. Cynthia redirected him to a tear in the chain link that allowed them into the flat industrial wasteland separating them and the bridge. Some slender ash trees and shrubbery shielded them from view. As they passed into the muddy field, Piers wondered if Aimesworth had cut that slit in the fence with his bolt cutter and had blazed the trail before them.

"Cynthia!" Piers grasped her hand. "This ground is charged. It feels like an electric field. Do you feel it too?"

"No, Pike, but I sense the energy inside you. This isn't supposed to be an ascension wahan—you're not ready for that until the seventh conjunction. It's got to be co-spatial or co-temporal. What do you see?"

"I can't explain it. It's more like a vibration, but I can feel an opening somewhere along this bank. The wahan is here, up ahead." He indicated a raised levee running along the river.

"You go, I'll follow. Just don't fall into the river, and whatever you do, do it fast. Some people are coming out of those buildings we passed, and I don't think they're altogether happy about us being here."

"Okay. Run interference for me. I'm going for the bridge, straight on." Piers moved into a strong current of energy that propelled him towards the bridge. It hit his solar plexus and rooted into his chest. It pulled him into an invisible eastward flow equal and opposite to the directional flow of the river. For the briefest moment, he could feel the sides of a fluid tunnel that led him along the embankment towards the opening swing bridge.

Instinctively, he knew he had hit a living tendril of the wahan structure. His body trembled in the current's surge. He was determined to follow it to the source, come what may.

A large freighter departing from the port of New Westminster neared from the east, and the swing span was almost open, perpendicular to the rest of the bridge. The last thing he heard was the ship's horn as it thundered then faded into the infinite. Normal vision flickered, then phased out into a dense fog.

His feet trod a great midden below him, as white shells and dry kelp crunched underfoot, voices surrounding him. Here and there the fog lifted and he saw the shapes of people near the fronts of long cedar lodges and along the river bank. Behind them, he could make out the immense mass of a virgin forest, and he could hear the sound of men felling trees with stone axes. Enveloped in dog-wool capes of intricate design, surprised women with elongated foreheads turned to watch him race by them. To his right, the river bank was littered with long handsome dugouts, their sharply-sculptured prows pointed inland. In the distance, he saw what seemed to be a forest of giant human shapes with raised arms. As he neared them, he realized they were great cedar sculptures that bore stylized expressions of rapture or amazement.

As he ran without a clear destination, he heard the unfamiliar language of the villagers drift in and out of range. Farther on, he dodged in and around crowds along the shore. The sounds of their cries became more alarmed and excited, mingled with the cries of seagulls flying above and around him. One man wore a conical woven cedar hat. He waved his arms and pointed to a whitewashed lodge front with many black and red ochre figures painted on it. Piers stopped to catch his breath in front of the lodge and walked slowly over to it. He squinted at the decorations, expecting to see the northwest coast whales, fish or mammal forms he had noticed on the other lodges of the village. To his amazement, this one was inscribed with legible brahan. He lost no time in deciphering the complex of glyphs brushed in over its entire surface. Among them he was surprised to see the glyph plex he had gifted to Cynthia in the coffee shop.

Only at this point he realized that he had successfully cleared the wahan and reached its far terminus. He touched the wallboards of the lodge, then dug his toe into the fine sand and broken shells at his feet. *Solid*, he thought. The smell of the damp salt air drifted off the ocean to the west, familiar and clean. Just beyond the crowd of onlookers who loosely surrounded him, he could see the brown jade arm of the Fraser river as it surged in front of an ancient pre-island, little more than tidal flats covered in mist. He thought of Sea Island, but there were no bridges, no industrial buildings or urban sprawl, and no airport towers to be seen. The lay of the land was familiar, but in no way identical to what he had left. The wahan was a transform, he suddenly comprehended, and that only he and the river itself were its tajis. Everything else had been changed, and, sadly, there were no gold ingots to be seen anywhere.

The man who had signaled him towards the lodge now advanced and spoke in perfect Dirshani. "Traveler! Do you understand me? You seek the Dahi?"

Piers noticed the fine workmanship of his clothing, made of cedar bark strips and dog wool. *Could this truly be the Monra Sunara?*

He panted, and just managed to reply, "Yes, is the Dahi here? In this house? Are you he?"

The man broke out in smiles at his inexperience and asked, "Do you know what a dahi is, traveler? Knowing your quarry is half the hunt." Piers recognized a verse out of the *Torvaaden*.

The word "dahi" meant a vessel, but it could connote a master or sage; it had connotations of being separate from the masses and yet one who helped, advised or taught others. It was not clear to him that a dahi would be sympathetic in any way to his quest for a gold ingot.

"This is the lodge of the Dahi Utanjil of the Durzh, and the place of his audience when he visits among us," the man explained. "Announce yourself. Speak loudly, traveler, and ask permission to gain entry."

The other men, women and children who had gathered to stare at him showed no comprehension of what the greeter had just said, but they were outwardly curious about the pale young traveler in strange clothing who had emerged from the wahan. Piers felt an emotion he had not felt since the funeral of Tom Aimesworth, when the Ordinath people pressed close to him and objectified him as a special personage. Likewise, these villagers had a sophisticated understanding of what had just transpired, accompanied by an appreciation that it was extraordinary. But to them he was no mere object. They seemed to naturally sense the *Torvaaden* Codex within him. Piers felt infinitely at home with them on the misty beach.

"Tewantsa! ... ah, Dahi Utanjil! I humbly ... humbly, ah, implore you to grant me the audience I humbly seek! I petition you to admit me to your presence!" Piers shouted in his most formal Dirshani as he faced the lodge front. There was no response, so he yelled even louder the same greeting. This time the crowd laughed. Piers looked around and saw what appeared to be a white-haired albino of childlike stature by the corner of the lodge, looking intently at him. The leather-skinned man who had spoken to him motioned towards the small figure and said, "May I present to you the Dahi you seek, traveler?"

Piers was momentarily silent. As he looked straight into the Dahi's face, he could see that this eminence was indeed not a child, but more like an aged dwarf. He knew what he must do. Piers knelt on the sharp shells and gravel before him, lowered his face and said, "Dahi, I disgrace myself! I did not see you standing there. I am Pike, a poor student of Brahan from the Orbis Primoris. I am ignorant of where I am and how I arrived here. I wish to know more of this, I mean obtain greater wisdom, that is, if I am able …"

This brought fits of laughter from the crowd, though few of the river people could decipher his Dirshani ramble. The diminutive Dahi murmured only, "Tewantsa, Pike-satjim. Arise. I know your true name and have been expecting you for some time. Your mentor, Tom-satjim, told me of you and accepted guidance from me concerning your path. I salute you for making the journey across the vast gulf of time. This is a great test and you have proven yourself equal to its rigors. Come into my lodge, satjim, and rest. There is much for us to discuss and learn." The word "satjim" took Piers by surprise. He recalled that it meant a close and esteemed friend, not an ordinary acquaintance. He was relieved at the welcome his host had extended and his willingness to accept him in friendship.

They entered the large single-room interior of the lodge, lit only by a smoldering fire in the center and light from the smoke holes in the roof. Around the periphery of the room were raised daises for sleeping and a single dais in the center of the room by the fire pit. A large sisiutl feast dish sat before the central dais. In an alcove he walked past, Piers noticed several fine stone carvings. Among them were a pair of crouched human figures, their arms embracing bowls, the like of which he had only seen in museums. Wherever ceiling-hole light could be found, women spun and wove at Salish looms. Near the looms were the large spindle whorls on which yarn of various colors was spun. The Dahi seated himself on the central dais and indicated that Piers could sit on a blanket by the fire pit. The incense of cedar and smoke surrounded him in the dim light and set him at ease.

"You may take refreshment if you wish," the Dahi said, and a young woman brought Piers a wooden grease dish of smoked sockeye with salmonberries in eulachon oil. Piers gave thanks to the woman with a Dirshani hand sign as she departed into the shadows, and then hungrily took small handfuls of the food as the Dahi looked on.

"You wonder about me, do you not? How can you know and trust my identity? Don't answer, Taighenkaatsuan. In that utterance I have confirmed myself as the knower of your secret name. You know from your mahir Tom what that means. That is sufficient to establish us both in each other's company," the Dahi continued as Piers finished the meal.

"Dahi, if I may now speak ... where am I?" he enquired.

"You are not in the Orbis Secundus, as you may be thinking. You are still in Monra Morasa, in the exact co-spatial locus that you left from. But the time is much earlier, approximately two millennia by your count. I had to meet you here in a friendly place so that we would not be directly observed by hostiles. Keep silence on the place of this meeting as the people of this place have been gracious enough to provide a venue for us. They should not be subjected to interventions by spies and djala operatives who would harass or punish them just to learn of your travels."

"Djalas, Dahi?" questioned Piers.

"It's high time you knew of them. They are a warrior caste who originate in the south hemisphere of the Orbis Secundus and are widely emulated by the Kopendres and others. Their allegiance is to the vir who commands them. There are two such virs who have taken great interest in you, one in particular. Until recently, you were under his ownership as a kravl, though the fact was kept from you. I have recently received word that he sold you to another vir for a large deposit. The deal won't be consummated until training is finished and you reach the sixth conjunction."

At this, Piers' jaw dropped. He could only assume that the Dahi was mistaken. It was completely contrary to everything he believed or had experienced, and he expressed this without reservation to the Dahi. Piers was a free agent and always had been, just like his father and Tom Aimesworth. However, the Dahi was quick to correct him. His father was an ex-slave of a djala syndicate, the Kopendres, and so was Aimesworth. Not only that, the daughter of Aimesworth was still a slave of Vir Draaxis of this powerful commercial group in the upper orb of Sunara. Draaxis, it turned out, was Piers' former owner as well.

Piers processed what he had heard, then asked, "Are you speaking of Victor Marron? Is he this Draaxis? And the Ordinath? He controls it, doesn't he?"

"Draaxis maintains projective presences in the lower orb, and this 'Marron' you speak of is one such. The 'Ordinath' is just a Kopendres front organization for his local operatives. To be a member of the *Ordo Stella Kopendres* is to be his kravl in the physical orb. Nothing more, really, though it's dressed up as a quasi-military mystical group," replied the Dahi in slow measured tones.

"So I'm dealing with slave traders." Piers said, half to himself.

After a searching pause, the Dahi continued, "I understand that you find all of this disquieting. Doubtless your father and your teacher have kept some of this from you. Don't blame them for this. They meant only to protect you. They cannot fight the Kopendres syndicate and survive, and nor can you. Now is the time for you to understand the veridos of this and take the road to a higher evolution. That is exactly what Tom-satjim wanted for you, as do I."

Piers could hear his pulse beat in his ears, in time to the rhythmic sound of the men in the forest as they pounded their stone mauls on wedges to split off planks from felled cedars. Slaves? They wailed a strange rhythmic song that he silently joined. He wiped away a single tear. *If the Dahi was right, I'm no different from them.* As his father once casually remarked as they left Tom's funeral, no different from livestock, uninformed when their ownership passes from one master to another. Here he was, being told his current master was an unknown tyrant in a barely-known upper world. Like his father before him, he couldn't afford to disbelieve, but he wanted to. With a passion.

"What if I never meet this vir, if I avoid him or escape, say, or he loses interest in me?" Piers asked as he pondered ways to avoid the consequences of this revelation. "Will I be free as you know it?"

"No, freedom is never obtained through the disinterest of others, and his interest in you will never flag unless you fail to perform the mountainous task set before you. And for the life of you, you cannot let that happen."

"And just what is that task?" Piers asked with a lingering tone of disbelief.

"Your identity is not subject to freedom or bondage. You are a ghenjil, from deep within you, Pike-satjim," the Dahi answered with a kind smile, but one that did not glaze over his inner resolve.

"Ghenjil?"

When he saw it registered a flicker of puzzlement on Piers' face, the Dahi continued, "The task of a ghenjil is to find the finest jaadentril in a race that only select masters of the art can participate. It is a run that some regard as sacred, others as profane. A ghenjil can be either bound or free, but they ofttimes begin as a kravl—even bought from specialized dealers who can spot their talents. They need the unlimited support and control of a vir patron to follow the arduous path of learning and attainment. This is a prerequisite for success in finding a jaadentril of exquisite quality. It is not an easy quarry, and though bullying, cheating, even stealing are tolerated, it's also won in how you achieve your win. Most candidates fail and are cut free as worthless or they are sold to another vir to try again. If they are lucky."

Piers' lower lip tensed at this. He could only respond humbly, "I have heard of jaadentrils, but I have no depth-teaching of which you speak. I'd easier fly to the moon than find one."

"There are jaadentrils in all lands of the three orbs of existence, some inside the veins of mountains or even leaves, some populating rivers and streambeds and some fully treelike, growing in secret places in the deepest forests and mountain crevasses. Their sap oozes with tril, the purest philosophical gold. There are even those who say a jaadentril grows in the heart of every ghenjil, and a ghenjil in the heartwood of every jaadentril.

Such is the bond between them."

"So, if you find it? What then?"

"If you find a major manifestation, it is called a strike. If you make two or more strikes, custom demands you must be freed by your master. Above all else, commit this to your heart, for this ghenjil's race, the Trilikon, is nothing less to you than a path to freedom. But that's only if you last the course. It ends when it ends and not when the runner tires. Remember also, the owner of the successful ghenjil is paid off by bets taken prior to the race. They who gamble on the ghenjil's run are addicted and crazed by it, and they may make wagers far beyond the dreams of the ghenjils themselves. Take this as a warning—you will not be held blameless if you fail them. Where you are going, the grandest of fortunes are lost and won, champions are freed, and losers fall deeper into kravlhood."

"Dahi, I'm not some kind of race horse, or whatever you and others believe me to be. I have no value as a kravl, not for this ghenjil-race you speak of," Pike blurted in anger. "And the whole thing is fake anyway. There doesn't seem to be any real running involved."

"The 'running' is metaphorical, Pike-satjim. You have opened a transorbulence and drawn down its Nexus that dwells, bound, within you. That on its own is not a strike, but a powerful portent. Some day you will know exactly how powerful. Draaxis himself boasted to his many buyers that you have a natural potency in the art of Ohan. That is the first great promise you have as a ghenjil. You've shown them a glint in the dark, enough to pique a bettor's intuition."

"There's more?"

"The Nexus accretion you sourced was not some ordinary object like a wooden spoon or a seashell, but a gold codex of great intricacy.

That is a rare omen of future return to your master. Finally, for those who know what to look for, your inner being directly reveals that you are indeed a ghenjil. You may try to mask this, but for the knowing ones it is there for the seeing. It prequalifies you for the Trilikon like a brand mark on your skin."

"You know? I've heard all this before in other words. You mean this is what they've all been plotting. Marron, er, Draaxis, and Cynthia, and even my own father — they want me to train as a ghenjil?"

"It was Draaxis' intention after the failure of your father and Cynthia. He was obsessed with the idea of acquiring a jaadentril strike, and all the more on bets, through you. I can only guess why he sold you. Perhaps he tired of your obstinacy and was vexed by the protective shield that Tomsatjim placed around you. I have doubts of that, knowing his willfulness. Rumors abound."

"So, why then?"

"Some say he could have lost you in a side-bet, or possibly needed to cull his stable of untested ghenjils. Draaxis is driven by profit, after all, and he reports to the shadowy Kopendres Syndicate Council. He's not a warrior vir who's built his own empire on the battlefield. He's more like the CEO of the Syndicate's corporation, and they can fire him if he doesn't bring in good coin on investments like you. Then again, it may have been nothing more than a shrewd transaction on his part, an offer he couldn't resist. Even so, be aware that he may still retain claims to your first strike in the Orbis Secundus."

"Dahi, I know I keep coming back to my theme song, but nobody hears the words but me. If a person believes in his heart he is free, then he is not a kravl, a slave—not in any orb. I gave all this up when I cut ties with Draaxis. He had nothing to say to me then. I have no desire to follow him or whoever else believes they own me. I'm completely in control of my life right now, and that's a taji that extends to all futures. The rest is just some cult fantasy as far as I'm concerned."

"Pike-satjim," the Dahi pleaded, "you are listed on the kravl registers of a grand vir as Taighen, and of the clan Uchundar, just as your father once was. His path to freedom cannot be yours, though. You may not believe it now, but you will attain your freedom only when you twice gain the jaadentril and the race adjudicators register your strikes. You have to make your own gold rush, twice, both of them big and flashy. The task is extreme, and only a talented and highly trained ghenjil can succeed. Seek this with diligence and you will attain favor with your vir and the freedom you crave."

"Why should I? It's not that I 'crave' freedom that I don't have; bottom line, I have always been free!" Piers now rooted his heel on the earthen floor and flashed a serious, almost defiant, look.

"I know why you've come here, Pike. You know gold well enough, I grant you. But tell me, do you know fool's gold when you see it?"

"What's that supposed to mean? Some kind of koan? We're talking about freedom, Dahi!"

"What you have, my satjim, is freedom's illusion. You share in the sweet delusion of the masses, a confection pleasing yet entirely nominal. I cannot blame you for holding to your naïve beliefs. They have served you well in the past, and that is refreshing to hear, I suppose. What you face beyond this orb is another veridos, though. I seek only to prepare you while your illusions of freedom still drip from the water clocks of Sunara. There will come a time ..."

"So, how do I see past this fool's gold?" Piers sensed there was a dark side to this.

"Know that a vir is an infinitely subtle and very powerful being. As princes of the upper realm, they know how best to deal with opposition such as yours. They may even encourage your belief that you are indeed free. By this they impose their will on the masses and hold on to their imperia. To many of the lower orb, their powers approach those of egotistic gods. False ones, to be sure. But that, too, attracts the masses like flies to carrion," the Dahi said with half-closed eyes, then looked up. "But I sense these thoughts have taxed you enough. Is it your intention to return to your customary time now?"

"Not yet, if it please you, Dahi. I need two answers," Piers replied. The arrogance blown away, his tone had changed. It was a plea.

He asked the Dahi for the identity of his new master but was only rewarded with a shrug. Few virs had the resources to meet Draaxis' price, yet to name one would have been speculative. The Dahi's answer only served to frustrate Piers more. The Dahi repeated that it would be made clear to him sometime in his future years when his master called him to duty. He was safe in the meantime to live a normal life.

Piers tried to move on. But he still brooded on the detestable thought of finding gold for the hoard of some tyrant to whom Draaxis-Marron had underhandedly sold him. Piers' second question was on the nature of the jaadentril: what it was, where and how did one find it.

The Dahi laughed. "How can I truly know or begin to tell you? I am neither ghenjil nor vir!"

"I know that it's a tree, *jaad*, and that its made, *en*, of gold, *tril*. Right?" Piers prodded.

"Self-evident, no? Your intellect is sound."

"But it's not near enough to go on, Dahi."

"As I said, it can take form as a vast entity in a tree-like structure, or it can be a tiny granule. It can materialize in mineral, vegetable or animal formations. Wæádra, who just served your food, is a free ghenjil under my protection. She made a first strike not far from here, in this very forest." The Dahi waved behind him in a northerly direction, towards the back of the lodge. "You should seek her counsel rather than mine. She can teach you how the ghenjil sees, smells, feels, hears, and tastes the jaadentril when near one. The seasoned ghenjil locates the jaadentril using instincts transcending those of a hunter. In veridos I say, the hunt is only part of the process. It is far more an act of creation—willing the quarry into being."

"So ghenjils can find jaadentrils in the physical world too, Monra Morasa, like Wæádra did?"

"Yes, but the tril of the Orbis Secundus is superior to any you can find here. It is fine metaphysical gold, a living thing far beyond the value of a mere metal of the lower orb. It reflects intimately the heart, courage and quality of the ghenjil who finds it. That is why you must aim higher and attain the greater treasure. It is a high art that demands knowledge of secrets and skills that you neither know nor have perfected yet. And behind that artwork there is more. You will find all that out, of course."

"I hope so. Dahi, someday your wisdom will shine in me and I will thank you with actions. Now, only words," Piers replied with appreciation, then suddenly thought of Cynthia. "But I'm expected. With greatest respect, may I take my leave of you? I entreat your indulgence, omzari." Flustered, Piers had ended the conversation abruptly, but along the lines of a Dirshani formal departure as Cynthia had once instructed him, with the proper term of respect, "omzari".

"As you wish," the Dahi smiled. "And don't worry about temporal hiccups when you return. We're in a unimodal causal loop."

"Wh—What?"

"This meeting was predestined and depends only on your future actions, all of which flow from this now-ness. That intrusive greeter in the Salish hat? The one who coached you to find my lodge? He's a future you. He, ah, thought you might run past it and get lost in the forest."

"That's not even possible. Is it? I mean the part about him and me being the same. And how do I re-enter the loop, wahan, or whatever? I really have to get back."

"Relax. It's all arranged. Someday you'll return here as him. And, as you saw, you did. That's a foretoken that tells us much: the work we've seeded here shall not fade. It will grow in light and deed, we know not how. Here's the important part. Can you catch it if I throw it to you?" enquired his enigmatic host.

"Yes," Piers replied, perplexed, then he smiled at the thought of a game.

"I'm ready."

The Dahi withdrew a small object from his robe and lightly tossed it towards Piers. It flashed brightly against the soft light of the lodge as it sped through the air. Piers instinctively snatched it in his right hand and held on tightly. As soon as his hand closed on the object, he caught his last sight of the Dahi, who hand-signed him bodiki vadya, "in all that you do let your motivation be pure." Then he lost consciousness of the lodge, the settlement and the compassionate Dahi who had propelled the brightness towards him. Without warning, the object had effortlessly pulled him into the cylindrical field of the wahan.

He opened his eyes to bright daylight and an open sky. He was on his back in the mud, not far from the Marpole Bridge. There was no trace of the ancient village, its thick fog, the scent of cedar and smoke or the Dahi's lodge. The freighter had just cleared the swing span and was ocean-bound. His head pounded, and his lungs heaved, as a high altitude might indicate. But he knew he had never left sea level.

He could just make out the forms of Cynthia and a tradesman dressed in denim coveralls. They strode towards him from the featureless industrial buildings lining Oak Street as though they had some urgent purpose.

"I'm nobody's kravl!" he muttered to himself with a blink and scowl, as the two figures came up to him. While Cynthia babbled a fabricated tale to the workman about Piers having a seizure, Piers glanced into his stillclenched right fist and saw the colors of a gold ingot nestled in his palm. His heart skipped a beat. It was Tom's ingot, the one he had been promised. Heavy, solid, beautiful and as golden as the afternoon sun.

Without pausing, he stuffed it into his pocket before anyone else could see what it was. "Occultus," he said to himself, while slowly humming aloud the logger's song he had heard in the ancient Marpole forest. Nothing he had experienced had been an illusion. His universe had expanded in a way he could never have thought possible. The wahan was real. The Dahi was real, a friend and a guide. And everything he had learned from Tom and Cynthia was as real a treasure as the ingot nestled in his pocket. And the kravl-ghenjil nonsense? It still tasted of dandelion milk in his mouth—a pill he wasn't quite ready to swallow. Not on his own. For that, he needed Cynthia's soft voice to sugar what he'd heard.

In the car, he showed her the ingot. Cynthia embraced him and praised him for his accomplishment, but he quickly corrected her. It was nothing he had done. It was a gift from Tom by way of the Dahi. She smiled and shook her head but let him have it his way.

"Congratulations, Pike, on your fourth conjunction. I know what my father would have told you. You've earned that ingot. What will you do with it?" she asked.

"It's pure tril. I have to learn how to make it into something of beauty or power. I'd be a fool to sell it for bullion."

"If that's your wisdom's counsel, it opens the door to the fifth conjunction. Keep all this a secret, Pike, and know that I will keep your secret too. If my vir knew of it, he would claim it from you. Never let that happen, for it would foul your momentum. It has a much higher purpose, and I know you will find it, even if its use surprises you. From here on, the power beings are watching you."

For a while, there was silence between them as Cynthia drove him home in the West Coast rain.

"You once said you were a kravl, Cynthia, didn't you?" Piers summoned up the courage to ask as they turned onto a quiet street.

"Yes, as your father and mine were at one time. Why do you ask, if you already know?"

"The Dahi. He told me." Then he looked squarely at her and said, "Someday I will set you free, Cynthia. I'm not sure when or how, but I will. I want you to know that."

She laughed at his innocence, then said, "Free yourself first, Pike, and become a master of your own destiny. Then you can think of me again."

"You know I'm a kravl too, then?" His voice broke despite his effort to appear controlled. This was his first admission of the fact to anyone.

"Yes. But many are and know nothing of it. You have self-knowledge, Pike. Know that your path will be a far different one from the many. You have not yet been called up for service. Be happy for that but be ready for it. You've mastered the teachings to lead you past it to freedom."

"I have?" He looked at her with widened eyes. Then he thought of Tom's song.

"That ingot in your hand proves it. My father wanted you to know yourself and prove yourself to yourself. In years to come, the lessons of today will remind you of that. You and I have come a long way, but my days of teaching you are over now. Others will take you down the high path of your calling."

Piers looked again at the gold bar in his hand. It seemed too pretty and small a thing to buy an abstraction like freedom. But then he knew nothing of its value or what he could use it for. He knew almost instantly that he would squander it, or most of it. It was in his nature. But at that moment he made a resolution: to save a remnant of it for a future day. It would be a day when he would make an object that would lead him to freedom, as sure as any lantern. He had no training or knowledge in the art required for this work, but he would gather it slowly and learn it well. And when the time was right, and only then, his trek to freedom would begin with the last fashioning of this ingot.

Chapter 8
The Serpent's Feather

As Piers walked across the crowded expanse of the Zócalo towards its north-east corner he caught a fleeting glimpse of someone he had not seen or heard from in a decade. It surprised him not so much as to whom his sighting appeared to be, but rather that this would take place by chance during a vacation in Mexico City. At first, his mind only registered that he had caught sight of a once-familiar face in an unexpected place. It was a shrill note. Then, milliseconds later, it came forth with an identity he had not expected. He looked again warily in the direction of the Palacio Nacional, along its northern extremity as far as the ruins of the Templo Mayor and examined each person in the crowd as best he could.

A scan of the restless mass of pedestrians proved fruitless. He had lost sight of whoever it was who may have looked like Victor Marron. In moments, however, the long-sleeping Codex had awoken within him and spread forth its sensory field. It confirmed on a much deeper level that the one he had seen bore the energy signature of Vir Draaxis, and worse, that the incident was not accidental. That was not all. Fully sensitized,

Piers detected an entrance to the wahan just ahead, somewhere in the Templo Mayor complex. It was active and highly charged, and it lay directly in his path. The visceral sting of its energy repelled him like the hot-spice feeling of electric shocks, though he sensed it was intended as an invitation. Or possibly a honeypot meant to trap him.

He immediately swung from his northerly course and carried on westward, away from the far north-east corner of the Zócalo and down a side street. It had easily been ten years since he had returned from his meeting with the Dahi, and with him the gold ingot. His life had drifted from virtually all things to do with his father, Cynthia and the tales of Sunara. There had been no further conjunctions, a fact that suited him entirely. To this he could add the Dahi, even Tom—they had all retreated into his past. And with unrestrained totality, so had his most troubling memories, those concerning Draaxis and the Ordinath. He wanted nothing more than to have a peaceful, hedonistic life tempered by monogamy, now that he was married. But the happening in the Zócalo had marred the surface of his shallow pond. It was the icy wind of an abandonned reality, one that laughed at peace, romance and bourgeois accomplishment. He caught himself glancing over his shoulder. Then he remembered his teenage years in persistent dread of the Ordinath. He would will himself to repress that past. He would look only at what was in front of him.

As he wandered down the Avenida Madero, he reflected on the years he had spent pursuing an education, student life, learning mathematics, science and literature so that he could impart to high-school students those same disciplines. A jewelry store with a sunlit window came into view across the street. Its glittering gold inventory caught his eye, and he was reminded of Tom's ingot. He remembered how he sawed off little pieces of it and studied with goldsmiths and jewelers the art of fashioning jewelry. He recalled every chain, pendant, brooch and ring he had ever made and every girlfriend he had given them to. They all bore brahanic motifs reflecting glyph plexes of the nexus. Of course, none were the wiser but he.

Now he had only one remnant left, a thin chain with an empty locket he carried around his neck, well-covered by his shirt. The miniature locket was unquestionably his best work, a sisiutl design, its multi-headed sea snake suggesting, but in no way appropriating, the Kwakiutl model. It was not something his wife found appealing, but it was the height of his skill and represented something within him that few others could appreciate. The circular aspect of it reflected not only brahanic inflections of the Northwest Coast sisiutl, but the Quetzalcoatl design from the Aztec calendar stone, the old world Ouroboros and several other serpentine references. As he walked farther away from the Zócalo, just past the Casa de Azulejos, the harsh vibrations that the locket had given off subsided.

For a while, Piers sat on a shaded bench in the Alameda. He drank in the soothing forms of the trees and cooling pathways. He could smile again, having exorcised his distasteful thoughts of Draaxis. He would speculate no further on the vir's intentions. His attention settled on the locket, whose vibrational energy had been so forcefully awakened in the Zócalo. Coincidentally, Piers noticed an elderly woman near a monument in the Alameda. She sold what looked like long shoe boxes of black and yellow gladioli.

Something about the place, the woman's serene face and the fresh splendor of the flowers awakened an almost-lost feeling in him. *I need to complete it. There must be some way. Another conjunction—it's coming like a freight train. Soon.* He understood that the locket cried out, its tiny interior needed a central motif to mark the new conjunction. *Something beautiful, like flowers in a shoe box, uniting dark and light, and powerful.* Nausea engulfed him, and he almost heaved. There was no way he was up to this work. Not here. *Not anywhere.*

On his way back to the hotel, he stopped at several jewelry stores and took his time looking for something readymade that might work. But he found nothing that satisfied him. The last store he visited had a few small gold pendants that he planned to take home as gifts for favorite students. He showed the proprietor his locket and explained in halting Spanish that he needed something that would fit in the tiny chamber. The man exclaimed when he saw the workmanship, "Señor, for work of this caliber, I have nothing that would suffice. I would suggest a miniature *filigrana*, perhaps," and then he jokingly confided, "But to construct such a minute thing is a forgotten skill, let alone to solder it in without melting it. These days, one would need a big microscope and a lot of luck!" Piers smiled agreeably and, with a polite *hasta luego,* left the shop with his purchases.

As he continued towards his hotel, he gave thought to what the jeweler had said. The man was right, of course. Working at extremely small scale was technically demanding and time consuming—he couldn't buy that type of work. Only the original creator could really complete his own creation. It could not be assigned to another. While traveling, perhaps, or after his return home, he would try to design such a completion. The execution of the design would be the greatest challenge he had faced, but deep inside him the seed of this work had germinated.

Piers could feel the roots of this new force spreading, seeking a source of sustenance. Grudgingly, he reflected it was Draaxis who started this. Then he wondered if that was the sole purpose of his appearance to him, as a catalyst to this work, or was there something darker? There seemed to be a mixture here, like the black and yellow flowers in the Alameda. He skirted the great plaza of the Zócalo along side streets, then made his way through the old center of Mexico City. He sensed it was a site of great creation and devastating destruction, and that the emanating wind that blew over him was the timeless breath of Quetzalcoatl.

The hotel was a former sixteenth century convent, remodeled and modernized in recent times. A double staircase met in the glassed-in atrium and a glass-walled elevator took Piers up four stories to the room. Near the room was a door to the roof garden, where a fountain gurgled water from a sea monster's mouth. Statues of angels were placed nearby, perhaps to rectify the impression that a baroque chaos reigned here. Beyond the retaining wall, the mist-bound city of Mexico spread in every direction, a mass of church domes and spires, antennae and vintage office buildings spiced with the occasional hyper-modern edifice. He walked out onto the terrace and up to a woman reclining on a chair. She had on a straw hat and sunglasses and a light cotton outfit. She appeared to be sleeping, but as he drew near, she stirred.

"Piers, is that you?" a sleepy voice enquired.

"Aw! I was going to wake you up. Or were you just pretending to be asleep?" He laughed.

"No. I'm dog-tired from a day at the museum," she responded as she took off the straw hat and sunglasses. "There were three seminars and a workshop on identification of artifacts. I have a thick wad of notes just for today. I think it will be worse tomorrow; we've got to do a panel presentation at the plenary session." It was clear Leanne was in a serious mood.

"Hey, sounds like the worst vacation ever! All we need is rain." He could not help a playful jab at her.

"It's only a vacation as far as you are concerned. This is work for me, and it will help me finish my thesis and make important contacts. You know that." She frowned crossly as she admonished him. Leanne got up from the divan and stretched. "Come on, we've got to get ready for a dinner my conference panel group is having at the Uruapan. I really need you to be on your best behavior at this thing."

"What's the Uruapan? A restaurant?" he idly questioned, following her as she marched towards their room.

"Yeah. It's just an informal group meeting. No speeches. Just a lot of talk about anthropology and linguistics, mostly. There will be mariachis, too, so it will be a lot of music, dancing and fun too." Leanne had fully recovered her wakeful state by now and was in planning mode. "There's a woman named Pru that I want you to not offend, if that's at all possible, okay?" she went on.

"What's the matter with her? Is she opinioned, frumpy or middle-aged?" Piers could not help a chuckle.

"All of the above. And she does *not* suffer fools gladly, I might add. I don't think she'll respond to your flirting, but if she does, don't lead her on. Think *ad decorum*." Leanne continued with the prepping as they reached the door to their room and she inserted the card key. The role to which he'd been cast for her new female friends was not unfamiliar to him—variances from the script were neither expected nor tolerated. At this conference, an academy performance was mandatory.

Leanne headed for the shower. Piers, shirtless to avoid getting lather on his clothes, shaved using a hallway alcove sink just outside the bathroom. The locket seemed to shimmer and vibrate as he glanced at it in the mirror. The wall alongside him had stonework along the edges, baseboards and crown molding, and was plastered over in the main areas between the stone edges. He briefly admired the restored colonial workmanship, then noticed a small defect in the plaster. The merest wisp of a feather's end barbs protruded from the plaster.

Curious, Piers put down his razor and tried to pull the feather or break it off. But it would not separate. It was incredibly resilient and had obviously been embedded in the plaster for a long time. Only recently had the plaster finally eroded enough to expose the tip. He gave it one more firm tug, and this time a thin surface layer of plaster fell onto the sink's marble counter, shattering. In his hand was something similar to a small peacock's feather, except that it wasn't exactly that. It had the blue iridescent sheen of a peacock's feather, but its overall shape resembled nothing more than a scaled-up antenna of the male Luna moth. It had fern-like combs of fiber, and they were tough, almost metallic. As he touched it in a childlike way, he could feel a deep awakening within his body core.

He held up the feather by the calamus as though holding aloft a quill pen. He studied the object and noticed his sisiutl locket sending him waves of energy unlike anything since the Zócalo incident. Instinctively, he opened the locket with his left hand. Immediately the feather replicated itself, producing a mirror image just below it. It now formed two vertically aligned feathers meeting at their quill-tips in the center. He let go in an instant, but the double-feather remained fixed, mid-air, without visible support, as though weightless. As he stared in wonder at it, he noticed the object darkening until it was as blue-black as the night sky. He was reminded of the Konespaar in the Aimesworth and Dixon cellar.

By now his hands acted in an entirely intuitive way. They moved around the feather complex and directed forces toward it that could only come from the tendrilations of its field. The feather responded with scintillating flashes of iridescent colors and a slow fade to ash-white. Another surge of energy came from his chest, through the locket and focused on the ever-whitening feathers. The vertical feathers now replicated a second time, forming a cross of ivory feathers meeting at their quill-tips. In moments, they glazed over with a metallic silver patina that spread like hoarfrost on a late fall morning. Then another surge burst from his forehead, chest and solar plexus. He was temporarily weakened.

Then delirium. He grasped the swirling marble counter-top with both hands. *None of this is real.* Yet it somehow was.

His consciousness flickered in and out as he fought the impetus to black out completely. Concentrating as best he could, Piers opened his eyes and witnessed the cross of feathers replicate at forty-five degrees. They hung in a motionless eight-petal formation. He recognized it to be Dixon's yantra that he had seen only once before in Aimesworth's store basement. The feather formation now drew his last strength from him as the lowest feather in the complex transformed into a thin trunk-like structure with its fronds concentrated at the bottom, radiating downward like stylized roots. Before toppling to the ground, he witnessed the final transmutation of the tree's color to a pure metallic gold amid what sounded like the strains of a thousand fairies.

Piers opened his eyes to a serious Leanne caressing his face and dabbing it with a cold water washcloth. He was lying on the floor and had no concept of how long he had been out.

"Honey, can you hear me now? Say something, please—anything," she was saying.

"What happened? Why am I here?"

"You must have fallen and hit your head. When I came out of the shower, this is how I found you—here on the floor."

"Maybe it's sun-stroke or something. I felt like vomiting earlier. Must have blacked out. Can you help me get up?"

"Sure, honey. You just take it easy. I'm going to help you get over to the bed. Are you feeling sick?"

"No. It's okay now, sweetie. Just a bit weak and dizzy. I need to lie on the bed for a few minutes. What a headache!"

"I'm getting a doctor to come see you. This dizziness and headache might be a concussion. You just stay there and don't move."

As Leanne phoned reception to enquire about a doctor, Piers fiddled with the sisiutl locket still hanging from his neck. It was closed, but he had no memory of closing it. As he lifted the locket so that he could see it better, it seemed marginally heavier. He opened it to see a miniscule tree-like filigree of the floating yantra he had seen just before losing consciousness. It was a perfectly detailed scale copy of the golden feather complex in its ultimate yantra form. It filled the entire interior of the locket. The execution of it in a red gold alloy was the same as Tom's original ingot. He immediately tested it with his fingernail. The filigree was so firmly fixed in place that he concluded it had to be soldered in. *But how could that happen? The conjunction?*

He quickly closed the locket and staggered over to the alcove where it had all happened. He recalled the high altitude feeling from the wahan a decade before, and this was it all over again. But he wanted to review the scene before it was cleaned up. There were plaster chunks and dust here and there on the counter and floor. But there was no trace of the original feather other than a vaguely fossil-like imprint in the exposed wall plaster. It certainly looked like he had slipped and hit his head.

Perhaps the feather transformation was just a dream. But how did the locket interior undergo such a physical change? That part was not of the normal causal world. Yet, most definitely, it was a *de facto* reality. Piers pondered this between the dull drum beats of his headache but got nowhere with it. Once more, a single question reemerged from his muddled thoughts. *Can this be the fifth conjunction Tom foretold?* He vaguely remembered something about binding to life's burden and decided to lay off all speculation.

He was back on the bed when Leanne finished her calls and checked on him again. "I've cancelled on us going to the dinner. The doctor will come at ten thirty tonight when he's finished his other appointments. We have to stay put until he gets here," she reported.

"Thanks, lovey, but you should go on your own to the dinner at the Uruapan. I'll be fine here with the doctor. I'm sure it's nothing really. And you have to plan your panel presentation for the conference," Piers pleaded. He felt a sudden guilt. He clearly was the cause of all this, but he could not explain it in rational terms to Leanne. And he really did not want her to lose the opportunity to work with some of the top people in her field. It was the only reason they were here.

"No, it's already arranged," Leanne insisted. "Pru will stop by here just before the doctor comes tonight. She and I can go over the plans for the panel and fine-tune the presentation. Besides, she really seems concerned about you and wants to give you her best regards. Isn't that sweet of her?"

"Yes," agreed Piers flatly, but he was immediately skeptical of this unknown woman who had insinuated herself in their midst.

Leanne continued work on her presentation in the small anteroom, while Piers took several aspirins and dozed off on the bed. From time to time she would leave for the media center on the third floor, returning with printouts. Hours went by, and then a knock at the door woke him up. Leanne was with her new friend Pru in the anteroom, chatting about what went on at the Uruapan and how each of their team was so sorry to hear of Piers' accident.

Yes, he thought, it would have to be cast in that light: *an accident*. His only concern was that the doctor might conclude that he had had a psychotic episode. Piers had already decided to withhold any incriminating details that might lead to such a diagnosis. And the locket would stay closed and hidden under his shirt.

Piers raised himself up on his elbows as the two women entered. Leanne spoke first. She addressed first Pru, then Piers, "Pru, this is my husband Piers, and Honey, this is Dr. Pru Harriman who I told you about. As you know, Pru, Piers had such a bad accident this evening, right here in the hotel room, and he was unconscious for a while, but he's feeling much better now, aren't you, hon?"

"Lovely to meet you, Pru. Sorry it's not under happier circumstances," he greeted the woman who had just positioned herself in front of him. Turning to Leanne, he went on, "but to answer your question, sweetie, I'm feeling a little better." Piers smiled weakly but sincerely in the direction of the middle-aged woman. He met her intent and somewhat critical gaze, then glanced discreetly at her print dress and stockings.

The dress caught his attention immediately. The cloth's bold pattern featured black and yellow gladioli. Piers could not believe his eyes, for either this woman had somehow anticipated his earlier thoughts in the solitude of the Alameda, or there was a certain ubiquity of black and yellow gladioli that Piers was blissfully unaware of. As she moved closer to speak with him, he noticed a heavy gold chain bracelet on her right wrist.

Pru extended her right hand to him, saying, "Piers, I'm so happy to finally meet you. Leanne has spoken so much about you that I feel I already know you. It's such a shame that you had this terrible fall tonight; all the group really missed you at the dinner. I only hope that it doesn't spoil any more of your vacation here."

Piers shook her hand with more vigor than usual, partly to convey that he had recovered his strength, and partly to raise the bracelet just enough to see the woman's wrist. As he suspected, the orange star was visible. She was a Kopendres djala. His heart skipped a beat, but he maintained a sardonic grin, his lips raised, revealing white teeth ever so slightly separated, his green eyes flashing the Codex openly present within him.

Pru took it as the warning shot it was. She withheld her firm grasp and in seconds gave him a Dirshani hand signal to the effect that they would speak later, not now. Piers laid his head back on the pillow and nodded, never resting his gaze from her. Among the three of them, only Leanne had no idea what had taken place, and she went on talking about how much better Piers looked already, but how they must get back to the task of preparing the panel presentation. Pru concurred like a concerned aunt, and the two of them resumed their discussions in the anteroom, bent over the laptop and flicking through the pile of printouts. After a few minutes had passed, Pru asked Leanne if she could print out fresh copies of some of the slides. Leanne promptly left on her new errand, leaving time for Pru to approach Piers once again.

"Well, ghenjil, you have created quite a stir with your energic outbursts tonight. Just what is it you have transmuted this time?" she said in a vituperative tone.

"I'd rather not say. After all, these things sometimes just happen on their own," he replied defiantly. "By the way, and for the record, which side are you on, Pru?"

"I haven't time to waste with you, Piers. You can see what influence I already wield over your unikari wife and her career. It would not augur well for her should you prove to be a problem for me. Remember, it's Vir Draaxis you defy, not just me. I merely follow his will," Pru parried.

He was familiar with the Dirshani term 'unikari', and though it fit Leanne to a tee, he disliked this Pru woman using it to describe her. Still, the woman had a certain power and was obviously a new force to contend with.

"Just look, don't touch," Piers acquiesced. He withdrew the locket from its safe obscurity under his shirt, allowing it to twirl like a pendulum.

"It's just a pendant, or some such bit of frippery. Just hand it over and let's be done with it," Pru commanded, though seeming a little disappointed.

"I am not the slave of Draaxis; my possessions are not his possessions," Piers shot back. "You're not entitled to this, Pru, so back off. Anyway, it may be a danger to you if you try to snatch it away."

"Very well," Pru relented, her eyes narrowing until they resembled those of a small bird intent on getting a breadcrumb. "Just let me have a look at it. I promise not to steal your bauble."

Piers removed the locket from its chain and handed it to her, giving her a hostile look. For her part, Pru sat on a chair near the bed and looked the pendant over. She recognized the motifs he had engraved so carefully into the external case and flashed him a sarcastic smile. Then she opened the locket casually, expecting a photo of Leanne or his mother mounted inside. Pru's demeanor changed rapidly when she saw the ensconced filigree of the jaadentril yantra. Her eyes belied any attempt to remain dismissive of the work.

"How did you come by this design?" she looked at him, astounded, then continued without waiting for an answer. "Did you execute this on your own or do you have a mentor? If so, who?"

"I have seen the design before, but I can truly say I had no part in its selection. As for mentors, I've studied with a few jewelers in Vancouver, but I have none at present. The work is my own," he responded.

"I have only seen this design in use among certain Mexican shamans in the mountains of Michoacán, and in some tantric schools of Northern India. You may have seen the old paper by Aston Dixon, perhaps? In Mexico it was once used to represent the feather of Quetzalcoatl. But you couldn't know that, of course. It's never been published." Pru, now in her academic mode, went on as though giving him a lecture.

"Have you ever seen the Aztec Codex Fejérváry-Mayer? In Liverpool? The first page has a motif like this around a fourfold axis. It's a common theme in Aztec art, of course. I needn't tell you, of course, what this means in western hermetics, do I?" Pru chattered on, unable to bridle her tongue.

Liverpool; it must have something to do with the Beatles. Piers inwardly laughed at the absurdity of her premise that he would spend days in library stacks or rare book rooms trying to rediscover what came of its own accord and in full possession of its own sovereign freedom. He had only been a passive channel, but he was aware she possessed no deep understanding of his role in its creation.

"So, would you say it's a Nexus?" he asked her, eager to get whatever information from her that he could.

"Yes, unquestionably—small but perfect. You had to use some locus, some initial energized object that truly relates to Quetzalcoatl somehow. There are so few remaining relics of that type."

"It was a mummified feather, embedded in the wall."

"You mean where the plaster fell off by the sink over there?" She scanned the wall above the sink skeptically.

"Yes. You can still see its imprint in the wall. I only supplied the energy. It self-transformed into what you see. Though I'd have to say it's everything I wanted, design-wise, and far beyond my skill as an engraver. The empty locket shell is my own work and I sensed that it was time to fill the void. But it was a call to action, not an act of will on my part."

"Did you know that this hotel was once the convent of Santa Maria de los Angeles?" she pointedly queried, as though he should have known this prior to booking a room here. When Piers shook his head, she continued, "It was believed to have been built on the leveled ruins of a minor pyramid dedicated to the Aztec god Mictlantecuhtli, just off the main precinct of Tenochtitlan. According to a folk legend, the convent became the refuge of an Aztec princess convert who had rescued a single feather of Quetzalcoatl from the Templo Mayor before it was demolished by Cortés. The feather was reputed to be indestructible and resisted all efforts by the church to destroy it. There are Nahuatl source traditions saying that it was hidden somewhere in this building during the late 1500s, but of course it was never found. Not until now, apparently."

Sometime during this interlude, Leanne entered the room, dumped some more papers on the coffee table, then entered the bedroom. "That sounds terribly fascinating," she broke in. "What have you two been talking about while I was gone? The history of this old hotel? I had a feeling when we arrived that there were many stories hidden away here."

"Yes, I was just telling Piers about the legends of this place. He's finding it quite interesting, he says," Pru smiled brightly at her, eyes twinkling, "and now we have to get back to work on your presentation. I've come up with some new ideas I think you'll just love."

Before Pru could get up from her chair, Piers stretched out his arm in her direction and opened his palm upwards, his fingers waving in a you've-gotto-be-kidding gesture. Showing mock embarrassment for being so forgetful, Pru reluctantly dropped the locket into his hand and went with Leanne into the anteroom to finish work on the slides.

The doctor came soon after, examined him, and pronounced that he suffered from nervous exhaustion. There were no signs of concussion or serious head trauma. He left a prescription and a small bottle of tranquilizers. Piers was to get plenty of bed rest and not go out the next day. But he began to hatch plans of his own. Pru left just after the doctor was finished with Piers. She wished Piers a quick recovery, then flashed a knowing eye at him, as if to say that none of this was over. After planting a cheek kiss on Leanne, she arranged that they should meet early the next morning at a nearby café, then go together by taxi to the museum.

Leanne woke Piers at six in the morning and quickly got ready to depart. He wished her a full and fruitful day at the conference as she opened the door of their hotel room and departed with her laptop and briefcase. They would meet again at the Uruapan at seven in the evening. As soon as Leanne had left, Piers then set about his day with a lucid mind.

His exchange with Pru the night before was dissatisfying. She had implied that there was something afoot with Draaxis but had not spelled out what it was. The only way to resolve this was to search him out, and that would mean tracking down the wahan. And he told himself he would damn well have to lose the fear and revulsion that gripped him the previous day. There was no way he would allow a Kopendres functionary to manipulate his wife because of something between him and Draaxis.

Chapter 9
Initiation in Cuzco

When Piers arrived at the south end of the Zócalo, it was still early and the morning rush hour was not yet in full swing. He could see clear across to the northeast corner and the entrance to the Templo Mayor. As he crossed the street and set out diagonally across the large square, he tensed himself and extended his sensors from deep within his solar plexus and thorax. It was clear to him that the wahan was hidden somewhere in the warren of passageways that ran through the ruins of the Aztec pyramids. When he arrived at the entrance of the ruins, he discovered they were closed and would remain so for a few hours. He sent out whatever remote feelers he could to determine the site of the wahan. Then he waited patiently for the gate to open. But he could detect nothing but low-level humming and the faint aroma of ionized air.

It was a cloudy day with the threat of rain, and no one but he waited at the wicket. Just prior to opening, he felt a slight charge building up in the locket as it rested against his chest. The wahan fluoresced its presence to him just as the physical gates to the ruins swung open for business. *Lucky me, I'm expected by the great one.* As he entered the complex, a replica of the dismembered goddess Coyolxauhqui seemed to plead with him from a huge disk on the wall. "Be wary," she seemed to say to him. Excited, he abandoned all caution and continued down the stairs to the ruins.

Soon he reached the public access paths in front of the pyramid excavations, quite alone. There were clear remains of the Quetzalcoatl cult with its giant stone carvings of plumed serpents aligned at the bases of stairs that once straddled the high edifices. He could feel their energies ping off the locket even though it was discreetly hidden from view. He wondered if the return of the feather to the sacred precinct that once contained it was an event foretold, a taji, perhaps. By now his entire nervous system was aligned with the grid of humming energies that gripped the ruin complex. He felt exhilarated but knew that serious work lay ahead.

He opened his hands and spread his fingers like multiple antennae to sense the origin of the wahan signature. It was not at the front of the large double pyramid that he had at first supposed. Instead, he followed the flux up a side path along the south end of the pyramid. Near the middle of the pathway, he felt the strong signature of the wahan, charged tendrils reaching out to him from the left. He looked around him and confirmed that he was alone and not visible from the administration booth. Then he jumped the low fence that separated the public from the archeological site and moved stealthily along a V-shaped juncture between two edifices. He dodged some stone human statues lying at random angles in his path, then picked up speed to enter the power vortex that he knew was in wait for him.

Enveloped by the wahan, he was free to run along its liquid corridor and glide like a surfer shooting the green room. Before he took many steps, dense fog surrounded him, then cleared. He stumbled over a dry cobblestone-paved street with distinctive Incan masonry walls on either side. Across the street the only notable feature was a door surmounted by a stone lintel with a bas relief serpent carved on it. As he gazed at it, the door opened. A short sun-weathered man called out to him, "Venga, Señor, por favor," and gestured that he should hurry across the empty street and enter. The feeling of high altitude swam through his brain and descended deep into his lungs as he hurriedly crossed the street. As the door opened wide for him, he made his way into a sunny courtyard of mixed Incan stonework and colonial architecture. The clothing of the smiling man reeked of coca. He could only be in the Andean highlands, he concluded, but the speed at which he had arrived here was beyond his own credulity.

"Monra Morasa? Orbis Primoris?" Piers queried the man.

"¡Si, Señor, por supuesto! Passe por acá, por favor. Sr. Marron le espera," affirmed the jocular doorman wearing a bright red knitted lluchu on his head. The man's directions and gestures indicated Piers should proceed down a sunless corridor and enter the brightly lit office at the end of it. He entered the office to find the familiar face of an amused Draaxis smiling at him from behind a large mahogany desk. Piers felt his nose wrinkle slightly. The room reeked of the infamous cologne. By now, Piers was feeling out of practice in Dirshani, so he decided to speak English.

"Vir Draaxis, if I may address you as such, and in this language."

"Yes, of course you may. I have been expecting you, and I thank you for coming at your soonest."

"I'm here to pick a bone with you, in case you were wondering. That djala woman Pru, who you injected into our lives, for example."

"You may have your private issues, of course, but since this is my place, it's my meeting and my agenda. We can get to your questions later." Draaxis smiled congenially while his blue eyes focused on some papers on his desk. "Sit down in that chair, will you, please?" Draaxis pointed out an ornate high-backed chair in front of Piers with an imperious gesture. Piers obliged him without complaint, for he was unquestionably feeling the ill-effects of the altitude. The uncomfortable colonial period chair squeaked as if in protest as he sank into it, its dense tapestry-upholstered seat pad compressing under his weight.

"If I can ask one small and potentially strange question: where and when am I?"

"Cuzco, and the time is effectively the same as when you departed in Mexico. This branch of the wahan is coeval. The end-to-end displacement is in spatial dimension only. So, the time here and there is the same, modulo the standard time zones." Draaxis yawned at the ennui of explaining such trivia, then added, "You seem to have some experience with the co-spatial branches involving large time displacement. Set up by an ally of Tom's, perchance? They open up the issue of temporal anomaly that must be handled with more subtlety, and there's no need for that right now as far as I'm concerned. And we're here for a very special reason."

Though a little confused, Piers lost little time in coming to the point, "So what is it you need to speak with me about?" he asked, adding, "As you already know, I'm expected back by seven this evening."

"There are several things we need to cover. Your impressive transmutation of the feather yesterday has further complicated matters." Appearing vexed, Draaxis looked him straight in the eye for a moment, then continued, "For reasons I'll explain, it's in your interest to keep it under wraps. I've already instructed Pru Harriman to say nothing more about it, including to your wife.

"I recommend you do the same. And keep the new-formed jaadentril talisman hidden from all. There are forces at work here that you have no concept of."

"Occultus?" Piers smiled back, suddenly reminded of Tom's love of secrecy.

"Yes, occultus," the vir snapped back, "and be warned that I can read the silly little thoughts that flit across your face. Tom Aimesworth was a worthy adversary you couldn't hold a candle to, and he was loyal to you, to a fault. Misguided, perhaps, but loyal." There was an uncomfortable silence. Piers sat chastened, even saddened, that he had forgotten that Tom had done all within his strength to help him. And now it had come to this.

"Frankly, you have been left unmentored in the ways of the ghenjil for far too long, and your new master now grows impatient. I myself had given up on you as useless for further investment of any effort whatsoever. But a sale is a sale, and contractual obligations compel me otherwise," Draaxis informed him, his gaze locked on the desktop marquetry inlay.

Then his look seared into Piers' face. "You're like your father, I might add, except that you show the odd flash of natural talent now and then. It's an enigma to me how you do it. At any rate, per the sales agreement, the time of your majority draws near and your new master demands that I prepare you for transfer to service," Draaxis went on matter-of-factly.

"Well, I'm not going anywhere with you today," Piers answered back, quickly raising his hackles, "and I'm not getting involved in any of this idiocy about being the property of another vir, either. The pair of you can just punt on this. I have never accepted the theory that your world, should it exist at all, has precedence here. I'm free and that's how I'm staying. You have no power over me anyway, or you would have made a move before now."

"Relax, Pike," Draaxis said soothingly, then laughed and went on, "if you were bound for transfer today, you'd be returned to me as spoiled and worthless merchandise. My client is an important one, and fastidious to boot. Your price is too high to allow him any displeasure. So, I'm taking charge of this transaction myself and not leaving it to underlings you may have met.

I'm renowned for the quality I deliver, and you will be delivered only when I approve the transfer."

Then he paused, flashed an ironic smile, and half-whispered, "But when it does happen, you won't see it coming. I can promise you that. You're far more vulnerable than you think, and your bravado doesn't alter that fact."

Piers said nothing but looked into the impassive face of Draaxis with doubt verging on fear. The silver-haired gentleman in his pin-stripe suit merely stated the obvious, "I see. Now I have your full attention."

Draaxis launched a long monologue in which he outlined the three orbs of existence, the three Dirshani artforms and their applicability to a ghenjil's education. To Piers it seemed stilted, pedantic and delivered primarily to satisfy Draaxis' sense of *noblesse oblige*. He took little notice of the details but tried to look studious, as if that might move the endgame forward. The thought that his own students did the same thing to him in his classroom made him smirk once or twice, an act that drew censorious looks from Draaxis. He mockingly failed to answer correctly when questioned by Draaxis, like a class dunce. Strangely, for a teacher in the role of a student, that didn't bother him at all.

Draaxis dryly summed up, "You are clearly deficient in Avda and lack both control and sophistication in ohan, but due to Cynthia's tireless efforts you have retained a satisfactory functional knowledge of Brahan. Your early transcriptions bear this out. And I assess that you are reasonably fluent in the Dirshani language, if a little rusty. To be a ghenjil, however, is to know the three arts including Avda and Brahan passably well, but especially ohan. And you will need a masterful teacher in the latter to overcome your present deficit. Precious little time or money for that, I'm afraid. So, you'll pick it up along the way." Piers knew Brahan backwards, but the avdani's power art concerned some kind of rod-like weapon he had never seen, and ohan was something across a martial art and balet, an art of leaping warriors and esthetes called ohanin. Nothing he felt drawn to.

Draaxis continued his analysis in a more thoughtful track. "Moreover, it is essential to unite them all in jilhaan, the ghenjil art of being. It's incongruous, but I believe you have an innate understanding of that aspect, because you keep showing depth in it from time to time, and without the slightest grounding or training in it. This is usually the last and most difficult thing an advanced ghenjil must learn." Then he added wryly, "Not that you are in any way advanced at this point."

Why is he harping on this ghenjil crap? I'm not going to cram more lessons just to please him—this whole damn fifteen-year experience has been a complete waste of time, a farce. As though he had said it aloud, Draaxis responded, "I'm not asking that you fill in these gaps now, or even be motivated to do so, but the time will come when that will be imperative. And you will be willing. Then."

The examination in ghenjil skills went on into the early afternoon, when Draaxis had lunch brought in. After a short meal, Piers was allowed to wander the streets for an hour while the vir sorted through his other business.

Piers entered the Plaza de Armas of old Cuzco, took in the panorama of cathedrals and fine mestizo baroque architecture, then looked up to the ancient Inca fortress of Sacsayhuaman looming high above the old city. There was no time to explore it, but he toyed with the idea. He had no money for a taxi and the walk up the great hill on which it rested could take much longer than the free time he had remaining. On reflection, he realized that there was no way, short of a spectacle or a crime, that he could either take with him or leave any evidence that he was ever here on this date in the center of Cuzco. Without a single Peruvian sol, he could not buy as much as the tiniest of souvenirs from the omnipresent vendors around him, or have a picture taken of himself. He felt a profound detachment, and a feeling of being isolated and alien. Just possibly, he mused, that was Draaxis' intention in letting him play out his aggression.

Dejected, Piers returned to the serpent lintel house. Then, on impulse, he overshot it by continuing down the street. There was something farther along that seemed to beckon, and he felt a glimmer of excitement. In a few blocks, Piers found himself at the Coricancha, the pre-Hispanic solar temple and once-repository of the Incan gold treasury. A spark of energy awoke in the jaadentril locket around his neck. He wondered at, and savored, the intricate echoes of energy as it fluxed between the tiny tree yantra within it and the long-denuded temple, now engulfed by a baroque church. A stone somewhere within the temple radiated a beacon of energy that transected his energy field as he stood outside on the street. He recognized that the beacon was a temporal taji that had remained unchanged over the passing centuries. Though he heard the street noises and bustle, his attention became fixed on the taji emanating from the Coricancha. He witnessed that each moment was a transformation that preserved the beacon intact.

Piers closed his eyes, and in the moments that followed, he discovered that the long-lost gold of the Coricancha was a purely symbolic entity. He understood. It was not the actual metal he detected. It was the erstwhile reverence for its worked forms, its Brahan, and the psychic force of a solar esthetic that permeated this place. The beacon was a white hole, an object destroyed by the melting of an original Incan jaadentril, but forever radiant on a different plane. He opened his eyes from the ecstatic stasis that had enveloped him, then turned and retraced his steps to the door with the serpent lintel. He knocked firmly and with a sense of purpose. Now, for the first time, he felt the spirit of jilhaan within him; he was ready to learn from his former master, an idea he had, up to now, despised.

The doorman responded to his knock and conducted him once more to the office. Draaxis was waiting patiently. His hard and impassive manner was softened in the afternoon light that came down from the atrium. For a moment, Piers felt that eternity had somehow descended on them in the inexpressible clarity of the Andean sun. Draaxis, ever inscrutable, simply waited for him to break the silence.

"I experienced jilhaan, Vir Draaxis, at the Coricancha," Piers volunteered, unsure how it would be received. He braced for a sarcastic remark followed by a put-down. But it never came. It was as if Draaxis could see the truth inside him.

"Congratulations, you have passed the most critical initiation test, the sixth conjunction," responded Draaxis. "You are now among the rare few to have detected the ghost of the jaadentril that once grew from the octagonal stone of the Coricancha. That was the prime purpose of bringing you here." His tone was jovial, almost sarcastic, yet tempered with respect. "There is much more you must endure and learn in order to achieve anything of value or to fundamentally matter in the cosmos at large. But this is an omen of what may happen, a beginning, and it proves to the unbelievers all I have boasted of you."

"I never thought I would say this, but if this day brings only this one experience, I will be satisfied," Piers said truthfully. "I want to learn more if I can, though. I feel changed and ready to listen and receive whatever I can from you, vir."

"Excellent," Draaxis exclaimed, his eyes sparkling, basking in the new sense of respect he was being accorded. "I can hardly ask for more from you. But we must work quickly. There is little time to prepare you, indeed."

Draaxis lost no time in reminding Piers that his new master-to-be, Sephros, was the most powerful of the virs of the higher orb in terms of territorial control and wealth. As Draaxis went on, Sephros emerged to Piers as an absolute imperator, a feared tyrant, controlling vast domains in the Orbis Secundus. He recalled Cynthia mentioning his viraaj, known as the Parúni dominion. While Draaxis was a commercial magnate operating under the aegis of an ancient consortium known as the Kopendres, Sephros had embarked on a path of military conquest and political control. The old Dirush empire had fought back but was now defeated and fragmented. The remnants of the Dirush imperial union existed in only a few northern territories, a patchwork of mere dependencies and vassal states of the Parúni vir, with one or two nominally free states. The Dirush imperium was all but finished.

Piers took this in without emotion and asked salient questions on the relationship between Draaxis and Sephros, and where he stood between them. "You are shrewd to ask me this, I must say," smiled Draaxis, not quite willing to be entirely forthcoming, but reluctant to burn his bridges with Piers. "Sephros and I are rivals in every sense of the word. In the Trilikon, the race you will train for, we are frequent adversaries, betting well beyond propriety or imagination, intoxicated by the plunder of the jaadentril. We gain and lose fortunes on the skills of our ghenjils who race for us and for the prize of their freedom."

"So you each have large holdings of ghenjils? Are you well matched in terms of ability and numbers?"

"Ha! I can only speculate on the exact holdings of Sephros. He is secretive, and he is my adversary."

"But more than yours, I'd guess," said Piers, as if sticking the knife in to pry open a tightly closed clamshell.

"His contingent may outnumber my own, but I would like to believe that my holdings are better in talent, verve and training than his. Both he and I are firmly committed to the race, its lore, its promise of rich treasures and its heart-wrenching failures that, one hopes, befalls all of one's rivals." Draaxis had waxed fondly on this subject again but caught himself before giving away clear advantages to his student. "You must understand that you and I are rivals too, understandably. But in a way, we are also covert allies. I can't instruct you too deeply in the secrets of the art or my strategies. It would only serve to curtail my own profits in the long run, as my ghenjils compete against you, even as we speak." Draaxis paused and cast a serious eye towards Piers.

"Be forewarned, however, that I lay sole claim to your first grand strike and will pursue it to the full wherever and whenever you make it. So, though you seem to compete with me as would any Parúni kravl, you are secretly my ally until the first strike." His demeanor began to harden as he continued. "The sooner you fulfill that promise, and I believe now that you will, the better it will suit me. After first strike, we will become enemies and I can brook you no quarter. You understand that?"

Piers nodded, excited, and almost relishing the thought of rivalry with one so powerful. It was as if, in the context of a formal game, a cat could indeed look upon a queen. Then sanity reared its head again. The sunlit courtyard had now turned shady as the afternoon progressed. It was important to quickly gather whatever information he could before losing contact with Draaxis again. He quickly recalled his most important questions and broke in, dangling the locket in front of him.

"Tell me, Vir Draaxis—this talisman, is it a proof of conjunction?"

Draaxis opened the locket, acknowledging the workmanship and the aura of its energy, then replied, "It is the primary artifact of the fifth conjunction of your apprenticeship, the joining of the gold calx of the Codex and the spore of an external power being, a fearsome one. It will be recorded as such in the Trilikon annals, you can be sure."

"Pru thought it was a jaadentril."

"Technically a jaadentril, yes, but the size of it is so insignificant we need not dwell on that aspect. I make no claim of it as a first strike for you, and Sephros knows better than to press me to take it as such."

"Well, I'm not offering it to you, so no worries. But I'm curious. Why not?"

"In doing so, I would forfeit all claim to your future strikes. That is a rule of the Trilikon. So, I ask you as a covert ally to respect my position. There is also a reason you should keep it occultus from the untrusted. The feather of Quetzalcoatl can be recovered from it, in a reversal to the conjunction that you blindly undertook to transmute it. In Sunara this feather is sacred to the Ruakon."

"Ruakon? Refresh my memory."

"They are powerful beings who are kin to Quetzalcoatl. They are the trusted servants of the Yondai, the dreaded agents of creation and destruction on every orb. You may need their pledge someday. The bearer of that talisman who falls into their clasp can buy his safety with it, or even pass through the higher wahans to the Orbis Tertius. All inter-orbal wahans are under their control."

"Powerful, but benign?"

"Powerful? Most assuredly. But the best advice I can give you is to stay away from the Ruakon at all costs. Virtually any confrontation with them will end in your annihilation or the destruction of others with you. If you see them flying overhead, take cover immediately."

"Flying serpents, feathered, like the Aztec god Quetzalcoatl?"

"Exactly. They are feared by all, and with reason. They are shrewd, merciless and they can turn on you at a moment's notice. Avoid them, but if they speak to you, listen. And if they teach you, learn as if your life depends on it. They have shown you great favor with that feather trick you pulled. Show them respect and you can only prosper."

"And the Orbis Tertius? You spoke of it this morning. You just mentioned it again. What is it?" Piers asked in a matter-of-fact way, but he had privately wanted to know more of this mysterious orb since Cynthia dropped a reference to it years ago.

"Well asked, indeed. Few know enough to pose such a question. It is occultly known as the Monra Arvana in the Dirshani tongue: the third and highest accessible orb. There is more that can be said of it, of course. But few are given to know such things, and the door of knowledge is closed to all but the most advanced initiates. It's the non-duality of much of the orb— such information simply can't flow to a dualistic reference frame like ours. It manifests as jibberish."

At Piers' urging, Draaxis gave a private briefing into the mysteries of Arvana. Draaxis admitted he had never reached this orb himself, or its lower portal to Sunara, called the 'Unadi Pon', or small room. This portal had enough dualistic traits that traveler's terse yarns made sense. His glowing account or these secret doctrines was not wasted on the younger acolyte and were memorized as quickly as they were spoken.

Draaxis peered suspiciously at the door and the crack of light at its sill, apparently to see if Eusebio was eavesdropping. A distant echo of footsteps and broom sweeps from the courtyard were all that could be heard. He looked again at Piers to see if further questions were brewing.

When none were asked, Draaxis went on, "Mark what I say, few travelers who have climbed to the heights of Arvana ever return. On that account, be prepared to stay if you find your way there—not for years or eons, but eternities and transcendental cardinalities of time beyond even that. It takes cunning art and strength beyond the willpower of most to return to the lower orbs. That is all I have for you, Pike, for there is nothing more that can be said of the Arvana. Little knowledge of it ever transits downward to us."

"Why tell me all this, then? How can I ever use this lore if I am just an ignoramus? It's casting pearls before the swine—or a kravl, which is about the same thing," Piers prodded the vir.

"Be assured: you are not what you think you are, my young traveler. Or even what I say you are at times. You hold a rare and fabled brahan within you that may be crucial to finding passage to this exalted place. And not just for yourself. This secret knowledge is universally applicable and transferable. You kept it from me by obscuring your Nexus transcriptions. Remember?" Draaxis now paused with his sardonic grin in place, his teeth barely showing.

"You disapprove?" Piers smiled knowingly.

"You acted in prudent self-interest. Who can blame you? And you followed the misguided teachings of that old misfit Tom Aimesworth. Fate can be capricious in granting the greatest of treasures to an ignoramus! But an ignoramus can be wise in keeping the treasure hidden until it is needed."

"That's a left-handed compliment if I ever heard one! Enlighten me, then, great vir!" Piers exclaimed with a laugh. "What is this great treasure I conceal in my ignorance? And what use is it to anyone?"

Draaxis eyed his irreverent student shrewdly, then responded with care. "I have come to accept that you are currently the only known possessor of this brahan codex in the lower orbs, though it's still uncertain who bestowed it on you, or whether it is entirely accurate, or even authentic."

"And what does Sephros know of all this?"

"Everything, and I can assure you he paid for that intelligence with roomfuls of gold coin. Your teenage scribblings are the only reason Sephros agreed to an even greater price for you. He has copies of all the transcriptions you gave to Cynthia and has acquired most of the other lost brahan plates in the Codex from wide and varied sources, including my own large collection. Both he and I, and our combined army of brahanin scholars, have studied your fiendishly-corrupted transcriptions—but with limited success, I must admit."

"Has he identified the Codex?" Piers looked at him with anticipation.

"I think we both know the answer to that. Yes, I would say—to his satisfaction, at any rate."

"Come on, Draaxis, just come out and say what you really think it is," Piers goaded him.

"Fair enough. Your Nexus comes from a lost collection known as the *Torvaaden* Codex. It's likely the entire primal indicial of that sequence, like a title page, contents and index in a book, but even more seminal."

"The *germinatus*."

Draaxis nodded cagily. "Tom taught you well. Fragments of its cortex are known. You can find it on gold tablets, cloth, parchment and glass bottles scattered over creation. But the entirety of the Codex is virtually incomprehensible and therefore useless without the indicial complex—like an enciphered text without the cryptographic key. Use this treasure discreetly and with care, and you will doubtless find the path to freedom and the essences beyond it."

"He wants it in the worst way, doesn't he?" Piers asked, already knowing the answer but expecting only obfuscation from his tutor.

"Obviously," Draaxis responded with surprising alacrity, "you are likely the only living embodiment of the most valuable thing Sephros or any other Mehenti can imagine. As your fame spreads, you will come to be addressed as the *Torvi*. Beware of fame and uniqueness, though. It can force you into compromise and confinement by those who covet what you have. T'will sooner be a cumbrance than a boon, I fear."

"Tell me honestly. Should I cooperate? Unveil the whole Codex to him?"

"As if I have been less than frank with you." Draaxis laughed. "Were you to fully transfer it to him in fair form he would use it to wield ever greater power—more than you can imagine. He might very well cast you aside at the end of your usefulness to him. As it is, he is committed to training you as a ghenjil. I can't conjecture why, exactly, but you have the aptitude and he has the plan. So, accept the fortune you have been given. Don't complicate your life with needless strife."

"He'll try to take it. Won't he?" said Piers, resigned to the inevitable.

Draaxis shook his head as though warning a child. "He already has—many times these past ten years. But surely you know, Pike, that no one, no matter how powerful, can extract it against your will without knowledge of your secret name. That lock can't be picked. Were that not so, I would have it in hand and you would be a broken man. If that's not enough, each conjunction you have achieved acts as a guard lock on the others. You're a Gordian knot to him."

"There's no way he can extract it, then, without my free will?"

"Sephros relies on your conscious volition to recreate it from raw materials he will supply: engraved sheets of gold, or with paint on a cloth or parchment. That's his only channel."

"Okay, but let's say I've ruled out that. So, he orders me to replicate it. What right does a kravl like me have to refuse him?"

"The rights of a kravl? None whatsoever, of course!" Draaxis snapped. "I can't believe I'm being asked to teach you this. Cynthia covered basic Sunaraic law with you, didn't she?"

"Bear with me. What defense does a kravl have against a vir?"

"Well, more than you might think, but it's all old hat to you."

"Answer, please," Piers pushed back.

"You may obfuscate, distort and confound the brahanic glyph codes if you are skilled enough to use veridos to escape detection—and we both know that you are. Your skill in this is far beyond mere palimpsest and text butchery. You're a veritable semantic surgeon when it comes to the *Torvaaden*. We may either thank or curse dear Cynthia for that! In that regard she was more faithful to her father, and you, than to me."

"Cynthia?"

"Thanks to her you know every trick in the book, and concocted trapdoors of your own that no one else grasps in the slightest. You force me to give you your due. You are a Torvi in every sense of the word, and the first of that rare rabble I've shared company with."

"It's not enough. He could use forceful extraction, torture, the harming of others." Piers looked seriously into Draaxis' eyes like a child pondering the mystery of iniquity.

"Nonsense. Coercion is equally useless to him. In the short term, he is defenseless against misinformation. Bend the light you hold within. Project distortions with your mind—in subtlety, of course. I don't know why I'm coaching you on this. You already mastered it long ago. But don't obsess about all this blunt force. He will not try such tactics on you—I'm sure of it," Draaxis coached him, his voice drawn to near a whisper.

"No? How can I be sure you're telling me the truth?" Piers responded, surprised.

"Because I know Sephros' plan, and I aim to thwart him. Why else would I be telling you all this but for your good and mine?"

"What's the plan, then?"

"His mind is corrupted by a grand abomination, and I'm beginning to fathom that you are a part of it. The call-up to service is the starting pistol's report. A lot of noise but just a blank. It's the race itself that matters, not the soundtrack. That's all you need to know at this point. Too much knowledge can be a grave danger."

"This doesn't help me, Draaxis. You've got to give me more."

"Believe me when I say: he will never harm you. But he will bully and test you to the edge. His next course is to gain your trust and promise a reward. Be wary of such offers, though. You will find him very subtle in that regard," Draaxis answered with an air of finality.

Not unlike yourself, Piers thought to himself.

Draaxis sneered openly. It was clear he read the thought, and Piers could see that his own impish disrespect had antagonized the vir. Inferring the revelations were at an end, Piers sensed it was time to give credit to Draaxis for going beyond a dogged adherence to contractual duty.

"Vir Draaxis, I never thought I would say this, but I thank you."

"For what?" Draaxis snorted.

"For your patience, this day, and for teaching me the Unadi Pon doctrine," Piers said in honest appreciation.

"Never utter that name or even think it when with fools like yourself!" Draaxis thundered, losing his patience. Gathering himself, he lowered his voice, "Only speak of it with the rare knowing initiate, or a trusted Ilyaan agent! Remember what I tell you. One day you'll know: I pass on these illuminations to you with the best intentions, far more than your master Sephros ever shall. So, oblige me and be worthy of my efforts: lock these secrets deep inside you! Wisdom protected attracts more wisdom and multiplies beyond all expectation. You will live to see that if you heed me."

"Yes, vir. I will, of course. Occultus many times over. But since you mentioned them, can you expound a bit on the Ily—" Piers blurted involuntarily, but Draaxis stopped him midsentence.

"In a word, no! There was a time you could have asked me these questions—those petulant teenage years when you wanted nothing to do with me. I have completed my contractual requirements and then some. So that's where the prattle ends. Many are the questions and few the ready answers. It's for others to show you your path and provide the necessities from now on. Not me. I can't afford it. I've already helped you enough to ruin me if you win the Trilikon."

Draaxis fell silent and completed the transcript bound for Sephros. The light began to fade, and the time neared for Piers' return. With the results of Piers' testing compiled, Draaxis completed his report to Sephros. He then presented Piers with a bag of Mexican souvenirs, which Piers familiarized himself with. He was now furnished with the alibi that he had spent the day resting, then, feeling much better, buying gifts for the trip home. There was even one special gold brooch for Leanne, and a black and yellow gladioli shopping bag for Pru. *How fitting*, he smiled, *Slightly more useful than a plastic candlestick.*

The alibi had to be completely credible. The word "Cuzco" could not fall from his lips. Draaxis made it clear that no one, not even his trusted djala operatives, would ever know what transpired at their meeting. The humble doorman, Eusebio, was the sole exception, and even he knew nothing of their private conversations. Or so it seemed.

"I'm encouraged by our discussion," Piers calmly addressed Draaxis with the air of an equal, "so I'm asking you as an ally to leave Leanne out of any rivalry you may sense between us. Please don't allow your djalas to manipulate her in order to get my attention."

Draaxis had recovered his composure and grudgingly agreed in principle. But he added, "Don't rule out any future maneuver should you forget your obligations. And soon you could be contending with the djala operatives of Sephros, once he makes the final payment on you. That is beyond the Kopendres sphere of influence. We are obliged to uphold the transaction from our end and can neither protect nor rescue you and yours."

"When will I be—"

"When the final agreed installment arrives from Sephros, but not a moment sooner. Then you are his. Pru will keep you informed. If you have any doubt or confusion, follow her instructions."

They shook hands on it in Dirush fashion, and Piers walked down the hall, asking himself what he had involved himself in. A part of him still disbelieved the strange reality of what had transpired over an Andean afternoon.

As he entered the quiet courtyard, the sun had sunk low enough in the sky that the purple shadows engulfed the antique stonework and potted plants. He looked back and saw the even darker shadow of Draaxis in the office doorway, regarding him as if balancing a gold trinket against weights in a pan. Piers noticed how he moved like a cat, sizing up the prey, assessing the fight or flight decision, psyching out the adversary.

"Still you have doubts, ghenjil? Have I spent a day with you for nothing?" The taunting voice was that of Draaxis, but distant, muffled by the hallway.

"I may have my doubts. But the day wasn't for nothing," Piers replied, focusing on Draaxis' dark shape.

"A vir cannot have doubts, nor can he waste resources. If I squander time, I will be defeated by time. I cannot waste a single day, a single hour, not even a minute. Yet I have spent a precious day with you. Think on that. Be ready."

"I am ready." Piers squinted at the dark shape and set his jaw forward defiantly. Then he laughed at his own fate and added with no small bitterness, "As for the day you spent on me, don't shed a tear. I'm sure it won't bite off much of your profit."

"Your initiation is complete," Draaxis called out to him in a plangent voice. "You have experienced jilhaan this day. That is your sixth conjunction. You are consecrated in the doctrines of the elect and are now a *ghenjil initiatatus*. Your old mahir Tom would be brimming proud, for you hold the wisdom of the alchemists and all artisans of ageless wonders. All that you need is within. Leave the gulls and dupes to pour over their dusty tomes. They have nothing to offer you, not now or evermore."

"I'm ready? For the race? The Trilikon?" Piers stammered, extrapolating from the vir's words and shaken by their meaning. It was like a myth become real but the more fearful a thing for that.

"I long ventured I would never say this to you, yet I say it now in full veridos. You are as wise as the cosmic serpent and immune to its venom. I judge you worthy of an accomplished run. And if scant blessings are called for, then here is mine: when the Trilikon eventuates its fullness someday, I hope not that you win, for that would be my doom, but lesser, yet greater still, may you be counted among the free, ghenjil."

Speechless, Piers signed a parting salute to the shadowed vir, then turned and continued across the courtyard. With an enigmatic smile, Eusebio unlocked the thick mahogany door for the last time and wished Piers well, signing to him in Dirshani hand signs. Then in the manner of a parlor magic trick, he produced what appeared to be a coin from between his fingers. He spun it in the air, caught it and pressed it into Piers' hand before shutting the door after him.

Souvenir bag in hand, Piers crossed the street and waited until it was deserted. On examination, the object in his hand turned out to be an antique token or mandalic disk of some sort, with serpentine edge perforations that accentuated the jaadentril yantra design in the center. He idly explored the designs, perforations and edges with his fingers. About half of the token had a sharp edge to it, as if filed to function as a makeshift knife. *What an odd initiation gift.* Piers shrugged and pocketed the strange disk, the only artifact of his sixth conjunction. Tom's riddle came back to him—a worthless coin that would buy his freedom. *Not in this world*, he smiled.

As he looked down the street, he recalled the unique state of jilhaan he experienced at the Coricancha. Then he smelled a singular ionization in the air and sensed the field of the wahan pulsing through the jaadentril locket and opening for him. He glanced back briefly but could see nothing of the street save the serpent lintel stone fading into a dense fog. In less than half a minute, he was back in the grounds of the Templo Mayor in Mexico City. Light-headed, he jumped the fence and hurried to the museum that adjoined the ruins. He left the building at the street exit with a few of the stragglers just as it was closing. There was ample time to return to the hotel, freshen up, and get a taxi to the Uruapan Restaurant.

Chapter 10
Intervention Intervened

As he arrived at the restaurant, Piers felt a small energy jolt. It channeled through the talisman and into his body core, like water trickling over a pockmarked rock, following rills and craters until it found its rest deep inside. There was an unknown someone inside the restaurant who gave off a liquid crackle of energic flow, as unique as any personal signature. He felt it but did not respond in kind. Instead, he had a strong impulse to conceal his own spectrum, to remain quiescent.

He suddenly remembered something he taught in physics class, the lightning experiment of Benjamin Franklin. Franklin's night storm version had metaphysical allure, but was beholden to the caprices of nature, lethal voltages and kitesmanship. The school version was a sterile lab mock-up, a Van De Graaff generator in a darkened room. A thin sliver of lightning flashed from its metal dome towards a tin key hung from a wire ground representing the kite string. Naturally, the Uruapan had none of the elements of his lab demo. But Piers detected the unmistakable feel of a night storm in the making, or something stranger and maybe deadlier.

He entered the crowded art deco style room and scanned for Leanne. She was at the back of the restaurant with a large table of her colleagues. He also recognized Pru Harriman, several chairs over from her. When he arrived at the table, he embraced Leanne and kissed her on the cheek, then presented her with the gold brooch Draaxis had meticulously provided. It was not his proudest moment, but he carried out the pretense that he had selected it to commemorate her presentation at the conference. To all and sundry it had to appear he filled the day with tourist wanderings and purchases. Leanne genuinely smiled at the unexpected gift and gave him another kiss and hug before they both sat down. Piers waved cheerfully at Pru, who reciprocated with a benign yet sophisticated smile. Did she know what he had been up to? Almost certainly.

Piers was soon engulfed in a stream of introductions to people he might have heard of through Leanne but had never met before. They all seemed to know about his "accident" in the hotel bathroom. They all seemed delighted he had recovered so well. He good-naturedly attributed his recovery to Leanne and the hotel doctor. But his thoughts drifted to the day spent with Draaxis and the mysterious beauty of jilhaan. He passed the shopping bag gift to Pru and thanked her for all the help and support she had given Leanne. He sensed that Pru was a face reader like her master, so he kept his gaze away from her. What passed between him and Draaxis was an alliance never to be shared. At least, he reflected, not with a djala spy who had no authority to intrude on his confidences with

Draaxis. Pru seemed to instantly pick up on his defenses and diverted her attention to another conversation in progress beside her. Piers noticed that she also seemed to cast glances at a table in the extreme corner of the room. But there was no one there except a solitary businessman in a suit, quietly attending to his dinner.

Beside him, Leanne had a conversation going with a husband and wife team who specialized in the folk music of Mexico and Central America. The three of them bantered back and forth on whether European colonial influences harmed or benefited the development of regional folk music. As time passed, the heatedness of the conversation increased until the wife of the pair went into a sulk and shook her head in barely contained rage. Skirting volcanic, it ended with a chill as Leanne casually enlisted the SapirWhorf hypothesis in a final swipe at her rival. Like a child trying to decipher the conversations of adults, Piers heard it as "Super Worf" and wondered if the discourse had shifted to sci-fi movies. He conjectured a laugh was in order and segued into a tentative guffaw. But the neighbourhood silence suggested otherwise, forcing him to cough his way out of a snicker. No one else offered any more response than a cool flutter of eyelashes over the salad and hors d'oeuvres. None within earshot seemed to grasp her point, but clearly, Sapir-Whorf was nothing to laugh at. Leanne's foray into ethnomusicology exhausted, she turned to Piers to launch a new conversation. He understood it as a rescue for his laugh gaff, and hurredly asked how her morning presentation went.

He only half-heard her response, following her more by her facial expressions than by what she was saying. Piers smiled at her pride and elation, his eyes empathetically responding to her reliving of the presentation. At the same time, he had become conscious of the man in the corner of the room. The latter now seemed interested in everything that went on at their table. He wore a blue suit and had dark curly hair. Piers noticed that he understood their English and was fluent in Spanish with the waiters.

Most of all, Piers was now aware that the energic flow he had experienced before entering the restaurant originated from this man. *It travels through time, like consciousness, thought. It seeps through mind and matter, a slow patient lightning, a snake seeking its prey, preparing the strike.* The token that Eusebio had given him shone in his pocket, vying for attention like a latter-day Franklin's key. Insistent, it became impossible to disregard and difficult to hide.

The waiters started to serve the dinner to the table and the mariachis mounted a small stage in the corner opposite the blue-suited man. Predictably, they began with "Cielito Lindo". In the chaos and confusion of the moment, the blue-suited man paid his bill and left the corner table. Alone, he calmly walked over to a position just behind Piers and quickly placed a small metal cylinder beside his plate. Then he melted into the crowd. A small incident, it just was enough to interrupt Leanne, who had been talking about her presentation appearing in the proceedings of the conference.

"What's this, Piers? That man just left you something," Leanne interjected, diverting Piers as the man escaped. She had already opened the cap of the cylinder and proceeded to take out a tiny scroll of parchment. It reminded Piers of the encapsulated messages conveyed by homing pigeons. Leanne could make nothing of the unintelligible script on the parchment, handing it to Piers. He took it from her delicate grasp and, with apprehension, read the brahan message. He recalled the sigil of Sephros that he had learned from Draaxis earlier in the day. The message seemed to be a signed order from his new master. The anonymous blue-suited man was, beyond doubt, a Parúni djala operative. Piers surveyed the crowd for others, but no energy signature registered anywhere near that of the blue-suited djala.

"It's a joke, I think," he said casually to Leanne. "Nothing to worry about."

"I'm showing this to Pru. There must be somebody here who can read this," Leanne said, grabbing the parchment before Piers could pocket it.

Pru pretended to look puzzled at the script, but Piers knew she was assessing a potential course of action. It seemed Draaxis had been true to his word and had kept secret the details of his meeting with Piers. Otherwise she would have known that the assessment report had gone out to Sephros and that a transfer to service had been approved pending final payment. It was a small distinction, but it would buy him time.

Pru handed the little scroll back to Piers without comment. As they finished the final course of the dinner, Piers noticed that she was hand signaling other Kopendres operatives in the room. She was orchestrating a defence. There would be a djala duty guard for Piers and Leanne as they left the restaurant and returned to the hotel.

Piers got up to stretch his legs and slowly moved over to Pru's chair. He smiled, as if talking about something innocuous, and asked her quietly, "Do you really think this is necessary? I think Leanne and I can slip out of here unnoticed and get back to the hotel in one piece."

Pru looked up in alarm. "So you think that's an option? How droll! I don't know what transpired between you and Vir Draaxis, but my last orders were to prevent any intervention from the Parúni without receipt of the final payment. I'm following the agreed protocol. That Parúni message was a rogue attempt on their part to abduct you."

Piers broke in with a whisper. "I think they only want to talk to me—outside on the street. That's all the message says. I'm not necessarily proposing that I do that, but—"

Pru's look was scornful and her voice adamant. "They planned to lure you outside, stuff you into a car, and then: poof! end of story, never seen again. It's a typical prize-grabbing maneuver by a junior djala commander to curry favor with Sephros and make a cheap show of power against us. They insist they have made good on the purchase, but they have not covered fees for Vir Draaxis' final report and your initiatus testing. They are trying to steal the piñata before the party starts. It will not happen on my watch. So, forget the pompous little message; don't leave this place without our protection."

Piers assented with a glum nod to show his distaste at being compared to a piñata. But the money squabble between Sephros and Draaxis could only buy him time. He glanced back at Leanne. Chatting with some of the conference folk, Piers casually made his way back to her. By now his sensitivity had peaked. Pru was right—there were other Parúni in the room. Waiters, busboys, customers; they all went about their business as if nothing else mattered, but a few of them leaked a curious energy that Piers began to detect. His talisman hummed against his chest, as did the token in his pocket against his thigh. Despite having eaten a multi-course meal, a strangely empty feeling in the pit of his stomach grew. It was a storm warning. Beyond anyone's control, a Kopendres-Parúni turf war brewed. And it centered on him.

He sensed the evening had tired Leanne. Her triumphant presentation had been accepted by all but a few of the old guard anthropologists. Among them was Prof. Raembert, who was renowned for his ability to sleep through half a lecture, then wake himself at the most critical moment to raise a deadly criticism of the speaker's main point. It was a skill he had polished for decades, and earlier that day he had used it against Leanne with aplomb. Yet as Piers arrived at her side, she and Raembert had reconciled over a beer and were laughing off the incident as they might a fond remembrance. As Raembert made his last unrepentant pronouncement, Leanne looked at Piers with longing. He knew it was time to get her away from this place.

"I think we can get a ride back to the hotel with Pru. They're leaving soon. Wanna go?" he said, guiding her away from the table.

"I thought you'd never ask. I'm officially wilted, and beyond my ability to stay awake. No wonder people like old Raembert sleep through the conference," Leanne weakly chuckled.

At that, Piers waved towards Pru and pointed to the front door. Pru nodded, signaling her forces to meet them there. Piers could feel the Parúni presence move in synchronous response, tracking them in lock step towards the front door. As he glanced down at his pocket, he could see Eusebio's token inside, its glow ever and ever brighter.

At the front entrance, Piers saw a black car pull up in front of the door. It was an older model with federal district plates, but he could not tell if the car was under Kopendres or Parúni control or was just some other car. He looked at Leanne to see only a tired shadow of her usual gregarious personality. She seemed to have faded rapidly since they left the table, and he wondered if she was influenced by the oppressive atmosphere as much as he was. Or had someone drugged her food? He held on to her and supported her as they navigated their way to the door.

The street outside the Uruapan was unusually crowded, and Piers sensed that the Parúni djala corps was well represented. He decided to wait inside, far enough away from the front door so that if there was an attempt to drag either of them out, the other could raise a ruckus and get help in time. He stared intently at the car, trolling for clues as to its disposition, but to no effect.

Pru arrived at the door with a motley handful of supporters, some kitchen staff and some diners. Her face was tense as she looked out on the street; all she would say to Piers was, "Not our car. Stay inside." To add to the confusion of the scene, departing conference people were saying their goodbyes, oblivious to the brewing confrontation. Pru and Leanne did their best to put on strained smiles and wish their colleagues well. Piers tried to create a feeling of normality by blending in where he could, but much of his attention was on the energic leaks from the street crowd and the black car. He toyed with the idea of negotiation as a way out of it, but there was little he could offer the Parúni other than himself.

Pru checked her cell phone on the minute for texts. Finally, her face brightened. "They're coming! They should be here in two minutes or so. Let's be ready to move in tight formation to a position about fifteen feet behind the black car. When I say 'Go', we go."

Leanne looked even more lost and asked why they had to be so military about it. Pru answered that the streets were dangerous, and she didn't want any unpleasantness to come their way. Piers said nothing but raised his eyebrows in agreement when Leanne looked questioningly at him. Pru and one of the waiters took Piers aside and withdrew a thick wooden staff about forty centimeters in length from a cloth bag. Piers had never seen anything resembling it. It had a bulb-like finial at one end and a small orifice at the other. He wondered if it was a musical instrument, or possibly a club of some kind. It gave off an odd energy like an old tobacco pipe, an aura that suggested much use.

"This is an avda. You will need it if they attack. You're right-handed? Then hold it with the reverberator bulb in the right hand and the receptor orifice in the left. Draw energies from within you on both ends, and when it builds up, release from the center. Use your heart, guts and hands to control it. Only small motions, okay?" Pru rapidly instructed him.

"I've heard of these, but I didn't know what they looked like," Piers said, fascinated by the object but untrained in its use.

"Don't attack with it. Leave that to us. Just use the energy from the center as a shield. It reacts to subtle body presence, and a wrap-around shield is easy to form. It's all you need. They'll try to knock you out, preferably, or kill your body on this plane. The part of you they want is alive to the upper orbs. They'll attempt to connect that essence through the wahan, so resist any attempt to traverse it," Pru explained factually, all the while on lookout for the car she knew was coming. For his part, Piers was eager to wield his new weapon.

"Not here, not now!" she quickly whispered, as though hushing a child. "Just hold it at your side and be ready, ghenjil. They'll get you someday, just not tonight."

A yellow rental car drove up fifteen feet behind the black car. As if scripted, there was a moment of silence on the street as the sidewalk area between the two cars emptied.

"Go! Go! Go!" Pru shouted. Piers grabbed Leanne by the shoulder, his left arm across her upper back and his right hand on the avda, stuck in his belt like a pirate's sword, pommel uppermost. Two of the Kopendres djalas opened the door and went before them. As they stepped onto the sidewalk, Pru scurried to the other side of Leanne and barked an order to the two djalas ahead of them. Then to Piers, she shouted, "Make a shield now, like this." She held the two ends of the avda and, eyes closed, churned up enough internal energy to channel through her left and right hands into the instrument. Piers saw a white glowing elliptical region at the center point of the avda, then witnessed it fan out over the three of them, like a semitransparent sheet. Temporarily letting Leanne steady herself between them, he tried to duplicate Pru's shield, but failed miserably. The glowing central region on his avda was a weak patch of glitter that sputtered and faded.

"Pretend like you're starting a gas-powered lawn mower. Crank hard on that cord in your gut and let it fly. Push it with both hands into the avda like you're holding the handlebars of a bike." Pru rattled on, her eyes not on him but on the black car in front of them.

They started across the sidewalk towards the yellow sedan but were stopped by a power blast from a group of three djalas emerging from the black car. The stream of green energy buffeted Piers on the side and knocked Leanne to the pavement. Piers quickly picked her up while Pru restored the shield around them. When Leanne was on her feet again, the three regained their balance and moved again towards the yellow car. Another triple green energy flow slammed into them from the three assailants. The simultaneous blast delivered a flattening blow. This time, Piers found himself and Leanne on the ground.

Pru and her two djalas fired back at the Parúni. They were joined by three others who had emerged from the restaurant. In a lull in the crossfire, Pru again set up a shield with her avda. This time, Piers got to his feet and tried to set up a shield as Pru had taught him. He felt the power of his inner Nexus, the talisman and the token in his pocket synchronize and flow down his arms into the avda. The center of his avda shone a diamond white with yellow auras around the edges. *Look at it! Pumps out power like a geyser!* Grateful, he tightened his grip on the avda and willed the fluid energy to spread around the three of them, melding with Pru's shield.

The Parúni had moved onto the sidewalk to cut them off from their destination. In the darkness that dominated the street scene, he made out glowing djala shapes with phosphorescent energy auras around their flesh and clothing and green and blue emissions around their eyes, brows and mouths. The only thing he had ever seen that resembled the energized djalas were the wrathful deities he had seen depicted in Tibetan tanka paintings.

At Pru's command, they moved a few more steps towards the yellow car. The two Kopendres agents fired back orange flares of energy towards the Parúni and drew counterfire. Roving tendrils and sparks of energic color flew above them in all directions, lighting their path like fireworks. Then, suddenly, all combatants fell to the ground together. Piers hit his head on the pavement, but he was only dazed. He regained his wits slowly and found his gaze on the chandeliers inside the restaurant. They moved in slow arcs like pendulums, all to the same rhythm. The mariachis, who had been oblivious to the street fracas, had stopped playing. At first, he was puzzled. Was this yet a new weapon? All the lights in the buildings and most streetlights suddenly extinguished.

Then he felt it: the tremor. First a jiggle, and then a jolt. Then it came to him as he heard the cries and deft reactions of local Mexicans. *What a moron*, he gulped, *it's an earthquake.* In the dark, the people frantically poured out of the Uruapan and into the street around them. The black car pulled out from the curb and the yellow car's back doors remained open. Piers got to his feet and lifted Leanne from the pavement beside him. Once she was steady on her feet, he reached down to retrieve the avda that he had dropped in the confusion. It still radiated a slight afterglow that guided him to it.

There was a rumble in the distance that resembled thunder. The Kopendres djalas fired again at the retreating black car. Power lines snapped and sizzled along the street and the avda energy beams spiralled into the fallen cables rather than hit their mark. Piers regenerated the shield over himself and Leanne with his avda, this time more easily. They had to get away from the fallen electrical cables, so he pulled Leanne towards the street. The yellow car gave them a short beep on the horn, and he quickly moved towards its open doors. Pru was already inside when they got in the back seat. Then the car cautiously moved into the lane, dodging the wreckage and fallen cables. Exhausted, he sat back in the seat and watched the buildings and streets whiz past. Here and there, lights were returning to the city streets.

Piers said only, "Wake up, baby, wake up," to his wife. She opened her eyes halfway then, smiling, then descended again into blissful slumber.

Otherwise, a kind of grim silence pervaded. Pru was lost in her thoughts and her driver concentrated on the single goal of reaching their destination intact. Though the wheels of the car hugged the road as a child her mother, the aftershocks, of which there were several, were largely undetected by the party. Piers realized that the car's motion and suspension isolated them from the surrounding unstable environment.

The route through the darkness back to the hotel stretched endlessly. They avoided the clogged main thoroughfares and took the secluded side streets in a twisted path that could only be compared to Brownian motion. They were safe, but it was not due to their random course. As the cityscape swept past, Piers became aware of a monstrosity: a dark gigantic being whose breath enveloped the skies above them. Its wings were fear and its body unimaginable power. The great vibration of its heart had rattled the city around them and scattered his Parúni enemies. At least for now. The jaadentril talisman around Piers' neck was linked like a salamander's tail to this cosmic creature. The being seemed to speak to him in low, barely intelligible vibrations.

Following the voice, Piers looked outside as the car stopped at an intersection. The wall of a brick building had partially collapsed into an alley, leaving a scattered jumble. He saw a commercial sign, boxes, broken lumber, bottles and assorted trash. The scene was meaningless to him. Then at the being's urging, he looked deeper into the dimly lit alley and its surrounding detritus.

A temporal wave had enveloped the car as he absorbed the scene. All action was suspended, allowing Piers time to be meticulous in his survey of the rain-swept heap. He eventually realized that the entire scene was a brahan with glyphs perfectly formed from bricks, cracked boards and even a lost umbrella. It was not easy to decipher at first, but it had a simple and direct message:

I am known across the orb of Morasa as Quetzalcoatl of the Ruakon. I address Taighenkaatsuan, no other, for he is my chosen holder.

After Piers translated this, he was afraid of what might follow, but he knew that the Ruakon was teaching him a new art, that of reading the landscape and its hidden messages. As he continued, the next brahanic sequence set him at ease. It was the heart and core of the text and was repeated in several places in the ruins.

The holder of my feather shall be protected from harm until fate brings him to the place of rebirth in the northern plains of Sunara.

The next sequence dealt with proscription and punishment, though, and his fear returned. Even so, his eyes became accustomed to the darkness, and they followed the glyphs concealed in collapsed brick walls and broken wooden beams that had fallen in the quake. The translation also came with greater speed and surety.

Theft or acquired possession of the feather talisman by any but the holder will result in great destruction in accordance with the widely-known code. This message is occult and, outside of the holder of the talisman, none but the Ruakon, Yondai, Soenai and Ilyaan chona will know of its content.

The rest of the message fanned out into the metal and plastic trash on the sidewalk and street. It redundantly referenced the earlier parts of the message, so he skipped over much of it. The message suddenly ended in a tangle of dry twigs and branches outside the car—a coda that sealed its authorship.

By the testimony of Quetzalcoatl of the Ruakon, the Great Heart wills this thus and so.

Of the Ruakon and other power beings, he had only the scant knowledge obtained from Draaxis earlier that day, augmenting the little that Cynthia had grounded him in years ago. He recalled Draaxis' warning of their dark might and winced. While the referential framework made little sense to him, the importance of the feather ensconced in his sisiutl locket was inescapable. *If you believe secret messages in the trash. It lines up with Pru's story about the feather in the convent.* He had been directly addressed as the holder of Quetzalcoatl's feather, no less. There was a certain eminence to it, but not something to dwell on.

With the decoding finished, time and motion resumed its normal course for Piers, and the voice faded. An aftershock rippled through the street and the fragile heap he had read moments before fell back into chaos. The message, like so many things, was occultus and now existed only in his memory.

Piers was wrapped in the unknowing of whether he dreamed or was awake. He heard only the echoes of thunder, rain and the car's nocturnal passage through empty streets. A final stroke of lightning lit their path, and he thought again of Franklin's experiment. In the after-moment of the lightning, he felt himself to be the key, glowing with the sky energy that suffused his body. The talisman nudged its way into this radiance as though it were the key and he, the earth below it. His arms around Leanne, he drifted into a dreamless sleep. The celestial experiment was over, and for now, so was the failed Parúni intervention.

The next thing he knew, Pru shook him and exclaimed, "Wake up! We're here. The hotel."

Piers had trouble regaining consciousness. He caught it only for a split second, then, against his will, drifted back into the magnetism of sleep. Pru shook his shoulder more roughly and dug her fingers in deeper. Piers sat up, opened his eyes and murmured softly, "Okay, I'm back from dreamland. Mission accomplished. I know we're here now."

"Watch the street. They could attack again. It's unlikely but possible," Pru warned him as he tried to wake Leanne and get her out of the car on her feet. That proved impractical, so he ended up carrying her towards the hotel entrance.

Pru told him that the manager had just assured her there was no earthquake damage to the hotel or their room. She accompanied Piers and the sleeping Leanne to their room and helped with settling Leanne on top of the bed. She couldn't help commenting that the plasterwork near the sink looked new and a marked improvement from her previous visit. Piers smiled ironically and thanked her for the escape.

"This is yours," he said. He offered her the avda.

"No, keep it on you for now. You may need it if they attack again," she said, adding, "Don't wander far from the hotel. The Ordinath will discreetly watch this place, so don't make it hard for them to protect you. I'll be with Leanne at all times in the morning."

For some reason, Pru didn't seem exultant about the skirmish and its outcome. There was something deeply troubling her and she could only look at Piers with an air of resignation. He was aware that she knew more than she was able to say.

"And what's the agenda tomorrow?" Piers asked, yawning.

"Conference ends at noon tomorrow, then we make for the airport. I'll supply the transportation, so be packed and ready at two sharp," Pru replied crisply, then made her way to the door. She waved goodbye, Dirshani style, and continued into the hall without further notice, flinging the door behind her.

As the door closed on Pru and her footsteps faded into the distance, Piers got ready to retire. He would have to pack in the morning, then check out by eleven. It had all happened too fast, but he took a moment to look down on the angelic form of Leanne on their bed. It was too cruel to wake her, but he felt he had to. Soon she chatted to him about the conference, the people there and the reception of her paper. *Yet again.*

She was especially grateful to Pru for her generosity in refining the presentation and helping her meet the right people.

Inexplicably, she remembered little of the events at the Uruapan restaurant other than what people had said at the table, and nothing whatsoever of the attack, escape and earthquake. *It's like we inhabited two different worlds,* Piers thought, listening to her reminisce. But it made no difference to either of them. Together, they fell asleep in each other's arms within minutes, reunited in the same world.

Leanne had already packed when Piers woke up. It was still early in the morning and the sun was just rising. After a shower, he dressed and began to help with filling the suitcases and travel preparations. Leanne had not spoken to him nor returned any attempt at greeting. At first, he mistook this for concentration on the task at hand. But it soon became clear that her brisk attention to packing had a hostile feel to it.

"Leanne? What's the matter? Why don't you say something?" he volunteered, swinging one of the smaller suitcases to a position near the door.

She looked at him with a hard-edged glare. "You really should know," she said scornfully.

"What is this about?" he asked without the slightest comprehension. "Last night? I don't get it."

Without a glance at him, she swiftly moved to the bag that was partially packed and withdrew a small brown box that bore the name of Joyería Monje Campero.

"You never get it, do you? Just who are these for?" she queried icily.

Piers relaxed his shoulders and back, for he knew now what this would lead to. "The gold charm is for Shauna and the silver tie clip is for Vince. They've practically carried the whole school drama production, and I felt I needed to show some appreciation for the effort they've put into the play, the rehearsals ... and over and above all of that they're the top students in my class."

"Shauna?" Leanne shot back at him. "You mean that well-endowed little bimbo you were walking home that night I came to pick you up after the socalled rehearsal?"

"Nothing, absolutely nothing untoward was going on there. That rehearsal was cancelled and neither of us knew. We didn't have a ride and I wanted to be sure she got home safely," Piers stated firmly. He intended to repeat his rendition of the event. But he was cut off.

"I've already heard what you had to say about it," Leanne said, her eyes narrowing to slits, "and I don't buy it for a moment. You may think you're pretty smart, Sherlock, but your story lacks a certain je-ne-sais-quoi called consistency. How come the rehearsal list you left on the kitchen table didn't have it listed? Seems funny just the pair of you forgot to read it."

Piers protested innocence again, but the argument went on until Leanne got her things and departed for the last morning of the conference.

"I can't see how you can dote on favorites like that. Buying secret little golden treasures for your princess student and her boyfriend, but nothing for the rest. I don't think your principal would approve of those ethics. It just doesn't pass any smell test that I know of," she said with a note of finality as she firmly closed the door. Piers was blindsided by her last remark and felt like the proverbial deer in the headlights. He felt chastened. After all, maybe Leanne was right about the gifts.

Piers finished packing and wandered the streets around the Zócalo one last time. He made sure to carry the avda in his backpack.

There was a calm quietude around the Templo Mayor, and he felt attracted to it. He no longer detected any emanations from the wahan. It was as if it had fallen into dormancy like the truncated pyramid it entwined. His jaadentril amulet gave the most distant whine like wind across a snow-covered field. He looked around to check that no one followed, aware it was too open a place to stage an ambush. Sparse aimless crowds shifted across the plaza. The whole scene felt vacant of Parúni presence. But he remembered Draaxis' warning—no portent when and where it might happen.

Even more compelling, he considered, Pru would not approve. Since the night's events he had come to trust her, especially where Leanne was concerned. The Ordinath was supposedly on guard and was ready to move in if needed. It was unappreciative, even self-centered, he realized, to lead them so far away from the hotel. So rather than go farther afield, he returned to the hotel, checked out with his bags and had brunch at the adjoining café. He read a newspaper article about the earthquake. The epicenter had been deep below an uninhabited place in the state of Oaxaca. Damage had been light in the city with some power interruptions. There were no casualties, nor any reports of a dark serpentine being above the city or a street altercation at the Uruapan restaurant. In an unrelated article, someone reported seeing UFOs over the city. He half-snickered, then suddenly remembered the Ruakon.

Around noon, Leanne and Pru arrived. They spotted him, then joined him at the table and drifted into an easy conversation about the conference, the people and ideas they shared there. For his part, Piers just smiled agreeably and enjoyed the peaceful conversation of the women. As Leanne launched a final peon of praise for Pru and her generous help, Piers gazed sincerely into Pru's eyes and signed to her a heartfelt message, "Thanks for protecting her." Just remembering something, Piers rummaged through his carry-on bag and took out a long wooden object.

"I'd have a hard time getting this through security, so I'm returning it," he laughed, handing over the avda to Pru.

"What is it?" Leanne asked, intrigued. "An Iroquois war club?"

"Yes, a replica, of course," replied Pru in a perfect deadpan. "Piers was fascinated with it, so I let him examine it. Actually, you should hold on to it for a while, Piers. The kids in your history class might find it interesting. Especially if you show them how it's used."

"Ah yes, the history class. And there's plenty of enemies lurking in the halls, too. All in all, that's more than generous, Pru. Thanks," said Piers with an appreciative smile. Inwardly, he realized what Pru was really saying. He was a fugitive, on his own now, and another intervention by Parúni djala was certain. He thought of resignation from his position at the school and dropping out of sight, maybe to resurface in a small northern community with a change of name. But that was futile. Leanne had to finish her degree, and she wanted to pursue a career of her own. He couldn't ask her to give up her dream, and he would not go without her.

The three left together in a bright yellow SUV bound for the airport. Once there, Piers and Leanne parted with Pru as they all prepared for baggage checks and boarding passes. Prior to boarding, they met again for one last coffee. Leanne wandered over to a duty-free store where she spotted an acquaintance from the conference, leaving Pru and Piers to speak candidly.

"I've learned a great deal this trip," Piers began, an admission that he had grudgingly come to trust Pru.

"How so?" replied Pru in a neutral tone.

"I know I will have precious little time left with Leanne. I guess that's the cruelest part of it," he choked on his words.

"You have already lost her."

"What do you mean, *already*?"

"She thinks you're losing it, crazy, insane. Did you know that?"

The candor with which Pru said it took Piers by complete surprise. He was momentarily silent, then restarted the conversation.

"I don't know what you mean, Pru. I've never told her anything about jaadentrils, the Orbis Secundus, what it is to be an untrained ghenjil and all that. I keep everything from that life separate from my life now. I curse the day my father tricked me into that after-school job that turned out to be"—he paused, choosing his words with care—"a metaphysical mine field."

"Maybe that's the problem. You try too hard to split yourself into separate lives. I can tell you from experience that it doesn't always work out. Even for spies and secret agents."

"But how much does she know?" he pleaded.

"She knows quite a bit. Even though it's clear you love her, she isn't as stupid as you must think. She hears your sleep talk. She reads your moods. She senses the conflict you have buried inside yourself. The subliminal channel between you and her is strong."

"And so she's told you in a few short days that I'm losing my sanity. Is that it?"

"You could say that. She was looking for someone to confide in, and it just turned out to be me, I suppose."

"And what would you suggest? Should I just confront her and tell all?"

"No, avoid confrontation and avoid telling what can't be accepted as truth. You and I know you can't escape obligations within the extended reality you have contacted. Telling her about that will not help either of you to deal with it. It will only confirm to her that you really are schizoid."

"Me? Schizoid? Only a shrink would think that!" he laughed ironically.

"It's the only way most people on this plane can interpret trans-orbal behavior. They are defensively bound to exclusionist thought patterns."

"So, then what?"

"Just be strong. Don't let her doubt that you are true to her. That's all she needs for now. No promises when you're pulled off to Sunara, though. You know the doctrine of Veridos?"

"It was taught to me long ago by a dear friend, though I can't say to this day that I fully comprehend it. She called it 'non-exclusionism'. The Dirush believe it's more than just a negation of Aristotelian logic. They see it as the key to everything. Never exclude variant realities in an open context. Small truths and falsehoods are illusory. The Great Intelligence transcends all, includes all."

"Then you know all you need to know, ghenjil," Pru said in flawless Dirshani as she rose decisively from the table. Then, almost as an afterthought, she continued in English, "One more thing. Make no mistake, Piers. There will be another intervention. Listen for the phrase 'behind the artwork.' It's a sign they will strike soon." She looked once more at him, eyes slightly narrowed, and in parting, said, "May you someday be free."

"Thanks. May you as well, Pru-satjim," Piers responded, reflecting on her words, then added, "And special thanks for the avda lesson last night. I hope to do you proud someday."

The PA system called Pru's flight for boarding, so she winked, with a slight rise of her left eyebrow, and moved in the direction of her gate. She waved to Leanne who waved back in grand fashion, then broke off her conversation to come over and give her a hug. In less than a minute, Pru vanished down the crowded corridor. Piers and Leanne rejoined and walked slowly towards a more distant gate.

Chapter 11
Behind the Artwork

As Piers drove into the high school parking lot, the sun broke through the clouds and the morning shower died down to a Scottish mist. A fresh breeze brushed over the puddles that surrounded him, leaving rippled wavelets in its wake. He hauled his much too heavy brown briefcase up the stone staircase and through the entrance and greeted students along the way.

Some knew that he had been on vacation and asked about his trip. Some heard he was in Mexico and asked how the beaches were. All he could think to say was "Out of this world!" Then he put on a satisfied smile and watched as their bored expressions turned to the merest suggestion of curiosity, even jealousy. If he had told them what really happened, they might have reverted to boredom or gone on to full-scale disbelief. *Better to play the beach angle.*

The path to the staffroom was similar, sprinkled with greetings and enquiries. The new school custodian, Gord Stevens, introduced himself and announced that Piers' home room had been fumigated and sanitized top to bottom in his absence due to a cockroach infestation. Mildly surprised, Piers expressed his gratitude to Stevens and agreed that no more lunches would be permitted in the room. But he sensed that the gaunt man was holding something back.

Looking upwards to register Stevens' facial expression yielded little. There was a definite subtext in what the man was saying. It was difficult to say what it was, though, so the thought vanished like a small cloud on the horizon. Stevens had heavy brows and a strong jaw. His eyes penetrated yet let nothing out in the way of emotion, approval or dislike. He seemed a quiet thinker, not given to unnecessary aggression. Everything about him was cagy and guarded, but power and calculation were there in equal measure. He resembled nothing so much as a predator, ready to pounce at the tiniest motion, but not unless success was assured. He was altogether different from the last custodian, Piers thought, in fact, any custodian.

Together, they walked to Piers' home room so that Stevens could show him where the spraying occurred. Piers noticed a slight odor of disinfectant that seemed new to him. They chatted sparingly and looked at the moldings and cupboards with awkward silences, then Piers smiled appreciatively as Stevens turned to go. Stevens' final words were subdued but stern, "These Infestations need to be reined in, I hope you understand."

Piers nodded in sober agreement, but already his mind wandered to thoughts of Kafka's Metamorphosis. Whimsically, he wondered if the students would appreciate the irony. Probably not. It was hard enough to empathize with Kafka's hero in the early twentieth century. He couldn't help but wonder if Stevens viewed him in the same light. But that was irrational, borderline paranoid, and he broke off his musing.

"Ah, Gord, where did you find them, the roaches?" Piers asked impulsively as the janitor left the room.

"Up there," Stevens replied, apparently amused to be asked. Then he pointed above the varnished wainscoting towards some student paintings. "Behind the artwork."

His response seemed innocuous enough to Piers. But moments after Stevens receded down the hall a sudden queasiness overtook Piers. He inhaled quickly, heart aflutter. His hands felt clammy and his fingers trembled. What had Pru warned him about this phrase? No. It had to be a coincidence. After all, he had asked Stevens a question that could have had a thousand other answers, all equally rational. It was an overreaction to assume this utterance had any significance. Piers argued with himself that no causal link could exist between Stevens' answer about a roach colony and an impending Parúni attack.

It was just a ludicrous panic attack. The kind he used to feel as a teenager whenever he thought of Victor Marron and the Ordinath. Piers waited a moment, but the feeling of being exposed intensified in the empty classroom. He realized that if this was the sign Pru spoke of, he had no idea who this humorless janitor was or which side he was on. Then he looked at his watch and started unloading his briefcase. As students began to drift into the room, he felt comfort in their presence. The void in his stomach gradually began to dissipate, and he regained his composure.

Classes were a return to something familiar and comfortable. For the most part, the substitute teachers had kept up with the curriculum and no massive recovery efforts were necessary. The mathematics classes needed some remedial attention, but the rest were right on schedule. In the English literature class for grade twelve, there was a choice of several short stories on the curriculum reading list. Piers was immediately drawn to "Tlön, Uqbar, Orbis Tertius" by Borges.

But the class launched into his choice with neither enthusiasm nor opposition. In retrospect, he regretted the choice after that first class. The closest teacher he had to a pal in this school was Gerry Means, who just happened to wander in as the bell rang. His reaction was immediate.

"It's more the kind of story you read at university, or in some upscale private school. Definitely not here," Gerry volunteered. "You may need to suggest interpretations from the get-go to keep this class engaged. Most of them won't have a clue what you are talking about, or what the story is really saying." Then Gerry added with his characteristic irreverence, "That is, if it's saying anything at all anyway."

"It's probably self-indulgence. I'm attracted to the other-worldly stories. What can I say?" Piers responded.

Gerry turned to go to his next class, but offered one more comment, "Okay, nice, but you'll have to elicit insights and allow them to reconstruct Borges' world as they see it themselves. Not necessarily what you see. It's a poem on manifold levels but the sad fact is half of them are never going to read it all anyway." At which point he winked and jokingly offered a last piece of advice. "Try Finnegan's Wake; they may find it more transparent!"

Piers just smiled and waved him off with a chuckle and a look of mock pomposity. "World reconstruction indeed. Don't we all have enough trouble reconstructing our own little normality?"

But Gerry had a point, though. Tearing the world apart and reassembling it was, Piers mused, the only firm reality accessible to most of us. For an instant, he could sense encodings of Brahan amble across his field of consciousness. It was as real to him as a pair of glasses or a pen that lay on a desk. Or the classroom window to his right. The window was transparent and allowed light from another place to shine within. The quality of this light might be diffused through a rainy mist, one that seemed to hug the school building in grey indecision, but it was light nonetheless. One that gave no defining shadows, only shades of grey.

He looked away from the window. There were only two students left in the room, and they stood in front of him. Their gaze rested on him. It was as if they waited patiently, and knowingly, for a Walter Mitty meditation to end.

"Shauna, Vince! Just the two I was hoping I could have a word with," Piers exclaimed.

"Hi, Mr. Ralston," Shauna beamed back at him. "How was the trip?"

As far as Piers was concerned, Shauna had a smile that could light up any room. All he could do was bask in its glow for a stolen moment. Then he gathered his wits.

"It was great," he smiled, "and speaking of which, before you two take off, I have something for you. But just keep this on the down low, okay? I don't have presents for anyone else."

Vince, who up to now had worn a featureless expression, cracked a grin and said, "Presents? Sweet. Finally, something that isn't more homework." Then, his brows knitted ever so slightly, added in a mock whisper, "So, where are they?"

Piers reached into the inner pocket of his sports coat and produced two small black cardboard boxes finished in mock leatherette. The two opened the boxes as soon as they were in their hands. Shauna's eyes shone, and her teeth flashed as she thanked Piers. Again, he melted in her glances, but tried to reveal only a look of avuncular affection. He offered her a final conspiratorial wink that said, "Let this be our little secret." None of this was lost on Vince, whose face had reverted to a glower as he stared at the silver tie pin, then the ceiling.

On cue they both thanked their teacher for his generosity and retreated to the door. Shauna departed down the hall with a final wave, but Vince lingered on after a "Catchyuh later, babe" to his girl.

Piers now found himself alone with the intensely red-haired Vince, wondering why the boy had dyed his hair that awful color when it was already a fine natural red to begin with. There was even a little electric blue streak on the left side that screamed for attention. Then he realized that Vince was talking to him, blue eyes flashing, and that the tone of voice was no longer so benign.

"I'm sorry, Vince, you said what about my wife?" Piers enquired, reentering the dialogue.

"You heard me. I said your wife called me this morning. Here, at school," Vince replied with emphasis on each word. He was clearly irritated.

"But I don't understand. Why would my wife call you here? She doesn't even know you."

"Oh, but she does, Mr. Ralston, because you told her about me. And about Shauna, too. Not only that, she caught you out trying to set up a little hookup with Shauna. She warned me that you might try that again."

"Leanne is mistaken about that, Vince. It's a misunderstanding about something that never happened. My relation with Shauna is purely correct, platonic, and I can truthfully say that I have never laid a finger on her, nor would I." Piers didn't need to act out his response. He merely allowed his voice to convey his shock that they were in open discussion of a career black hole.

"Ain't so sure, Mr. Ralston, having seen the eyes you have for her. When she's around, you can't think of anything else, and it shows. Seems to me your wife has it spot on."

Piers was dumbfounded. What had started as an innocent meeting with his favorite student and her boyfriend had soured into a confrontation. How had Leanne summoned the rancor to mix in his work life and make false allegations that could lead to his ruination? Even if she really believed it, this wasn't like her at all.

And this boy. How could he seem emotionally crushed, even angry at a supposed rival, yet so cunningly toying and calculating in his remarks? There was a catlike beauty to the way he looked at Piers as he spoke, as though enjoying every moment leading up to the kill. Piers had admired those same qualities in him on the school stage and drama club. It was stunningly clear he had just witnessed the fruit of his own teaching.

"I can't believe this is happening. It's a total shock to me, Vince. I don't know how Leanne could take it upon herself to talk to you like this, but Shauna herself will back up what I say. Have you asked her about it?"

"Not yet. And I don't think I'll have to," Vince spoke softly to no one in particular, eyes fixed on the translucent mist outside the window.

"What do you mean, Vince? Of course, you have to talk to her. She will completely back up what I've just told you," Piers stated in calm, measured tones to make sure his case was brought home to the teen.

"You will soon be far from here anyway, Taighen. Isn't that your real name?" Vince shot back. "Vir Sephros is calling you to service, slave, so you'd better obey before his patience runs out. And it's not to Tlön, Uqbar or the Orbis Tertius. Understand? It's behind the artwork." Vince's tone had taken a swing to the malevolent, and he looked straight into Piers' face as he spoke.

Silence filled the space around them. *Coldcocked, and bold as brass.* Piers had barely begun to process what swirled around him: the allegations that Leanne had apparently thrown into play, and now this clever teen actor, a mouthpiece for Sephros, no less? He was shattered and without words but tried to rally a response. He wanted to know what part that janitor played in all this too. Then he noticed the red-haired boy was gone and that he was alone in the otherwise empty classroom.

It was unclear to him how long he had been lost to the world. He was reminded of the time gaps he experienced as a teenager in the Aimesworth and Dixon store. But now his mind was sharp and on high alert. He had been served notice twice in one day from what could only be Parúni djala operatives. It was evident that Sephros had wasted no time. The school had been infiltrated and primed for an imminent abduction attempt. Without hesitation, Piers took the chalk in his hand and quickly turned to the blackboard. He drew the brahan glyph he had once composed for Cynthia, but he gave it a recessive-passive mood. There would be birth and transformation, grinding and washing, but not just now. The ghenjil was otherwise engaged, it suggested. He smiled at it ironically. Vince wouldn't have a clue what it meant. It was directed to the man who cleaned the boards at night. He seemed to be the puppet master here.

Although it pained him, Piers immediately tracked down fellow drama teacher Selma Kendrick and pitched the proposition that she take over the drama club's Ubu Roi production as manager and director. She filled that capacity while he was on vacation and was more than qualified for the job. Her reaction was one of resigned acceptance, but Piers knew she fancied her name on the program and would save multiple copies of it forever. This, he assured her, was her ticket to fame. She laughed it off, but there was a hopefulness to her glance that signaled tacit agreement with him. This was all he needed to forego the dress rehearsal that night and avoid further entanglements with Shauna and Vince.

He also arranged a confidential meeting with the school principal, Mrs. Cole, and Gerry Means, to ask to exchange English Literature classes with Gerry. This would covertly ensure that he would no longer be in direct contact with Shauna or Vince. Naturally, Gerry vigorously questioned the whole thing, particularly the choice of curriculum that Piers had laid out for his class. But in the end the principal readily accepted the phony mental stress explanation that Piers pitched and simply offered him a health-based work reduction to drop the class. That would be pending a certificate from a qualified healthcare professional, of course. Piers would now have to follow up on the psychiatrist visit Leanne kept harping about, if only to get a letter that would satisfy Cole. It would keep everyone focused on the positive action he was taking.

In the meantime, he could assess his next move. He would have to exit the teaching profession in general and this school, in particular. But before departing, he had to find out more about Gord Stevens and Vince Lang—as strange and unlikely a duo as any he had encountered. Who were they in contact with, and how did they communicate? He was certain there was a nerve center somewhere in the school where djala could freely speak and receive commands from Parúni control. And he would have to level with Leanne about leaving this place for another locale. That would be the most painful part.

When he arrived home, Leanne was busy with dinner. Their eyes met as he opened the apartment door and took off his shoes. The steamy atmosphere of the small kitchen had saturated the entrance area and lent an indistinct smudge to shadows and light. Her face was hard to read, so he tried dialog.

"Leanne, we need to talk about Vince Lang. He says you phoned him this morning?"

Leanne took her time before she issued an answer. She stirred a pot of noodles, then another of stir-fried vegetables.

"I think that's between him and me. Wouldn't you agree?" Her voice was nonchalant as she continued to monitor the cooking.

"No. It involves me, my job and our future. I have to know what you told him. If you said the things he says you did, I am up to my neck in trouble. So, I need to know." Piers was tired and his desperate plea came out in a monotone. He was aware it carried little of the distress he felt.

"Well, I'd say that you have your secrets, so I have mine, too," Leanne answered him back more quickly now. She hit a wooden spoon on the rim of a pot to shake off a noodle stuck to it. It made an aggressive "bong" that was not lost on Piers.

"Fine. I'll spill all the beans. I'm leaving the school, and I'll have to leave town. It's not your fault, but I need to know if you want to come with me or stay behind," Piers put it more bluntly than before, but this only elicited another silence from Leanne.

He wandered into the living room and turned on the lamp by the couch. He thought about telling her he had dropped the theatre production, but that seemed so beside the point that it would make her laugh. Sarcasm was not what he sought from her, nor was another tirade against Shauna.

They ate supper in silence, with barely an exchange of looks. As Piers got up to leave the half-eaten plate, Leanne finally spoke.

"I'm not going with you, if that's what you're asking me to do. I have a future career to think of too, and I'm not giving it up on one of your whims, Piers. If that's what you expect from me, it's absolutely not on."

"No. I understand you. I'm not asking you to go anywhere."

"You need help, Piers. Really. Did you try to get an appointment with Dr. Feldman?"

"Yes, I talked to his receptionist—you know, that woman you know. She had a cancellation for tomorrow morning. I'll see him then."

"Okay, this is a start. Maybe you can get some help now. Maybe you don't have to leave town. Maybe you can learn to separate your overactive imagination from reality. And maybe even manage your paranoia. Or even just a few of those things."

Piers smiled with mock cheer, then replied, "That seems like a very long laundry list. But I'll try my best."

He decided to speak no further of leaving his teaching job at the high school or of his impending disappearance that would certainly follow should he stay there. To Leanne, that was paranoia, he knew, the fear of imaginary things. When they finished the dish washing and Leanne left the room to work on her course assignments, he took out the locket that hung around his neck and looked at it again.

The feather of Quetzalcoatl was there—the one that he somehow extracted and transmuted from the wall of a hotel in Mexico City. He squinted at it and pressed it against his palm to make sure that he was not merely imagining its miniscule presence. He could feel its imprint prickle against his skin. It was as real as the grain of sand an oyster feels within its mantle before nacre is layered around it. But unlike a pearl, he did not create this reptilian feather. Its intricate textures were well beyond his skill with the graver. And it had a life of its own—a life he was attached to with a golden chain as thin as it was unbreakable.

His fear returned, and he quickly put the locket away under his shirt. For the first time since Mexico, he felt it buzz against his chest. He wanted to take it off, throw it away and be done with it all. But to escape from this vortex was becoming increasingly difficult. Where could he go to avoid the Parúni imperium and its unrelenting djalas? Now at least one and maybe more of his students had joined their ranks and perhaps even faculty were becoming coerced into their sphere of influence.

The locket subsided to a low-frequency pulsing against his skin, having delivered its warning to him. He relived that event in a dark Mexico City night when the earth had trembled and he read the ruinscape. He could never discard it while the Ruakon had extended their protection to him. Even virs feared their cold vengeance. It was assured that none could take it from him. But just as clearly, he would be chained to this object until the sky beings relieved him of its burden on the northern plains of Sunara.

The next morning, Piers arrived for his first class and sailed through the lesson according to plan. As he left the school by the front door, he saw Gord Stevens finish sweeping the worn limestone steps. Gord wore his customary drab overalls and chatted with Vince, who was attired like a goth prince. They fell silent as he descended on them, so he beamed at them with facetious warmth.

"Good morning, gentlemen, but my, don't you make an unlikely pair? The prince and the pauper?" Piers joked, but to no reaction from either of the pair. Given that the forced allusions were questionable, he continued, "Excuse my attempt at humor. I'd love to chat, but I'm off to an appointment."

From the bottom step, Gord simply looked up at him in benign silence as he passed by. It reminded Piers of a steely-eyed hunter whose eyes never leave his prey. Vince's eyes darted away from Piers' face and his lips zipped shut. *Clearly, he's mute in the presence of his commanding officer*, thought Piers as he left them. One thing caught his eye before he turned towards the parking lot. Vince had already added a slender hook to the tie-pin Piers had given him. The whole thing dangled from his left ear lobe like a trophy. Leanne had been right about gifts for students: hardly worth it.

Piers opened the car door and looked on the pair once more from a distance. Gord listened impassively to Vince as the teen emoted and gesticulated. *No doubt,* Piers imagined, *the pair of them discuss me. Or is that just me being paranoid?* He wondered if Gord had taken the time to appreciate his brahan on the blackboard last night. Of course, like all blackboard graffiti, it had vanished by morning as though washed away by the night tide. *Like so much of life,* Piers thought as he turned the car key and shoulder-checked his right of way.

He arrived at the second-floor office of Dr. Feldman and announced his arrival to the receptionist. She was pert, attractive and smartly dressed, a dark-haired woman barely older than his students. She shrewdly smiled as she sized him up, though, and gave him a look as if to say "your wife told me all about you." She asked him to fill in a 'welcome form' and take a seat until the doctor was ready for him.

Ten minutes later, Piers found himself in Feldman's office. It was an austere room with mint green walls, a desk, chairs and a mahogany bookcase. But there was no couch. This was Piers' first such visit and he reflected that a lot had likely changed since the days of Freud. Feldman himself resembled nothing like a standard model of a psychiatric practitioner. He was a middle-aged man, clean-shaven with slightly greying hair, and he wore a casual pair of jogging pants and plaid shirt. The tie and suit were absent, a thing that Piers obviously had been conditioned to expect. He felt overdressed for the occasion, but there was nothing he could do about it.

"Hello, there. I'm Dr. Feldman, and you must be Piers Ralston. Can I call you by your first name?" the doctor greeted him with a smile and indicated he take a chair in front of the desk.

"Yes, of course," Piers replied with a nervous grin as they shook hands. Just over Feldman's shoulder, his eye settled on a familiar object atop the bookshelf. It was an antique porcelain phrenology bust with territories of consciousness charted over the smooth dome of the head like little countries on a globe. Piers had seen specimens of this oddity during his teenage days working at Aimesworth and Dixon. Perhaps this was even one of those he had dusted on the shelves there. The thought comforted him and gave him an unexpected feeling of connection with the place.

"Well, I'm puzzled, Piers," Feldman continued. "According to your welcome form, it seems that you are happily married and have a solid career as a teacher, but significantly sense you are under considerable pressure from people around you. Is that an accurate statement?"

"Yes, I think so," Piers responded with a more serious face. "Some people actually think I'm paranoid and that I exhibit lapses from normal reality."

"Really?" the doctor's eyes opened somewhat, and his voice inflected to a higher pitch, but Piers knew this to be a clever theatrical ploy. The man was clearly not surprised by anything. They both knew that the planned outcome was a prescription for pills and a letter that would justify reduced hours for Piers. Piers had hinted as much on the welcome form.

"And who are the people who believe you have these problems?" Feldman continued.

"My wife and ... I guess that's it," Piers admitted after thinking it over.

"So, you are here because your wife was concerned about your behavior or statements you made to her? Anyone else?"

"Yes to the first question. No to the second," Piers allowed, thinking that his case was not coming across very convincingly.

Dr. Feldman began to question him on the fears that he harbored. It was clear that Piers would have to tell him something close to the truth. He was a notoriously bad liar, and it would show to a trained listener like Feldman. Then it came to him in a flash: alien abduction. If he dressed up Sephros and his functionaries as aliens attempting to take him to another world, the psychologist might simply draw on the common mythos and relent from probing for the details. *After all, everyone knows about aliens and their compulsive abduction of humans,* thought Piers. *It should quickly lead to the letter and pills.*

Feldman calmly took in Piers' monologue about an alien being named Sephros who ruled a planet far away. Sephros had acquired rights to Piers from another alien named Draaxis who ruled a different distant planet. In Piers' adolescent years, certain people in his family and community were connected to a conspiracy against Sephros to keep Piers from being taken then. But on a recent trip to Mexico, the aliens had struck with a vengeance. Piers had narrowly escaped being captured and transported to work as a slave on a faraway planet forever. His wife had been present during the attack but had no memory of it, of course. He explained this by her having been induced by alien technology to forget the incident.

Feldman had listened with professional diligence to Piers' rendition of his secret life, one that his wife had apparently gleaned scant fragments from his episodes of sleep-talking and verbal slips. Aliens were even showing up at his workplace and harassing him there as well, Piers added. He finished up by confiding that he had finally agreed with Leanne to seek help when he noticed the stressful effect it was having on his teaching responsibilities. The school principal was also concerned, of course, but knew nothing of the details.

After a thoughtful pause, Feldman wrote a few notes, then looked up at Piers.

"You're an imaginative man, I would say, and highly inventive. I would further say that your study of drama and literature must have fed that ability and brought it to fullness in your adult life."

"But what has that got to do with my imaginary fear?" Piers fought back. "Are you saying that I just make up things too easily and then believe them?"

"No. I'm saying that I don't find your story convincing, entertaining as it is. And I suspect neither do you."

"Why not?" Piers protested, ready to put forward more arguments. "What do you need to be convinced? It's as true as the day is long."

"Well, first off, alien abductions have been studied to death, as a man of your intelligence might imagine," Feldman rejoindered, "and much of what you have to say about your experiences lacks connection with the known features of these narratives."

"What do you mean? There's not enough sex, or something like that?"

"That's one motif that's lacking. For example, you say nothing about being held immobilized on an operating table in a spaceship and penetrated with instruments."

"That's a cliché. If I'd talked about that, you would have known I was making it up," laughed Piers. He came to a sudden stop, realizing his ruse was falling apart.

Now it was Feldman's turn to grin, and he did so with a restrained smugness.

"You know, the biggest tell is your focus on presentation and abstraction," he explained, then gave Piers a penetrating look, saying, "You present a comic book version of your life but conceal the underlying actualities and motivation. That's all right, of course. It just means we'll need multiple sessions to strip away the layers of artifice. You obviously excel at storytelling, brilliant, coloristic and entertaining. That's an admirable trait in a teacher. But I need to go deeper: behind the artwork."

The last phrase set off an alarm bell in Piers' brain. A tethered hound, his fear was suddenly unleashed and his locket flashed a searing impulse against his chest. He broke into a sweat. His heart drummed in his chest. Without a word, he abandoned the verbal chess game with Feldman and bolted from the chair. Piers emerged from the consulting room like a gazelle bounding across the open veldt. He startled the receptionist from her typing and several other patients from their magazines. But before any of them could blink, he had cleared the waiting room and was halfway down the hall. His adrenalin rush easily took him down the stairwell to the foyer in the time he would have waited for the ponderous elevator.

Once in his car, he screeched out of the parking lot and took off down the street without regard for the speed limit. He was nearly at the school before he realized he had no prescription and no letter for Mrs. Cole. It was of little consequence. He had no intention of taking any pills anyway, leastwise not from a djala operative masquerading as a psychologist. He could just take sick leave until he was ready to disappear off the Parúni radar. He had escaped the Parúni djalas once more, and that was all that mattered to him.

Chapter 12
The Cord in the Labyrinth

The locket's burning sensation abated. His heart rate gradually returned to normal and he reduced speed accordingly. He smiled as his car coasted into his favorite spot in the school parking lot. The fleeting bliss of triumph filled him, and that was enough to sustain him for the moment. It was oh-so-clear what was next. It was time for the magician to show the audience his vanishing act and leave them dumfounded. The thought made him smile, but it was a grim smile.

Piers got out of his car and opened the trunk. He took out the avda and slipped it into a small backpack to conceal it. He would need protection from unforeseen djala attacks from this point on, so the avda would accompany him wherever he went. He thought about strapping it to his belt like the gunslingers of old, but that seemed ridiculous. It would be carried over one shoulder. He turned towards the school and entered by a side door.

As he walked down the school hallway towards his home room, he saw a print of the Franklin kite experiment that he had put up months ago. It triggered thoughts of the mysterious coin-like talisman that Eusebio had given him. Where was it? It was no longer in his pocket, and he had no recollection what had happened to it. He made a mental note to look for it at home. Perhaps it would come in handy to indicate when its owner was under attack, as it had in Mexico City. He knew by now, though, that it would prove to have some other future purpose. But what that purpose was, he had no inkling.

As he turned the corner to enter his home room, a lone student looked up from a front row desk. Teary faced, she was obviously troubled.

"Shauna! What's up? You look like you've lost your best friend," Piers exclaimed.

"Mr. Ralston, Vince gave me this thing and told me that he found it. He said it was on a waterlily pad, then he said sidewalk, but I don't believe him. I think it might be yours." Shauna choked out the words.

She opened her palm, and to Piers' surprise, he saw her reveal the talisman he had just been thinking about.

"Why, yes! It is mine, or at least it was given to me by a friend while I was travelling. You say Vince found it on the sidewalk?"

"No, I'm sure he found it on the floor in this room. I saw him pick up something when he was poking around in here yesterday. He waited until today to give it to me. I told him I didn't want it if it belonged to you or someone else. Then he got mad at me and we had this big blowup right here in this room. He just stormed out of here five minutes ago," she sobbed.

"It's alright, Shauna. You did the right thing. You know, it really is a strange coincidence. I was just thinking of looking for it moments ago, and I thought it might be at home. I'm really impressed that you would guess who it belonged to and return it in person," Piers genuinely responded.

"It's such an artistic thing," Shauna went on. "I was sure you must have got it travelling in Mexico. It was just a hunch, but I went with it."

"Thanks, with all my heart, Shauna. It was given to me for some reason, and I have a feeling that I'll pass it on to someone else someday. I promise to take better care of it," Piers smiled, hiding the talisman in his pocket.

Shauna hesitated, then said as if in confidence, "It's a winikos—that's what Vince called it. He said it directs power from some kind of field, amoeba fields, I think, to free a friend from danger, I think. But only when they are really in need of it. And it must be given to be effective, so I'm giving it back to you."

"Amoeba fields? That sounds like high-power bio-engineering," Piers questioned her, choking back a chuckle. "Ambivalent? Ambidextrous? Amniotic? Ambient?" he gently suggested with a serious facial expression.

"Yes! That's it," Shauna cried out in delight, "the last word you said. That makes sense, doesn't it?"

"It does, Shauna," he said approvingly, then continued in an innocent voice, "Ambient fields would make the most sense, indeed. The only thing I wonder is, and perhaps you can tell me, how would Vince know all this? I know he's a very smart guy, but even so, this knowledge is not at all commonplace."

Shauna gave him one of her Mona Lisa smiles and was silent for a moment. Then a slight furrow in her brow signaled to Piers that a moral dilemma was brewing.

"Of course, Shauna, if you don't want to go there, then don't," Piers said softly. "I understand that there may be private confidences involved here. There's no need to answer. And don't worry about Vince."

While he waited for a response, Piers thought about Vince and his wild accusations the day before. He surmised from the expression on Shauna's face that all Vince's recent revelations about Leanne's call were also off the table for this conversation. A voice from within warned him not to push in that direction. *Let's just pretend it didn't happen.*

Shauna came out of her thoughts, then replied, "You're right, Mr. Ralston. I can't go there. But I will say Vince knows a lot and learns very fast, so I wouldn't, ah, try to mess with him. Never tell him I said that. Please. And please don't tell him I gave that disk thingy back to you. Vince said he wasn't happy you had it. It was like it got in his way or something. I'm just glad it's back with you. Hope it brings you luck."

"Thanks for your kindness. I'll take your words to heart. And no, I won't betray the trust you've put in me. This is between us only."

Shauna moved towards the hallway with one of her delicious smiles that still melted Piers inside, though he well knew it was not in his interest to either feel this way towards her or show it. Then, as she was about to turn and say goodbye, something jogged her memory and she pointed her index finger in the air to get Piers' attention. As his eye was drawn to her signal, he noticed that Shauna wore his gift charm on her bracelet. He smiled instinctively, then caught himself quickly. She was saying something to him. "Mr. Ralston, while I was waiting for you, Mrs. Cole came by, looking for you."

"Really? Was it urgent?" He tensed his jaw mildly.

"Yes, important, I think. I'm sorry I just about forgot. She wants to see you in her office right away."

"Okay, Shauna. I'll head right down there. And by the way, I look forward to seeing both you and Vince perform in the play tonight. You must be excited. I certainly am."

"I'm so glad you are coming, and yes, I am very excited. I didn't know if you'd be there or not, but it means a lot to me. You were the one who showed me how to emote and create dramatic tension with voice ... all that wonderful stuff."

"It's a proud moment to see my best students perform in public. I wouldn't miss it. I can only hope Vince and you patch things up before the performance," he said with an open smile, but quickly moved on to the new matter at hand. "But I have to go now, and so do you, I guess. Thanks again for the winikos. And I'll see you at the opening tonight."

Piers took only a moment to watch the girl leave the room and disappear down the hallway. Then he sped off in the opposite direction toward the principal's office, his backpack-concealed avda over his shoulder. Most likely, this would be about his request for time off, but why the urgency? he wondered. Something about this did not sit well with him.

As he entered the school office secretarial area, he greeted the lone secretary, then asked if the principal could see him immediately. The woman scarcely looked up from her computer screen and waved him towards the office door of Mrs. Cole. He knocked and entered. Cole wore one of her favorite outfits, a hot pink and white checked suit with a chartreuse blouse. On her lapel she had a small gold brooch. Its design seemed familiar to Piers, but he couldn't place it. The rest of her outfit did not flatter the hefty woman, Piers thought, but he was determined not to dwell on that.

"Hello, Piers, how are you feeling now?" Cole asked. Her face showed only the trace of a smile, but her eyes projected a practiced benevolence Piers had seen before. She was a teacher and administrator with a long career, one who was acquainted with his father Jim when they were both young. She knew Piers since he was a child, and she had hired him straight out of university.

"I'm fine, Trudy. Never better, really. Just need a little time off, I guess. I'm working on getting that letter for you," Piers offered, guessing at the purpose of this meeting.

"That's all right, dear. Dr. Feldman faxed me the letter. He also had the pharmacy courier over a prescription. Here it is." She handed over an envelope with a bottle of pills inside.

Piers took the envelope. There was little he could think of saying, so he just responded with a soft "Thanks."

"He phoned me, Piers, and we had a long conversation about you—entirely professional, I might add," Cole continued, her ever-calm eyes scarcely blinking. "You and I go back a long way, so I thought it only fair to have a heart-to-heart talk with you. Please close the door behind you."

Piers turned to close the door that he had negligently left open and noticed the secretary peering at them over her screen. He quickly smiled at her as the door shut. The thought impinged that she could well be a subordinate djala, but he tried to stifle it while he turned his attention to Cole.

"I'll just come out with it. You're relieved of all classes until further notice, Piers. Here's the signed form. It's a leave of absence that can be extended indefinitely, as long as you wish and we both agree there is a point to you coming back to teach here," Cole said with a forced smile and passed him the form. He felt butterflies in his stomach as he took it from her hand.

Piers asked her calmly about the statute of limitation on the agreement and other details, just to appear interested in resuming his career in the future. He listened to her drone on about a maximum two-year leave of absence, reinstatement without penalty clauses, compulsory waiting lists and substitute teaching options, but his eyes were elsewhere, as was his mind.

She concluded the monologue in a matter-of-fact tone. "You can leave right now if you want, then come back in a day or two to clear out your locker."

"I'd like to see the opening of the play tonight, if that's all right? I told Shauna Byrne that I'd be there for moral support," Piers asked.

"I have no objection, but I'd keep it very cool and formal if I were you. There's been some talk about you and her. Given her age, I might need to get the authorities involved if I hear any more of it. You know what I'm talking about, and you know I want to avoid it," Cole replied in a low and measured voice.

"I can't believe I'm hearing this from you, Trudy. It's rumor-mongering of the worst ilk, and I have a good idea who's manufacturing it. It certainly isn't Shauna."

"That may be, so far. But I warn you, the more I hear of this from you or anyone else, the more I have to be concerned. So, let's focus. You've approached me about time off and backed up the need with a psych report. That's all we're talking about here and now. Just be careful what you casually say to me, even if it's not related to our purpose here. It can all be used against you at a later date. Y'follow me?"

She looked up at him with a stern glance, then went on. "And in case you haven't considered it, if someone gets that girl to go public with a story that vilifies you, made-up or otherwise, your career and life will shift for the worst, and fast. There's nothing I can do for you then. Nothing." Her tone rose in sync with Piers' emotions.

"I'm trying to tell you that there is an agenda in all this. It's not based on truth, either." He shot back at her.

"Fine. I know you are under pressure and my apparent jumping to conclusions doesn't help. I've consulted some of the people around you and one professional. Based on what they say, I can help you. So I'm doing that.

You're on leave. End of story." Cole was more controlled again, and Piers was taking more time to consider what his next words should be.

"I take it you talked to Leanne?"

"Yes, she came by here a half-hour ago to pick up your car. She dropped by my office to say hi and, of course, we chatted about things in general and about you in particular. As you well know, she was one of my students before my administrative years."

"I can't believe the degree to which you can pry into and control things that go way beyond your concerns, Trudy. What could Leanne tell you that I haven't?"

"Plenty!" she hooted, then burst into mini-paroxysms of giggling, allowing some unflattering facial wrinkles to show. Resuming her professional self-control, she explained, "I know that you are planning to vanish and leave us for parts unknown, for example."

"That's none of your damn business, and there's nothing you can do about it. I don't even know why you care. What's it to you where I go?"

Piers was visibly disturbed by the sudden laughter over his private plans. *How could Leanne be so easily coerced by this controlling woman?*

"Oh, Piers, your welfare is one of my biggest priorities. If you only knew!" she exclaimed, and then whispered to heighten the sense of drama she was spinning, "That's why we can't have you falling off the edge of the known world, can we?"

Piers was at once repulsed by the contorted smile Cole flashed at him. It reminded him of the sudden spasm of a shell-shocked soldier. Her hands now gripped the edge of her desk in a predacious show of domination, her brow misted with tiny beads of perspiration. His locket was activated by the field fluctuations he sensed. He saw pale blue light rays streaming from his pocket where the winikos lay nestled. Every fiber of his body was tensed for action, but he forced himself to maintain a calm exterior. *Why had Leanne taken the car?* He felt trapped here without the speedy exit it would have given him. The school was obviously filled with enemies. Even the secretary outside the door might be on the ready to attack. *This isn't paranoia. I'm not surrounded. I can defend myself and walk right out of this place.*

He slowly moved his hand toward the backpack still draped over his shoulder. As it edged nearer, he smiled and said, "Trudy, there's no need to take offense. I meant nothing when I spoke to Leanne about possibly relocating. Nothing is planned, really. Nothing at all."

"I'd park my hand away from that bag if I were you. It's not that I fear your skill with a decommissioned avda, but I'd rather not injure you with the one I keep under my desk. Vir Draaxis insists I deliver you in prime condition to his customer. You know, for the Trilikon." She let it sink in, then added, "speaking of which—Its starting, I can assure you, and you are a part of it, ready or not."

"So, you're of the Ordinath. That explains a lot." Piers almost choked on the words. Then, half to hide his shock and vulnerability, he continued in a smooth and jocular way, "And a djala at that. Congratulations, Trudy. After all these years I never suspected that you wore the star under your wrist bangles, but I guess you must."

Cole pulled up the bangles to expose her wrist and wiped off the opaque skin-colored compound that covered her star. She continued to gloat at him with the same menacing smile.

Piers shrank from the sight of the hated symbol, gagged slightly and continued, "My father tried to warn me about you when I started to work here. He said he knew things about you that would make my hair curl. I regret that I was so excited about the job that I didn't listen."

"Ah! The errors of youth. You should have asked your old friend Tom Aimesworth about me. We were adversaries from the old days and he had the bruises to prove it. 'Biggest witch in the country', he used to call me! My regards to your father, by the way, but I understand you two have not been on speaking terms for some time," Cole said with mock concern as she allowed the bangles to fall over the tattoo once again.

She tilted her head just slightly, and the sunlight from the window reflected off the brooch on her lapel. Piers suddenly recalled where he had seen that design. It was the yantra from Dixon's collection—the one that Aimesworth had destroyed just after Piers started work at Aimesworth and Dixon. He had not seen that pattern since the locket transmuted in Mexico. He was tempted to pump Cole for how she came by it. Then he thought better of it and moved instead to more recent events.

"Astute observation. So, tell me, Trudy, were you involved in that fiasco in Mexico City?" Piers calmly began to put things together.

"As a matter of fact, I had a major role in planning it. But we don't see it as a fiasco at all. I sent Pru Harriman to oversee the job. She was given the directive to make it look like the Kopendres and Parúni forces were battling over you. I think it had the overall effect we were looking for."

"Yes, without a doubt. Fooled me. But why?"

"Oh, come on, Piers, I expect you should have figured it all out by now." Cole continued to gloat.

"It makes no sense," he said, still puzzled. "Why set up an intervention, then contrive it so I escape anyway?"

"The Kopendres-Parúni joint forces developed a plan we coded 'Black and Yellow'. Its mission was to use your nascent ghenjil powers to locate and capture the Quetzalcoatl feather. A kind of qualifying test of your worth, you might say. That part worked spectacularly well. We had you booked into the exact room—the one our research indicated should contain the empowered relic. And sure enough, you found it like a pig to the truffles and triggered its transmutation. It's been centuries since anything like that has been carried out so flawlessly."

"The whole thing was enervating, but I never thought it was that remarkable at the time," Piers murmured in surprise.

"The Aztecs wound tight knots of protective energy around that godfeather. Presumably spun and coiled from the last energy fluxes of human sacrifices, but who knows? A dark business! Reeks of jinn involvement, I'd say. Speaking from modernity, they removed it from normal space-time by sealing it off in a pocket that no one could find, let alone perform an extrication on. That is, until you came along. I must say that the two virs were duly impressed with your performance."

"I still have it. And I don't see you trying to make a grab for it. So, how did the rest of the plan crash and burn?"

"Pru fumbled the initial retrieval. Remember? We couldn't foresee exactly what form the feather would take, and it was too hard to keep up the academic charade with Leanne while making off with your locket at the same time. So, we came up with the street battle scam to separate the locket from you. You were supposed to be unconscious from a Parúni stun blast."

"Kudos to you, Trudy! Brilliant plan," chuckled Piers ironically. "Vintage cops and robbers."

"I'll allow it was brilliant enough, but it turns out you were just too good at the defensive use of that beat-up avda she gave you. So, you made it to the car with the locket still on you. Our Plan B should have allowed us to grab it when you fell into a drugged sleep in the car. But then came the clincher. Unforeseen by us, the Ruakon intervened and sealed it on you during the earthquake. We were effectively stymied by an unbreakable taji—in dramatic terms, a deus ex machina, you might say. At least for the time being."

"So, I'm worthless to you now, courtesy of the Ruakon."

"Not at all. Sephros wants you even more, my dear. Due to the Black and Yellow exercise, you're a valuable pre-ghenjil asset with validated credentials. That will bring in a tidy profit to my dear master, Vir Draaxis, and that's what we're all here for. I'm even getting a sizeable bonus thanks to your excellent performance, and I thank you for that, Piers. Sincerely."

"And what if I do escape, Trudy. Say I just disappear off your radar. Am I worth chasing?"

"Definitely, but within a certain limitation."

"Tell me more."

"The sale is final contingent on successful delivery, so even a temporary escape would increase our costs unnecessarily. That's why we planned a little low-cost flick starring Shauna and you."

"Don't tell me you have a storyboard sketched out."

"Of course. The main premise: you won't get too far if the police are hunting you down as a ruthless pedophile. We'll do the moral thing and stir up a public outcry in act one. I'm sure Vince can ensure an on-camera sob from Shauna, and her new supportive friend Leanne will play with the press interviews in act two. Act three: they find you, jail you, and we just grab you in the prison exercise yard. The contained environment is an even easier intervention locus from our perspective. At least that's our current thinking on the pre-production side. Any thoughts or comments?"

"There's just one flaw in your synopsis. Shauna would never condone, let alone participate in such a travesty. I know her too well, and I trust her character."

"How touching! Well, the girl is naïve, but she's proven to be quite ductile and completely under the control of her keeper, Vince. Surely, you're aware of that. He feels he can induce her to deliver a convincing scenario along these lines. Unfortunately for you, I think you've turned out a great little actress, but hardly the heroine you imagine. We've already filmed some of her sobbing scenes."

"I'm amazed. You people have really been taken in by little Prince Vince, haven't you? It's almost as if he's really become MVP for the Parúni team."

"I'll grant you, Vince Lang is a precocious and a rising young Parúni djala with direct access to Sephros, no less. That means he's a power player. A rock star, you might say, were he not so underappreciated around here. We have been instructed by Vir Draaxis to consider his ideas and opinions seriously, or at least appear to do so."

Piers involuntarily coughed at the word "precocious". It had once been used to describe himself and he gagged on it even then. For just a moment, he felt sorrow for Vince. Then he hardened his heart and glared with frankness at the smug, calculating face of Trudy Cole.

"Yeah, he's ruthless and power-hungry, but as I see it, there's nothing in it for you if he wins the endless war, and much to lose if he can't deliver in the end."

"I have to confess, Piers, that many of the ideas we used on you in the Black and Yellow caper were his. He's proven himself to me time and time again."

"Somehow that doesn't shock me. A word to the wise, Trudy. He's a user and he'll play to your greed and use you too."

"If his star rises in the Parúni firmament, we rise with it. If he falls to earth, we disavow everything and do damage control. You should really consider currying more favor with him. Once you are firmly localized in the Parúni corral, you do not want him for an enemy."

"Me? Suck up to Vince Lang while he struts down the hall in his goth outfit with a tie-pin dangling from his ear? I'm sorry—not my style. True, he was my star student, and I will always be impressed with his bright young mind. But look at the whole picture. Believe me, he's got feet of clay. What about his commander, Gord the janitor? Should I curry favor with him too?"

"You could definitely do worse," she laughed outright for the second time, "but I'll leave that for you to discover."

The in-joke humor was more than Piers could stomach from this woman. Before her hysterics subsided, Piers walked out of Principal

Cole's office and slammed the door. As he left the school office, the secretary dutifully popped up and called out to him as he passed, "Please remember to take your pills, Mr. Ralston." He ignored her and tossed them on her desk.

Piers walked slowly down the hall. He noticed only its darkness and aimlessness. The students followed a current of sorts, some in small groups or pairs and some singly. Like him, they seemed to have no idea where they were really going—like salmon fry swimming downstream in search of the distant ocean. Of course, he knew most were on their way to their next class to obtain infinitesimal packets of knowledge that would soon be forgotten. Most knew nothing of their own identity, nor would they ever believe they had one. He, too, had tried to reject that idea for the longest time, but he had reached the threshold of acceptance. Never before had he understood the futility of endless disconnection from core being. To reject this core, to 'escape' from it, was nothing more than clutching that willful ilusion that actors affect on stage—the wise among them knowing that greater reality lies outside the backstage door.

For the first time since the evening of his name-giving he voicelessly incanted with intent, "Taighenkaatsuan! I am that! And I don't care if I'm paranoid and delusional."

Piers immediately felt a resultant influx of energy and recalled one of his classroom demonstrations: luminescent pale white ink seeping into wet blotting paper inside a shadowbox. The influx to his body penetrated him in a likewise manner; he sensed it as fluid lightning. His being was somewhere else, high-flying yet grounded, reminiscent of Franklin's ribbon-tailed kite. But on second thought, Franklin's glowing, electrified key captured even more of his experience. It was the core, the jaadentril. He realized these thoughts were of mere static electricity experiments.

He had reenacted them in the classroom more times than he could count and watched them being transcribed to quad-lined student lab books. What he now experienced could not.

The talisman, the jaadentril locket around his neck, gave forth a pulsed radiance within him from his heart outwards. He slipped easily into ecstasy while the oblivious world tumbled and transformed around him and down the high school hallways to nowhere. Like Franklin's key, his heart felt surrounded by sky and filled with light. He could barely sense the taught cord that linked him to stationary ground. Time seemed to flow like water in a mountain stream somewhere far below him, beneath the cloud-like jilhaan.

Then all consciousness cascaded down a temporal hole, leaving him suspended in the boundless void.

Chapter 13
The Curtains Open

Though early, the stage hands had triple-checked the electronics, sound and lighting and the cast was in costume. Piers momentarily thought of Shauna and imagined her in the wings, ready to emerge on stage. The student actors were under strict orders not to dart out into the halls or peek around the stage curtains or show themselves in any way. Piers had taught them about the magic of stagecraft and of how they could destroy their spell over the audience merely by appearing in costume in a public area before the curtain rose or during intermissions. He had every confidence that Selma had reminded them; he saw not the slightest trace of any actor. The magic was intact.

The echoes of their voices were another thing: soft excitement drifting from behind the curtain-shrouded stage and punctuated by nervous laughter. But that, he knew, was the sound of another magic they would soon weave. The leaking of it into the rustling of chairs and early audience chatter only added to the heightened state of expectation.

Piers roused himself and took stock. He knew he was in the school auditorium but had no recollection of how he got there. As he looked around, the first recognizable face he saw was Gerry's, immediately to his right. He had the sense that Gerry had been earnestly talking to him, without response. Piers laughed at how ridiculous the whole thing seemed but couldn't pin down why it was so.

"So, you can hear me now?" Gerry said with a grave look on his face. He noticed Gerry had been rubbing his hand, but now stopped.

"Yeah, sure, am I ev'r wiped out! What time'z'it?" Piers said, languid.

Gerry told him it was a half-hour to curtain. Piers started to focus on the lost time but it was too hard to remember exactly when he left Trudy Cole's office.

"I found you in the hall. You were propped on the floor with your back to the wall, completely spaced out. So, I walked you down to the office. Trudy gave you a pill that she said you were supposed to take by doctor's order. Here's the bottle."

"No! I don'wana take 'em. They w'r sen t'over by some Parúni quack an' I don't wan 'em." Piers struggled to get his diction back, but words still came out slurred.

"Well, anyhow, she asked me to take you down here and find a nice seat for you. So, I sort of became your babysitter for the afternoon—between the rest of the chaos, that is. I kept thinking we should phone the paramedics, but Trudy nixed that."

"The hell with 'er! She's a damn Kopendres djala. Fer cry'n' out loud."

"Piers, darling, dial it back a bit," Gerry hissed. "There are parents coming into the auditorium now. Try to keep a lid on it."

Piers found his friend's entreaty laughable and started to giggle again. Then he stopped himself. It was possible that Gerry was unaware of his plan to escape and he may not have known that Piers was on leave. It was hard to know how much Trudy had told him, or exactly what his alliances were.

"Sorry, Gerr. I'm not in my right mind, really."

"Nah, you're okay, just a little disoriented. Let's just keep it real, though. Remember, I'm only here to help, so act like you're being helped." Gerry fiddled with his watch and looked nervously at the stage, then as if just remembering something he'd forgotten, reached into his pocket.

"Piers, I took something off a kid in the hall. I know it's yours. From the end of the hall where I was, it looked like he was trying to unfasten it from your neck and run off with it. When I reached you, I stopped him and made him give it up. You weren't conscious."

Gerry pressed the jaadentril locket into Piers' hand. Piers looked at it, felt its familiar energy signature and gasped at the thought of it being stolen so easily. Something about Gerry's tone seemed rehearsed and even disingenuous to Piers. He wondered if the story was real or made up. Or more likely, Piers thought, Gerry had been told to retell this story. He had never thought Gerry a player in the grand scheme of things, but perhaps he was. The best agents are the most ordinary folk, after all. *If that's true*, Piers thought, *Gerry could be a master.*

Then he turned his mind to the problem of what they had tried to do with the locket. *Trying to break the taji put on it by the Ruakon? Good luck*, he thought, *hope they had fun trying. More than likely, they burned their fingers before they gave up.*

"Thanks, Ger, dunno what I'd do if this were gone."

"It's very artistic, even powerful, and I know it's important to you. Fact is, I've never seen you without it," Gerry replied casually, with an indulgent smile. It was hard to plummet how much he knew, but he knew something.

Piers began to speak again, and having the locket again had a decided effect in regaining his speech. The energetic flux was like mother's milk. He could see that Gerry could sense it as well.

"Gerry, I think you know more than you are letting on. Who would call a locket powerful but one who knows its powers? I hate to sound paranoid, but are you a part of an intervention, one that's aimed at me?" A part of Piers was appalled that he had just uttered those words.

Gerry stirred in his uncomfortable metal chair and tried to look away, his gaze darting around the ceiling.

"I can't answer that, Piers," he finally answered softly, then after another long pause resumed in a lower voice, "and I think you know why. That's the only insight I can give you. I can't answer questions about if, when or where, or anything like that."

"Why not? I always thought of you as a friend." Piers played his trump card, then waited for an answer.

"I'm not your friend, Piers. Not in the warm fuzzy way you mean," said Gerry quietly, as he looked towards Piers with little humor left in his eyes.

Gerry paused as if thinking about his next words, then continued, "Maybe I will be someday. So, I'll level with you, Piers. I'm a low-level functionary of a large empire in the Orbis Secundus, but you already know what I'm talking about, don't you? I was posted here to act as a friend and confident to you over the past three years. A spy, in other words."

"You—a spy?"

"Don't be surprised. You are an object of incredible value to them. I am far less so. Not that I dislike you, but to me you are just the property of my master, and I am here to assist your passage to his domain. They call it 'transfer to service', and I'm told you've been briefed about it in their anal retentive way. Our paths will part, you to another place. And me? Let's just say that my work here is far from done. But I may be of service to you, someday. If you ever make it back here."

Piers was crushed, but he didn't allow himself to show it. It was a shock when he found that Trudy Cole was a member of the Ordinath only hours earlier, but it was something he had adjusted to without emotion. She now was a declared enemy, and he was relieved the uncertainty was over.

Gerry was different: sharp and youthful but possessing an old soul. He was a lovable curmudgeon when it came to literature, and he cherished all talk and thought-sharing about media, characterization, semiotics and critical theory. Normally it was hard to get him to stop once he got started. He was someone Piers admired, fought with, acquiesced to, and shared insights with. A real brahanin, and the only friend of his that Leanne liked to have over for dinner. And now it emerged that he, too, was a puppet of the enemy.

Gerry got up without a word and only stayed when Piers reached over and pulled him back by the wrist. He sat down again, looked at Piers with resignation and a sigh bordering on a moan, then whispered a Dirshani monologue into his ear.

"Lean on my shoulder, pal, as if you're having a fainting spell. Now listen! Keep the winikos with you. You may need it to escape once you get there. If it's lost, it will come back like a bad penny—unless you gift it to one who depends on it more than you. Also, that defective avda in your bag —you seem to know how to use it. So defend yourself when you need to, but it's useless for attack."

Gerry nervously scanned the auditorium, then continued, "Seek the free lands, Piers. They're in the north, so always take the northward roads, never south or west."

Gerry was speaking of another domain, not this sod-bound world. He seemed to know Piers' itinerary, the one Sephros had set for him.

"The frontier is the first and last chance to get away from the Parúni. Head north to find a town called Durgos. Have something to give the old man who keeps the gate at the palisade. Give up the winikos or the avda if you must. Otherwise he'll turn you away from safe refuge. The forest is dangerous, the rain and surface waters deadly, so try to enter the settlement at any cost or find immediate shelter wherever you can."

"Why is the water dangerous?" Piers interjected, popping his head up in surprise. Gerry just opened his lips in a wide smile and rolled his eyes skyward at the question.

"Because it's time. Real, visceral time! It's the same time that passes as we talk here in Morasa. And time equals endpoint when too much of it passes too quickly."

"But time is here, Gerry. It passes slow and easy like water, but you can't see it, touch it or taste it. You're the first to say it's not just a metaphor, or some relativistic fiction."

"In the next orb it materializes as water and it's concentrated. You'll need to take small amounts of distilled water to support your life there, but the acid rain and polluted groundwater of south Sunara is toxic. It's the same in much of the midlands and north. Each drop burns up your life force and ages you on contact until you shrivel up and enter a mummified stasis, or even endpoint death. If you're dry enough to be immobile, only experienced healers can hope to save you, otherwise endpoint is endpoint. Omega. No return." Gerry's usually limpid brown eyes were serious and focused on Piers, intent on him getting the point. He was like a parent teaching a child not to drink poison.

"Really? No one ever told me that," Piers said, genuinely intrigued yet appalled by his own level of ignorance.

"Why doesn't that surprise me! They think you're actually going to stay with the sweet tram trip to Zirindar and go through kravl orientation shit at the ghenjil academy. That way you are completely dependent on them. But I say: don't do that, Piers. Go rogue!"

Gerry methodically scanned the crowd as they took their places in the auditorium. There was something about them he feared and distrusted. Then he continued his whispered instructions.

"Remember all this stuff I'm telling you, and never forget that the djalas will spy on you, follow your movements and monitor your progress without relent, both Kopendres and Parúni. Stay away from their power centers, the Parúni imperial city of Zirindar and the Kopendres capital Irupaan. You're in the Trilikon, a race that has already started, Piers. The Kopendres candidates are on the field as we speak and all the other Parúni ghenjils are veterans. They've left the gate, word has it. Worse, you're ranked pretty much in last place at this point and nowhere near deployment. Worse still, and beyond all reason, Sephros has big money on you. It's beyond crazy, like you needed another obstacle."

"So, what do I do? It's hopeless, isn't it? I mean, I'm not even trained yet. I wouldn't know a jaadentril if I tripped over it," Piers asked self-mockingly.

"You need to get training on the run from whoever will teach you the art. Talk to the ghenjils and ohanin you meet: healers, dealers, dancers, whores, and warriors, you name it. Even the odd traditional brahanin and avdani can give you an advantage. Use food, gold or sex to pay for it, or get your vir patron Sephros to foot the bill if you can. Maybe your old sugar daddy Draaxis can help you from the side, but not after the first strike. And don't be naïve enough to place your trust in the unworthy. Avoid capture until the second strike: then freedom is yours. If you are captured or sidelined, always negotiate based on your future value as a ghenjil. And never divulge that I told you all this. According to the oddsmakers, you're not supposed to know much, and it may start a minor war when the bets are paid. Occultus, okay?"

Piers could only say, "Sure, occultus, but very little of this makes sense to me, Gerry. What kind of sex are you talking about?"

"Ya know? I think I'm about done now, Piers. I'm out of time and can't explain any more to you. Just go with the flow like a dead fish. Be cautious all of the time and brave only when there's no choice. One way or another, everything I've said will be clear to you later when you get out there."

"But I'm not going there, Gerry. I can beat this thing."

"Get real, Piers. It's like talking to a total greenhorn. They are going to take you, so be ready. That's what 'behind the artwork' means. These are hardened soldiers of an imperium in a constant state of conquest. You know by now they've all but taken over the twinky little school: it's little more than their tactical operations center. For them, this is just a little hunting party where they show off their skills to their vir. Nothing more. They run the prey ragged, and when your energy is depleted and your spirit low, they move in. The locals will never know they were here or what happened to you. Just another disappearance, or if you're lucky, another comatose body." Gerry turned away from Piers in frustration, then felt obliged to look at him one final time out of grim compassion.

"So's that it? No good news from you, Ger?"

"Okay. Remember this, because you may need to know it someday. My calling-name is Jaeron of clan Vaalsenor. My woman is Irindai. If you need help, find her or any of the free Vaalsenor and ask them in my name. They're honor-bound to help you. Your father's clans people are low-class kravls in the southern forests and are few and far between, so don't count on them."

Gerry reached into his pocket and produced something resembling a fragment of dense lace. He closed Piers' hand over it and told him to keep it with him always.

"What is this for, anyway? Some kind of subversive nosegay?" Piers whispered in mock conspiracy.

"Not. It may save your butt or get you what you need. If you meet Irindai, give her this—but only her. It's a knotwork message. The encoding can't be read by any outside the Hodenvaal. She'll know it came from me."

Piers looked at the little ecru square and its precise arrays of knots. It resembled finely executed brahan, but none of its glyphs made any sense to him. He quickly stuffed it into his front pocket. Gerry was clearly getting ready to leave, but the skeptic in Piers countered him with a last question.

"One last thing before you go: how do you know these things, Gerry? You seem to be speaking of the Monra Sunara I've heard of, but few have gone there and come back to tell of it."

"Well, I'm one of the few, then. I was there, little brother. I was a wretched kravl in the pens of imperial Zirindar. I arrived there a promising youngster at the academy, a pampered brat who thought he was on a school holiday. My devoutly cultish parents had even staged a mock funeral to explain my disappearance here on the Orbis Primus. Complete with death certificate from a cult doctor."

"What happened, Gerry—when you got to Sunara?"

"Later on, at the academy, I acted out a few times. Then I failed a single validation level: ghenjil principia-intermediate. So, I know your fate if they take you there and you fail or step out of line as I did."

"Yeah? What?"

"May the Great Intelligence preserve you! I escaped and made the long trek out of the Parúni imperium to the Hodenvaal, but not without the help of underground alliances. That's your only hope if it ever comes to that. That's what that little doily-thing is good for, but Irindai is the one you give it to— no one else. To anyone else it's just a doily."

"So how did you get back here? And working for the Parúni too?" Piers was genuinely curious now, but Gerry was getting increasingly nervous, scanning the crowd and stage from the corner of his eye.

"That's another story," Gerry responded with tightly pursed lips. "I was captured in the north at the battle of Tilgaat, imprisoned, pardoned by Sephros himself and retrained as a Parúni watcher djala."

"A spy."

"This is just another posting for me, and no, I'm still not free, and I'm constantly watched by the others." He passed his line of sight towards the side doors of the auditorium, then added, "In fact, we are being watched right now, and if they have a clear enough sight to lip read us, you'll definitely never see me again. Gotta go. Enjoy the show, and may you be free, Taighen-Uchundar. Burn everything I just told you into your memory. They'll try to suck it outa yuh."

Gerry quickly got up from his seat and, without a glance towards Piers, he made his way towards the exit. Then just before he left earshot, he turned and said, "Hey, I saw that brahan you wrote on the blackboard last night. It was uncommonly fluid, masterful. A poem on manifold levels."

That phrase was the highest praise Gerry ever bestowed on anything. Before Piers could break a smile, his avowed Parúni watcher had waded through the crowd and was half-way to the exit. It seemed to Piers that in the seconds that followed, Gerry vanished by degrees, obscured by the assorted parents, relatives and students coming through the door and milling down the aisles. At some indeterminate point, he was simply gone. Whether he was friend, foe or double agent was sheer veridos. Whatever he was, he had stepped out of the shadows, revealed himself and left for collateral a lacework message to an unimaginable woman. Piers chose that bittersweet moment to remember him as a true friend.

When the final minutes had passed, the auditorium darkened, and the stage lights brightened behind the curtain. The bright spot lights were aimed on the central stage. The curtain was about to open. The audience became quiet. By now, Piers was coherent again and could think only of Leanne.

Where was she? Why did she take the car? Why did she talk to Trudy Cole? He had lost contact with her for a matter of hours. On a normal day this was not an enormity. But today was not normal and Piers was beginning to panic. If he delayed his departure any longer, the Parúni might act before he could. He had to reach her and plead one more time for her to come with him.

With a smile he remembered Gerry's parting wish, that he enjoy the show, but Piers now knew that this was not the show. The real show was elsewhere. *Nothing to see here. Move along.* Just as the curtain began to open across the stage, he tripped his way over the feet of the other people in his row, then bee-lined for the auditorium door. He felt saddened by the fact that he would not be able to congratulate Shauna on a fine performance, but her boyfriend and his new master were clearly orchestrating events that extended far beyond the stage and into the real life of Piers Ralston, former teacher and present refugee of the Parúni dominion.

It was a cool dark night outside with a full moon and a clear sky. It didn't seem that any of the watchers were on to him yet. From behind a hedge of oversized junipers, he tried to phone Leanne, but only got her voicemail greeting. He left her a message saying he was late getting away from the school and to stay put at home and wait for him. He had something important to discuss with her. *Please just wait. Don't phone me. Be there soon. Love you always.*

Piers had a few choices. He could walk all the way home, but it would take about forty-five minutes. Unless he jogged. The other realistic choice was to call a taxi, but the mere thought of that caused such a violent surge from his locket that his paranoia struck again. *What if the driver's Parúni?* He would fall into the enemy's clutches before the real escape could even start. Or the taxi dispatch system could be monitored by Parúni djalas. All roads led to capture, it seemed.

So, despite wearing the wrong type of shoes and a ridiculous two-piece suit, he started the jog homeward. He loosened his tie, took off the jacket and stuffed both of them into the backpack, then moved into an easy loping cadence along the sidewalk with frequent back-checks for watchers. It reminded him of the night he ran home from Tom Aimesworth's shop after the fateful meeting with Marron and the secret name-giving. That was the last time he saw Tom. This night seemed to be another of the same sort of last times. He quickly banished the negative thoughts and jogged on.

He could have phoned his parents, asked them to pick him up, then take him to Leanne. That would be the sanest way, he reflected, as he crossed the first intersection. But he and his father had not spoken in three years, and the flagrant awkwardness of such a confrontation was a major strike against that idea. Added to it was the near-impossibility of their attempts to understand his current predicament. Especially his mother—he had to rule it out. The success of his plan depended on speed of execution.

He could contact them from the safety of a new haven. His mother, at least, would come to accept that. Perhaps. But his thoughts turned to the inevitable Parúni reprisals against his parents or Leanne. The more he stewed over it, the more he understood he could not contact his parents under any circumstances for a long time. The less they knew, the better. Leanne, too. Leanne would have to vanish with him, for her own safety.

These thoughts funneled through his mind as he ran in the dark streets and avoided the lights of the main thoroughfares and public places. Between the thoughts and plans, he would look over his shoulder, above and below, left and right. Every vehicle on the road represented a potential ParúniKopendres raid aimed at taking him. And under the tunneling action of paranoia, he framed these into imaginary encounters in which he hid, used his avda for defense or his fists and feet to escape capture. But none of the cars, vans, trucks or buses that passed by him so much as slowed to show interest in his thin form against the urban landscape. To them he was cloaked in transience, like a spider scuttling across a cellar floor.

As he neared his apartment block, his sense of fear heightened. He looked for signs of abnormal formations in the nearby grass and foliage. Human forms in wait were suddenly imagined and then dissipated in the shifting city lights. He approached the building cautiously and silently and took cover where he could. It was imperative that he reach Leanne before they did. Even more so that he convince her of the danger that surrounded them both.

He was elated to be so near to her, but he harbored a growing apprehension about what he might find as he entered the painted concrete building. The vacant lobby offered no clues, so he proceeded by elevator to the sixth floor. He would have preferred taking the less vulnerable stairwell, but he was bent-over breathless by now and his heart pounded. He understood the need to conserve what endurance remained and clasped his knees, breathing deeply. In seconds, the elevator doors opened on his floor. The locket tingled, pricked and sparked against his chest as he walked the empty corridor that led to his apartment door. The hollowness that had invaded the pit of his stomach became more intense as he neared the door labeled 622. Something was gravely amiss. He drew the avda from his backpack then unlocked the door.

The flat was dark and the creaking sound of the door hinges had an odd echo that he had heard only once before, on the day they moved in. He flicked on the light in the entrance hall and called out, "Leanne? You here?" There was no answer but the echo. She was not there. In fact, as he quickly entered the rooms of the apartment and flicked on the lights, it was clear nothing was there. There was no furniture, no pictures, no pots or pans, no silverware nor clothing of any type. The watercolor paintings Leanne had done two summers ago were gone. Even Piers' teaching certificate had vanished, leaving only a ghostly dustprint on the wall. There was only the detestable olive-green carpet and the beige walls of an otherwise tomb-like emptiness.

He phoned the superintendent on the ground floor without success. Then he pounded on the door of 621. A normally friendly woman named Lola answered, but her stark face told Piers another story. She had seen movers early that afternoon. There was a moving van parked in front of the building for an hour or two. That was all she knew, but, ah yes, she noticed a redhaired youth of eighteen or so directing the movers. She didn't see Leanne at all, but she concluded from the sounds coming through her wall that apartment 622 was vacated.

Piers thanked his neighbor without further question. As she said goodbye, she suddenly put an envelope in his hand and shut the door, quickly chaining it from the inside. He took it back to his empty flat and opened it. It was a letter written in longhand by Leanne, signed and dated.

To Piers' best recollection, for the first time since childhood he wept inconsolably. He felt the pang of loss in a way that he had never conceived possible. As had happened earlier in the day, the intensity of experiencing his own deep consciousness pushed a wave, a tsunami, a solar prominence into the space of his phenomenal existence. He could only retain one phrase, "I am leaving you." A time dilation swept over him. Like a tide after a storm, lucidity returned. It was past midnight by the wall clock.

It had been raining outside, but the worst was over. He was sitting on the floor, back against the living room wall, still wearing his crumpled wet suit. Facing him was the large window now covered in rain drops that scattered street light illumination into the dark room. He waited five long minutes to make sure that full rationality had returned to him. In that interval, the full moon emerged through a rift in the clouds like a white chrysanthemum in bloom. For some unknown reason, it reminded him of the night he first went with his father to meet Tom Aimesworth—but a full burnished, platinum moon this time.

Nothing seemed right to Piers about either the tearstained note or the sudden and complete disappearance of Leanne. The whole thing seemed too contrived and vindictive for Leanne. The unusual use of the passive voice and the phrases like "without any interference whatsoever" seemed stilted and uncharacteristic of her. It was not something Leanne would write. And who are the "new friends"? The presence of a red-haired youth cast further doubt on the event being carried out by Leanne alone. Parúni involvement was almost certain. *Was it her independent will that she move out? Unlikely in the extreme,* he thought. *Was Vince a key player in this?* With certainty. *So, find Vince, and you find Leanne.* But that tracked back to the school. *Didn't it?*

The other oddity about the letter was the way it ended, on the phrase "at the school or wherever." If he had been asked to mark the letter as a class assignment, he might have commented that the phrase seemed out of place and irrelevant. He wondered if Leanne had added it in a final attempt to tell him something. She knew they were taking her to the school, perhaps? Or he would learn of her whereabouts there? It was pure guesswork, but intuition was all he had to go on. He needed to feel that Leanne was trying to direct him to where she was, no matter how hidden by the general tone of the letter.

Piers now came into his second wind. There was no way he could curl up and sleep for the rest of the night, so certain was he that he could find Leanne and rescue her from the Parúni camp. In the back of his mind was the second realization that they had a key and could have stormed the apartment any time while he was unconscious or sleeping. Why didn't they? He needed to leave this place soon and keep moving. This was shaping up as cat and mouse, the kind of game that a smart mouse could sometimes win. That was his only sliver of hope.

He searched the refrigerator and found enough to recharge his depleted energy level. While he wolfed down a crudely made sandwich and drank water straight from the tap with his hand, he noticed a single framed picture in an awkward corner of the kitchen. He was sure that no pictures had remained on any wall when he entered the apartment earlier. But this one was so tiny, perhaps he had not noticed it before. It was one of his collection of tiny literary scenes, and the only one that had been left to him. Ironically, it was a print of the initial scene in Kafka's Metamorphosis, where the protagonist Gregor Samsa realizes he has mysteriously transformed into an insect. The symbolic impact was not completely wasted on Piers. He allowed himself a grim smile as he remembered Gord Stevens' comment regarding the cockroaches and the need to rein them in.

The djalas left it to taunt me? He was sure it was absent when he first entered the apartment. But it was not the sort of thing he would notice in a state of shock. He carefully thought over the alternate theory, the one he called "game theory". They entered the apartment after he had passed out and remounted the picture as a kind of message. They may have done other things, too, so he started to search the rooms for changes. The first surprise was the clothes closet in the bedroom. It was no longer bare. There were jogging clothes and a fake leather jacket he often wore on weekends, running shoes too. *They want me to change*, he thought. Then he checked the bathroom and a used bar of soap had been returned, along with a favorite green towel. It was as if they were sending him commands like "take a shower," and "change clothes." *Kravl commands. Seriously? No frigging way, assholes!* Then he calmed himself.

He debated whether to follow the visual commands or show defiance and stay in his sweat-soaked white shirt and suit pants. It was uncomfortable to remain as he was, though, so he eagerly went along with the script he'd been given, starting with the shower. As he was about to leave the bathroom after his shower, he noticed one other change he hadn't noticed before. Feldman's prescription pills were sitting on a glass shelf above the sink. Startled, he was almost certain they had been placed there within the timespan of his shower, but again, he couldn't be completely sure. Whatever the event sequencing, that was one reminder he would cheerfully ignore.

He quickly dressed in the fresh clothes and got ready to leave. It seemed that they wanted to chase him. Why else allow him to believe he could escape them? Otherwise, they could have taken him easily in the hours he was unconscious. Ergo, he was the mouse in this game and had all the speed, wiles and aptitudes of such. And something of a head start, it seemed. Confident in that realization, he quietly left the apartment without locking the door. There was nothing worth taking inside, and the djalas obviously had the key anyway. He headed down the hall with the winikos in his pocket, the avda and Leanne's letter in his backpack and the jaadentril locket around his neck. Nothing more. This time he took the stairs down to the lobby, then descended one more level down to the basement parking lot. The side door on that level had a touch bar on the inside that would allow a discreet exit. He scrambled up the short external stairwell to a shrubbery area behind the building and from there he squatted and observed the lay of the land.

The full moon afforded him broad visibility of the surrounding grounds and street, and he saw no evidence of lone watchers or suspicious cars parked nearby. It was as if Coyolxauhqui, the Aztec moon goddess, had spoken to him—as if she had given him assurance that his enemies were not lying in wait for him, that she had led them to sleep and dream while he looked over the peaceful urban landscape. He well remembered her sacrificial corpse carved on a large stone disk replica at the templo mayor in Mexico City. His mood darkened at the thought of her deathly agony, only her head resurrected to light the night sky.

As if on cue, thick clouds drifted over the night sky. The moon quickly darkened like a snuffed candle. At once, Piers took this as a sign. He set out under cover of darkness in the direction of the school, jogged at an easy pace and kept his eyes on all his surroundings. The sense of purpose, danger and desire ignited the jilhaan within him. With each step, he slowly gave in to the instinct that pulled him into a race that his heart and mind rejected, but that his inner being had embraced as crucial. He repeated the mantra: *This is for Leanne.* Deeper within, however, a more mysterious process was beginning. A process as natural and autonomous as breathing, and somehow just as necessary. He couldn't put his finger on what it was, though.

Chapter 14
The Seruwani Council

He stopped to catch his breath. After a scan of the environs, he identified dark masses of foliage and grass. It was a small park, dotted here and there with broadleaf maples and thin wooden-railed benches with pig iron legs. The benches were empty and inviting, the type you could sleep on with newspaper padding, but he knew he couldn't rest. The will to go on was stronger than any other; he balanced himself against the back of a bench, ready to depart again at any moment. He used the moment to look around the streetscape and park with its modest playground and sand pit. There were few vehicles on the road and no people, either in the park or along the street. All businesses were long closed. Piers allowed a sardonic quip to himself, *Deserted as paradise after the expulsion.* It was something Tom Aimesworth would say on a slow afternoon at the store.

Then he noticed a flickering light coming from the far corner of the park. He darted behind a maple tree and stole a careful glance for any human presence or motion in its vicinity. Sure enough, people moved about, but it was hard to say how many. They seemed to carry a large yellow box or walk near it as it moved towards a small alley on the other side of the street. The procession was slow and had a dignified air. As a teacher, Piers knew the known gangs operating in the area, and he had been briefed by police on their names and profiles. Even their rituals. The behavior of this group seemed very different from any of those. If anything, this was more like a covert midnight funeral.

Perhaps it had nothing to do with Piers and he could continue his jog towards the school unnoticed. Maybe it did have some connection to him. Or it was a Parúni trap, and he should move on while he had time to put distance between him and this group. The jaadentril locket told him nothing. The group seemed neutral, but he took out the avda from his backpack in case of attack.

Piers moved slowly from tree to tree, hoping he had not been seen. The light they used was a flashlight or maybe an old kerosene lamp. He watched as it moved in advance of his cautious approach, away from the far corner of the park and up the alley. He could pick out four or five people in rag-tag clothing surrounding the box, then even more of them in the rear. *Not djala*, he conjectured. *Street people, quite possibly.* And it was now definitive: they did nothing to hold or support the box in any way. He was mildly astounded. It floated above the ground by no more than a few inches, as though it were a hovercraft riding a cushion of air. He could think of no other rational explanation.

Who are these people? Did they build or invent this amazing device, or steal it? He smiled at the thought that they might well be a nocturnal robotics club fielding their latest creation. But it wasn't that, either. His curiosity had taken hold of him, and he was hopelessly drawn to them.

What about Leanne? His conscience prodded him, and he stopped behind the last of the maple trees, torn between the responsibility of finding her and the ongoing spectacle of the floating box procession. There was still time to return to his mission. Shame was beginning to overtake him, and an inner voice warned him: *stay on course!* How could he embark on the rescue of his lover then be so easily diverted by random happenings in a night alley he had never noticed before. No matter how engrossing the apparition of the floating box was, his sense of a deep, unforeseen ambiguity was rising.

The group was now building a small fire on a corrugated iron sheet in the alleyway, and were gathered around it, warming themselves. His mind immediately jumped at the legality of the fire, forcing him to again reconsider whether he should remain. If police were called in by neighbors, it might be another way the Parúni could take control and trap him. He would be much safer blending back into the dark night, but the fire-lit glow of their small company now attracted him like a beacon. He was a fugitive like them. No job or income. Branded by a psych report. His relationship in shambles. Pursued by enemies intent on his capture. There was something appealing about their marginality, and he felt a deepening kinship.

He tentatively crossed the street towards the shabby little alleyway and its nocturnal flock, taking a position at the juncture of the alley with the street and half-hidden by the bricked corner of a store. He felt like a birdwatcher seeking a blind from which to observe a new-found species. Weird though it was, they seemed more than just aware of him. It was as if he had been calmly expected. The avda was discreetly stowed in the backpack again.

He stepped out into plain view, hands at his sides, and a few of them looked his way without alarm. They evidenced no problem with his being there. He felt the momentary thrill of acceptance, but knew his reaction could be spurious, and all the more dangerous to trust. Continuing up the alley, he fixed his eyes on them and the mysterious box. As he drew near, he could make out faint brahan inscriptions painted on the box. He stopped. *This could be another Kopendres-Parúni trap*, he thought, *like the one in Mexico*. Tactically, it was transparent: the djalas lure him into a cul-de-sac then cut off his exit. *Game over*. Or the box itself could have been a glorified rabbit trap. He recalled Trudy Cole's cold lingo: intervention locus. It gave him an involuntary shiver, but he shook it off. There was still time to reverse his steps and get away.

For a few moments, he stood there on tenterhooks considering his options, when he was suddenly overwhelmed by what happened next. The weathered yellow box simultaneously collapsed and opened in midair, revealing none other than the Dahi in a gold-embroidered blue robe. There was no puff of flash powder that might have accompanied a magician's trick, but the event left Piers just as speechless as a child in a church basement magic show. The devoted throng surrounding the white-bearded figure exclaimed, "Tewantsa Dahi!"

Piers relaxed and smiled sheepishly at the Dahi, repeating the same greeting to him in his mind, but delivering from his mouth only a choked-up version. The Dahi fondly returned his smile, nodded in approval to all and spoke softly in the rapt silence that took over as he raised his hands.

"Tewantsa satjimri, trusted ones—Greetings to you all. My satjimri—listen! Tonight, we are here for one purpose: to help our dear satjim Taighen. He stands before us at the crossroads, alone, forsaken and in fear of powerful enemies. We must aid, protect and advise him in his journey. You all know this journey and its dangers. You all have been kravls in your time, but now are free. You all have great honor in my heart. I seek your voices of assent. May they unlock his destiny."

A murmur of approval passed through the dozen faces trained on Piers. Though poor in clothing and material possessions, the assembly took on an air of august deliberation. The discussion had begun among small subgroups, some animated and some thoughtful, whisperings that rustled through the gathering like wind through the autumn leaves, even voiceless exchanges of opinion and sentiment that passed from one pair of eyes to another.

For Piers, a new realization dawned as he witnessed them at work. These people had a stature that transcended their low estate in the Orbis Primus. He understood that they were masters of the three great arts of Sunara: indeed, they were Seruwani. Each of them had mastered Avda, Brahan and Ohan and had specialized in one of these artforms. Cynthia had once told him of the Seruwani in a tone of awe and respect, and she warned him of their capricious and sometimes unpredictable behavior. They were a clan apart from all others and the imperators of the old Dirush empire were always chosen from the Seruwani. In the old order, judges, generals and administrators were also of their number. Their counsel was above price or reward and their devotion to truth unwavering. Though tacitly vouched for by the Dahi as trustworthy, their ragged appearance spoke otherwise. What they were doing in the parks and run-down streets of Vancouver, he could not imagine. In a middle-class district? Even more out of place.

Just as it seemed to Piers that no consensus would evolve, a stout grizzled bear of a man in patched pants and threadbare dinner jacket stepped forward from the center of the group. His broad face bore the scars and skirmishes of his hard life like a battleground. The peace he had was hard-won, and Piers could see the others looked to him with respect.

"We can't rule on this case, Dahi, until we know more of this man. More than what we can see here. What is his past? What are his intentions? Which vir lays claim to him, and what are the grounds of that claim?"

"Wise words, Bartemus-satjim. Let the man speak for himself before the council," the Dahi replied, turning his gaze to Piers.

"My name is Taighen-Uchundar. I now follow the ghenjil way. Without my knowledge, I was made a Kopendres kravl at a young age. I later learned this was to avenge the freedom taken by my father earlier in his life, freedom from the ritual abuse of the *Ordo Stella Kopendres*. Unlike him, I was given a protected and peaceful life. I have three great souls, the Dahi, my exmentor and my father, to thank for that."

Piers paused and looked over the group again. The silence was hardedged, so he continued.

"Early on, I showed promise to those who know the high arts. I performed an exchange transmutation through a transorbulence I activated at age fourteen. What I tell you is in confidence." He looked at the Dahi to get the nod to proceed. It came without hesitation.

"It was a tril copy of a critical section of the *Torvaaden* Codex. The accretion was debased to common gold and the essence transferred to safety. Even so news travelled, and it reached the virs. Since then I rebelled from the path set before me. I have never pursued a major strike, and my slavehood was never repealed. My former master Draaxis-Kopendres sold me to Vir Sephros. Now Sephros has called me to service in the Trilikon. I have ignored this call and am now a fugitive running from the Parúni djalas. They have taken everything from me but these clothes, an avda and what I have on me." Piers wondered if he had gone on too long with his personal history, but all eyes continued to be trained on him.

"I am convinced they have taken my wife too. She's *unikari*, doesn't understand the non-Mehenti world, and I think she has been deluded by the Kopendres and Parúni djalas. They may be holding her at the school where I used to teach. They are running their command post from there. If I can reach her, and she is willing, I mean to rescue her and take her with me to wherever we can live in freedom from the forces of Sunara. Somewhere far from here."

Piers took a moment to let his words sink in, then added, "I know this is a lot to ask of you, but if any of you can help me, I'm in your debt."

As Piers scanned his small audience, he saw only serious faces now. They were focused and centered on his words. Bartemus stood and asked for would-be responders to signal him. A slim oriental man of perhaps forty years raised his index finger. Unlike most others, his sleek black clothing was not of the street but suggested a worldlier source.

"Council recognizes Mencius Wah. Speak, Mencius-satjim, and share your wisdom," Bartemus responded. Piers got down on his haunches to listen, his arms folded over his knees. Mencius rose to his feet and stood feet shoulder-length apart in a martial stance. To Piers, this man was manifestly ex-djala and his bearing still carried the rigors of his training.

Mencius looked squarely at Piers and spoke without emotion or haste.

"I was a Parúni djala for many campaigns before my return to free life here in the Monra Morasa. I earned my freedom from Vir Sephros in payment for service at the battle of Tilgaat, in the north of Sunara. I know the djala strategies and methods. From much practice, I feel the martial energies when a commando operation of the djala is in progress. A few weeks ago, I sensed a confluence around here in the south city. It was a power surge I have only ever detected prior to a Parúni battle or raid."

"What was that?" Piers interjected, interested in what Mencius could be hinting at.

"All I can say is that for the longest time I have felt at ease with the absence of my former vir in these environs. But I sense now that he walks among us. There is no question in my mind that Sephros is close. For what reason, I know not. But now that I've seen you and heard your story, I'm convinced you have something to do with it."

"Why?" Piers asked, already knowing but wanting confirmation.

"He has never had the territorial ambition to show more than a token presence here in the lower orb. This place simply doesn't interest him. But people with unusual strengths and capabilities do. You seem to be the prime object of this hunt. I'm afraid your woman may be either collateral damage or bait, to put it bluntly. Hard to say which at this point."

"Mencius, can you come with me to the school? I need your experience and ability to identify him," Piers asked in complete sincerity, virtually ignoring the other's blunt assessment.

"I ... I can't do that, Taighen-satjim," Mencius replied with equal candor. "For me to appear even beyond visual range of the vir's campaign post would alert him to both my presence and yours. He and his forces are on high alert. And his subtlety in field sensing is uncanny, in the physical world as in Sunara."

"I'm asking a lot. It's just that I'm one man alone against an army."

"The most I can do is to help you decide whether to submit to him now, run far from him or mount a stealth reconnaissance of the facility he operates from. Anything more and I could be a greater danger than a help to your mission."

"Can you guide me to his location and confirm his presence?" Piers entreated him, trying to find at least some role for Mencius. It was clear he needed collaborators like him, but it was next to hopeless to find them.

"Yes, but as I said before, it's dicey to enter his core domain. My mere presence would give away your plan and could implicate the Dahi. I won't do that without his approval. There's more: my freedom can be terminated if he associates me to your escape. I'm talking about something more than the Sunaraic law codes of sentient property theft."

"How so?"

"It makes me his enemy—my neutrality pledge to him would be broken. And until you are in his possession, he sees you as an enemy as well. He's just toying with you now, but I sense the hard knocks are to come. And they won't be pretty when they do."

"So, you're saying that you can't help me achieve anything?" Piers blurted out, his inner tension verging on outrage.

Mencius was calm and without a ripple of emotion as he answered Piers in a low clear voice. "No, I can help you decide, Taighen-satjim. That's the first objective of this council. And if you have already made your decision, we can help you plan and effect the plan into action. The rest is for you. If you plan to attack the most powerful vir of the upper orb in his local fortification, I can advise, but I cannot commit to be present. Not unless the Dahi overrules me."

"Okay. Advise me, then. What's my best option?"

"If you plan to run into obscurity and relative safety, I can act as your guide and put my experience at your disposal. The mountains to the north of here are as wild and intractable as any on the planet. There are safe havens there, and I can take you to them."

"And if I turn that down?"

"I hate to say it, satjim. In the end, you are on your own."

"That's bullshit!" another voice rang out. It was one of the young men among the Seruwani. He had stood up while the discussion was going on and was ready to contribute his views. All eyes were on him, so he took the center stage. Mencius slipped back to his seat on a concrete block without a word, arms folded around his knees and eyes closed.

The young man surveyed the gathering and held their attention with a voice that matched his piercing eyes. "Taighen can't rescue his woman all by himself. It's suicide. And he's not ready to submit and go meekly as a Parúni kravl. He needs our help, not talk. Together we have eons of knowledge and experience, and some of us know the battlefields of the Parúni expansion like we know this alley. The only plan is to infiltrate the school, get his woman and get out. C'mon! Where're all the heroes?"

"Spoken like a seasoned general, Turell," Bartemus broke in with a wistful smile, "but our council is one of realistic advice and moral help in Taighen's time of need. We haven't the power or the means to direct an attack on Sephros undetected, and then bring off a rescue on top of that. We could help with a basic escape from the city, but even that may just be putting off the inevitable. Can our wise ones give us their reading of this? And voices down! There may be watchers in that park or around the corner."

Piers watched the embers of the fire as silence returned. If he wanted to achieve his goal tonight, the thought occurred that he was wasting precious time. Over his shoulder the moon came out again, casting its silvery light up the alley and washing its coolness over the reddening coals. The Dahi, too, was taking in the play of light. As Piers looked into his face, he could hear the Dahi's voice speaking from a place within his own mind. "Patience is the gateway to accomplishment. Drink in the pureness of the time and it will multiply within you. Eternity has no haste," it told him.

Piers phased out of the group discussion and tried to duplicate the telepathy in reverse: he would think of something to "say", then project it mentally and see if the Dahi picked it up. He tried the phrase, "Forget what you know and go with the flow." In no time he caught sight of a thinly disguised smile on the Dahi's lips. The Dahi hand-signed back to him, "Forget the flow, it's all in what you know." Piers first nodded in agreement, then shook his head with a smile and rejoined the group discussion.

An aboriginal woman from the north coast they called Lady Bea had been given the podium. She apparently suffered from aphasia and appeared neither cooperative nor communicative, especially when separated from her precious cargo—a shopping cart laden with plastic bags containing the sum of her worldly possessions. It was more than a hoard. It was her house, Piers realized, one that travelled with her along the streets and alleyways of her life. There was great magic in its recesses and depths that only a true nomad of time and the orbs could know or access. With melting reluctance, she finally acceded to Bartemus' entreaties.

Vocally, Bea could manage little more than moans and grunts, but she turned out to be very adept in the use of Dirshani hand-signs. Turell and a hippie street-vendor named Shandy were trying to convince her to make a prognostication using stones in a small brass box that she kept in her skirt pocket. The deal was sealed when Shandy produced two joints from his pocket and pressed them into Bea's hand. She handed them back with a wise smile that treasured Shandy's gesture, yet all the while shaking her head. Turning her eyes to Piers like a sparrow in flight, she gave him a rapid signing of something that could only have been a Dirshani children's song:

> *Kravl or Vir,*
>
> *Do you wish to see,*
>
> *What it is, Wehanti,*
>
> *That you shall be?*

Charmed by her silent song in which he seemed to be cast as a wehanti or child, he grinned back. Bea lost no time studying Piers' face, her dark brown eyes rapt, as though conducting an orchestra, then she withdrew the battered box from the folds of her skirt. At first, she turned it gently. Then she shook the box like a shaman's rattle, swaying in rhythmic swoops and dives. With each motion there were deep guttural whines then soft high-pitched hums, leading into clicks and groans. Suddenly all sound and movement stopped, and Bea flipped the box lid, revealing the contents of the oracle before her in perfect stillness. It took her only seconds to study the pattern in the bone-dry, lightly spread gravel. Immediately, her eyes closed. Her soul entered a geomantic trance, her box shut as it vanished once more into her skirt pocket from whence it had come.

"Lady Bea, if you please, bring us, with your seer's vision, the times to come for this man Taighen," Bartemus asked. She opened her eyes, looking first at Bartemus, then at Piers. Using her fingers and hands, she started to rapidly sign a story. It concerned a young man, a truth-seeker, carrying a heavy burden, crossing a stream to avoid thieves who pursue him.

He wanders in a grove of birch and alder trees for cover. There he drops his burden at the base of a grand alder laden with myriad cones. Unbound by time, the alder is the keeper of a rare wahan that reaches all places and times. A way opens in the distance as the countless lesser trees move aside to make a path—one that no thief can follow. He finds a fortified town, a place of both learning and oppression, a woman's love and an enemy's duplicity, endless woodlands, dark prisons, and the flags of peace and war. Not all he trusts is true. A powerful ally proves deceiver and binds him with the coiled rope of time. But a strange boy with sky-blue eyes and hair as fair as the sun guides him to a place in the stars. From there alone, by his own art, can he return to his homeland bearing his truth.

To Piers, the story was dreamlike, symbolic and on a par with folk and fairy tales he had read in class to his students. But he found it inconclusive and the connection with himself seemed tenuous at best. He signed her a query, "What happens at the end? Does the seeker rescue his beloved from the vir and his army?"

"I know not. I only read the figures in the river stones, nothing more," Bea signed back to him, her eyes blinking as one who has returned from a far place.

"Am I the truth-seeker?" he asked her with his hands.

"Yes, always one figure in the message stands for the seeker of knowledge, love or fortune."

"Who is the woman? My wife?"

"I think not. The stones favor another lover. One with powers and teachings you lack but need. She is already known to you, but darkly, in these times of shadow."

"Where will I find her?"

"In the place where water is time. I see her dwelling among the warriors and dancers, the magi who are reborn through her. They follow her in learning and war. You will do likewise, and yet again without her."

"Lady Bea. Tell me of this place I will travel to."

"Ask nothing further—all that the stones give me to know, I have shared. You must find another guide at another time in another world. Perhaps the woman I speak of. Perhaps the strange boy."

A hush fell over the group, only to be broken by Turell. "Sweet, I wish someone would tell me my fortune for a change." It was little more than a whisper intended for his girl, but the whole circle heard it and laughed.

Bea's replies only left Piers more puzzled than before, and oddly chastened, but he reluctantly accepted that the questions were over. He turned to the Dahi and asked, "Does this story help me make the decision before me now? Frankly, I can't see it."

"It carries much meaning. But only you can unlock it for yourself," the Dahi quietly replied.

"How?"

"Veridos. Non-exclusion. That is always the truth you seek. It is like fine metaphysical gold, but more excellent. There is nothing like it and it is everywhere. Yet it is the hardest thing to find."

"I don't need multi-dimensional truth. I need survival."

"The excellence of the one may provide the other," chuckled the Dahi. "Keep the winikos I sent you. Among its other properties, it can buy you truth or freedom, but not both, and only once before it passes on to another. Choose your moment wisely."

While their conversation continued, the council silently disbanded without ceremony, the members aware their task was done. Soon only the two of them were left in the alley.

"You sent the winikos? Through Eusebio?" Piers whispered to the Dahi.

"Yes, he is one of my agents. I tell you this in trust—tell no one. It can't get back to Draaxis or his operatives."

"Understood, Dahi, I won't blow Eusebio's cover. Occultus!"

"Occultus squared—I beg of you! Know that we are observed here, even those lips you use to shape words and the fingers you use to sign them to others. You may assume the virs know much more now than when you entered this alley, for it has been a mine of intelligence to them. But the alliance you have forged was by far worth the risk of disclosure." The Dahi impressed his words on him with an intense gaze, as if looking for a reciprocal level of comprehension.

"I'm ... mindful of that, Dahi, and I'm in your debt. I thank you for all you have done for me, here, tonight," Piers replied haltingly, trying to take in what had transpired in this place.

"And now all signs indicate the time for action has come," the Dahi continued. "The virs know from observing us here that I champion your cause. They know that Mencius and my other Seruwani are your allies. They all know we must act as if it is so. Mencius has mastered his fears over the fire of the ages and is in the park if you need him, along with Turell and some of the others. They will loyally serve your cause if you accept them. They will even conduct you to the school if that is your will, but I counsel you that hardships will follow."

"Did I hear right? They could get Leanne and I to safety, as well?"

"That is contingent on a chain of flawless successes. But, yes, that is the essence of what I mean. Yet if it happens otherwise, you will all grow in power and knowledge. I say this: one day, you will see all who you love, and we will be there to sing your praises. What happens this night will not alter that."

"Dahi, from all my heart, thanks. I will go now with whatever strength my allies and I have, to break through the vir's defenses and rescue Leanne."

"I understand your heart, and it is pure. Go! Meet the destiny that awaits you and your lady. May all transpire as you hope. But if another outcome arises, meet it with the same courage you now grip tight within your heart. Know that it will mean a separation into the dyad of flesh and soul. The drink is bitter, a toxin to the ignorant, but down it and release the burden of your memories. That is all I can ask of you. The seventh conjunction draws near you this night like a snake set to strike. It is the wahan to Sunara."

"I can't lie to you. When you say 'Sunara', it's still a myth to me— some cultic delusion that's hopelessly remote from anything I understand. My hopes and dreams are all here, Dahi. And they bind reality to me in a way denied to any bundle of dry words."

"I speak no dry bundles. Sunara is the marriage of heaven and hell, of peace and war, of transience and stasis, of bondage and freedom. And it is far from myth, for its blood is life and its water is time. Its pull on you is stronger than the earth you stand on, stronger than any destiny you hold dear.

I fear you will yield to that gravitation before this night succumbs to day, satjim. Yes, fight hard. Fight hard if your soul still dreads it and loves the garden of transience that enfolds us here. But if paradise be lost and defeat should befall you, master it with grace. For like a beast of prey, Sunara will engrave its lessons of beauty and terror on your heart before you and I speak again."

Before Piers could say a parting word to him, the Dahi returned to the place where the yellow box had collapsed. *It's not even me. It's the Codex. It's being pulled to Sunara.* He suddenly recalled another bundle of dry words about the path of Measureless Essence and the topos of the *Torvaaden. Tom*, he thought. *The seventh leads beyond this world.* He felt a sharp tug from a realm outside anything he thought real and strove to share it with his compassionate friend. It was not to be. Piers was dumbstruck as he watched the Dahi raise his hands and reanimate the fragments of painted wood. Immediately the box reassembled itself around the Dahi Utanjil of the Durzh as though caught in a time-reversal of its earlier destruction. As before, it floated above ground, lifted by an unknown force. Piers watched as it slowly moved off under its own power into the dark landscape of the park.

He felt a slight chill the moment he realized the darkness had swallowed it.

Chapter 15
Drag Race

Piers turned away from the last embers of the fire and headed towards the roadway and park. He was alone again, but he knew that the maples concealed his new Seruwani allies. He had only to set out towards the school. While he jogged through the park, others were beside him. He saw Mencius in the corner of his left eye, and to his right were Turell and Shandy. Behind were three others, Bender, Chill and Denz, all members of Turell's circle. *Now we are seven.* His heart gladdened for the first time since he left the apartment block.

They moved into synchronous pace along their moonlit path. As their feet touched the concrete sidewalk, their progress along the street echoed like drumbeats. They now drew into a single file formation with Piers at the lead. Mencius had fallen just behind Piers and flanked him to the right. The others fell farther back, their rhythm constant. The precise beat of their footfalls gave Piers a surge of pride in his new team. But he also wondered whether the steady vibration could be picked up by the Parúni detectors. He turned to Mencius and signaled that a stop was needed. Mencius dropped back to signal the others.

"It's time to break, catch our breath and strategize," Piers addressed the group, hands on knees. The others squatted on the sidewalk, ready to hear their orders. It was as though Piers was in the classroom again, but his students were not students. They were more like hardened soldiers who had already seen the battle before them. Their silent, somber faces reflected a watchful determination. There really was nothing he could teach them, but he knew it was his role to lead them. If only this once.

"Fortune smiles, Taighen-satjim, no attack yet. They can hear our voices and footsteps, but something holds them back," Mencius spoke, breaking the sound of panting breaths. "I sense the presence of the Ruakon here. They seldom come down to this plane, but they are here, high above us. The virs wait to see their intentions. What interest could the sky creatures have in us, Taighen?"

"Their purpose is not open knowledge. Their will is the will of the Great Heart, but I believe their presence is benign and they intend to protect us within the bounds of their precepts. This gives us time to make our strike point, given the Parúni can't detect our exact position," Piers answered.

"The Parúni do more than detect us, Taighen-satjim. At this point, they track us step by step. It is just eerie that they do so silently and without show. I sense a trap in the making," Mencius warned.

"But if the Ruakon keep harrying them, does it matter if they know our position?" Piers responded.

Mencius was about to answer when Turell broke in.

"Listen!" he cautioned them. "Don't you hear cars in the distance? Sounds like cars racing. Just out of range, but I hear them."

Piers was about to redirect Turell's attention to the matters at hand. Cars careening along the southern streets of Vancouver had no bearing on the goal before them. Then he attuned himself to the sounds of cars in the moderate distance. He wondered if Turell was onto something. It was known that clandestine street racing was carried on in this area in the early hours of the morning. The revving of motors, the sound of accelerating cars turning hairpins and gaining speed on straight sections of road, it was all there in the soundscape. But there were no police to be seen, no one at all, on the face of it, but the seven of them. He decided to downplay it.

"I hear it, Turell, but it's common at night around here. It doesn't concern us as long as they stay where they are," Piers offered, more as a way to quiet him than deal with what it meant.

"Change course, Taighen," Mencius interjected. "The drag racing may be a device to lure us off course or surround us. Following the present course adds nothing to our purpose, only greater risk." Then he added after a meaningful pause, "And we can't afford to take that on."

"Mencius's right. This race thing's a sham," added Turell. "It's Parúni trickery, and they're coming for us. I just feel it in my gut."

Wide-eyed, Shandy and the others nodded in agreement. Piers knew he could only accept the group consensus or face loss of confidence. They had to treat this as a threat whether it was or not. He abruptly told them to move out and follow him. He led them to a quiet street two blocks west, away from the noise. It was a wooded residential street with low levels of lighting. Even the moonlight was excluded by the lush walnut foliage high above their heads.

"We proceed south along this street, parallel to the first route. Stay under the tree cover and go into silence. No talking, no noise, unless absolutely necessary. Avoid visual exposure at all crossroads, and that includes signing to each other," Piers whispered. The dark shrouded street would provide better cover for his small force and offer safe mobility.

They progressed for another three or four blocks in protective darkness until the noise of the races had edged so close that Piers signaled another conference. The sound and light of the accelerating vehicles came from the area just two blocks to their west, in the direct path of the initial route. By now the whole area they had fled from had become nothing less than a midnight car rally. But it bore little relation to any real street race he could imagine.

Even without direct visual confirmation, the sheer power and speed of the vehicles was beyond Piers' belief. That, together with the prodigious number of customized cars, represented a potent barrier to their progress. Hideous crashes and agonizing screams were heard in the distance from time to time. Some sent flames above the trees and buildings that screened them from direct view. Some ignited the surrounding buildings themselves. Occasional whiffs of smoke and even the sickly scent of burnt flesh assailed Piers and his runners as they continued towards their destination.

High-speed sounds and lights to the north and south of their position indicated races were in progress there as well. Out of earshot, the lightshows sprouted in the eastern reaches of the city as well. But how did they do it? No answer came to mind. This was nothing like conventional street racing. They had stumbled into a fiendish dragnet of vast proportions, designed to isolate and entrap them. There was a twist, though. It was a game. He could only compare it to a gigantic video game capable of lethal threat should they try to engage it. Turell had seen through it and called them out. This bore the trademark of the same Parúni tactics Piers had witnessed on the streets of Mexico City.

"It's no use. They know our position. They've staged new raceways to the south and north to hem us in," Piers called out to the increasingly wary team, barely able to reach them over the increasing volume of noise.

"We need to move west, say two blocks, then break through on the south. Move out now!" he yelled and hoped his voice would not be picked up by the enemy.

The team zig-zagged westward and southward into a residential area, then carried on south again. Their tentative goal was now to breach the new south raceway and push towards the school. As they cautiously traced their way towards it, an insight jumped out at Piers like a tiny sharp-angled stone in his shoe.

In a word, it was Vince. It could only have been Vince who designed this theatrical stage they had blundered onto. It was bizarre, noisy and destructive just like the Black and Yellow operation on the streets of Mexico City. In retrospect, a little like his own Ubu Roi production too. The specter of Vince came to mind in a flash, in his usual strut across the dress rehearsal stage as a goth-inspired Ubu, spouting obscenities and commanding attention. Mulling over the happenings of the past hour led Piers to the same conclusion: it screamed Vince's unmistakable stamp.

Evidently, Sephros had indulged the wunderkind again, egged on, no doubt, by Trudy Cole and Gord Stevens. Half apprehensive, half amazed, Piers marveled at the raw power young Vince Lang now wielded over him. It was cat and mouse once more. But this time Piers took heart in having stumbled onto the obvious. It meant that flaws could be more easily identified and exploited. Moreover, it meant the element of surprise that had gripped Piers and his band of rescuers had been loosened. He understood now exactly who he was up against and what game they were playing. The oppressive sensation of fear left his body with each breath and his courage returned. He remembered again the last words the Dahi spoke to him and took comfort in them.

Piers and his strike team found themselves in an alley that flanked two rows of down-at-heel three-floor houses. Plenty of dented garbage cans, colored plastic bins of various sizes and the occasional bald tire set were dotted along the alley, and these gave Turell and his friends an idea. They set about to fashion a crude fort that would provide more concealment, enough to prevent them from being spotted from the raceway directly to the south. The stench of garbage soon concentrated in their tiny enclosure, but the team welcomed the chance to rest and have a smoke.

After a short private discussion, Piers and Mencius rejoined them in the fort and listened to the ongoing discussion on alternate plans. A scant twenty meters away, the chaos and cacophony of the race was in full progress. It had a cinematic quality to it, as if it was nine-tenths illusion and soundcrafting. The scent of death by impact and incineration saturated the air, brashly obscene yet grandly formidable. Vince had more than earned his theatrical kudos on this performance.

The consensus was that a diversion was needed to allow Piers and Mencius to cross the raceway in progress across their southern route. The rest of the band would not proceed farther but remain concealed in the neighborhood. The main force would continue to create diversions here and there to attract Parúni attention away from the two south-bound infiltrators. Their first operation, however, would be to break the flow of traffic and force an interruption in the race. It was a tall order, but Turell and his companions were quick to respond. They were up to it.

Piers and Mencius scurried off to the west until they were perched inside a dense hedge, aided by a painter's step ladder. As they surveyed the southern raceway from up close, Piers said, "Mencius, I think this is the work of a certain student of mine. He's a bright kid and has some standing among the Parúni djalas. Even the Kopendres Ordinath take him seriously."

"Quick. Tell me his weaknesses," Mencius said.

"Vanity, ambition and a certain compulsion to impress the virs, I'd say," Piers answered with a smile.

"And his strengths?" Mencius continued, as though balancing an equation.

"The same!" Piers answered glibly, then added, "But I'd have to put his chief strength as the ability to adapt to new circumstances. They've come to depend on him to invent new attack scenarios. This race theme is just the kind of thing he would dream up. He tends to see these campaigns as some kind of theatre production. All the world's a stage and all that."

The Shakespeare reference did not register with Mencius and brought only a puzzled look. Worlds and stages were apparently separate categories for him.

Piers tried to rephrase, but nothing came to mind so he just summed it up, "It's karmic retribution—my fault for teaching him to think that way, I suppose."

"Forget karma," Mencius impressed on him. "If you're right about him, he's under intense pressure and has his own karma to tweak. My old master Sephros will push him to his limit and beyond. Remember: he's expendable and you aren't. So, this wonder boy may just overextend himself and make a mistake. That's his real weakness, and it could be fatal for him."

Piers muttered, "I hope it doesn't come to that."

Mencius grabbed his arm and said, "Let's be ready to take advantage if it does. This is war, Taighen-satjim, not a stage play! So, don't pity him in his delusion. Mercy is weakness in the game we are playing, and the weak don't survive to the end."

Piers felt the impact of these words and steeled himself. It could come down to lethal combat. But he had to be ready to see it through, if need be. Vince had no compunction about capturing him and sending him off to the Parúni slave camps. Piers knew that he would need to be just as callous to win his freedom.

As they looked down the street, they saw a prodigious array of lights installed on the power poles and beamed on the pavement. Neon blue, pink and green, they formed a constantly moving stream of patterns that blended with the racing cars that flashed past in either direction. On average, every three to four seconds another powerful vehicle shot by at high speed in either lane. Piers estimated they now numbered in the hundreds. And in the west, another brightly-lit raceway had been set up, just out of direct sight. *Another leg of an absurd race to nowhere.* He shook his head, hoping it escaped observation, but the others were too mesmerized by the light show to notice him. *So, this is Psych warfare?*

The strike team was now fenced in on all sides by a pulsating ring of noise and deadly color. How the Parúni flawlessly synchronized the accelerated flow of vehicles at the intersections and consistently tightened the noose around them was beyond him. Even beyond physics or mathematics as Piers understood them. But he was more intent on understanding how he and his team could use the perfection of the seething vortex against itself.

"How do they do all this, Mencius? So fast, so bright, so big," Piers asked, like a youngster on his first visit to the county fair.

"Don't be fooled! It's all an illusion, satjim," Mencius replied with a brave laugh. "Part of the ohanic war art is the exploitation of the real; part is about mastery of illusion, making it seem real. Try not to invest too much in what you see, hear, smell or touch. They play directly with your mind and senses to induce fear and the sense of futility. We are in a house of mirrors where the glass is like the air around us. We must discover how to smash the glass and clear the air."

Piers shook his head in doubt. He wondered if he had sent them all on a fool's errand. There was little time left to strike through the enemy's closing noose, but no clear path seemingly led them to victory. That was the beauty of Vince's counterattack, of course. Defense and offense in one stroke.

"I know well how they do it, yet just the same, I am as vulnerable as you are," Mencius went on softly. "Just tread carefully. Underneath the illusion is a hard and real trap. It has teeth. It's very hard to isolate. Yet that is our immediate task: to find it, avoid it or disable it. Either way we escape it."

"I think they gave me pills, Mencius. Could that be part of it, the trap?" Piers asked in a self-questioning way, as his mind wandered over the possibilities.

"Yes, Taighen-satjim. Like everything, the pills may be real and induce illusion, or they may be placebos with only the power of suggestion. Either way, they're part of the circus we animals perform in. Either way, compensate with your own strength of mind to cut through the sensory window. That's Ohan—the way of all warriors."

"So, what can I do to help the rest of you?" Piers pondered aloud. For the first time in this mission he floundered, and Mencius could see it. Soon fear would cripple him.

"Let the rest of us do the grunt work. You concentrate on that one thing— the one and only thing that matters. In the end, you alone must fully trust the reality that we deconstruct here and now. After that, there can be no indecision. You alone must act!" Mencius said slowly and emphatically.

After hours of quietude, the jaadentril locket sent forth a potent shock against his chest that jolted him out of his black hole orbit. Without hesitation, Piers said to him, "I'm ready—ready to cross over. Signal the team, Mencius. Start the diversion. Smash the glass," then he looked into the pupils of Mencius' eyes and said, "We attack now!"

Mencius melted out of sight as Piers leapt into a full sprint. His own race against the illusion had begun. In the near distance he was vaguely aware of Turell, Shandy and the rest. They flew up and over the raceway and released garbage cans and tires like bombs over the passing cars. They were flying like avenging angels! *True* ohanin, he thought, so unlike himself. Mencius, too, had taken flight and blasted streams of energy from his avda into the opposite lane. A momentary path in spacetime immediately opened across the street just as he entered it. Piers ran for it like a deer pursued. The air was like glass, just as Mencius had foretold, shattering everywhere as Piers ran. With it, the race cars splintered and the gaudy floodlights faded away into the darkness.

Piers looked up the now-darkened street and saw a new threat. The beatup green Ford that Vince drove to school bore down on him at top speed. Piers couldn't stop, so he strode longer and faster, unsure if the car would adjust and meet him dead-on. Avda thrusts from the flyers seemed to bounce ineffectively off the car, now within a stone's throw to his left. Piers neither could nor would stop. He set his goal on the sidewalk scarcely ten feet away. There was no time to retrieve his avda from his pack or reverse course.

Then it happened. Vince's Ford smashed into him. Like a rag doll, Piers was yanked away from his course and sent airborne by the sudden impulse. His gaze was back on the car as he flew down the street. The car had been immobilized by something Piers couldn't identify. It wasn't an avda blast, but more like a large black extension of the sky. Vince's body flew out the front window and travelled in a parallel trajectory to Piers.

Inexplicably, Vince flew past him as Piers decelerated. The black sky being had caught Piers like he was a softball snagged in a midnight-black baseball glove. He descended to the road surface with a bump that pushed the air from his lungs. Perhaps another twenty feet farther, Vince's body struck a street-side tree and fell mangled to the ground. Though Piers could see the whole sequence detailed in slow motion, he had trouble believing it. He stood on the far sidewalk like a spectator entranced by the theater of reality. Then he looked down and saw his own motionless body lying crumpled against the asphalt surface of the street. The sight neither bothered nor engaged him, no more than looking at a crushed container might. He had no trouble moving and no pain whatsoever, so he dashed over to where Vince lay. The boy was lifeless.

He looked back at his own inert, yet living, body. The separation dyad of body and soul had been achieved by the unlikely alliance of a dead teenager and the Ruakon. Mencius, Turell, Shandy, Bender, Chill and

Denz gathered around it. They showed no sign of seeing him as he moved towards them. Mencius was talking into a cell phone, but his words were inaudible. The others were speaking amongst themselves, and he heard only one Dirshani word: "dulati", being uttered softly, ever so softly. *Hah!—Newcomer, noobie, first-timer, greenhorn.* They seemed to be reciting some kind of chant or prayer of ascension. The fact that their quickly executed hand signs mentioned Sunara meant little to him, but he took it to be a parting token of respect from his flying Seruwani commandos. Turell and Shandy started to head back up the alley, soon followed by Bender, Chill and Denz. In an eyeblink they vanished as warriors do when the times call for it.

It felt odd to him how time passed in jolts and languid pools, now dilated, now smooth and rectilinear. Within moments, two ambulances and several city police cars arrived. Vince's body was covered with a dark blue tarp. One ambulance left empty. By then only Mencius had stayed behind and was answering questions to the police. They seemed to regard him as a midnight jogger who witnessed an accident. His words were inaudible as before, and Piers noticed that all the other people there communicated likewise. Increasingly deaf to the entire soundscape, he saw only their lips moving and heard only muffled low-frequency vibrations that held no meaning for him.

A coroner's car arrived later, then more cars, more people. Some of them photographed the scene. Some measured skid marks and body positions with a tape. Some talked on their cell phones or car radios. Some applied spray paint from hand-held pens to the pavement, marking in arrows and body outlines. Vince's car was towed away in short order. Piers saw his own body being strapped to a gurney and loaded into the ambulance. Then it was gone. Before he knew it, Vince's body had been removed in a black bag and the response teams were vacating the site. Soon, little remained of the fruitless night mission but a few spray-paint markings on the ground and scattered litter from the attack. Unobserved and silent, he laughed at the human comedy of it. There was no hard evidence that a street race ever took place. Perhaps it didn't.

He looked for Mencius, but he was not with the departing police. Then Piers saw him, farther up the street where the actual crossing was, facing him. Mencius was standing near the empty south-bound street they had earlier planned to take to the school. He looked towards Piers and signed to him that he saw him. As Piers moved towards him, Mencius turned and began jogging the final leg of the trip. Over the course of the night, the full moon had moved towards the western horizon like the hands of an astral clock. Whatever was to transpire, its time was already meted out.

Chapter 16
Strange Attractor

Piers caught up and ran beside him. No words were spoken. They jogged along silently, passing one house after another, one cross street after another, block by block, approaching the school. They were completing the mission according to plan. But it was in no way the Charge of the Light Brigade—no longer a bold attack aimed at victory over superior forces. Neither was it a furtive raid. More a parade of honor into certain defeat.

Piers mentally checked his few possessions: the jaadentril locket, the winikos and the avda. The little lacework Gerry gave him. They were all with him, but quiescent. Even as he approached the empty school parking lot, no radiance came from any of them. Like his body, these objects were no longer of the Orb of Morasa, but core emanations of some other kind. It was as if they had been extracted from any physical reality they once may have had.

Just as the yantra had transformed into a seed within him after the first conjunction, and the Nexus of the second conjunction had coalesced with it to become the *germinatus* of the Codex, so his secret name had bonded as an internal shield for the dichotomy. These things that he carried within him were more than accoutrements of his being. Planted in style, as Tom's song said, they were fundamental to his core identity. He rested easy in that realization as he repeated his secret name as Tom had taught him.

Mencius stopped by the bottom of the front steps of the school. He looked in the direction of Piers and said audibly, "Leanne is not here, Taighensatjim. Our retreat is cut off. Your choices are endpoint or defeat. There can be no rescue and no escape."

Piers said nothing but, concentrating on the building, tried to pick up the presence of Leanne. Without knowing how, he was able to defocus his consciousness and let it spread over the school campus like a blanket. He sensed many energy signatures in and around the building, but none of them was the one that he hoped for. He knew grief and defeat, but he was not yet ready to invite them into his soul.

He stopped scanning the building and admitted to Mencius, "She's somewhere else. I can feel it too. It pains me now that I brought you here, Mencius. I'm truly sorry."

Mencius was unresponsive, yet stoic. He gestured with his right hand that no apology was called for. Then he calmly looked up to the front door as it opened. Five or six darkly clothed figures emerged and quickly descended, holding the last of Piers' commandos firmly by the arms and escorting him away to the rear of the school. *Uleg djalas, the lowest kravl-level djalas.* Piers watched Mencius depart with them. He found it odd that, unlike Mencius, they seemed not to have the slightest interest in him, nor did they show any awareness that he was standing there. *Not much more than flesh automata.*

The senselessness of it all enfolded him. It had taken all this time for him to realize what he could only now lament, that he should never have asked Mencius on a mission this far into the Parúni domain. The brave man had sacrificed his freedom for nothing. Even young Vince would be alive if Piers had submitted to Sephros instead of running. It was time to face the futility of resisting the inevitable and the consequences it entailed. Wasn't this what Mencius had tried to tell him? Even the Dahi had hinted the real battle was to be won not here, but in a higher orb.

"By nature, freedom justifies itself, hence the struggle for freedom is self-justifying even in the face of certain failure," he rambled aloud, convinced no one was listening. The golden glyphs of the *Torvaaden* swept across his mind like leaves falling on a rain-swelled stream.

Even if they were deep and meaningful to him, the philosophies of a kravl were of little interest to the mighty potentate who had called him to service. Inwardly he laughed at himself, remembering a half-forgotten philosophy class on Nietzsche. Piers mused: could he fully embrace fate through laughter? Then something broke through his pointless introspection. It felt like pinpricks going up his spine and forced him into a full alert.

Though Mencius was gone, Piers was now aware he was not alone. He felt the force of a hundred or more avdas behind him in the parking lot. He could feel them *en masse*, pointed in his direction. Each of them dribbled a tiny irregular stream of energy that converged on his back. He glanced over his shoulder and confirmed the presence of a large djala contingent standing at the ready in the area he had just jogged through. There was no escape now—these djalas were of the elite Kaaghen corps. They could plainly see him. If he tried to run, they would converge and capture him effortlessly. Piers shuddered involuntarily then reluctantly trudged up the familiar steps as the school door opened for him. His legs seemed tired, laboring with each step. Night was starting to wain and the full moon was soon to set in the west. It was the last thing he saw before entering the building.

Passing through the open door, he expected to see another band of djalas waiting to take him to some functionary of his master, probably Gord Stevens. But there was no one. The familiar checker board of the hall floor had been cleaned spotless and waxed to a sleek gloss. Though the hall was sparsely lit, it was obvious that very few djala feet had been walking over this floor in the last few hours. *A shame to risk marring the shimmering surface.* Yet it seemed the only thing to do. Piers' sneakers would leave little trace on the hard wax surface in any event, so he set out down the empty hall. The dark humor came back to him and he snickered aloud despite his wish to remain solemn. *Why worry about messing up the floor, anyway? Would it upset Gord? Do I care?*

A chill realization suddenly seized him, and he stopped. He had taken a few steps but left no tracks. He walked with more force, trying to stamp and dig his heels in the wax. Nothing. No imprint whatsoever. Then the fool in him threw up his hands and allowed wisdom to take over. It was Ghost Science 101. He was no longer a physical Morasa-being. Separation, the opposite of conjunction, had occurred. That part of his separation dyad left in an ambulance earlier in the night, and the remaining half of the dyad was his thinking and emoting soul. He pressed his hand against the wall, but it no longer offered more than a spongy resistance, if that. The floor was solid enough to walk on. But that was because he believed it was solid and would support him, like the ground he had jogged over with Mencius.

Then he thought back about the front door. He didn't physically open it, but perhaps it opened because he wanted it to. He had never had the power of psychokinesis before, nor believed in it at all, but he did now to a greater degree. It was obvious that he was a fish out of water and he needed to get to his natural environment, wherever that was. Piers went past his home room without looking in. It was no longer his and he had lost all interest in it. He willed the door to close and it did so.

Doors and hallways led to the office, the cafeteria and the auditorium. These too, he left behind in disinterest, knowing there was no one there. The doors closed as he passed them. Here and there were the posters that advertised the theater production of Ubu Roi. Vince and Shauna were still listed on the roster of actors. There was the slightest feeling of nostalgia as he passed them, but he knew it was critical to move on and find the right door to his new life. The whole school was just a tomb to him now, a cavernous monument to pass through and leave behind as a snake leaves its molted skin.

He stopped before a nondescript double door that led downstairs to the basement storage areas and furnace room. He had never used it before and, as far as he was aware, it was always locked. The basement was normally off-limits to students and teaching staff alike, but it was one of those places where Gord Stevens was known to hang out. Piers knew that someone was down there, and that the command center for this entire intervention had to be there too. The door opened for him. He started his descent down the dimly lit stairs.

At the bottom of the stairs, he followed a hallway past dusty shelves of cleaning supplies and several rooms filled with old textbooks and lockers and one with a vintage upright piano and assorted band instruments in their cases. He followed the light and it led him to the furnace room and a dusty teacher's desk at which Gord Stevens was sitting. Beside him stood three djala operatives wearing the teal Parúni uniform. He felt a sudden chill from their cool blue presence.

"Taighen-Uchundar, ghenjil-to-be!" Stevens exclaimed. "And not a moment too soon, I must say. My attendants have just finished your safe conduct tags for the immigration station at the Parúni frontier, and your travel clothes are here as well." Stevens welcomed him with an autocratic smile, then after a pause he winked and added, "And may I say, you've given us a worthwhile chase—all to your credit, of course. Your inventive mind and powers of observation are justly acclaimed. And why not? A lame quarry makes the hunt pointless. Sounds like something from the *Torvaaden*, wouldn't you say?"

Piers gave him a defiant look but said nothing. He would not be discussing the Golden Codex with this fake janitor.

Stevens pointed to what appeared to be a pile of dusty sackcloths lying on the floor near the furnace. Piers turned his gaze to the engraved metal tags on the desk. He was impressed with the swirling brahanic forms so effortlessly engraved into the silver and gold tags. Then he looked at the drab grey rags he would be expected to wear and flashed an ironic grin to Stevens. This was the custodian who was so concerned about reining in the cockroaches, he recalled.

"You may place the tags around your neck using the attached chains," Stevens went on, as though a festivity was about to begin, raising a glass of what appeared to be whisky.

"Gord, or whoever you really are," Piers beamed back at him in mock appreciation, then took a more acidic tone, "you really shouldn't have gone to such trouble: tags and togs! And such lovely ones too. What more could a defeated kravl ask for? But I think I'll keep my old clothes. It's a matter of comfort over style. If you don't mind, of course."

"Ah, you disapprove of our selection?" Stevens replied with an equally sarcastic tone of forced solicitation, then laughed, "I'd have to say that your present clothing is simply out of place in Sunara. And not everything will survive the passage through the wahan. The clothes you have on are just a virtual projection of your subtle body image, and quite temporary. They will perish on the way, I'm afraid, thread by thread. Do you wish to arrive at our academy naked? It's not recommended, given the public decorum expected of you."

"Hmmm," Piers thought out loud, "I guess not."

"And another thing: you should practice being a little more deferential, as well. It's the kind of thing they groom into you in training. So, get used to it now and you will have one more advantage later," Stevens continued while Piers disrobed and put on the rags from the pile.

So, the conditioning starts already. Stevens caught his thought and answered him silently with a wry expression and a nod.

Stevens flashed another carnivorous smile and nonchalantly asked if he had a secret name. It was not usual for a kravl to have such a thing, but if it existed, it was needed for inscription on one of the brahan documents bound for Zirindar. It would, of course, be kept in confidence, he explained to Piers with a veneer of concern. Piers made no reply but smiled knowingly.

Stevens stealthily met his gaze and seemed transfixed by what he witnessed in Piers' eyes. *Looking for the Torvaaden?* Piers stared straight ahead in quiet defiance, his adrenalin flowing. He kept absolute silence. His mind was fixed, hard and impenetrable. The shield of the name held firm as he internally chanted it.

Stevens looked away, baffled, unable to read him. *Two points for me*, Piers thought. *One for the name and one for the Codex. Score 2-0.* Demoting it to a game made it winnable.

Piers finished dressing himself in the rags and stood at ease, though the tense confrontation had tired him beyond words. He desperately wanted to focus the conversation on something mundane and totally unrelated, but knew he had to appear blasé to Stevens, with nothing contrived. It was vital that Stevens not feel any weakness in his wall. He would only thrust deeper.

"May I take my avda and other belongings with me?" Piers enquired, indicating the little pile on the concrete floor that included the winikos and avda. The balled doily Gerry gave him was there, too. The jaadentril talisman was around his neck. It had never left him, nor was it touched or tampered with in any way.

"I allow you those articles you carry. The avda is forbidden to non-djala kravl and subject peoples, of course, but yours is hobbled so it matters little. Remember, though, the Vir Sephros gives you preferential treatment in this and other courtesies. You have absolutely no expectation of further entitlement in the Parúni realm. Understood?" Stevens answered sharply. His mood had shifted since the confrontation over the secret name and he no longer projected any hint of unctuous concern.

"Yeah, right, Sunaraic law on sentient property and all that shit." Piers let his voice trail off as he adjusted the locket around his neck and pocketed his other belongings.

"Well and good. Any questions, Taighen-Uchundar, ghenjil? Be quick about it if there are."

"My wife, Leanne? Is she well, safe...?"

"Yes," Stevens replied in a clipped tone, his eyelids raised slightly. "She has been relocated, as you have recently discovered. She will be seen to by the local Kopendres operatives, from a discreet distance of course. That Ordinath woman Pru and her trainee girl you know as Shauna will visit and report on her needs. No reasonable request will be denied her. In good time, she will be taken to visit your body on life-support in the hospital. If it is her wish, that is. Just remember that much depends on your good behavior and progress."

"And my parents ... my mother, especially?"

"Same. I'm informed they are with your living remains as we speak. But never forget my warning to you!"

"Can't thank you enough ..." Piers said, relieved. *We'll give him a point for that, 2-1.* He felt encouraged to ask more favors to stretch out his onepoint advantage. But he was cut off in a curt interjection from Stevens, who had finished his whisky and tossed the glass to an attendant.

"Then let's drink to this. It will help you transition to your new life and it will help us all in keeping you keened on the things that matter," Stevens sneered, taking full advantage of Piers' forced spirit of cooperation.

A djala gave him a faceted tumbler filled with a cloudy translucence. It gave off a dank, faintly rotten odor. *Aged, perhaps, but not whiskey.* Piers gagged at the thought of drinking it.

"I can't drink this bitter crap," Piers protested as he flung the glass to shatter on the concrete floor. The odorous liquid splashed everywhere, but nothing was said.

Another glass was immediately prepared, and in seconds Piers found himself bound to a chair with his head tilted back. A much-used speculum clamp was inserted between his teeth, his jaws forced open with an inserted screw-key. The presiding djala carefully poured the contents of the glass down a thistle tube directed somewhere near his esophagus. Piers thought of turning his head, coughing and sputtering in an effort to resist. But he could see that his captors were as determined as they were methodical. He downed it passively. *The score's even now: 2 all.*

Almost immediately he felt a pain shoot from his jaadentril locket and fan upward to his head. Then a deadness set in. It was as if he had two natures. The new nature was quickly finding its way around him and rooting itself. Cool ghostliness fell over him and he shuddered. In moments the sense of otherness had seeped so completely into every conscious fiber that he could no longer discern it. Separation of the magisterium, Tom had called it, separation into the dyad of the white ethesia and calx. The earthly calx, his comatose body, would be left behind like an empty flask, and soon. Now, his psyche was the purified ethesia—a solvent bearing a precious but invisible sublimate: the Golden Codex.

By the time he noticed Stevens barking at him, the mouth-clamp and rope bindings had been removed. He heard the muffled tirade, but it seemed far away.

"Y'know, I'm like that glass—just an invisible container. Guess you'd know about that, Gord. But d'you know what's inside the glass?" Piers said, desperately wanting to set Stevens on edge.

"You protect your identity well. I can only say disclosures of that nature may reveal my own, and that is not expedient at present," Stevens replied with his chin lowered and eyes leveled at Piers.

"So, really, who the hell are you, Gord? Why'd they stick you in this house of bondage?" Piers laughed, feeling loopy from the drug soup bubbling through his gut.

"The Custodian. That's all you need know."

"Yeah, right. Great wax buff on the ground floor, by the way. As fucking usual, of course."

"Thanks, but it wasn't me." The tone in Stevens' voice was imperious, even pained, as if he was naturally disinclined towards menial labor.

"Don't suppose it was. Too busy running the fox hunt, eh?" Piers jibed.

The "Custodian" showed signs of getting riled at his drilling. *This guy's patrician, not some low-life djala plebe. A commandant, or maybe more?* His intuitions were reinforced by something aural: the faintest accent. Unnoticed before, not North Dirshani like Cynthia or Draaxis—it hailed from the south of Sunara. It even reminded him of his father's rustic Dirshani exchanges out by the wood shed. *Is this man an Uchundar? No. Unthinkable.* He remembered Tom mentioning the Ilyaan's adversary, the Uchundar he wanted excluded from the sanctuary. The thought gave him chills. He strove to remember more that Tom or Draaxis might have told him, but Tom, Cynthia, Draaxis, Leanne, his parents, Shauna … they all swam in a swirling river bound for a forgetful sea—a place where grief and joy were distant clouds. *It's that stinking potion. It's stealing everything I was.*

"Is that it? No more questions? And don't stall! Accept what must be. The conveyance must depart on time—just as the full moon sets," Stevens snapped. Now it was all Piers could register—that damned Uchundar accent.

Piers could only just make out Stevens' words, but was unable to deliver a riposte. A pent-up remorse flooded his mind. He felt like a sobbing drunk, unable to hold back. One penultimate memory persisted. "I am sorry for Vince Lang. I regret any part I had in his—" Piers hurriedly confessed to Stevens, who immediately lashed back with impatience.

"For me—just a djala kravl who expired in action for his vir. Self-important and difficult to handle at that! He delivered your separation dyad intact, but only with the help of the meddling Ruakon. It blew up in his face—nothing more to be said." Stevens' tone had slithered from irritated to indulgent.

"But for me, he was—"

"For you he was an ingenue, an actor taking to your silly little stage productions. But not as stunning a student as you may think. Aside from the technical display, his final performance was barely competent."

It was an icy eulogy. When Piers looked away mournfully, Stevens gruffly admonished him, "The Parúni imperium has many such, and we grind through vast supplies of them in an endless state of conquest. It's a waste of thought pining for him. Fail your vir and be assured, you'll face a painfully similar fate."

"I understand, omzari," Piers tried to placate him with a show of respect. It did nothing to help the situation or ease the new tide of displeasure in Stevens' eyes, however.

"I have no patience for your sentimental blather! Concentrate on the Trilikon, ghenjil," Stevens went on, still annoyed and ready to set him straight. "Do you actually cultivate the art of posing tedious and ignorant questions? If so, you miss the point entirely. Your master, the vir, can in no way afford attitude from you. Draaxis trained you on this, did he not? He wheedled an extra fee for it, so you could at least play along."

Once more, Piers assented, this time with his eyes alone. Something in them caught Stevens' attention. A glimmer of things to come?

"More to the point, you've been bought and paid for. Much has been invested in you and continued indulgence is not a right. It's earned milestone by milestone, and the road's a rough one. So, run the race. And win the race—any way you can, *ghenjil initiatatus testificatus.*" Stevens spat out the last three words in unconcealed contempt.

Yet, tucked in there was a note of grudging respect, even fascination, as if for a rare, bejeweled acquisition. A mechanical bird, perhaps, that could take commands and speak amazements. That, but then some. Piers was instantly reminded of a poem by Yeats that he once taught in a class, but could only catch one fragment as it passed him in the flood, "... of hammered gold and gold enameling / To keep a drowsy Emperor awake; Or set upon a golden bough to sing." Was he sailing to a Byzantium like the seeker Yeats extoled, or to a refuge where a kravl could toil his way to freedom? Gerry's earlier reproach came back like a fishing float bobbing on his crumbling memory. *Go rogue!*

"Yes, omzari," Piers replied. He sensed the conversation was over. There would be no more talk of Vince or any other facet of the orb he was leaving behind. He watched his thoughts of them erode in the river as it raged, leaving weirdly shaped beach stones bereft of any clues of their origins. Like Lady Bea's river stones, they spoke only of a watery, uncertain future.

A longcase clock chimed a sonorous "bong", jerking his attention to it. Piers noticed the sun, moon and planets, ascending and descending above and below the horizon line on its face, the full moon just touching the horizon. It was an ornate mechanical planisphere with an eighteenth-century Dutch look, an instrument he miraculously recalled having seen only once at Aimesworth and Dixon. Yet here it was again, like a long-lost friend come dockside to see him off, aboard a new ship of industry. And his most precious possessions—his life-memories—going and gone—dripping like blood and bile over a slaughterhouse floor.

Stevens turned to his startled attendants, waved his hand towards the wall and bellowed, "Moonset! Terminate! Close operations. Take down the ensign. Pack up. Escort the kravl to transport. Now!"

The ensign that Stevens had flailed his hand towards was an exquisite cinnabar velour and gold-leaf banner on the wall. It was inscribed "Behind the artwork" in skillfully-executed brahan. As he was strong-armed from the room by two of the uniformed djala, Piers realized that he had seen this exact glyphic complex long before. In hindsight, he had been too busy overreacting to it to notice what it was: an obscure phrase from the *Torvaaden* Codex.

"Behind the artwork lies the path of glory—only in destruction is it born a stone, and the entrance to the stone is sacrifice," he mumbled under his breath, inwardly reconstructing it from the indicial complex.

The Codex responded, filled him, heart outward. He reflected on how it was born a stone of Konespaar, how it was transmuted in the cloud of his unknowing, how its separated elixir was transferred to him by his dying mahir. These were memories no potion could dissolve or corrode. Remnants of its ingot now hung from his neck, a talisman encasing a Ruakon feather bound for Sunara. *Yes, there is sacrifice.* Tom's face sprang back to him like a drowning man's hand. He thought of Tom's selfless labors on the separation of the Nexus and of how it prefigured his own marital and bodysoul separations this very night. Like the tril he once breathed to life, now wore and would seek again in yet unknown realms, freedom is metaphysical and unbound by passing things. The ageless simplicity stunned him.

From a newfound maturity, he felt his own concerns recede like the petty intrigues and debacles of childhood, absorbed into the golden innerness that filled him. He spoke silently the secret name that sealed his path—he knew not why, only that he must. The journey ahead was the jaadentril within, its life-seed planted in rich soil, its leaves and tendrils groping towards an emerging luminance.

He fell back into silence as one of his guards glanced impatiently and yanked him forward. Stumbling, pushed and dragged by his guards through the dark hallways, Piers put on a long face to mask his thoughts, though it was scarcely necessary. The dim red light of an exit sign lit their way only momentarily, then shadow took over. *Exit. Exodus.* His chattering mind sank into numbness. His memories of this world were soon to trickle away entirely. Even Stevens and his underlings were swept from sight like the creatures of a sour dream. The cadence of marching took over.

With no choice but to stumble in the pre-dawn between two lumbering djalas, Piers glimpsed past the colossal failure of his night mission. It was time to embrace the reality that, like the feather of Quetzalcoatl swaying from his neck, he was and always had been Sunara-bound. To his surprise, he felt buoyed, energized and renewed in his calling to the Trilikon and the liberty it promised. Determined, even passionate, he was ready for the last of the unions foretold, the seventh conjunction. He recognized his impatience and longing for the trip through the wahan. It was his undeniable calling, persistent, and growing as the minutes passed. What had once been an anathema to him was beginning to pull him forward like an unseen magnet.

THE END

ABOUT THE AUTHOR

William Sandberg is a Canadian writer whose concentration is fantasy and metaphysical fiction. From early years and onward, he was enchanted by stories bound to other worlds and hidden realities that crystalize to a transpersonal hardness.